FOR KEEPS

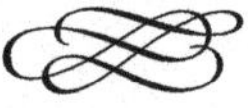

TIFFANY PATTERSON

A special thank you to There For You (thereforyou.melissa@gmail.com) for editing.

PROLOGUE

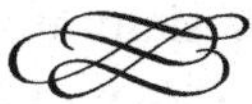

Destiny

"I look like shit," I mumbled to myself as I stared at the woman with the vacant, dark brown eyes in the mirror. The deep-set bags surrounding my eyes, my skin that was usually a glowing mahogany looked ashen, and the deep frown that I couldn't turn upside down even if I wanted to, all served to make me unrecognizable to myself. Inhaling deeply, I pushed myself away from the mirror and granite countertop in my bathroom and thought about stumbling to the kitchen to make a sandwich. I couldn't remember the last time I'd eaten. The rumbling in my stomach was a sure sign that it'd been at least twenty-four hours since I'd nourished myself. But the work to trudge all of the way down to the kitchen, take out the food to make a sandwich, and then actually eat the damn thing felt like too much effort. I'd much rather go back to bed.

Slowly ambling my way out of the bathroom, I trekked across the bedroom that I'd always thought was too damn big for just two people. Along with the house. But my husband, Darryl, would always remind me that he'd purchased an eight-thousand square foot home for all of the children we would fill it up with one day.

"Bastard!" I cried out, as the thought of children had me nearly crumbling to my knees, while clutching my abdomen. I just made it to the bed as I collapsed in a heap of tears, cursing Darryl as I wailed. I cried myself to sleep for probably the hundredth time in the last three weeks.

I don't know how many hours had passed when a loud ringing sound jerked me awake. Looking around the dark bedroom, it took me half a minute to realize the ringing noise was that of the doorbell.

"Who the fuck?" I cursed, slamming my head back against the pillow and covering the other side with another pillow to seal off the noise. Whoever the hell it was would get the hint and leave. But after what seemed like an eternity, the ringing didn't stop.

"This better not be Darryl again!" I huffed as I pushed myself up and out of the bed. I had to hold on to the cherrywood bedpost to steady myself. Days of not eating were obviously catching up with me. Yet, the ringing of the bell persisted. Pushing my disorientation to the side, I moved out of the bedroom and down the hall toward the staircase.

"Darryl, I told your sorry ass to stay the hell away from me!" I yelled as I descended the steps, moving quickly to the door. Through the glass door I could only make out a figure but was too filled with rage to clearly see what was in front of me. That is, until I yanked the door open so quickly and harshly that I startled the person on the other side—the one who'd been ringing the goddamn doorbell like a lunatic. It wasn't Darryl.

"Who the hell are you?"

"Where is he?" the woman snarled down at me. She had at least four inches on my petite five foot, three inch frame.

I was too stunned to even make a move when the woman quickly moved past me, stepping around me, inside my house.

"Darryl! I know you're here! You can't keep running from me!"

Her yelling finally snapped me back to reality and I swiftly spun around in her direction.

"Bitch, who the hell do you think you are walking up in my house like you're crazy?"

"I'm your husband's baby mother!" she shouted back at me.

I whirled backwards at the same time my eyes dropped to her midsection. For the first time since this little encounter began I realized what was happening right in front of me. I blinked, hoping beyond hope my tear-swollen eyes were just deceiving me. They weren't. This woman had to be around six months pregnant. For the past three weeks I'd been living in my own personal nightmare and I was certain it couldn't get any worse … until that moment.

My body began shaking with all of the pent-up anger I'd been feeling for weeks. When my gaze lifted and the smug smile across that bitch's face grew as she rubbed her belly, I couldn't refrain any longer. I lunged at her with every intention of wiping the look of superiority off her face. However, just before my fist connected with her jaw, I was pulled back against a hard chest, strong, familiar arms bracketing my body. Revulsion shot through me.

"Gina, what the hell are you doing here?" Darryl shouted at the woman while still holding me back.

"Take your goddamn hands off of me, Darryl! I'll kill both of you in here!" I yelled and fought to get free of his grasp, but my small, malnourished body was no match for his six foot four, athlete's grip.

"Calm down, Destiny."

More nausea consumed me when his lowered tone made its way to my ears. It's the same tone he'd used to console me on many occasions throughout our almost eight years of marriage.

"Get your fucking hands off me!" I screamed again.

"Tell her the truth, Darryl! This is our baby!"

I lunged again, but Darryl held firm.

"We don't know whose baby that is. Get out of my damn house!" he yelled at her, still struggling to hold onto me.

"Let go!" I managed to turn around to face Darryl, doing my best to attack him instead of the whore behind me. After all, it was him I was truly livid with. Him, who'd betrayed our marriage vows. Him, who'd destroyed everything we'd built together. And him, who'd killed *our* baby.

"You dirty son of a bitch! I hate your fucking guts!" I yelled as I kicked and tried to knee him in his dick.

"You need to leave!" he shouted above my head behind me. "I need to talk to my wife."

"I'm not your fucking wife, you lying piece of filth!" I barely registered the woman's words as she moved from behind me toward the door. I was sure she said something about coming back or getting what was owed to her and her baby. I didn't give a shit. She could have it all. As far as I was concerned, I was done.

Not until the door slammed did Darryl release me from his arms.

"Destiny, you have to calm down! The doctors said you needed to rest."

"Fuck you!" I yelled, lunging at him again, pounding on his chest only because I was too small to accurately reach his face. "You got another bitch pregnant while … while …" I panted, suddenly feeling woozy. I grabbed for the wooden bannister to keep myself from falling.

"See, you probably haven't eaten in days. You look like you've lost ten pounds since getting out of the hospital. You need to take care of yourself."

"Ha! Like you took care of me?" I snapped back. The only reason I didn't try to take his head off again was because he had the decency to look ashamed. I stepped back, staring at the man I'd once loved with my entire heart. The man I knew I was going to spend the rest of my life with. The man who'd asked me to be his wife when we were just twenty-one years old, and I hadn't hesitated in agreeing. His normally neatly trimmed beard was overgrown, his clothes were disheveled, and the bags under his eyes mirrored the ones I'd seen under my own when I'd looked in the mirror. But none of that made me feel even an ounce of pity. He deserved to be living in his own personal hell. I didn't. I'd stayed true to my marriage vows. He hadn't.

"You killed us." My grip tightened around the bannister. "Everything we built is dead. It was all a lie."

"Our life wasn't a lie!" he retorted. "I've loved you since I was nineteen years old."

"Is that what you tell all those other bitches you've fucked over the last eight years? Did you laugh with them about how naïve your fucking wife was to think big time NBA star Darryl Wright could ever be faithful?"

"I never—"

"Never what? You lied to me all these years. I invested *everything* in you! I gave up my dreams and career for you! And for what? This big ass house that was built on your bullshit!"

"Don't say that." He stepped closer.

"I might be half your size, but if you take another step closer I will take your fucking head off!" I snarled at him.

Though an unfaithful, lying, cheating bastard, Darryl wasn't a fool because he didn't take another step.

"All I see when I look at you is death and destruction. You destroyed everything we had and killed our baby in the process." I stared at him with all of the disgust and hatred I felt at that moment.

"Destiny, baby, I'll spend the rest of my life making this up to—"

"Shut up! I don't need or want anything from you except for you to sign the divorce papers my attorney sent to you."

"I'm not signing those."

"The hell you won't!"

"Those papers say you don't want anything from me."

"And I don't!" I reiterated. "Trust me when I say you've given me plenty!"

His honey brown eyes widened. He obviously understood my reference. Darryl had given me the sexually transmitted illness that ultimately killed the baby I was six months pregnant with.

"I don't need anything else from you. Not your lies. Not your money. Not your fucking house. And most certainly not *you!* Sign the papers and we'll end this fucking sham of a marriage and I will move on with my life! Now get the fuck out!" I yelled at the top of my lungs before turning and charging up the stairs.

"Destiny! Don't do this! You're being selfish. What about your mother? She's going to need money to—" Darryl couldn't get the rest of his sentence out before I'd turned, ran back down the steps, and slapped the taste out of his mouth.

He stood there, eyes wide, hand to his cheek, staring at me, as if he couldn't believe that I'd just hit him.

"Don't ever mention my mother again," I stated through gritted teeth. "You didn't give a damn about her health before and you damn sure don't give a damn about her now!" I knew Darryl. Not as well as I'd obviously thought I had, but I knew him when it came to money. He saw money as a means of controlling. He didn't give a shit about my mother or her health condition. He only cared in terms of how he could use my love of my mother to control me into taking something from him. I didn't need shit from him. Not alimony, not the big ass house, not a lump sum. Nothing.

With one last look I turned and headed back up the stairs and locked myself in the bedroom before finally crumpling to my knees in the middle of the floor. Right on top of the pile of dirty clothes that'd accumulated there over the previous three weeks. These would be the last tears I'd shed over Darryl Wright and the deception he'd spun over my life to make me believe that our marriage was real. These very likely wouldn't be the last tears I'd shed over the baby I'd lost.

However, when I was done crying that time around, I would pick myself up off the floor, call my cousin and best friend, Resha, who I just knew was anxiously waiting by her phone, to come get me. She'd been staying with me ever since I left the hospital but I couldn't take her hovering. It had been a week since I'd sent her back to her apartment, telling her I'd call her when I needed her. That didn't stop my bossy ass cousin from coming by a few times throughout the week and calling daily, but at least it'd given me some space.

By the time I got up off of that floor, I wasn't healed by any means but I was ready to end this chapter of my life.

CHAPTER 1

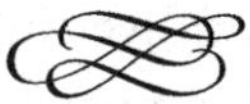

Destiny

Beep! Beep! Beep!

"Ugh!" I groaned as I rolled over in my queen size bed, swatting at the alarm that rested on the wooden stool I used instead of a nightstand. I knocked it to the floor, effectively silencing it. With quiet once again filling the room, my eyes drifted closed and I fell back into a dreamless state. Unfortunately, it wasn't to last.

"What?" I groaned into my phone that began ringing some thirty minutes later.

A deep chuckle moved across the phone lines. "I'm going to make a morning person out of you yet."

"Grr!" I growled at the cheeriness I heard in my personal trainer's voice. "JT, I am going to kick your a—"

"It's too early for such a beautiful woman to use such foul language."

"Whatever," I grumbled at the same time I pulled the covers away from my body and sat up, stretching my free hand over my head.

"I knew you'd sleep in. Let's go! Meet me at the park in twenty minutes!" *Click.*

I pulled the phone from my ear to see he'd disconnected the call, and rolled my eyes at the time. It was five-forty in the morning. Nobody should have that much energy at that ungodly hour. Pushing out a heavy breath, I rose from the comfort of my warm bed and grabbed the workout clothes I'd carefully laid out on my windowsill the night before. This was my usual routine, two out of the five weekday mornings. I'd set my alarm in hopes I would get up early enough to beat JT's call but always fell back asleep, leaving my personal trainer to call around five-thirty to wake me up and make sure I made our six o'clock appointment on time. Since it was summer, JT and I were meeting at a local track instead of the gym.

I quickly brushed my teeth, carefully placed the sweatband around the edges of my hair to keep them laid as I worked up a sweat, changed into my workout clothes, and grabbed an apple to eat as I made the ten minute walk to the track. In all, I was out of the door in ten minutes, leaving me to arrive at the track at six on the dot.

"Thought I was going to have to make you run an extra lap for being late," JT chuckled.

I rolled my eyes. "You wish."

JT's forehead wrinkled some more as he let out another laugh. I found myself smiling as well. JT was extremely handsome with his five-eleven, solid build, tanned olive skin, and dark hair. He'd been my personal trainer for close to six months, and as far as trainers went he was one of the best.

"What am I in for today?"

"We're going to incorporate some strength training with some HIIT and bodyweight training. Think you can handle that?" He nudged me with his elbow.

"I think I can manage."

Over the next hour I worked up a sweat as I squatted with a thirty pound sandbag, did countless wind sprints up and down the football field encased within the track, and countless shoulder presses, back rows, and more with the kettlebells he'd brought.

"Your form is looking good," JT said smoothly as he spotted me while I did a two armed back row with the weights.

I glanced over at JT whose eyes had narrowed. "Easy there, tiger," I warned causing another chuckle from him. We'd been down that road once before and we weren't going back.

"Nice workout. You still feeling the tenderness in your hamstring?" he asked as he stood above me while I laid on the ground and he stretched my right leg.

I shook my head. "Not since I took that week off and iced up like you advised."

"Good." He nodded. "Switch legs."

I lowered my right and lifted my left for him to stretch. Five minutes later, I was back on my feet, feeling loose and ready to head home to start my day.

"See ya' on Thursday." JT waved as we parted.

"Thursday." I said and headed in the direction of my condo. Once home, I swiftly stripped out of my sweaty workout clothes and made my way to the shower. I took my time getting out, dreading the new client I'd agreed to take on that day. Reluctantly, I picked out my white and black polka dotted silk blouse and paired it with black pants and my sky-high Kessie pointy toe mesh boots. Hell, if I was going to take on a less than desirable client, I was going to at least look cute doing it.

After tossing the boots into my bag, I put on my pair of black flats to walk the mile distance to the space I rented for my office. I grabbed my premade oatmeal and banana muffins made with agave instead of sugar, slathered on some crunchy almond butter, filled my coffee mug and was out the door.

"Five, four, three, two, and ... one."

Bring!

"Hey Resha," I smiled and answered, not needing to look at the screen to know who was calling.

"Hey, girl. On your way to work?"

"Where else would I be going on a Tuesday morning at eight a.m.?"

"Don't get cute."

"I was born cute."

"True!" Resha answered and we both cracked up at our usual conversation opener.

"You work out with that fine personal trainer this morning?"

"I did."

She sucked her teeth. "As gorgeous as he is and you keep him on your payroll to have you running some damn laps. I'd have that man yelling my whole name."

"Resha!"

"What?" she questioned innocently.

"I don't mix business with pleasure. Besides you already know what happened the one time JT and I actually went out on a date."

"Yeah, I remember. He talked about his ex the entire time."

"Yes. Good thing they got back together." JT was certainly a flirt and loved women but he was also deeply in love with his girlfriend.

I rolled my eyes. "Anyway, what're you up to over there? Still scoping out locations for your fashion week event?" Resha was a successful fashion blogger and co-host of our weekly podcast, *Fashion and Finances.* She and I had both grown up with a love of fashion, and within the last five years we'd decided to combine my love of personal finance and money and her love of fashion to create a podcast that spoke to women. She was currently in Europe for the next few months working with a few designers to host events and drum up promotion for their spring and summer lines.

"Yeah, I think I found a couple of places that are in my price range. Now, to make it all come together." She sighed heavily.

"It will. You always work your magic."

"I do, don't I?"

We laughed as I pulled the glass door of my office building's lobby open.

"You walked to work today?"

"I walk everyday," I answered.

"I know, but don't you have clients way across town today? How're you going to get there? Your cheap ass better not be hopping in no damn Uber."

I giggled at her silliness. "First of all, I'm *frugal* not cheap." Looking down at my outfit, which altogether cost in the five figure range, I frowned. I sometimes wondered if I was even really all that frugal.

"And secondly, I drove in yesterday because I met another client for lunch so I just left my car in the office's garage and walked home. I'm driving myself to my meeting, thank you very much."

"Oh well, I wouldn't put it past you to try and walk all of the way across town just to save the ten dollars that half a tank of gas might cost you."

"I'm not that damn bad," I laughed.

"No, you're not. I'm just messing with you. Hey, we're still recording tomorrow, right?"

"Same time as always," I answered. We recorded our podcast every Wednesday so that it'd be ready for a Thursday morning release.

"Cool. I'll call you later."

"All right, Resh. Love you."

"Love you, too. Bye!"

I smiled as I entered the elevator to head up to the eleventh floor where I rented an office space in communal office setting. I enjoyed the energy working with other people provided even though I was fully self-employed. My office neighbors ranged in their professions and were everything from bloggers to event planners—one woman ran a nanny business for high-end clients.

"Hey, Dawn," I called, acknowledging the office's receptionist as I entered. Dawn was in her mid-twenties, had short hair like mine except hers was in its naturally curly state while I wore my hair relaxed, and she was as efficient as they came.

She nodded and greeted me, "Good morning. I've printed out your schedule for the day, and you wanted me to remind you that you'd left your car parked in section B6 of the parking garage."

"What would I do without you?" I disliked driving and did it as little as I could, but sometimes the job required me to get in my car to meet clients. I would often forget where I'd left my car parked. The day before I'd written it down and told Dawn to remind me.

"Lord only knows." She smiled before laughing.

Dawn wasn't officially my receptionist. She took calls and did a lot of administrative work for a number of the other businesses that ran out of this office space. She was paid by the building's owner out of the collective rent they received. However, on more than one occasion I'd considered hiring her full-time to work solely for me.

"I may have to make you an offer you can't refuse." I wiggled my eyebrows in her direction, pointing my hand with my coffee mug in it at her.

"As long as I don't wake up with any dead horses in my bed, I'll consider it."

I picked up my schedule from Dawn's desk and instantly groaned at the sight of my two hour mid-morning client meeting.

"That's the same face you made yesterday when looking at the same client name."

"I should've never agreed to taking on these clients."

"Then why did you?" Dawn questioned.

I wrinkled my forehead before raising my gaze from the schedule in my hands to Dawn. "Because when the woman who mentored you, helped you get a highly coveted position, *and* gifted you the seed money to start your own company asks you to do her a favor, it's not all that easy to tell her no." I sighed before taking another sip of my coffee.

"Better you than me. I hate athletes." Dawn shivered before turning back to her desktop.

"Me too," I mumbled before heading back to my office. I checked the time on my wrist watch as soon as I reached my desk and booted up my desktop. Sitting down, I waved at one of the male owners of the event planning company as he walked past. Sometimes the fact that all of the office walls were made of glass could make one feel like they were working in a damn fishbowl, but for the most part, I liked my office space. I got a kick out of opening my door that read "Destiny McDonald, Financial Advisor."

I got lost in checking and sending emails when the phone on my desk rang.

"Destiny McDonald, Financial Advisor, how can I help you?" I answered in one breath without taking my eyes off the email I'd been typing.

"Are you ready?"

My hands stilled over the keyboard. "I still don't get why you couldn't take on this job."

"There's no way Mike would allow me to teach his guys. He says they think of me as a sweet mama bear and they'd never listen to my advice. They're a tough group," she answered, hints of her southern accent, derived from her Nashville, Tennessee roots apparent in her voice.

I snorted. "So I'm the sacrifice."

Brenda McClellan's giggle moved through the phone lines. "Hardly, honey. Those boys will take one look at you and not even realize they are the ones who better stay out of your way or get eaten alive."

"Oh, but they'll find out soon enough."

"I'm sure they will. They're all good boys. Just need a little guidance."

"These are grown ass men who've been coddled their whole lives." I rolled my eyes, being all too familiar with the lives of professional athletes.

"They're not that bad. Just whip 'em into shape. Mike's really concerned about how these guys are handling their money. You read the report that came out a few years ago citing that most professional athletes—"

"File for bankruptcy within five years of ending their careers. Yes, I'm familiar with it."

"And after Denny's suicide last year, Mike took it really hard. He still feels like shit that one of his former players didn't feel he could come to him to talk about his financial troubles."

I did my best to ignore the pang of sadness that filled my belly but I couldn't. Mike McClellan, Brenda's husband, was the head football coach for the Williamsport Cougars and had been for the previous decade. Denny Wilson had been a star player whose rise came quickly, and burnout came even quicker. After years of being hounded by financial problems due to the mismanagement of his money, Denny took his own life.

"Great. Lay a guilt trip on me to get me to do your bidding."

"How's it working?"

I smirked. "Like a charm. I'm heading out in about twenty minutes."

"Good. And don't go soft on them either. These guys need a hard reality check and you're just the one to give it to them."

I nodded even though she couldn't see me. "Later, Brenda."

"Bye, Destiny."

After hanging up, I pulled up the research I'd done on the Cougars football team. I'd already known most of the players. Despite my distaste for athletes in general, I loved sports and was a big Cougars fan. It'd been imbedded in me since I was a child to always root for the home team. My father wouldn't have had it any other way, and as a born and bred daddy's girl, I wouldn't either. For the fiftieth time I looked over the pictures, names, news articles, and anything else I could find regarding the Williamsport Cougars' players. From this information I was to build a three-week course around financial literacy and management to teach these players.

My eyes somehow landed on an image of the Cougars' star quarterback, Tyler Townsend. Not for the first time, I found myself staring into those hypnotizing hazel-green eyes of his. He wasn't smiling in the picture but his eyes held a certain mirth. It was as if he was a part of some secret joke he wasn't about to let the world in on.

"Whatever," I mumbled to myself as I stood. No need wasting anymore time staring at pictures of these players when I'd be standing in front of them all in less than thirty minutes. I didn't give a damn about smiling hazel-green eyes. I needed to get my head in the game so I could push through the next four weeks and get this job over with as seamlessly as possible.

* * *

Tyler

"Someone was training in the off season."

I turned and peered down at Jack, the assistant to the head coach, and nodded. "What'd you expect?"

Chuckling, he shook his head. "Nothing less from silver spoon."

I frowned, narrowing my eyes at Jack. I hated that fucking nickname. I'd gotten it my first damn year in the National Football League and still couldn't shake it.

"Don't take my head off, Ty," Jack laughed.

"Don't give me a fucking reason to," I warned.

"Easy, double T. You know Jack just likes messing with you," Kelvin Maynard, our team's star wide receiver and the closest thing I had to a best friend, stated as he clapped me on the back.

I shrugged his hand off me. "I can't stand that nickname."

Kelvin laughed some more. "That's exactly why they continue to use it, silver spoon."

I whirled around on Kelvin but he ducked the jab I shot at his jaw. Ever since my induction into the NFL as the fifth overall pick by the Williamsport Cougars, I'd been plagued with this damn nickname. Seeing as how I was born with the proverbial silver spoon in my mouth, my counterparts didn't seem to think I could or would hack it in the league. Despite my outstanding collegiate accomplishments, to some I was just the rich kid that'd bought his way into the league. I guess my reputation over my time in the NFL hadn't exactly tamped down on those speculations. But my performance on the field should've long put to bed any bullshit about my not earning my spot.

"Let it go," Kelvin yell-laughed after I took another swing at him.

"Do I look like fucking Elsa to you?"

Kelvin froze and cocked his head to the side, raising a dark, bushy eyebrow. "The fuck is Elsa? That chick you banged last—"

"No, jackass," I laughed, holding my stomach muscles, "she's a Disney princess. The coldest …" I paused when I saw the confusion on his face grow even more. "Forget it." I waved him off.

"See, you spend too much time around all those kids in your family. They got you watching Disney movies and shit." Kelvin pointed at me.

I shrugged. "Guilty as charged." And I wasn't about to apologize for it either. I loved every moment I spent with my niece and nephews. If Kennedy, the only niece in the family so far, wanted me to spend a few hours watching Disney movies while she talked my ear off, so be it.

"Man, if people only really knew you're not as much of a trouble-maker as they say you are," Kelvin stated, patting me on the shoulder again.

I winked at him. "What people don't know won't hurt me."

"Let's go! We don't have all damn day!" Coach McClellan yelled from down the long hall that lead past the locker room to the lecture hall where we spent the mid-mornings and early afternoons going over news plays. It was the third week of July and we were just starting the second day of our whole team's training camp, hosted at Williamsport University. The college had a stadium and field large enough to house our team's practices, along with available lecture halls for the off-the-field study.

"We're coming, we're coming," I called ahead.

"Then move your ass, Townsend!" McClellan barked back, causing me to laugh.

"What's this session about again? Why're we all in here?" Kelvin asked as we made our way into the classroom with stadium-style seating.

I glanced around the room, noticing that the entire team was beginning to fill out the seats. That included both offensive and defensive lines, along with the special teams. Our sessions rarely consisted of the entire team coming together.

"Hell if I know," I answered Kelvin. I made my way down to a middle row, following Kelvin. He sat a couple of seats in while I chose an aisle seat. Sitting in a lecture hall already had me on edge as it was, no way I was about to sit in the middle of the row.

"Money management?" Kelvin read out loud from the screen at the front of the classroom.

I sat back in my seat, arms folded, and pushed out a hefty breath, ready to be bored to fucking death. Glancing up at the ceiling I decided to count the cracks above to pass the time until this shit was over.

"Gentlemen, the coaching staff and myself, as well as the team owners, have decided that making money management lessons a part of training camp would be a great idea. The problem is ..."

Wah. Waah. Waah. Wah.

That's exactly how Coach McClellan was starting to sound, just like the teacher from *Charlie Brown*. My eyes narrowed. *Have Kyle, Kennedy, and Diego ever even watched an episode of* Charlie Brown*?* I wondered as I continued to stare at the ceiling. Kids these days didn't know good television. I'd have to try and find some episodes on Youtube or somewhere to show them. I doubted their parents would go out of their way to introduce the joys of Charlie Brown and his gang to my niece and nephews, so it was up to me. *Uncle Tyler to the rescue,* I mused, grinning to myself as my eyes remained transfixed on the ceiling above.

Just as I trying to recount my favorite *Charlie Brown* episode my nostrils were hit with a smell that had my stomach muscles tightening and the hairs on my arms and neck standing. I popped my head up from the back of the seat just as a petite figure blew past me, her heels clacking against the linoleum floor as she confidently strode toward the front of the room.

As if it had a mind of its own, my body sat up out of the laid back, lazy position I'd been in mere seconds prior. When the figure turned around, my heart rate picked up speed as if it knew I was just preparing for another grueling workout.

"Daaamn, shorty is fine!" Kelvin whistled under his breath but loud enough for me and a few of the other guys to hear.

"Hell yeah."

"I'd hit that."

My hands tightened into fists and my jaw clenched for a reason I'd never experienced a day in my life. *Jealousy.*

"Team, I'd like you to meet a good friend of mine, Ms. Destiny McDonald. Ms. McDonald is a certified financial advisor with years of ..."

The coach's words again fell by the wayside as I took her in. She was little, probably around five foot three, but the heels she wore gave her at least three or more inches. The white and black polka dot silk blouse she wore stopped right at her waist, revealing the curves of her hips. Her mahogany skin held a healthy glow, and her oval face stood out thanks to the short haircut she wore. The woman was beautiful. For the first time since entering the lecture hall I regretted not sitting closer to the front of the room. Her physical beauty was only heightened by the fact that as Coach McClellan talked she stared around the room, hands clasped in front of her, completely unintimidated by the fifty or so sweaty jocks in the room. Including the team's players there were about fifteen on our coaching staff. That meant in a room of close to seventy men, she was the only female in the room, and she held her ground, staring at and studying every single one.

When her dark brown eyes finally connected with mine, my gut clenched again. My fists tightened, and a sensation I'd never felt started at the top of my head and moved through my entire being. Her gaze lingered on me for just a second longer than she'd intended. I don't know how I knew that but I did and it caused a grin to open up on my face.

"I expect you all to give Ms. McDonald your full attention," Coach McClellan finished up saying.

She took a step forward and her perfectly plump lips that were coated with a clear gloss opened slightly, preparing to speak. I leaned in, needing to hear her voice for the first time, but she was cut off.

Immediately, I grew annoyed and agitated when instead of a feminine voice, I heard, "What the hell can this bi—" The voice cut off as the woman at the head of room raised a perfectly arched eyebrow, daring him to finish that word. "Female teach any one of us about money? Was that your ten-year-old Honda Civic I pulled up next to in the parking lot?" Leonard Riggs asked before breaking out into a round of laughs. Snickers from around the room began to join in as well.

The tops of my ears began to heat up as the anger that'd come from nowhere grew in my belly. I shot a death glare in Leonard's direction. That kid needed to be shut up. He was just beginning his second season in the league as our team's cornerback and he had a mouth on him that needed to be closed. That moment just solidified for me that I'd be the one to shut it, eventually.

But before I or Coach McClellan could respond to Leonard's statement, the Ms. McCloud—I hadn't caught her first name, too caught up in staring at her when coach had first said it—held out her hand, warning coach off. She stepped forward.

"Yes, Mr. Riggs, that is my ten-year-old Honda Civic you so lovingly parked your Bugatti next to. I would've thought my Honda was more your speed since it's foreign and all. Isn't that what your rap star friends always tote? Having foreign cars? But," she moved even closer to Riggs, stepping up one then the second stair, "unlike your *leased* Bugatti and your friends' vehicles, my Civic is both foreign and paid off. Do you know what that means, Mr. Riggs?" She paused.

"Nah, what?" Leonard challenged.

"It means that over the last six years I've had my car, the three hundred dollars that would've went to car payments went to my investment accounts instead. Along with the other funds I've saved in costs for higher car insurance deductibles, gas, and more. And over the course of the last six years, I've more than quadrupled my net worth by not spending on extravagant, luxury items that depreciate as soon as they're driven off the lot. And do you know what that means, Mr. Riggs?" She paused again.

No answer.

"It means that I could stop working tomorrow and never have to worry about having a roof over my head or about where my next meal is coming from. And *that* is what this *female* can teach you about money." She stared at Leonard for another second before moving back to the front of the room. "Now," she clapped her hands, looking at the rest of us with a heart-stopping smile on her face, "are there anymore questions?"

A banging sound sounded as my back bumped against the seat behind me. I was, quite literally, knocked over. I stared at the tiny, slip of a woman who had just stunned our entire football team and coaching staff into silence. I was pretty sure my fate had been sealed in that one moment. When I finally tugged my gaze from her face to peer up at the screen behind her, I knew. Emblazoned across the screen was her name, title, and picture. Destiny McDonald, Certified Financial Advisor.

Destiny indeed.

"I fucking knew it," I heard Kelvin say to me in a low voice.

In spite of my not wanting to take my eyes off the woman at the head of the class, I turned my head slightly in Kelvin's direction. "Knew what?"

Chuckling, he shook his head. "Man, any black woman with that Halle Berry 90s haircut and that Nia Long swag don't have time for the bullshit. She's the type you wife up, quick."

My lips curled into a scowl. "Don't even think about it."

"Who? Me? Nah, man." Kelvin shook his head, chuckling. "Chicks with short hair don't play. They don't have time to waste doing their hair, and they sure as hell don't have time to put up with my bullshit."

My head began nodding in agreement before I realized what I was doing. "She's more beautiful than Nia Long."

"The fuck? The hell you know about Nia Long?"

I cut a look in Kelvin's direction before turning back to the beauty at the front of the room. "Don't worry about it."

I spared Kelvin little more attention as Destiny McCloud began with her lessons by first explaining her professional background. I got wrapped up in the melodic sound of her voice as she spoke about budgeting and living beneath your means. My eyes followed everywhere she went in the room. And move around she did. My chest tightened when, on more than one occasion, a player would ask a question in an obvious attempt to flirt. Time flew by in that lecture hall as Destiny handled herself well among some intimidating looking men, answering questions about money management and informing us all of the syllabus over the next few weeks. She'd actually written up a syllabus that was passed out to all of us. Had this been anyone else, I wouldn't have glanced twice at the paper. Hell, I'd barely looked at any of the syllabi I'd gotten while I was actually in college. I'd hated school and just barely gotten by. I'd done the minimum needed to be able to continue playing sports.

Looking over the weekly lessons, I grinned when a question formed in my head.

"Excuse me?" I raised my hand.

Destiny's head lifted, and our gazes colliding. Her eyes widened just slightly before they returned to their normal size.

"I see next week we'll be discussing the basics on investing. I was wondering if beforehand you could just answer for me, what is the difference between a stock and a bond?" I asked in my most charming voice, and prepared myself for the verbal assault I'd knew my question would bring.

Destiny didn't disappoint when her back went ramrod straight, eyes narrowing, pouty lips forming into a frown that made me want to lick all of her remaining lip gloss off, ever so slowly until she begged me to take her.

I'd gotten somewhat lost in that little fantasy before realizing that she'd begun moving up the stairs until she came to stand directly over me. I inhaled deeply and that fresh scent of lavender and mint flooded my airway again.

"The difference between a stock and a bond," she repeated, arms folded across her chest.

My grin widened as I nodded. "Yes, that's what I asked."

"Sounds like silver spoon needs to learn more about money." A round of laughter in response to Leonard's joke sounded.

"Hey, Riggs," I called but my eyes never left Destiny, "do yourself a favor and shut the fuck up before I shove one of these chairs up your narrow ass." I cut my eyes in his direction before returning to the woman before me. I grew even more pissed when I saw that her gaze was no longer on me, but across the room at Leonard.

"I'm sure what Mr. Riggs meant to say was that it's interesting you of all people, Mr. Townsend," she turned her attention back to me, squelching the heat of jealousy in my chest that'd begun to grow, "don't know the difference between a stock and a bond."

My eyes made their way from her face down her petite frame, admiring every dip and curve along the way. "Guess I never paid attention to all that stuff." My voice had dropped low. "Maybe you can teach me."

She blinked before taking a step back and lifting a perfectly arched eyebrow. "I'll be teaching you exactly what I teach the rest of your teammates, Mr. Townsend." She pivoted on her heels, starting for the head of the lecture hall again, but paused and turned to glance at me over her shoulder. "And I suggest you bring a paper and pencil to take plenty of notes because I don't enjoy repeating myself."

With that, she turned and walked away, leaving me to watch the sway of her hips.

"I've got something you can repeat, over and over again," I mumbled, feeling energized by our brief exchange. My body felt as if I'd just awakened from the best eight hour sleep I'd had in a long time, instead of having just coming in from a grueling two-hour, early morning practice. I smiled down at the woman who'd just sealed her own fate and didn't even know it.

CHAPTER 2

Destiny

"Brenda told me you'd be able to handle this group but I was worried. I should've known better."

I laughed and smiled at Coach Mike McClellan. "Yes, you should've." We were in his temporary office on campus, debriefing, as he called it, after my first money management course with his team. Mike took his role as head coach of the Williamsport Cougars very seriously. There was serious talk of the team going all of the way to the Super Bowl this year. But Coach McClellan didn't just care about his players' performance on the field, he cared about them as individuals, hence the reason he'd approached the team's owners to fund this short money management course. Despite my initial objections, I had to say, the team was paying me very nicely to teach their players what I knew about managing money and planning for the future.

"I don't think I've ever seen Leonard Riggs stunned into silence like that. Hell, I don't think I've seen my whole team stunned into silence like that. Not by a—" He stopped.

I lifted my brows. "It's okay, you can say it. Not by a woman."

He chuckled and cleared his throat. "I didn't say it, you did."

I shrugged. "It's fine. Just speaking the truth."

"I can't believe you actually handed out a syllabus." He stared at the paper on his desk.

I shrugged. "It helps us all stay organized. I think today's lesson went well, but I'm really looking forward to seeing how they answer the homework I gave them."

Mike chuckled. "You actually gave my guys homework. During training camp."

"Sure did, and they better do it, too." The first assignment I'd given the team was to track all of their expenses over a seventy-two hour period. Three days. That's all I needed them to do, but I was sure most of them wouldn't.

"We'll see. Brenda wanted me to nail down a date with you to come over for dinner. You know how she is about this stuff."

I giggled. Brenda McClellan could be the sweetest woman you'd ever met, but ask her six foot, muscular, former football player turned coach husband, she was the biggest bully around.

"How about next week sometime? I'm open any evening except for Wednesday."

Mike nodded. "I'll tell Brenda and get back to you."

"I'll give her a call. You've got enough on your plate."

He pushed out a breath. "Thanks."

"I—" I was cut off by a knock on the door.

"Hey, Coach, you needed me?"

"Yeah, Ty, hang on." Mike held up a finger as he answered his ringing cell phone.

I peered over my shoulder, seeing Tyler Townsend's big, six-foot-three frame filling the entire doorway. I turned back to Mike. "I'll see you next week," I told him as I picked up my black leather Kate Spade briefcase to exit. I turned toward the doorway but was stopped from exiting when Tyler remained in place.

"Excuse me?" I glanced up at him but avoided staring directly into his eyes.

"Am I in your way?" he drawled.

I pinched my lips, anger mounting. "I only see one doorway, and since you're standing in the middle of it, yes, you *are* in my way."

My body stiffened at the sound of his deep chuckle. "You are feisty, aren't you?"

"Mr. Townsend, cats are *feisty.* I am a woman who is in a rush and has some work to do. So if you'll excuse me." I stared over his shoulder, emphasizing my desire to move past him.

"Tyler."

"What?" I snapped my head backward, finally looking up at him in his eyes. I ignored the tremble in my knees that one look caused.

"Tyler. Not Mr. Townsend. No need for the formalities between us. Right, Ms. McDonald. It is Ms., correct?"

I worked my lower jaw, gritting my teeth. I just needed to leave this damn office and this damn gymnasium with all of this testosterone swimming around in it.

"Have a good day, Mr. Townsend." I rolled my eyes and pressed past him. He moved just enough to let me pass, but his arm brushed up against my waist.

"I'll definitely be seeing you around, Destiny."

My steps faltered as I heard my name coming from his mouth for the first time. I urged myself not to turn around to steal one last look, but that's exactly what I did. A tiny gasp escaped my lips when I saw Tyler watching me as he bit his lower lip, running a large hand through the right side of his red beard. Those magnetizing eyes of his actually sparkled. The mirth I'd noticed in previous pictures was intensified tenfold in person. And those eyes were unabashedly planted on my derriere until they rose to meet my eyes. A grin that looked like a warning and an invitation all in one spread across his face. And that look alone told me I needed to stay as far away as possible from Tyler Townsend.

I continued down the long hallway, only feeling safe once I rounded the corner that headed to the parking lot. I knew I was out of Tyler's hungry gaze. I rolled my eyes, feeling both irritated and relieved at the same time. All professional athletes were serious womanizers. It was a by-product of having the world handed to you on a silver platter all because you could throw or catch or put a ball into a hoop really well.

"Well, well, well, Ms. McDonald."

Sighing, I rolled my eyes at the condescending tone in Leonard's voice. He was unfortunately in the parking lot heading in the same direction I was, since our cars were parked right next to each others.

"Mr. Riggs."

"Need a ride anywhere? Your little hooptie ain't gonna make it around the block," he laughed at his corny ass joke.

"No thanks. I've got Uber right here on my phone in case my Honda decides to poop out on me." I wouldn't need it, of course. My car was only ten years old and ran in excellent condition thanks to my keeping up with the necessary maintenance. But to men like Leonard Riggs a ten-year-old, paid off, reliable car was unsightly. It didn't meet the standard his year and a half old, multi-million dollar contract in the NFL had afforded him. Laughing, I shook my head at the ridiculousness of the situation. Leonard Riggs had come from very humble beginnings but was now looking down on my car because it wasn't up to his baller status standards.

"You'll need it with that piece of shit."

"If you say so, Mr. Riggs. Just make sure you have your homework done for next week's class."

"Man, fuck that—" His retort was cut off once I slammed my door shut and started my vehicle up. I didn't even spare him a second glance as I pulled out of my spot and maneuvered out of the parking lot.

Fucking athletes.

* * *

Tyler

I watched as she walked away, my head cocked to the side, admiring her going as much as I'd admired her coming. She held her head high, back straight, shoulders back as if she knew she owned the attention of those around her. As if that was how it should be naturally. The fact that she hadn't shown even the slightest bit of intimidation in the lecture hall had left me intrigued. Her refusal to say my first name left me compelled. But her response when I'd called her by her name for the first time left me in awe. I rubbed my lips together just as she turned the corner, disappearing from my line of sight, leaving a burning desire to learn more about her in her wake.

"Tyler," Coach McClellan called, snapping me back from the edges of reality.

I turned in the coach's direction, and finally stepped fully into his office.

"Don't even think about it," he warned.

I wrinkled my brows in confusion.

"Fuck that look. You know exactly what I'm talking about. Leave Destiny McDonald alone. She's out of your league and Brenda would kill me if anything happened to her. She's very fond of that girl. And when my wife gets upset, I get upset."

I chuckled. "You sound like my father."

Coach grunted. "Robert and I have a lot in common."

I waved him off. I didn't draw too much attention to the fact that my father and my head coach were good friends.

I was, however, tempted to ask for my coach to tell me everything he knew about Destiny McDonald. And I meant *everything*. But I doubted he'd be receptive to my request. I had other ways of finding out what I wanted to know.

"Look, Ty, this season's important for our team. With you, Riggs, and Maynard in the lineup, we're unstoppable on offense. Our defensive line is stronger than ever, and we haven't had a chance to take this team all of the way in a long time. I need your head in the game."

"My head's always in the game, Coach. You know that."

Mike frowned, lifting a suspicious blond eyebrow. "The past few years say otherwise."

I grunted. "None of my off-field bullshit has ever affected my on the field stats."

Mike nodded. "I am aware. But this is deeper than your performance on the field. You and I both know your desire to become a coach one day. Your antics could get in the way of that dream."

I inhaled and pushed all the air out of my lungs. I didn't want to hear what Coach McClellan was saying but I knew he was right. Not many people knew of my desire of becoming a head football coach one day. I loved playing more than anything but I wasn't stupid. Most professional athletes didn't play more than a decade at the highest level. And in spite of my family's wishes, going into the family business at Townsend Industries just wasn't my calling.

I snorted. "I'll rein it in coach."

"You need to do more than rein it in, Townsend. You need to step up."

I furrowed my brows angrily. "I bust my ass every time I step out on that field."

Coach nodded slightly. "I never doubted your commitment to this team, but what I'm saying is, as you're entering your fourth season, third season as a starter for our team, the younger guys are looking up to you. I know how big of a pain in the ass some of them can be, trust me. You were one of the biggest."

I pulled my head back in mock offense. "Coach, I'm hurt you would even—"

"Cut the shit, Townsend." He waved me off with his hand.

I couldn't help the chuckle that escaped my lips.

"There was that night in Vegas with the strippers halfway through your rookie season."

I snorted. "Minor misunderstanding."

"The DUI at the end of your rookie year."

I held up my finger. "I wasn't driving, and in my defense, I didn't know Cindy had been drinking that night."

"And let's not forget about the brawl you started your second year between our offensive line and the Lions' defensive team, on another wild night out."

I grunted. "They deserved that shit."

"Tyler."

I held up my hands. "You won't have any trouble out of me, Coach. Scout's honor." I held a thumbs-up.

"That's not the fucking ... forget it." He waved me off again as I laughed. "Anyway, my true concern is you looking out for the other guys. If you want to prove yourself as a future coach and leader of a football team, you've got to step up. Not just on the field by running plays, which you do very well, but by showing these guys how great they can be. They respect you as their quarterback. Channel that in other ways. Riggs—"

I grunted at the mention of his name. Leonard Riggs was going into his second year with the team and while he was shaping up to become one of the best cornerbacks in the league, he was an over the top asshole. I mean, a much bigger asshole than I ever was.

"I get it, he's not your favorite guy on the team, but you two on the field are magic. And since you know more than anyone what it's like to be the underdog on this team, you could take him under your wing."

I snorted again. "Don't count on it."

"Ty."

I pushed out a breath. I didn't like Riggs. His first season it was just a minor irritation but I could handle it. But since that morning the condescending remarks he'd made during Destiny's lecture pissed me off. Why, I didn't know. But I didn't need to fucking know either. Something possessive took ahold of me from the moment I first laid eyes on her, and Riggs had fucked with that.

"Do it for me, for the team, and for your future as a coach. You will encounter more than your fair share of players who you can't stand. But as their coach you will have to work with them, teach them, and mold them to reach their full potential as athletes."

I tutted and cut my eyes at my coach. "If you say so. I'll see what I can do."

He nodded. "That's all I ask. Now get the hell out of my office. We've got our second practice of the day starting in thirty minutes. Don't be late!" He pointed in my direction.

I shook my head. "Wouldn't dream of it, Coach." I backed up a few steps before turning toward the door to head out.

"And, Ty?"

I stopped, turning back to my coach, raising an eyebrow.

"I mean it. Stay away from Destiny McDonald."

My lips spread into an instant grin. Just the sound of her name brought back the image of her perfectly shaped oval face, intense brown eyes, and fully-glossed lips. I gave my coach a wink. Stay away from Destiny McDonald.

Not a chance in hell.

CHAPTER 3

Tyler

"So, Wendy, tell us about the way in which finances played a part in your recovery process. I know with any illness, especially a sudden illness as in your case, money is a huge factor ..."

I listened intently, my eyes drifting closed as I paced back and forth in the hotel room where the team was staying during our training camp. I was on my third episode of Destiny's podcast named *Fashion and Finances.* Apparently, she hosted the weekly, hour-long podcast with her best friend, Resha, who was a fashion blogger. The women's keen interest in money and fashion played off one another, and they used their knowledge in their respective fields to provide information to young and middle-aged women on how to get their finances right, and look cute while doing it. At least, that was the tagline they used as an intro on all of the recordings I'd listened to thus far.

This episode they were speaking with a journalist who was a financial correspondent for one of the big cable networks, who'd had a sudden major illness a year and a half prior. The woman was lucky to be a live, let alone doing as well as she was, having recently returned to work full-time. I listened aptly as they discussed the need for long-term care insurance, emergency funds, and the like. The facts and ins and outs of navigating money matters during a medical crisis didn't interest me much. It was Destiny's voice that held my rapt attention. I always found it deeply intriguing hearing the passion in someone's voice as they spoke on matters that lit a fire underneath them. I heard that ardor in Destiny's voice as she asked questions and relayed sometimes complex information in a way that her listeners would comprehend. The more I listened the harder I fell.

"Man, will you sit your can't-sit-still ass down somewhere?"

I stilled, quickly pivoted, and aimed the Nerf ball I'd been tossing up and down in my hands at Kelvin who laid on the bed. He caught it easily.

"Nice hands."

"All that damn pacing. What're you listening to?" he finally asked, sitting up.

Reluctantly, I pulled my phone out of the waistband of my shorts and paused the recording.

"A podcast," I answered.

"The crime and theory one I told you about?" His eyes grew wider with excitement. Kelvin was a true crime buff. He'd told me about a popular podcast that traced a twenty-year-old crime from start to finish, questioning whether or not the wrong person had been put away for it.

"I'm telling you, man, I think it was the best friend who did it. No way it was the ex. He got a raw deal," Kelvin blathered on, shaking his head.

"No, I'm not listening to your true crime shit," I grunted. "I'm listening to Destiny's podcast."

He scrunched his eyebrows. "Destiny," he repeated her name before snapping his fingers. "Oh, right. Fine Nia Long chick from this morning."

I narrowed my eyes on him. "Watch your mouth. She's not a damn *chick*. And I already told you, she's more beautiful than Nia Long." The actress was gorgeous, but Destiny was … Destiny.

Kelvin pushed out a long whistle. "Whoa," he stated as he stared at me.

I decided to ignore him and went to press play to continue listening.

"How many episodes have you listened to so far?"

"Almost on number four."

He shook his head. "That's nearing four hours. I don't think I can remember the last time a woman has held your attention that long."

I gave him a middle finger but he was right. Most things didn't hold my attention for very long, save for football. The fact that I'd spent this long listening to her voice, hadn't escaped my attention. But as I was about to hit play my phone rang. A smile crept over my face when I saw my oldest brother's name pop up.

"Diego!" I answered. It was almost eight o'clock, close to his bedtime. He always called me right before he went to bed on the nights his father was home from the station. My oldest brother, Carter, was a firefighter in Williamsport.

"Hey, Uncle Ty! Guess what?"

"What?" I questioned, sounding just as enthused as he was.

"Mama and Daddy said we can come visit you on your family day at training camp again. And this time, Kyle and Kennedy can come. Isn't that awesome?"

I laughed at how excited he sounded. "Hell yeah, little buddy."

"Watch your damn mouth when talking to my kid!" Carter's voice bellowed from the background.

"I was wondering when your nosy ass was going to butt into the conversation between my nephew and I," I retorted.

"Good thing I was, too. Remember, you're talking to a nine year old. I know that's only a year or two beneath your mental age, but—"

"Fuck you!" I growled to Carter's laughter.

"Ooooh, Uncle Ty you said a bad word. My daddy makes Uncle Don, at the fire station, put money in a swear jar whenever he swears in front of me."

I chuckled. "What's the matter, Carter? Firefighting not paying the bills so you gotta hustle your fellow firefighters out of money now?" I teased.

"Nope. Trying to teach barbarians like Don and yourself to show some damn respect."

"Oooh, Daddy you said damn."

"That's not a real curse word, son."

"Since when?" I intervened.

"Since I said so," Carter growled.

"Diego, your daddy is doing what we adults call moving the goal-posts. One day I'll teach you what that means. For now, tell me about camp. How was it?"

I continued to pace the room, as Diego recounted his day at camp to me. He, as well as my niece and nephew from my second oldest brother, Aaron, attended the same camp. Though Kyle and Kennedy were nearly two years younger than Diego, the trio were thick as thieves. I grinned at the memory of Carter and Aaron both telling me how Diego stepped in when a bully was targeting Kyle and making fun of him because he was a poor reader. I laughed my ass off when Aaron added in the fact that while Diego and Kyle tag-teamed the third grade bully, Kennedy, my only niece, had run over and kicked the boy as well. I laughed so hard at the image of my sweet niece kicking the boy, my stomach ached. Kennedy was as kind as they came but don't mess with her brother. She reminded me of her mother in that way.

While Michelle and Patience, Carter and Aaron's wives, had forbade them from taking the children out for ice cream after the fight, I along with my brothers had taken the children out and allowed them to get whatever they wanted. I wasn't the uncle that would lie and tell my nephews and niece that fighting was never the answer. Sometimes it was necessary to put a bully in their place with your fists. And I'd be damned if I didn't let them know they'd done a hell of a job in doing so.

"Okay, Uncle Ty, Mommy says I gotta hang up now."

I grinned at the sadness in Diego's voice. "Okay, champ. I've gotta go myself. I've got another early practice in the morning. I'll see you next week for family day, all right?" I didn't doubt I'd be talking to Diego again before then, but I wanted to leave him with a reminder to wipe away some of his sadness.

"Okay, love you. G'nite."

"Love you back. Night, buddy." I hung up and tossed my phone on the bed. I glanced over to see Kelvin just turning over, headphones in his ears, probably listening to one of his true crime podcasts to drift off to sleep. Like Diego and Kelvin, I should've taken my ass to sleep. I had to be up early for another grueling day of two-a-days, that's two practices in one day, followed by lectures and watching videos to go over and perfect our plays. Training camp was meant to be grueling. It was how we prepared for the ups and downs of the next six months of the season. At least we hoped it would last for six months, putting us into the playoffs and the big game.

But even as I daydreamed of the possibility of winning that coveted ring, the satisfaction I often felt just envisioning that day was tampered. Something felt as if it were missing. That's when I picked up my phone, pulled up the podcast I'd been listening to, and hit play.

"Welcome back. We've been talking with ..."

A calm settled over me as her voice welcomed the listeners back from their commercial break. I strolled over to my bed, turning off the lamp that stood on the wooden nightstand between our beds, before getting into my own. After thirty minutes or so, I drifted off into a peaceful, dreamless sleep to the sound of Destiny McDonald's voice.

* * *

Destiny

"So, what's today's hot topic?" I questioned, speaking into the microphone I had set up in my home office. It was Wednesday evening and Resha and I were recording our podcast so that I could post it on our website the next day. Since Resha was still in Europe, we had to record long-distance over the phone which wasn't ideal but it worked out. Our podcasts garnered hundreds of thousands of listeners every week, something that I'd never dreamt was attainable when we first started. But fours years later it was very successful for the both of us. There were so many women, young and old alike, who hungered for financial knowledge that wasn't being passed down by condescending men or by someone who wasn't trying to sell them something. Couple that information with both Resha and my love of fashion and we had a hit on our hands.

"I was thinking of taking the shame out of shopping at consignment shops or thrift stores."

"I love it," I stated into the microphone. "How did you come up with the idea for this topic?"

Each week Resha and I switched off on choosing the weekly hot topic ideas. They were always a surprise to the other, because we didn't reveal our topic until the recording. I felt it made the podcast seem more authentic, to get one another's natural, off-the-cuff reaction on-air. It was Resha's week to choose the topic and I loved what she'd chosen.

"Since being here in Europe, I've passed by so many consignment shops. And the people are not ashamed of going in and looking around or buying from these places. A Parisian fashion blogger I met the other day, practically gushed over the outfit she wore that she'd gotten from a second-hand shop. So my question to you, Destiny, is why do you think Americans are more leery of thrift stores and consignment shops?"

"I think you know my answer to that, Resh, but I'll tell you anyway," I began. "There are many reasons, and some of them are legit, of course. We all want to pay for quality, and when buying second-hand, we can't always be sure of the quality or of the care the previous owner took with the item, right? But I think it goes deeper than that. It goes hand-in-hand with the keeping up with the Jones' mentality."

"Here she goes, y'all."

I laughed. "No, hear me out ..." I went on talking about some people's obsession with new, flashy items and how buying second-hand or from thrift stores didn't fit that standard. Resha and I volleyed the topic back forth between us over the next ten minutes before moving on to reader questions. This was my favorite section of the podcasts. I thoroughly enjoyed hearing our listeners' questions on everything from saving for retirement, starting a fashion blog, paying off student loans, money and relationships, and more. We went through about five reader questions that I'd chosen for that segment, before closing out.

"One week, we should do a whole podcast solely answering listener's questions. I only pick out three to five per episode but we get hundreds each week," I told Resha right after we ended our recording and I turned my mic off. It was only us on the phone now.

"Yeah, that's a great idea. I know we can't get to all of the questions each week, so taking on as many as possible in one segment would be a way to get to more," she agreed just before letting out a huge yawn.

"It's late over there, huh?"

"Almost eleven and I have to be up early tomorrow."

"I won't hold you too long," I responded, pressing the button on my phone to turn on the speaker and walking toward the kitchen.

"No, it's fine. I wanted to ask you how it went with the football players yesterday."

"Pssh." I rolled my eyes.

"That bad?"

"It wasn't bad, actually. There were some jackasses, of course, but I got my point across and I didn't have to slap anybody, so that's good." I shrugged and laughed along with Resha.

"Girl, you know you can call me if you need to go upside anybody's head."

"My ride or die."

"For life."

"Love you, Resha."

"You bet your ass you do. So that's it? It was cool. Didn't have to tackle anyone? The footballers played nice?"

At her question, the oddest thing happened. An image of Tyler Townsend's hazel-green eyes came to mind. I swallowed. "Yup. Well, there was one, Leonard Riggs."

"The showboat."

"That's him." Riggs had a reputation on and off the field for being flashy and cocky. It's partly what made him so good, but it's also what made him an asshole. "He tried to play me in front of the whole team but I got him together quick, fast, and in a hurry." I laughed when Resha chimed in on the last part.

"I know you did."

"No, but seriously, he's a handful. However, it's guys like him that need my help the most. He's young and doesn't even realize he may have another five to six years left at the top of his game, to earn the bulk of his lifetime income. That's if he's lucky. And the way he's spending, if it's not reined in, he'll become one of the statistics." I frowned, biting my lower lip. I wasn't a fan of Leonard Riggs, but the idea of a young man like him making it out of the proverbial "hood" all of the way to the NFL, only to land on his face and back to poverty because of poor spending habits, wasn't something I took joy in at all.

"I hear you but that's why you do what you do, right? To teach people how to get their money right?"

"Sure is. You of all people should know."

Resha had been my first client in my side business, which is what would go on to become my full-time job. Once she became a blogger and her business began growing she needed help managing her finances. I was working for a huge corporation as a financial advisor but continuously growing uneasy with the products we were encouraged to push our clients into. I wanted to help people learn the best way to manage their money, not just sell them the portfolio that was going to earn me or the company the highest fees as their advisor. So, I took Resha on as a side-client, eventually taking on another and another. Between my personal clients, the podcast, and my full-time job, I became overwhelmed and had to make a decision. I chose me and hadn't regretted it since.

"I do know. That's why I believe that boy is in good hands, whether he likes it or not. But let him know, you've got a cousin who doesn't play when it comes to her family."

I grinned. "I'll tell him that. Go to bed," I urged after I heard her stifle another yawn.

"I am. Tell Aunt Donna I'll give her a call this weekend."

I nodded even though she couldn't see me. "I will. Bye."

We hung up and I placed my phone onto the white and grey granite countertops before heading to my fridge to choose one of the pre-prepped meals I'd had delivered to eat. I wasn't big on cooking, especially since I worked late so many days at the office, so I made room in my budget for a meal delivery service to have fresh and healthy meals on hand throughout the week.

I chose the roasted broccoli, rainbow quinoa, and grilled salmon meal, and popped the dish into my microwave to heat up. While the food was warming, I strolled over to my kitchen's countertop and found myself again reviewing the files of the Williamsport Cougars' team. I didn't question why Tyler, the star quarterback's, file was at the top of my pile, opened with his picture staring back at me. He was the one person on my team that didn't need my help. Even without his multi-million dollar NFL salary he'd fair pretty well in life, having been born into the one percent.

I slammed his file shut. The Tyler Townsends of the world didn't need my help. No matter how charming, good-looking and deliciously … Nope! I wasn't going there. I had a job to focus on. Men like Leonard Riggs and Tyler's other teammates needed my help. I didn't need to worry about or focus any of my energy on Tyler.

CHAPTER 4

Tyler

"All right let's bring it in for a break! Hydrate yourselves. I don't need any one of you passing out on me in this fucking heat!" Coach McClellan yelled out after blowing his whistle.

I grunted heavily as I tugged the helmet from my head. It was hot as balls out on the field and it was barely nine o'clock in the morning. I tucked the football under my right arm and carried my helmet in the left, turning in the direction of the large table at the sidelines that held cups of Gatorade. I actually hated the stuff but it's what was kept for us players to hydrate and replenish the electrolytes we sweated out.

I'd taken about three steps in the direction of the table when I lifted my gaze and paused. Moving assuredly past the table was the woman I'd fallen asleep listening to more nights than I cared to recount, over the last week. I licked my lower lip, admiring how the black skirt she wore cupped her ass nicely, along with the silk leopard print top she had on. As my eyes trailed up her body, I noticed the top had a matching scarf that she'd knotted around her neck. My grip on my helmet tightened as I stared at the choker-like adornment. I blinked my eyes closed, willing my breathing to steady itself. Destiny McDonald was almost too good to be true.

"You all right?" Kelvin questioned, coming up behind me.

I cut my eyes in his direction, irritated that he'd interrupted the fantasy that'd been developing in my head. But grateful also. I didn't need to take a trip down fantasy lane, when the real thing was standing there, just waiting for me.

I grinned.

But when I turned back to Destiny, my smile was replaced by a frown. She was now talking to Mitchell Jones, one of the defensive linemen.

"No, I'm not," I answered Kelvin, not even looking his way as I picked up my pace toward the drink table.

"Hey, Ty," Mitchell called.

I clamped down on my desire to put my hand around his neck for standing too close to Destiny. A thrill shot through me when she lifted her head and her eyes widened just a minor amount.

"Mitch, would you mind if I interrupted your conversation with Destiny here to ask her a few questions?" I'd kept my eyes on Destiny while speaking to Mitch, wanting to see her reaction to my mentioning her name again. Sure enough, the telltale uptick of the pumping of that tiny vein in her neck demonstrated that I got to her as much as she got to me.

"Uh, no, not at all."

Not a glance was spared in Mitchell's direction as he walked away. My gaze was trained on Destiny. When she turned angry, narrowed eyes on me, my heart rate kicked up.

"That was rude, Mr. Townsend." She folded her arms across her chest.

My eyes fell to the small amount of exposed cleavage. Not nearly enough to be lewd but just enough that I could envision what it would look like to run my tongue over the smooth, soft skin of her body.

"Still calling me Mr. Townsend. You don't take direction very well." I cocked my head to the side.

Her eyes narrowed even more. "Direction? I certainly don't."

I licked my lower lip again. "That's going to be a problem … for you."

She lifted an eyebrow. "Mr. Townsend, I don't know what kind of game you're playing."

"I play a variety of games, Destiny." I began, moving closer. "Football, for one." I tilted my head toward the field before turning back to stare her down. "But you knew that. I play games with my niece and nephews. I grew up playing all types of games on my older brothers. I'm used to games, Destiny. But this," I waved a hand between our two bodies, "this isn't a game."

"I have no idea what you're talking about, Mr. Townsend, because there is no *this*." She mimicked the same hand movement I'd just done. "The hell is so funny?" she angrily questioned at my laugh.

"You're fucking adorable when pissed. That little wrinkle in your forehead."

She pushed out a heavy breath, stepping back, and shook her head. "Athletes."

"So you have a thing against athletes?"

She rolled her eyes upward toward the sky. "What is it with you and the word *thing*. There is no *thing* between us and no, I don't have a *thing* against athletes. I just know you are mistaken. You seem to believe that my being here is an invitation for you to hit on me but it's not. I am only here for one *thing* and that is to do my job. The Williamsport Cougar owners hired me to teach their athletes about financial management and planning and that is what I intend to do. That is *all* I intend to do, Mr. Townsend."

I whistled low in my throat. "My you are—"

Destiny held up a finger, jutting it in my direction. "I swear if you call me feisty again, or sassy, or—"

"No." I shook my head. "Those words are much too … subtle to describe all that you are."

I grinned harder when her mouth fell open for a full second before she clamped it shut. "Does this usually work for you?"

"What?"

She waved a hand, gesturing it in my direction. "This, you, the whole charm and bedroom eyes *thing* you're doing. Does it usually win over your next conquest? Earning them the coveted spot in your bed for the night, or if they're lucky a few nights before you move on to your next acquisition?"

I stood up fully, moving in even closer. "So you think I have bedroom eyes?"

Her shoulders sagged as she pushed out a breath, her face turning incredulous. "Wha—"

"Townsend!"

I glanced up to see my coaches waving me over. *Fuck.*

"Saved by the bell," Destiny mumbled and started to back up to walk away.

I caught her by the elbow, my own breath hitching at my body's physical response to our contact. I leaned down farther to get closer to her ear.

"You don't have to worry about any past conquests, Destiny. These bedroom eyes are exclusively for you from here on out. I suggest you drop the Mr. Townsend bullshit and get used to saying my first name. You'll be using it a lot more frequently from now on."

"Townsend! Let's go!"

I bit back a curse toward my coach as I lifted my gaze to see them staring expectantly at me. I dropped my eyes again to Destiny who's dark, umber-colored irises were pinned on me. I forced myself not to lean down and take her lips the way they were begging to be taken. I squeezed her elbow before releasing her and heading over to where my coaches stood. If it wasn't for the cup I wore during practice, I was pretty certain the entire team would've noticed the semi hard-on I'd earned just from that little exchange.

* * *

Destiny

Stay away from boys like that. My daddy's warning rang in my ears as I watched Tyler jog off in the direction of his coaches. The man had left me at a loss for words, and that was no easy feat.

I needed to pull it together.

But even as I stared at his tall, strong frame beginning to run drills with a few other players, I couldn't pull my eyes from him. He was magnetic. The exact type of boy my father warned me about way back in middle school when I'd developed a crush on the school's bad boy. *They'll ruin your life*, he'd said. I hadn't listened that time around, and again, years later, upon entering college, my father's advice faded by the wayside and I'd fallen for the ultimate bad body, and still had the emotional scars to prove it.

"Nope," I mumbled out loud, shaking my head. I wasn't going down that road again.

"What's up, Ms. McDonald? Scoping out your next meal ticket?"

My head swung around and instantly my hackles rose at the condescending remark and expression on Leonard Riggs' face.

"What was that, Mr. Riggs?"

Leonard slowly eyed me up and down before turning toward the football field in the direction Tyler had jogged off to. He turned his gaze back to me a smirk on his lips.

"You heard what I said. Checking out your next meal ticket?" He made a laughing sound and shrugged his shoulders. "You might as well hang that up. That whitebread, rich boy ain't going there with you. He might fuck you though. Hell, if he don't I might let you get a taste." His brown eyes narrowed lasciviously.

My head jutted back and disgust rolled through my belly at his remarks. Unwittingly, I took a step back to create more distance between our two bodies.

"I'm going to do us both a favor and pretend I didn't hear what you just said."

"What's the matter? Truth hurts?"

"Truth is relative, Mr. Riggs. And your truth isn't necessarily my truth. Like, for instance, you believe that because you make a few million a year, you're doing well financially and can spend as lavishly as you want. *My* truth is that I know, if you keep up the way you're going, you'll be lucky not to be working, bagging groceries once you hit forty. Do yourself a favor and worry about your own damn life and not mine."

Leonard took a threatening step toward me. "Listen, bi—"

"Everything all right over here?"

I looked up to see Kelvin Maynard moving in front of me, between Leonard and I.

"Everything's great. Just informing Mr. Riggs of the financial planning services I offer." I gave Leonard a scowl.

He worked his lower jaw, obviously pissed. "Yeah, yeah, everything's copacetic."

I pushed out a breath, rolling my eyes.

"I was just asking *Ms. McDonald* why she's even here. Her services aren't needed. My agent hooked me up with a dope ass financial advisor. Has me earning double my money each month."

I furrowed my brows. "No one doubles their money in a month."

"Ha! See, I knew you was a phony. My financial advisor did. So you can take your—"

"Hey, man, how about you head back on over to the field? Coach looks like he wants us all to huddle up anyway," Kelvin interjected, patting Leonard's chest with the back of his hand.

"Yeah, whatever," Leonard stated as he backed up and eventually turned and headed in the direction of the rest of the players.

"Hey, you all right?"

I glanced up to see Kelvin staring down at me, concern etched in the lines of his dark forehead.

I nodded. "I'm fine."

"Don't let Riggs get to you. He's young and got some issues with women."

"Pssh. You think?"

Kelvin chuckled. "Ah, shit."

I frowned, giving Kelvin a strange look, but he was looking over at the field, not at me. I turned my head in the direction he was staring to see what appeared to be a pissed off Tyler Townsend staring back at us. His eyes were narrowed, face taut, and though he was quite a distance away, the energy he was giving off had displeased written all over it.

"The hell is his problem?" I mumbled.

Kelvin chuckled. "I'm gonna have to sleep with one eye open

tonight. I'll catch you later, Ms. McDonald," Kelvin stated before heading over to the rest of his team.

I briefly watched Kelvin before my gaze was pulled back to Tyler. He pivoted angry eyes from Kelvin back to me. His mouth softened just slightly as he continued to watch me with hungry eyes. I shook my head warningly, and much to my chagrin, a mischievous smile broke out on Tyler's face. The flip flop in my belly was enough to startle me back to reality.

"Not going there again. Ever," I mumbled, turning and moving behind the water table to head back to the lecture hall where our weekly class was held. I'd shown up a little early to meet with two of the assistant coaches on the team about their own financial planning and ways I could help them. After those meetings and Mike saw I was here, he invited me out onto the field to watch practice for a little while before he called the team inside. I'd meant to just sit on the side-lines and make some calls and send some emails. That was before Tyler interrupted my plans.

"I'm going back inside," I insisted to no one but myself, since I was the only fool out there on the sidelines. I'd head back inside, make sure my PowerPoint presentation was set up correctly, and make my phone calls inside, where it was safe because I wouldn't have some young, twenty-something jock staring me down. Without my approval, my eyes darted across the football field to see the players all taking a knee as Mike stood over them, instructing them on something or other. My gaze zoned in on Tyler's who was at the front of his team, seemingly listening to Mike, but when my eyes found him, he turned his head to catch my gaze. As if he just knew I was staring at him.

I shook my head, trying to ward off the growing feelings that were beginning to warm my insides from just his captivated look alone. I turned and made my way inside, at least, for a little while I'd have some sort of reprieve from being underneath that penetrating glare. A few minutes alone should give me enough time to reconstruct the mental brick wall I'd put up against men in general, and athletes in particular.

CHAPTER 5

Destiny

"I hope you know you're paying tonight," I chided Brenda from across the table.

She smiled brightly at me. "The boys giving you that much trouble, huh?" she questioned before giggling and pulling me into a hug.

I'd been waiting for only a minute or two before Brenda joined me just outside of the French restaurant we'd agreed to have dinner at that night. It was one of our favorite places to eat good food and catch up. And since she and I hadn't found a time where I could go over to her place for dinner, this was where we'd chosen.

"They're actually not that bad," I conceded as we passed through the restaurant's door that was held open by the host.

"Welcome to Le Bec Fin. May I have your name?" the young host questioned.

"McClellan, sweetheart," Brenda answered, her southern drawl making its appearance.

The host ran his finger down the side of reservation list in front of him. "Ah, here we are. Right this way, please." He grabbed a couple of menus and waited for us to fall in line behind him. We passed through the dining space, passing people, Brenda and I both waving or nodding at a few dining patrons that we knew.

"What's the matter, Mike thought I was going to ream him out so he decided to skip dinner?" I teased once we sat down. Thankfully, the classical music that played in the background was low enough that conversation across the circular table wasn't impeded. The overhead pendant light were low as well to create a warm yet classy atmosphere.

Brenda laughed. "He might be hiding from the both of us. I told him if any of his boys give you trouble, I would pitch a fit all over his butt!"

I held my belly, laughing at her southern vernacular. Even after more than two decades away from the south and working in the corporate world Brenda had refused to give up her southern colloquialisms.

I waved her off with my hand before placing the cloth napkin onto my lap. "*The boys* as you call them are fine." I still couldn't believe how she referred to these grown men as *boys.* She didn't mean it in a derogatory way. She just thought of her husband's players as her family, for the most part. Mike and Brenda had opted to remain child-free throughout their nearly thirty-year marriage. Some people questioned their decision but Brenda had assured me it was a dual decision. Neither one had really wanted children and both were ambitious in their respective career fields, choosing to put most of their energy toward their professions and marriage rather than parenthood. I respected their choice not to bow down to societal pressures and to do what was right for them.

"Even Riggs? Mike told me how he challenged you that first day."

I nodded while swiping a piece of bread from the basket that'd been placed on our table. I dipped it in the flavored olive oil, sopping it up before taking a savoring bite.

"Mm," I closed my eyes and moaned.

"Destiny McDonald eating carbs after six p.m.," Brenda gasped, causing me to giggle while wiping my mouth with the napkin.

"I know," I began after swallowing. "I had a crazy day and forgot to eat lunch. Haven't had anything since breakfast. At this point, I'm ready to chew your arm off."

"Well, you eat up, doll."

"I intend to," I responded just before biting off another piece of the olive oil drenched bread.

Our waiter arrived a minute later, taking our orders. I decided on the crab cakes with roasted vegetables and some sort of cream sauce. Brenda had the beef tenderloins and caramelized carrots. I opted for one of my favorite red wines while Brenda chose white.

"Back to what I was saying …" She leaned across the table and began once our waiter left. "Riggs isn't giving you anymore problems is he?"

I shook my head. "Nothing that I can't handle. He's young and a showboat. His ass has been kissed his whole life because he's really good at catching a football. Women have probably been throwing themselves at him since he was twelve. I don't expect him to behave any differently toward me than he would any other woman."

"He'll come around. He's a sweet kid."

I rolled my eyes at that. Leonard Riggs was anything but sweet. Nor was he a kid at twenty-three years old.

"He did mention something interesting the other week that I wanted to ask you about."

"What's that?" Brenda questioned as she held her wine glass up to her lips preparing to take a sip.

"He said something about his agent introducing him to a financial advisor that had his investment doubling within a month's time."

Brenda lifted a perfectly arched, brunette eyebrow.

"Exactly." Brenda, having worked in the world of finance for close to twenty-five years, knew how unlikely doubling an investment in such a short amount of time was. She'd been my mentor since her time as an adjunct professor of one of my finance classes in college. She'd encouraged me to go into a career in personal finance from the very beginning. *We need more women with smarts, savvy, and integrity like you in this field,* she'd said to me early on. It took me a number of years to take her up on the offer. Luckily, by the time I was ready to actually put my degree to use, she and Mike were living in Williamsport as he'd become head coach for the Cougars and Brenda had moved up the corporate ladder to manage her own division in one of the major investment banks in the city. She was one of the only women in her company at such a high level and she personally vouched for me when I applied for my position as financial planner with the company.

"That doesn't sound right. Are you sure he said it doubled?"

"I heard what I heard, Bren. Now, he could've just been showboating, trying to one up me ..."

She nodded. "I wouldn't put it past him."

"Right," I agreed though it still nagged at me. Riggs was the type to say anything to get a rise out of someone or to prove he had one up on them. However, the way he'd mentioned his financial advisor was suspicious to me. He'd sounded so sure of himself.

"Trust me, I love many of Mike's players like they're my own, but I wouldn't put much past any of them," Brenda continued.

"Any of them?" I questioned.

She nodded.

"Does that include Tyler Townsend?" The question was out before I had a chance to stop myself. I had no idea where it even came from.

She let out a belly laugh just as our food was brought to the table. She waited until our waiter left to answer my question.

"Tyler's a doll. Mike and his father have been friends for a long time now. Some people thought that was why Mike decided to recruit Ty four years ago which is stupid. Mike would never jeopardize the quality of his team just to appease an old friend. Ty had it rough those first couple of years."

I snorted. "Yeah, real rough with all of the drama he got himself into." I wouldn't dare tell Brenda out loud but I'd read the articles of Tyler getting caught in a hotel lobby with a couple of strippers, the fight he'd supposedly started between his team and an opposing team during a night out, and a couple of other skirmishes.

"No, really. Don't believe all of the stuff you read in those gossip articles about him. Ty was the best player on his college team, you wouldn't find another player who gave their all the way Tyler does, but because he's a Townsend he had to prove himself. Everyone from coaching staff to fans and even fellow teammates doubted his commitment to the game. Imagine being a player from some of the roughest neighborhoods in the country. You fought tooth and nail to get to the league and 'make it out'." She used air quotes around the last phrase. "Only to have this guy who was born with all of the money in the world at his disposal, had the best opportunities in life, try and be your leader on the field."

I nodded. "I heard a few of the guys refer to him as silver spoon."

"He hates that nickname." She chuckled. "But he's come a long way. His numbers and show on the field are more than enough to prove that he's as committed to the game as anyone else."

"That's obvious," I mumbled, taking a bite of my crab cake. Tyler's stats didn't lie. On the field he was a beast. I'd often wondered why it took him two full seasons to rise to the level of starting quarterback for the Cougars, but what Brenda had just stated explained it. Professional sports was cutthroat, and as a quarterback if your teammates didn't believe in you, you might as well give it up. But Tyler had hung in there, winning them over with his love and passion for the game.

"Tyler giving you trouble?" Brenda asked, frowning across the table.

A flutter in my belly happened when I thought about the way he'd watched me in the lecture hall the day before. It'd been over a week since our encounter on the field, and since then he'd taken every opportunity to flirt and invade my personal space.

"No." I shook my head. "No trouble at all. Just still trying to get a feel for the players." A little bit of guilt rose in my chest at the lie but I wasn't about to spill the fact that I was beginning to find Tyler more endearing than annoying.

"You've got what? Two more weeks with the team? Have you taken any of them on as clients?"

I finished chewing a bite of my vegetables and nodded. "Yeah, two weeks left until the end of training camp. I've gotten three players, two on the offensive line and one from the special teams that contacted me for my services once camp is over." The three additional clients were well worth the time I'd put into preparing for this four-week seminar with the team. "A few more have shown some interest, so we'll see if they follow up. All in all, it's been a pretty good endeavor."

"That's great. I knew it'd work out for you. I'm so proud of how you struck out on your own."

I smiled, feeling a sense a pride at how she complimented me. "I wouldn't have had the courage to do it without your support." Though Brenda firmly believed in climbing the corporate ladder and showing the men that women were just as capable—if not more so—of working in our field, she wholeheartedly encouraged me to strike out on my own when I first approached her with the idea. She could tell that after four years in the corporate sector, I wasn't happy and had grown uneasy with some of the products I was pushed to sell our clients.

"You would have. I'm just glad I was able to help you. Great show the other day, by the way." Brenda was an avid listener of the podcast, often complimenting Resha and I on the topics we discussed. "I had a client come in the other day. She's going through a nasty divorce. Finding out her husband hid money from her for years." She tutted, shaking her head. "I recommended your podcast to her." She gave me a wink. We often discussed handling money and financial planning before, during, and after a divorce.

We talked some more about work and our plans over the next few months while we ate our meals. As we headed out of the restaurant and waited for the valet to pull up with Brenda's Mercedes, she pulled me into a warm hug.

"I can't believe you're still walking everywhere. That's why you're as tiny as you are." We laughed.

"I only live about a mile from here. Plus, I'm stopping by the cake shop to pick my mama up a slice of her favorite raspberry, chocolate truffle cake before heading over to visit her." It was just around seven-thirty so I knew my mother would still be up for a visit.

"How's she doing by the way?"

"She's doing well. The medications she's on help with the tremors so they aren't too bad. She loves the housing she's in. It's me that you need to be worried about."

Brenda grinned. "Still feel guilty for letting her live in a senior facility?"

I nodded. "She insisted so I had to let her but I feel like I gave up on her or something."

"Hush!" Brenda chided. "You visit your mother three times a week and are on the phone with her every other day. She is in one of the best facilities in the city of Williamsport thanks to you helping to pay for it. Your mother is well taken care of because of you. Let that guilt go."

I nodded. "You're right."

"But still..."

"But still," I agreed. Letting the guilt go was easier said than done.

We parted ways and I watched Brenda pull off, waving in her rearview mirror at me. I tossed her a final wave before crossing the street to head into the bakery. I'd placed my order earlier in the day, knowing that I'd be over this way around dinner. Once I picked up the dessert, I decided to catch a Lyft over to my mother's place. On the way over, I couldn't help but replay my and Brenda's earlier conversation regarding Tyler Townsend. No matter how much I wanted to stop thinking about him, the man would often creep into my thoughts. That was not a good sign.

* * *

"Look at what my baby girl brought me!" My mother grinned and clapped in delight when I opened the bakery box that had two slices of her favorite cake and another slice of vanilla bean cake for her close friend, who lived next door. "Ida is going to love this. You know her daughter still hasn't come to see her." My mother made a clicking sound with her tongue, shaking her head.

"I'm sorry to hear that." From what I knew, Ms. Ida and her daughter had a strained relationship. The younger woman also lived three states away, making it rather difficult to drop in on a whim as I could.

"Do you want to eat now or should I put it in the fridge for tomorrow?" I questioned.

"Chile, I want my cake now."

I laughed, already knowing what her response would be. My mother loved her sweets. I moved from the table, grabbing one of her smaller ceramic plates from the overhead cupboard, and then a fork from the drawer, bringing them to the table. I plated my mother's slice of cake for her and took it over to the wooden coffee table that sat in the center of her relatively small but comfortable living room.

"Did you want to eat it in here?" I asked only after realizing she may have wanted to eat at the dining table.

"No, here's fine." She shook her head and I stood, admiring her as she slowly reached for the fork and the plate.

I had to tamp down on the urge to help her, remembering that my mother was just as strong-willed as I was and she often wanted to do things on her own. The ache in my heart started when I watched the plate in her hand wobble a little as her hands trembled. But she managed to bring the first bite to her mouth without spilling any of it on her.

My mother was an older version of me. We were the same height at five-feet, three inches and had the same warm mahogany skin tone. Over the years my mother had gained about thirty pounds to her small frame thanks to not being able to move around as much, and of course, her notorious sweet tooth. A few years back she'd cut her mid-back length dreadlocks and opted to wear her hair in a natural twist out most days. Her hair was mostly grey as she chose to skip the dyes a long time ago. My mother was always immaculately dressed, as well. Resha and I had both garnered our love of fashion from her.

"Resha said to tell you she'll give you a call this weekend," I said over my shoulder before turning back to open the refrigerator. I looked around and saw the carton of vanilla almond milk I'd bought for my mother the previous week. Lifting it, I saw that it was half empty. "You like the almond milk, huh?" I questioned, pulled a glass from the cupboard.

"It's good. I didn't think I'd like it but I do," my mother answered as she slowly brought another bite of cake to her mouth.

"I told you, you'd like it. They also have chocolate. I'll pick that up for you to try next time I'm at the store." I placed the glass half filled with almond milk on the table next to her plate before pulling out my phone to add the chocolate almond milk to my list of groceries. Once that was completed, I finally sat down on the couch next to my mother.

"How was your day, Mama? Do anything fun?" I asked, sitting back against the comfy sofa.

"Just rested today," she answered. "The play we went to yesterday was so good. It was the first time it was being performed ..." She went on telling me about the play written and directed by a young, up-and-coming female African-American playwright. My mother's facility housed about fifty seniors, all in various levels of health. Some were extremely spry and healthy while others had a number of health conditions. My mother was somewhere in the middle in terms of her health. The Parkinson's she'd been diagnosed with nearly seven years prior had grown worse over the years but she was determined not to let that stop her from enjoying what parts of life she could. While it was a challenge to get around, the facility frequently hosted outings and events for their residents, and my mother was often first in line to attend. She was still in good spirits for a woman in her early seventies with a debilitating illness.

"What else did you do yesterday?"

"We went to the Museum of Natural History. I love that place. Oh, I'm trying to get the managers to take us to the Fashion Museum. I'd love to show Ida some of my favorite fashion trends over the years. She loves Resha's blog posts."

I giggled. My mother was so proud of Resha's blog. She showed everyone that stopped by her apartment. She had a desktop computer that I'd bought and had set up for her on the desk by the entryway to her apartment. It'd taken some time to teach my mom how to navigate the internet and how to locate Resha's blog, but over the last few years she'd warmed up to it as it helped her keep up with her niece turned daughter when Resha was out of town.

"Resh and I FaceTimed the other week."

I nodded. "She told me."

"Said she picked up a couple of pieces for me while over there but she won't tell me what she got." My mother pouted.

"You know she likes surprising you."

My mother smiled. "I do. Between you and Resha my whole apartment is bursting with gifts, food, computers, and more."

"We're not that bad," I teased. "You done with that?" I asked, nodding at her empty plate.

"Well, I could go for—"

"No," I admonished. "You will not be having two slices of cake tonight, Ma. You can have the other tomorrow when Ida comes over for lunch."

"Hmph!" My mother pouted again.

I shook my head and smiled although a pang of sadness coursed through me at the role reversal that'd taken place over the past six years. While my mother was still very upbeat and had most of her mental capacity, I'd had to step in and handle her finances, set her up to live in the facility she now lived in, and do her grocery shopping, or at least arrange for the groceries to be delivered to her. One reason it wasn't totally overwhelming for me was because my father had been determined to take care of both of his girls before he died. He'd worked for the government for years and that provided a lifelong pension of fifty percent of his salary to his widow, as well as retirement savings and life insurance he'd left both of us. While there were still some costs I had to take on to have my mom live on her own, they were minimal compared to what I would've had to pay had my father not cared for her the way he had. With or without my financial contribution, my mother would've been fine.

My father was the first person who taught me about handling finances in a responsible way. Although his belief was that I needed to find a good man who would take care of me the way he'd always taken care of my mother and I.

Yeah, right.

"What was that face for?"

I shook my head, freeing myself of my straying thoughts to glance over at my mother. "Nothing," I lied.

She frowned, obviously not believing me. She was still keen when she wanted to be. "You were thinking about Darryl."

I sighed, closing my eyes. My mother was the only one who ever had the courage to mention his name in my presence.

"I wasn't thinking about him, not really."

"What do you mean *not really*?"

"I was just thinking how Daddy always wanted me to find a man to take care of me the way he took care of you ... and how I failed at that. My ex," I paused, "wasn't Daddy."

"No, he wasn't." She shook her head.

"As much as I loved Daddy, he was wrong. I didn't need a man to take care of me. I've proven that."

"Yes, baby, you have. You've proven yourself to be strong and rather independent, able to support yourself. But are you happy?"

I refrained from rolling my eyes toward the sky. As a child that would've garnered me a smack across the face and I wasn't too sure my mother wouldn't try to let me have it again for such rudeness, but I hated that question. As if the only way a woman could be happy was to have a man in her life.

"I'm happy, Mama. Life is great. I have a thriving business and career, Resha and my friends. Brenda."

"But you don't have a man."

"I date, Mama."

"Who? I haven't seen anyone."

"That's because I haven't met anyone that I felt compelled to bring over for you to meet." That was the truth. I dated quite a bit over the past five years but hadn't met anyone that I seriously considered introducing to my mother. I even had one long-term relationship with a guy that lasted well over a year, but the thought of introducing him to my mother had never sat well with me. That's how I knew our relationship wasn't going to last into the second year.

"You need to find someone."

"I don't *need* to find anyone. I'm happy, Ma." I had plenty of male suitors and lots of opportunity to go out or have someone warm my bed when I wanted. "I'm busy building my business," I finally stated, sitting back against the couch.

"I know losing Darryl and the baby was tough—"

"Ma, please. Can we not talk about this?" I insisted more angrily than I'd wanted to show but I hated that she'd brought up the loss of my son. That was a conversation that was off limits, even with my own mother.

"Okay, I'm sorry, baby. I just worry about you. I want you to find someone to be as happy with as I was with my Daniel."

In spite of myself, I let out a small smile at the way my mother said my father's name. Theirs was a true love story. Growing up, our house was always full of love because of how deeply they cared for one another, and had no problems showing it.

"I know, Ma. How about you tell me about the Fashion Museum you're just dying to show Ida?" I encouraged, changing topics.

I remained at my mother's for another hour talking with her about fashion and thumbing through the latest *Vanity Fair* magazine. I helped my mother get undressed and into bed before turning her light out and locking up behind me. I promised her I wouldn't walk since it was dark out, so I ordered another Lyft to drop me off at home.

As much as I hated to admit it, my mother's words about finding a man had rattled me just enough, that sleep was a difficult chore to get to that night. Which was how I found myself sitting up in bed, combing through yet another sports blog, periodically stopping when articles about Tyler Townsend appeared. I found myself wondering about this athletically gifted, incredibly good looking, intense, yet somewhat dopey man. That was when I knew it was time for me to force myself to shut the computer and get to sleep.

CHAPTER 6

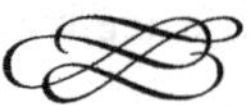

Tyler

"All right, you two, uncle Ty has to go but I'll see you in a couple of days," I told my niece and nephew. I'd just spent the last twenty minutes on the phone listening as they recounted their day at camp to me. It was just after eight, and Kelvin and I were headed out to a local lounge for a few hours. Since training camp was almost over, we were given a short reprieve for a night out.

"Okay, Uncle Ty, don't forget next time you babysit you said I could paint your nails again," Kennedy reminded me.

I laughed into the phone. "I did agree to that, didn't I?"

"Yeah, and Daddy says a man should always keep his promises."

I smirked. "Sounds like something Aaron would say."

"Yeah, but he says I don't need to worry about any promises from any other man besides him, my uncles, and my grandfather. He says no other man will matter to me until I'm at least forty. What's that mean?"

I bent over laughing since that *definitely* sounded like something my brother would say to his six-year-old daughter.

"It means your father talks too much," Patience, Kennedy's mother and Aaron's wife's voice pushed through the other end of the line.

"He's right though, Patience. My niece doesn't need to worry about any man that isn't related to her."

"Whatever, Tyler. Tell your uncle to have a goodnight you two."

"Nite, Uncle Ty."

"Goodnight, Uncle Tyler."

Kennedy and Kyle both said in unison.

"Good night. I'll talk to you all soon."

"Stay out of trouble, Ty," Patience warned.

"Where's the fun in that?"

She laughed. "Bye."

"Nite."

I hung up and stuffed my phone into the back pocket of the jeans I'd chosen to wear that night.

"You finally ready?" Kelvin asked from the side of his bed, looking impatient.

"Fuck you," I tossed back at him.

"Ah, man. You still upset?"

I narrowed my eyes on him.

"I told you I wasn't talking to that girl about nothing but business."

"Stop calling her a *girl*," I warned. I was still pissed about the exchange I saw between Kelvin and Destiny the previous week on the sidelines of our practice field. I questioned him about what they were talking about. He'd said he'd been asking her about signing on as one of her clients but I knew he was lying. Call it instinct but I didn't believe that was the full story which nearly led to me putting my foot up his ass. He'd called me insane for going all crazy on him over a woman I barely knew and hadn't even gone out on a date with yet, but I wasn't going to explain myself to Kelvin, best friend or not. The fact that he was my best friend was his only saving grace. I knew he wouldn't go behind my back to hit on Destiny, but that didn't stop the anger from welling up inside of me at just seeing them standing so close to one another.

"Whatever, man. Listen, it's our one free night before the season starts, and the last thing I want to see is you in here pacing back and forth listening to yet another four episodes of that girl—" he hesitated when I gave him a deadly glare, "*woman's* podcast. We need to blow off some steam before the season starts."

"Whatever," I retorted, shrugging his hand off my shoulder and moving toward the door. I was already on edge when it came to Destiny because she'd spent the last few weeks purposely avoiding me after each of her lectures. I hadn't been able to get the information on her that I wanted since I was at training camp and the Townsend head of security was caught up, helping my brother, Joshua, with some bullshit that was going on with the real estate company. I'd have to wait until I could stop by Townsend Industries myself to speak with Brutus to have him look up the background information I wanted on Destiny McDonald.

"Man, fix your face. You'll scare all of the women off tonight," Kelvin chided as we arrived at the door of the lounge. A friend of Kelvin's agent was part-owner of the place. It was named *Indigo* and had various shades of the color for its leather seats and walls. Though it was more lounge than nightclub there was plenty of pop music playing along with people on the dance areas in between the seats and low sitting tables.

"My face doesn't need fixing," I retorted, cutting my eyes back in Kelvin's direction.

He just pushed out a breath and shook his head. "We need to get you laid."

I grunted as I followed Kelvin up to the VIP area that was already tied off with about five of our teammates. From the looks of it, they'd been there for some time, having both an abundance of drinks and women there to accompany them.

"Hey, stranger."

I turned and squinted at the blonde who'd greeted me. She looked familiar but I couldn't remember her name.

"Do I know you?"

She had the audacity to look affronted. "Candy? Remember? We spent that beautiful night together last summer right before your training camp."

I gave her a deadpan expression before shrugging. "I'm sure it was great, sweetheart ... for you."

She gasped at my harsh words. Typically, I wasn't so short with women, but I simply wasn't interested in rekindling whatever Candy thought we had, and I didn't feel the need to sugarcoat it. Besides, the way she quickly looked from me to another one of the player's led me to believe she wouldn't have such a hard time getting over being dismissed.

No longer wanting to be in her presence, I pushed passed Candy and headed over to an empty seat. Unfortunately for me, I didn't notice that it was right next to Leonard Riggs, who was too busy getting a lap dance from some random woman to even notice me.

I didn't mind. I called the waitress over for another bottle of the champagne that was already being served along with more glasses. I wasn't in the mood to get into any pussy tonight, but I could definitely take a few drinks.

"Hey, Silver Spoon. I didn't think you'd make it out."

I rolled my eyes over to Riggs who finally noticed me. I frowned as he gave me a stupid ass grin while the same woman still shook her ass on his lap.

"That's not my fucking name."

"My bad." He held up his hands in mock surrender. "Don't want to piss off the leader of the team and all," he chuckled.

I was doing my best to rein in my temper. Coach was right. I had dreams of becoming a coach one day and it wouldn't bode well for me if I assaulted a fellow player.

Instead of showing my hand, I leaned over, closer to Riggs so he could hear me clearly. "You can't piss me off. You don't have the power to do that. Just make sure your shit is tight on the field and you and I got no issues. Got it?" I gave him a stern look.

He narrowed his eyes on me and I stared back, unflinching.

"Yeah, I got it."

"Good." I nodded and swiped my glass of champagne before moving to the overhead outlook. From there I could see the rest of the lounge's first floor.

I let my eyes scan the crowd below. There were people dancing, talking, some were eating at their tables. Movement out of the corner caught my eye and I glanced up, my breath catching in my chest.

My night just got a whole hell of a lot better, I thought to myself as I carefully observed Destiny McDonald dancing and laughing with another woman. I stared for some time, admiring the sway of her hips and the movement of her compact body in the orange, sleeveless, shorts romper she wore. Suddenly, it wasn't enough to just watch her from a distance. Especially when I noticed another male patron in the lounge approached her, licking his lips as if he was about to make a move.

Not today, asshole, I thought as I slammed my champagne flute down on the nearest table and practically pushed a few of my teammates out of the way as I headed down the stairs to the first floor of the lounge.

* * *

Destiny

"Come on, D! I heard Indigo is the place to be. Oh, that rhymed!" Leslie giggled as she clapped.

"You're drunk already," I laughed and teased my friend, Leslie. Leslie was another good friend of mine, though we didn't get to see each other as much since she lived out of state. We'd met freshman year as roommates at UCLA, cheered together on the same cheer squad in college, and had been tight ever since. We were sitting in Leslie's hotel room at one of the fanciest hotels in the city. Leslie's husband, Jerry, had business in the city and he and Les had decided to make a short getaway of it.

"I'm a little tipsy. Come oooon, D," she whined. "Do you know how hard it is to get a night out with three kids at home? You owe me."

"I owe you? How so?"

She shrugged. "I don't know, you just do! We're going out tonight." She pointed a finger at me.

I laughed, knowing that it would end like this. Leslie was always the life of the party. One couldn't help but have a good time whenever she was around. Ever since she'd called me earlier in the week to tell me she and Jerry would be in town without the kids, I knew we'd find ourselves out somewhere, at least one of the nights she was in town.

"Fine. I hear Indigo's not too crazy anyway."

"Yay!" She clapped, reminding me of the preppy cheerleader she was when we first met.

Just then Leslie's husband entered the hotel suite's bedroom from the living room where he'd been on a conference call.

"Hun, Destiny agreed to go out to Indigo with me tonight."

Jerry looked over at me.

I had to work hard to keep my lips from forming into a frown. Jerry and I had never been more than cordial with one another.

"That's cool. Y'all have fun. Hey, Destiny." He nodded in my direction.

"Hey, Jerry."

"Aye, I saw your husband the other day. I've got some business with him here in the city. I'll let him know you're still looking good."

My face instantly morphed into a scowl. "You saw my *what?*" I questioned with a narrowed gaze, pinning him.

For his part, Jerry's lips twitched, just barely keeping the smirk off his face, and his dark eyes sparkled as if he'd made the funniest joke in the world.

"Jerry, what the fuck is your problem?" I demanded.

"All right, you two. Back to your corners," Leslie intervened, getting both physically and verbally in between her husband and I. She was at least five inches taller than me, but I stood up on my tiptoes to peer over her shoulder at her jackass of a husband. Jerry and Darryl had been good friends, both having played sports for UCLA. While Darryl played basketball, Jerry had spent his four years as UCLA's leading running back. He'd spent six years in the NFL before an injury sidelined his athletic career. Leslie had been with him through it all. Including his many infidelities. In Jerry's eyes, I was the one who betrayed Darryl by divorcing him, not the other way around.

And every chance he saw me, he opted to take a dig, often still referring to Darryl as my husband, even after six years.

"Come on, Destiny. You know I was just messing with you," Jerry argued.

"You can keep your little digs to yourself. Matter of fact, shove them up your a—"

"Jerry, don't you have a late meeting you need to get to?" Leslie questioned, turning to her husband. She rushed over, pressed a kiss to his cheek, and began tugging him by the arm to encourage his movement out of the room.

"Yeah, I'll see y'all later."

"Not if I can help it," I retorted as he strode out of the room.

"You two," Leslie turned to me, exasperated.

I rolled my eyes. I'd never understood why Leslie put up with Jerry for all these years. She was beautiful with her sand-colored skin tone, curly hair, and light green eyes that so many men ogled over, but she'd been loyal to Jerry from day one. As loyal to him as I'd been to my own husband. The main difference was, once I found out about Darryl's infidelities, I dropped him like a sack of hot potatoes and never bothered to look back. That wasn't the case for Leslie. But then again, maybe Jerry's cheating had never caused Leslie to lose a child, as evidenced by the three kids the couple had together. Some things a relationship just couldn't get past.

"Tell your husband to keep my name out of his mouth and we'll be fine."

"You know he's just teasing. He doesn't mean anything by it."

I waved Leslie off. She always defended him and I wasn't in the mood to get into an argument with one of my best friends over her dumbass husband.

"Anyway, let's discuss something that really matters. Like, what are we wearing tonight to *Indigo?*" I asked, changing the subject. As much as I'd protested earlier, I was looking forward to a night out.

"Yes!" Leslie clapped. "I'll text Jackie and Stacey so they can join us."

Jackie and Stacey were also friends of ours from college who'd made their way to Williamsport in the years since we'd graduated.

Leslie got dressed in a pair of black leather shorts that showed off her long legs, and a dark, sleeveless top that displayed a risky level of cleavage. Once she was ready we took a Lyft over to my place where I chose to adorn myself in my orange shorts romper that criss-crossed at the neck, exposing both my arms and shoulders. It was going on the beginning of August and the weather was still in the high eighties.

"Ready?" Leslie questioned once I had on my six-inch strappy heels.

"Ready."

We made it to *Indigo* about twenty minutes later. As soon as we entered, I spotted Jackie and Stacey waving us over from one of the corner tables. We made our way to the two women who greeted us with champagne flutes that were filled to the top.

"To a night out with no kids, no men, and no work!" Leslie cheered, and we all laughed and clinked our glasses together before tossing them back as if we were taking shots. While I'd enjoyed the toast, my heart ached when Leslie mentioned no kids. I knew she loved her children with her whole heart. She was a stay-at-home mom who deserved a break. But the little pang of envy that moved through me couldn't be helped.

I shook my head, not allowing myself to slink down into the mire of self-pity for what I'd lost in the past. I had a great life and I wasn't about to let myself forget it.

"Oh, I love this song!" I cheered to the table once Maroon 5's "Girls Like You" came on.

"You always did like that type of music," Jackie chided, laughing.

I tossed my head back, laughing, because although Jackie herself was a strawberry blonde, blue eyed, white woman herself, she loved hip hop over anything. Our musical tastes were very different. Maroon 5 was one of my favorite groups and I had a special thing for Adam Levine.

"Leave my girl alone. You know she wants to put it on Adam Levine something fierce!" Leslie teased.

"I sure do!"

Placing my glass down on the table, I tossed my arms in the air, and began singing at the top of my lungs.

"'Cause girls like you run around with guys like me!" I sang and danced, swinging my hips in time with the music. The rest of the three women laughed and cheered me on. I was in my element, feeling happy that I'd conceded to Leslie's wishes and went out for the evening instead of staying home or catching a movie in her hotel suite.

Maroon 5 soon gave way to Bruno Mars' "That's What I Like" and I continued dancing, swinging my arms in the air and doing the same dance moves Bruno performed in the video for the song.

"Woohoo! And you didn't want to come out tonight!" Leslie chided over the music, now dancing herself.

"That truly would've been a shame."

My dancing faltered at the sound of the deep, male voice behind me. The hairs on the back of my neck stood on end. I glanced up at Jackie and Leslie to see their eyes widen with delight as they gazed at the man behind me. I didn't need to turn around to know who it was; but, on its own accord, my body did a one-eighty to see a glaring Tyler Townsend staring down at me. The same hunger I'd seen in his eyes on more than one occasion was apparent again that night.

A smile eased its way over his pink lips and not for the first time my fingers twitched to run through the strands of his low-cut beard.

"Destiny McDonald. Imagine my surprise to see you out on the dancefloor."

My jaw flapped open but no response came out.

"Are you kidding? Back in our cheerleading days Destiny was the first one on the floor!"

Tyler peered over my head, behind me, to Leslie. "Cheerleading days?"

"That's right. You're looking at UCLA's class of 2004 cheer squad's captain and co-captain," Leslie reiterated as she placed her arm around my shoulder.

"Is that so?" Tyler dropped those goddamned magnetizing eyes back to me again.

"You bet your ass. We were runner-up at nationals. I still think we got robbed if you ask me."

"But nobody asked you!" I snapped at Leslie who was talking too damn much.

"Well, I can't pass up an opportunity to dance with class of 2004's cheer co-captain, can I?"

I felt myself being pulled farther out onto the dancefloor. It hadn't been until that moment that I realized Tyler's big hand had mine firmly wrapped up in it. My feet moved as if he was the one instructing my brain what to do instead of me. At that precise moment another Maroon 5 song came on. "Moves Like Jagger" began playing and instinctively my body began swinging.

"That's it," Tyler encouraged, clapping to the music.

I rolled my eyes. "Whatever. Embarrass yourself if you want," I responded cockily. If he wanted to set himself up in front of all these people to get staged up on this dancefloor, it was his funeral. I turned and shimmied my hips lower, nearly touching the ground before coming back up and tossing my hands overhead to clap in time with the music. My intention had been to keep my back to Tyler during the entirety of the song, but unable to keep my eyes off of him, I turned around. To my surprise, Tyler had no problem keeping up with me just fine. When his hand reached out, pulling me by the waist, closer to him, I went willingly, our hips making contact in rhythm to the music. I should've been shocked that he was so good at dancing but I was starting to learn that Tyler was full of surprises.

"And I thought tonight was going to suck," he leaned down and said low in my ear before nipping my earlobe.

The shiver that ran through me knocked me off balance but I was steadied by Tyler's strong, competent hand at the small of my back.

"Easy, Destiny. We'll take this round nice and slow," he whispered soothingly in my ear.

I swallowed and inhaled deeply, trying to steady my heartbeat that had become erratic. Not due to the dancing but due to the man that I was now pressed up against.

Only by the grace of a loving being did that song finally end and was replaced by The Pussycat Doll's "Don't Cha". A screeching Leslie ran over to me, pulling me by the arm that wasn't wrapped around Tyler's waist … *When the hell did that happened?*

"Sorry, Mr. Townsend, but this is one of our theme songs. Right, D? We have to do the dance to this. Show these young girls we still got it!" Leslie exclaimed, pulling me free from Tyler's hold.

I ignored the feeling of loss I felt when he willingly let me go. But instead of leaving the dancefloor as I'd expected he would, he turned, folding his arms across his broad chest and blatantly watched. At one point he narrowed his eyes and glared dangerously at a man who looked like he was heading in the direction of Leslie and I. Obviously, using his sense of self-preservation, the man veered off course, and steered himself clear of us.

"Let's go, D!" Leslie yelled, shaking me by the shoulders, pulling my attention from Tyler to her.

Soon enough, Jackie joined us and we began performing the coordinated dance to the song that we'd come up well over a decade prior. Something happened to me when I remembered that Tyler was still watching me as I danced. I bent at the waist, poking my ass out, and came up swiftly, glancing over my shoulder to see him still smirking in my direction. Leslie, Jackie, and I spun in a circle before dropping low and picking it up, biting our pointer fingers. I threw caution to the wind as I fully embraced my inner stripper that this, and any song by the Pussycat Dolls, brought out in me. Knowing I had an audience made it all the more fun.

"Woo!" Leslie exclaimed.

"We still got it, ladies!" Jackie panted once the song finished.

We all turned and bowed and waved to the patrons who were standing around clapping for us.

"That was fun!" Leslie stated.

"It was even more fun to watch." Tyler's deep voice cut through the surrounding sounds of the lounge, reaching my ears. How he was able to do that, I had no idea. "I still can't believe you were a cheerleader," he stated, eyeing me as if challenging me to prove it.

"Believe it. Look!" Leslie butted in, pulling out her phone and bringing up a picture to show Tyler.

He peeled his gaze from me and peered down at the screen Leslie had thrust in his face. His smile increased. Reluctantly, I sauntered over, but even in six inch heels I had to lift up on my tiptoes to see the image Leslie was sharing with him. It was a picture of one of our cheer competitions. Leslie and I were front and center, me at the top of the pyramid due to my being one of the smallest members on the team.

"Good to know," Tyler stated before eyeing me suspiciously.

I narrowed my gaze, wondering what he meant by that, but was too bound by pride to ask. At least, I was too proud to ask in front of Leslie because as soon as she walked away, once her phone began ringing, I questioned, "Why's that good to know?"

Tyler looked down at me, lifting his auburn eyebrows at me before leaning over close to my ear. "Good to know as much information as possible about my future wife."

If I'd thought my steps had faltered before, that had been nothing next to the stumble I'd almost taken at that comment. Again, however, my unsteady body was kept upright by the steady embrace of Tyler.

"See? Falling for me already."

Clearing my throat, I mentally gathered my wayward emotions, physically pushing out of his embrace. "Mr. Townsend, I—"

"We're way past the Mr. Townsend bullshit, Destiny."

Another lump stuck in my throat at the sound of my name from his lips.

"Tyler. It's only two syllables. Say it. Ty-ler," he urged.

"I-I, what?"

"Ty-ler."

"Ty-" my mouth began to recite without my permission, "-ler."

"There it is." He grinned, the desire in his gaze practically burning me. "Get used to calling it, loudly, softly, in between. Practice makes perfect, and you'll have plenty of practice with it."

"Tyler, what the he—"

"See how easily it falls from your lips already." His eyes dropped to my lips and he ran his tongue along his own bottom lip.

Moisture pooled in places that were indecent for public exposure.

He bent lower, completely crowding my personal space. "How long do you think I'm going to let you play this game?"

My eyes widened as I pulled back and stared up at him. "Excuse you?"

"You heard me. How long do you think I'm going to let you keep this up?"

"Tyler, what are you even talking about?"

A heart-stopping, lascivious grin spread over his face. "Avoided saying it for so long, now you can't stop saying it. I knew you could take direction if pushed a little."

I scowled at him, not willing to admit that I did indeed enjoy saying his name.

"I don't take direction from anyone," I hissed.

"You will, Destiny. You will."

Another pool of moisture wrenched from my body at the assured tone he'd said those words. I blinked my eyes closed, needing at least a short reprieve from his penetrating gaze.

"Destiny, we have to go."

I pushed out all of the air in my lungs, extremely grateful for Leslie's interruption.

"I'm sorry, Mr. Townsend," Leslie stated, looking over at Tyler, apologetically.

"No worries." He kept his eyes trained on me as he responded to Leslie, "I needed to head out myself. Practice tomorrow. Destiny, I'll see you next week."

It sounded more like a warning than a parting.

"Sorry, girl," Leslie stepped in as she wrapped her arm around mine. "The husband got upset that we were out so late."

Her words barely registered as I watched Tyler back up and slowly turn to walk away.

"Wh-what?" I turned to see Leslie eyeing me, cocking her head to the side. I cleared my throat. "What were you saying?"

"Since when do you know Tyler Townsend?"

I shrugged. "Uh, I don't *know* him. I was hired by the Cougars for their training camp series on financial planning. No big deal." I shrugged again.

"Uh, huh. Shit," she cursed and glanced at her cell phone in her hand. "Jerry is freaking out. I go out for a few hours and the man loses his shit."

"Probably thinks you're doing the same thing he's doing when he's out of your sight," I mumbled.

"What was that?" Leslie peeked over her shoulder at me.

"Nothing. Tell your husband we're on the way." We both grabbed our clutches and hugged Jackie and Stacey good-bye.

"We're still on for the hip hop dance class tomorrow morning, right?" Leslie questioned before she climbed out of the Uber we'd taken to her hotel.

"Nine a.m. sharp. Don't be late," I added, sliding over in the backseat.

"Cool. See ya in the morning." She closed the door and waved as we drove off.

I sat back in my seat, closing my eyes, only to have them pop open again when the image of Tyler smirking down on me as we danced appeared in my mind. I squirmed in my seat, hating to admit to myself that for another night, the possibility of my falling asleep without the memory of Tyler's gaze was more than likely an impossibility.

CHAPTER 7

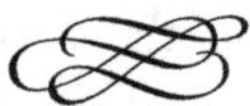

Tyler

"What the fuck are you calling me so early about?" my older brother, Joshua, growled into the phone.

"How nice to hear your voice in the morning as well." It was six-thirty in the morning and everyone in the family knew Joshua was not a morning person. It's why whenever I called him, I made sure to make it bright and early. Just to piss him off. But whereas the other early morning calls were just to get a rise out of him, this call was important.

"Fuck you, Ty. What do you want? Wait, hang on..."

I paused, listening intently as the hushed tones of a feminine voice sounded in the background.

"It's just Ty. Go back to sleep."

"Please give Kayla my regards."

"Fuck off. What do you want?"

I chuckled into the phone, still enjoying the ability to piss my brothers off, before clearing my throat. "I need to ask you about the house."

"What house?"

"My house."

"You don't have a house. You've got a fucking plot you picked out nearly two years ago but refused to build anything on it."

"Yeah, details. Whatever. Listen, what's the build time on it?"

"It depends on the square footage. Your plot is almost two acres so you can accommodate a house up to eight to ten thousand square feet. The larger it is the longer it's going to take to bu— Wait."

Fuck. I could hear my brother putting two and two together in his head. I'd partially been hoping the earlier time would prevent him from thinking so sharply. No such luck.

"Why the sudden interest in building now? You've gone the last twenty-three months without so much as even stopping by the property to—"

"For someone who doesn't like mornings, you sure do like asking a lot of questions in the a.m. Just answer my damn question and I'll let you get back to Kayla."

"First of all, don't fucking worry about Kayla. She's—"

"Ha! So that is who's in your bed. I knew it. You don't let any woman over your place."

"Didn't I tell you to mind your fucking business?"

I shrugged. "Probably, but don't ask for privacy if you're not willing to grant it, big brother."

The opposite end of the phone was silent for a heartbeat. "Touché."

"Now about that build time."

"Like I said, it depends on size, but it typically can take twelve to eighteen months."

I frowned, not liking that answer. "What if I put a rush on it?"

Another pause.

"Well, I suppose we could hire extra men to expedite the build. We could probably get the build time to a little as ten to twelve months."

I nodded even though he couldn't see me.

"Anything shorter than that and I wouldn't dare put my stamp of approval on it, nor would I have my brother living in a house I didn't absolutely know was safe."

"I hear ya," I told Josh.

"Do you know what you want in terms of square footage and design?"

I pondered his question for a moment. "Not quite yet. I'll have to think on it some more."

"I can have my assistant resend you some different designs and details."

"I'd like that. Thanks, Josh. I gotta go."

"Don't call me this fucking early again unless your ass is in trou—"

I didn't let him get the last word out before I hung up. He always ended our early morning exchanges the same way.

"Let's go!" I stepped into the hotel room, calling Kelvin who was still sleeping in the bed.

"The hell?" he grunted, sitting up slowly from the bed, rubbing his eyes.

"We've got practice."

"Man, I can't wait 'til camp is over and I go back to living *alone,*" he groaned.

"You say the same shit every year. Where would your ass be if I wasn't waking you up for practice these past four years?"

"Well rested!"

Chuckling, I tossed a towel at Kelvin. "And out of a damn job. Let's go." It was one of the last few days of training camp. We had our first pre-season scrimmage the following weekend. Which meant, this was the final day that Destiny McDonald would be teaching her seminar. After the previous Friday night's outing, she'd pretty much been the only thing on my mind. I'd meant every word I said to her Friday night, which had led to this morning's early phone call. I'd sat on the property I bought for the last two years, opting to utilize the condo in downtown Williamsport as my main residence when I was in town. I was often on the road during our season, and during the off-season I was constantly on the go doing commercials, photoshoots, or other events for sponsors. But now, I had a reason to slow down. To finally settle on the type of home I wanted to live in permanently.

Destiny McDonald was in a world of trouble and she didn't even know it.

* * *

Destiny

"Well, gentlemen, it's been a pleasure sharing with you what I know over the last few weeks. You've made this a rather enjoyable experience." I peered around the lecture hall at the entire Cougars football team, my eyes landing on Leonard Riggs. "Most of you, anyway."

A few snickers sounded around the room. At the same time Leonard's eyes squinted in my direction. I mentally brushed his look off. My eyes swung to the far end of the front row but I wouldn't let them venture to the final seat in the row. I knew *he'd* be staring at me intently as he'd done ever since my first class in that same room. After Friday night, thoughts of Tyler threatened to consume me at every turn. I just needed to get through that final lecture and hightail my ass out of there, to never have to see him again, save for Sunday afternoons or Monday nights when I turned on the football game.

"You all have one last opportunity to ask me any question you want. Wait," I paused, seeing a few hands go up a little too eagerly, "not *anything*. It must pertain to financial planning." Two hands dropped instantly. I dipped my head and had to keep my head from turning in the direction of Tyler.

"I got a question."

"Yes, Mr. Johnson," I answered the team's leading tackle.

"I get all of the budgeting stuff you talked about. It makes sense. My lady and I started to use of it actually."

"That's great." I perked up. "So what's your question?"

"You mentioned something about some type of account or fund to save up for things in the future. I forgot what you called them. Uhh …"

"Irregular expenses?"

"Right, irregular expenses. I'm confused on what type of account I would use to save for those."

I nodded. "Yes, the concept is called a sinking fund because the idea is that you put money aside in an account, or *sink* those funds for a time when you need them. You have my card right, Mr. Johnson?" I remembered giving him one of my business cards the previous week.

"Yeah."

"Great. Give my office a call and we can have you and your wife come down to talk more about it. I'll even give you two a free first time consultation."

"That's what's up." He nodded. "'Preciate it."

"Any other questions?"

"I've got a question."

My toes curled in my high heels at the sound of his voice. Slowly, I turned my head in Tyler's direction, regretting that I even opened myself up to any more questions.

"Yes, Mr. Townsend."

His smile dropped and a frown formed. Instantly, I felt chastised and he hadn't said a word. I knew it was my using the formality of his last name instead of calling him Tyler, as he'd instructed. *Instructed.* There's a word I would have cursed any other man out for trying to do with me, but for some reason I felt the compulsion to apologize. I shook my head of just silly thoughts.

"I didn't receive a business card. You must've forgotten to give me one."

My eyes narrowed and I clenched my teeth. "I don't have any—"

"What are those on the desk behind you?" He nodded in the direction of the desk.

I turned to see a stack of business cards I'd set out on the table earlier sitting front and center. I couldn't make a scene. Not in front of the entire football team and their coaching staff. Without another word, I turned toward the desk, sauntering over and picking up one of my business cards before turning back.

"Here you are, Mr. Townsend." I went to place the card on his desk when his large hand covered mine. I rush of air escaped my mouth.

"Tyler," he reiterated just loud enough for me to hear.

Pulling my hand free, I moved to the other side of the lecture hall, still feeling his eyes on my backside. "Okay, well, it's been a pleasure. Don't hesitate to reach out if you have any questions and are just too shy to ask in front of your teammates. Thanks again, guys. And good luck with your upcoming season. I'll be rooting for you from my living room."

With that last parting comment, I turned to my briefcase and began stuffing my business cards and belongings back inside to get out of there as quickly as possible.

"Destiny, can you hold up for a minute?" Mike called.

Dammit. I was almost out of there. "Sure," I mumbled to Mike.

"All right, fellas, we've got practice in about forty-five minutes. Make sure you refuel up with lunch and are back on the field. On time," he stressed the last part, looking directly at Leonard.

He waited for the team to disperse before turning his attention on me.

"I wanted to thank you for these last few weeks."

"Brenda tell you to say that?" I teased.

He chuckled a little. "No. But seriously, I'm sure it wasn't easy walking into this lions' den. These guys can be tough, and don't always take direction easily, but you handled yourself well."

"Don't sweat it, Coach. They weren't that bad, and once they realized I knew my stuff, most of them settled down long enough to listen."

Mike nodded. "Hey, we've got our first scrimmage next Saturday. Afterwards, we're going out to celebrate the start of the season. Just dinner at a local place, nothing fancy. Brenda will be joining us if you'd like to come."

"Uh …" My eyes traveled around the empty room. "Let me think about it."

"Fair enough. Thanks, again." He nodded, patting me on the shoulder before heading out of the lecture hall door that the other coaches had passed through a few minutes prior.

I looked around the room again, both relieved and slightly disappointed to see that it was empty. While I had told myself I wasn't looking for Tyler to hang around, the little pang in my chest told me that I might've been lying to myself.

Just as I was picking up my briefcase to head out, my phone

chimed with an incoming FaceTime. It was Leslie. Knowing I had some time before I needed to be back at the office for an afternoon conference call, I placed my briefcase back on the desk and answered.

"You've barely been gone twelve hours and are already calling. Missed me that much?" I answered.

"You know it," she responded, giggling. "I had a great time this weekend. I missed hanging out like we used to. With me in LA and you in Williamsport."

I pouted. "I miss you, too. This weekend was fun, wasn't it?" After our Friday night outing, Leslie and I had met up for a Saturday morning hip hop dance class, then had brunch, featuring bottomless mimosas where we talked and reminisced on our college days. We parted ways Saturday afternoon because she'd had a packed schedule with her husband for the rest of the weekend. They'd just left the previous evening.

"It was. We need to do it again and soon. And maybe then you'll tell me what's going on between you and Tyler Townsend."

My eyes widened as Leslie looked on through the screen with that *gotcha* expression.

"What are you talking about?"

"Hmmm, bitch, don't give me that dumbfounded look. I may have been preoccupied with Jerry's whining ass but I saw what was happening on that dance floor Friday night."

"It was a dance floor. There was dancing that was happening. That's it."

"Yeah, dancing hot enough to damn near burn the rubber off a pair of tires."

"What? That doesn't even make— Never mind. There was no—"

"Don't deny it." She held up her hand. "I've got twenty-twenty vision. And the fact that you're purposely avoiding answering my questions proves it even more. Have you two gone out on a date yet?"

"No." I shook my head. "You know my rule about dating men with beards. Shit. You do remember what happened the last time I dated a man with a beard, right?" I rolled my eyes.

"Girl, you are insane."

"I'm not. And he's got a red beard. You know what they say about those damn redheads."

"No, what?"

"They say we have no soul."

I startled so much I nearly dropped my phone as I whirled around to see Tyler hovering over me.

"Though, I like to think of my beard as more of an auburn as opposed to red," he stated, running a hand through that very beard.

I scrunched my lips up and stared down into the screen of my phone. "You were facing that direction. You couldn't have told me he was there."

Leslie was too busy giggling to even answer.

"I'm hanging up now. Bye!"

"B—" Her parting was cut off when I hit the end call button.

"Do you always eavesdrop on personal conversations, Mr—" My words caught in my throat when he angled his head as if daring me to finish my sentence the way I'd intended. I had half a mind to do so but what came out was, "Tyler."

A satisfied smirk appeared on his face. "Only when the conversation is relevant to me."

"It wasn't relevant to you. It was a friend of mine asking *me* a question about my life."

A chuckle escaped his lips and my stomach muscles tightened.

"Anything involving you is relevant to me, Destiny." He said my name as if it was meant to fall from his lips and his lips alone.

"Don't you have another practice to get to?"

"Not yet."

I shook my head. "This is ridiculous."

"What is?"

"You. This whole ... whatever you're doing. It's not going to work."

"It's already working, Destiny."

There went my name out of his mouth again.

"I'm not a jump off."

"A jump off?"

I rolled my eyes. "I'm sure you're familiar with the term. I'm not a groupie who chases after athletes looking to have a baby with them for the child support check, or the girl who's willing to play second fiddle while you parade your main woman like arm candy on TV."

"Nor would I expect you to be." He stepped closer.

My breathing increased.

"I-I'm too old for you," I blurted out.

His eyes scanned my body, causing heat to rise in my belly.

"You were born in June nineteen eighty-two, making you thirty-six. That's perfect."

I furrowed my brows. "You looked up my birthday?"

"You mentioned it in an episode of *Fashion and Finances*."

My jaw dropped open. I shook my head. "You did not actually listen to an episode ..."

"Every single one."

"I don't believe you." I folded my arms over my chest.

"How about you quiz me on any episode you want while we go out to dinner?"

I grinned. "Are you asking me out on a date?"

He shook his head and my grin faded. "Not asking. I'm letting you know we're going out. I'm asking what you'd like to discuss once we're on that date. You can question me on my knowledge of your podcast, or we can talk more about your days as a cheerleader, or—"

"Or we could cut this conversation short because there will be no date."

Tyler took a step forward and grasped my chin in between his thumb and forefinger, lifting my head up to meet his eyes. "Destiny, your feistiness is fucking adorable, but I wouldn't keep poking the bear if I were you. A man can have only so much restraint."

I clamped down on my lower lip with my teeth and inhaled deeply when his eyes noticeably darkened, his mouth tightened into a stern look. My nipples hardened painfully. My body's response to his commands was unrecognizable. No man, and I mean *no* man has ever had that type of impact on me.

Suddenly, Tyler took a step back, releasing my chin, a look of satisfaction appearing on his handsome face. "I'll see you next Saturday night, six p.m. at Mar Belo. I would highly suggest you not force my hand and make me come look for you." His eyes hungrily scanned my body one last time before he turned and confidently strode up the stairs and out of the door of the lecture hall.

I was left standing there with what felt like a damn geyser had gone off between my legs.

Maybe I was in trouble.

CHAPTER 8

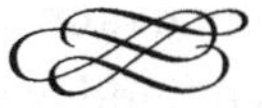

D*estiny*

"Yes! Go! Go! Go!" my mother chanted as we watched the Cougars' first pre-season scrimmage against the Tennessee Rams. Though it wasn't a regular season game, our local news channel was airing it.

I laughed when my mother waved her fist in the air as Leonard Riggs ran his second touchdown of the game, into the endzone. "That boy's good," she smiled and started in her slurred speech. The Parkinson's sometimes made it difficult to understand her but I knew what she was saying.

I nodded. "He is."

"You said you were working with them in training camp, right?"

"Yup. I taught a financial planning seminar to the entire team. Gained a couple of them as clients."

"That's good, baby. I hope that Riggs boy takes some of your advice."

"I think he's beyond my help, Mama."

"And that quarterback … woo!"

My back stiffened as I watched my mother's lips twitch into a grin at the thought of Tyler.

I knew the feeling but I wasn't going to be sharing that with her.

"I guess he didn't need any help with his finances considering where he comes from."

"No, guess not."

"Think they're going to win the superdome this year?"

"Super Bowl, Mama," I corrected. My mother hadn't been a football fan for very long. She'd only started watching after my father died. He was a diehard football fan and I think it helped her feel closer to him to watch the games each Sunday.

"Super dome, Super Bowl, what's the difference?"

"Well, the Super Dome is where they play in New Orleans, and the Super Bowl is actually the championship game. So, that's kind of an important distinction," I teased.

"Don't get smart with your mama, girl."

I laughed. "Sorry, Mama. You want anymore of this cake before I put it away?" I asked as I headed over to the table.

"No, I'm fine. Doctor says my blood sugar was a little high."

I stopped short from packing up the carrot cake with cream cheese icing I'd brought my mother. It was her second favorite type of cake.

"What? How high was it? Why didn't you tell me?" I immediately felt guilty about all of the sweets I brought over when I visited. I should've known better than to keep bringing a woman her age, and in her condition, all this junk food.

"Don't do that," my mother chided. "Stop that. It was only a little high. Nothing to worry about."

"How high was it, Mama?" I'd forgotten to ask her how her doctor's appointment earlier in the week had gone. I'd gotten so distracted with work that it slipped my mind.

"Only a few points. The results are over by the computer, see for yourself. Doc says it's nothing to worry about since I did have the last slice of that chocolate cake right before the visit."

"Mama, your doctor's appointment was ten o'clock in the morning. You had chocolate cake for breakfast?" My eyes widened.

"I had it with the almond milk."

I sighed. In that moment I made the decision to add on the option to have the certified nurse assistants who worked in the building, to come in for meal times to make sure my mother was eating right. Up until that point, I had put it off at my mother's insistence that she didn't need the extra help, but no longer.

"Ma, you can't have cake and almond milk for breakfast. I meal prepped some oatmeal for you for five days. All you had to do was warm it up and have it with the fruit I left."

"I wanted cake." She rolled her eyes at me and looked back to the screen. "Shhh, game's back on."

I didn't even bother arguing, instead placing the carrot cake on the bottom shelf of the refrigerator and tossing out the week-old oatmeal that'd gone untouched. I busied myself, prepping three more days worth of oatmeal, and cut up some banana for her to put in the oatmeal in the morning. I set a reminder in my phone to stop by the front office before I left to add on the CNA service to start the next morning.

I watched the rest of the game with my mother, cheering along with her once the Cougars beat the Rams, twelve to zero.

"I'm heading out, Mama."

"Good. You got a date?"

I angled my head. "Why would you ask me that?"

"Because it's a Saturday night and my baby girl is a beautiful, successful woman. What man wouldn't want to snatch her up?"

I laughed, shaking my head. "Bye, Mama. Call me if you need anything."

"Girl, hush! I don't need nothing. You enjoy your night out."

I didn't bother telling my mother that I wasn't going out on a date. I was just meeting my mentor and her husband out for a celebratory dinner. So what if it was the same dinner that the team's star quarterback had invited … no, insisted I attend? That surely did not make it a date.

Besides, I'd decided that I would make it a point of speaking with Leonard Riggs that night. His mentioning of his financial advisor and the returns he'd earned still nagged at me. And in spite of myself, I wanted to get to the bottom of that issue. See? Tyler Townsend had absolutely nothing to do with my decision to attend the team's dinner.

* * *

"THANK YOU," I told the Lyft driver as I handed her the cash tip.

"Thank you. Enjoy your evening," She smiled at me over her shoulder as I exited the vehicle.

I had been dropped off in front of Mar Belo, a popular Portuguese restaurant on the outskirts of Williamsport. The restaurant wasn't too far from the stadium where the Cougars played their home games. It was easy to see why Mike had chosen this location to have dinner with his players and their guests, to celebrate the opening of the season. Mar Belo had a reputation for its exquisite and authentic food, which was the result of its owner's Portuguese heritage. And while the restaurant wasn't over the top with its prices, it was pricey enough to give off a certain feel of exclusivity.

I inhaled deeply when I peered into the front window of the restaurant, noting all of the team members mingling and laughing with one another. The Cougars had won their scrimmage, and while the win didn't count toward their actual season's record, it was against the team that had knocked them out of the playoffs the previous season. It was more of an emotional victory than anything else. My eyes rose and ended up lingering on the man who'd led the Cougars to their win.

Tyler.

It prickled at me that I had become more used to referencing him by his first name than his last. He was right, I was getting used to calling his first name, and in spite of myself, I actually liked the way it rolled off my tongue. My breath hitched as I continued to watch when he tossed his head back, laughing at a comment a teammate of his made. He was tall, in shape, and wore the light grey suit pants with a tucked in royal blue dress shirt like nobody's business. The sleeves of his shirt were rolled up to the elbows, exposing his forearms. I grinned. Even at this distance I could see the light touch of the auburn hairs along his arms. With that thought, my gaze quickly climbed his body, taking in the low-cut auburn beard that outlined his square jaw, the freckles that ran along the tops of his cheeks, and to those damn eyes that were so goddamned captivating. If one were to squint while looking in Tyler's direction, he would remind you of Prince Harry—at least, that's what some entertainment blogs had claimed. To me, Prince Harry had absolutely *nothing* on Tyler Townsend.

"Excuse me," a giggling female voice sounded, pulling my attention from Tyler.

I glanced up to see a tall brunette, covering her mouth with her hand. "No problem," I stated, stepping aside so she could pass through the front door of the restaurant.

"Well, lookie here, *Mz. McDonald.*"

I blinked, looking from the woman to Leonard. His eyes were narrowed on me, mouth contorted into that smirk he always did when he thought he had something over the person he was talking to.

"Mr. Riggs," I greeted. I was all set to dismiss Leonard when at that moment I remembered that I needed to speak with him. I glanced between him and the woman who was now draped all over him. "Uh, could I speak with you a moment?"

The woman had the audacity to suck her teeth. I snapped my neck, grilling her before dismissing her and looking back to Leonard.

"It'll be quick. I just need an answer about something you said a while back."

"Leonard, I'm hungry," the impatient woman whined.

"Gon' ahead, baby. I'll be in soon."

I sighed in relief at not having to argue with Leonard or this woman.

"Make sure it's quick," she called over her shoulder before tossing her head in my direction, then lifting her nose in the air as she pushed through the door.

"Whatever," I mumbled, shaking my head.

"You finally decided to take me up on my offer. Females like you always do."

I frowned, pulling my head back. "What offe—" I stopped, remembering the words he'd tossed at me a few weeks prior about him letting me screw him. I let out a humorless laugh. "Yeah fucking right. Look, I said I'd make this quick, so I am. The other week you mentioned that you were getting some great returns from investments you made through a financial advisor you worked with. I just want to know their name. That's it."

He frowned, standing to his full height, looking down on me as if trying to figure out my angle. I would've gladly told him I didn't have an angle, but I knew that would've fallen on deaf ears.

"I see what this is," he stated, snapping his fingers as if he had me all figured out. "You're salty at the money I'm making. I'm getting more than that little seven percent shit you was talking, over the long haul, and it's eating you up." He began chuckling. "Nah." He shook his head and my shoulders sank. He had this all wrong.

"Leonard, I'm not trying to hustle you—"

"Because a bitch like you can't," he growled.

Instinctively, I took a step back. "That was unnecessary."

"What's unnecessary is females like yourself who try to eat off good men like me."

I shook my head, not understanding where his anger was coming from but not really caring either. I just needed a name.

"Fine, Leonard, you can keep your financial advisor a secret. But you said your agent hooked you up with them. Can you at least tell me your agent's name?" I figured with that information, I could make an appointment with his agent to gather information. If worst came to worst, I could do a little digging to find out Leonard's agent.

A smile I didn't like parted Leonard's lips as he stroked his goatee. "You of all people should know him."

I lifted an eyebrow, wondering why I would know his agent.

"Darryl Wright."

My stomach plummeted. I bit the inside of my cheek. Of fucking course, Leonard's agent would be my ex-husband.

"Yeah, I thought you'd know that name." Leonard looked me up and down with a disgust I was certain I hadn't earned.

I mentally shook off the surprise of learning my ex-husband was representing Leonard. "Thank you," I spat out and stepped aside to let Leonard pass through the doors. I didn't have anymore questions for him, none that he was willing to answer, at least.

I expelled a full breath only when I the door closed behind me. I'd heard that Darryl had become a sports agent once he retired from the league, the very season we'd gotten divorced. But that was it. After some time, I'd done my best not to make any inquiries into his life and I forbade anyone from telling me about him.

"Shit," I cursed realizing I might just have to speak to my ex again. I took another deep breath before tossing my shoulders back, and refocusing on where I was. I didn't need to make any decisions concerning Darryl right then. That night, I was just going out to have dinner with my mentor and friend, her husband, and the football team he coached.

And Tyler, my not-so-subconscious mind quickly added on.

* * *

Tyler

Nothing and I mean nothing could've had me in a better mood than when I saw Destiny walk through the doors of Mar Belo ten minutes after we were seated. Not the fact that we'd just beaten the team that'd ended our playoff run the previous season. Not the fact that I'd passed for close to two hundred yards this game. And especially not the fact that our team had shown the best pre-season showing in over three years.

Nope.

None of that mattered when Destiny walked through the double doors of the restaurant wearing a pair of black leather pants, a sleeveless cream top, and a black and gold choker, highlighting her elegant neck. It was the choker that had my hands balling into fists under the table.

"Destiny," Brenda, the coach's wife, called out getting her attention.

"Here's a seat." I instantly elbowed Kelvin, urging him with my eyes and a head nod to move his ass to the chair across the table. Destiny was sitting next to me. I moved out of the way, noticing as she glanced around, checking to see if there was space for her to fit anywhere else.

"Sit," I commanded.

Her eyes widened briefly before she pushed out a breath, conceding that there was no other space for her to plant her ass.

"Glad you made it," Brenda greeted, pulling Destiny into a warm hug.

I wondered how the two women knew each other. That was another question I put in the back of my mind to be answered later about this woman that had me enraptured. I inhaled deeply, savoring the sweet scent of some sort of fruit concoction. I typically didn't like too much scent on a woman but for her it worked.

"You smell good," I leaned in close to her ear to say.

She glanced over at me, peeking up through long lashes. "Hello, Tyler."

A warm feeling spread throughout my stomach. "You're finally getting it."

Her smile dipped slightly. "Getting what?"

"Used to using my name. Amongst other things."

"What're you even—"

"Finally decided to join the rest of us, *Mz. McDonald?"*

My mood instantly shifted at the sound of Leonard's voice from two tables down. I turned a sharp gaze on him.

"Yes, Mr. Riggs," Destiny greeted before taking a sip from the glass of water that'd been placed in front of her.

"I would've thought this place was out of your *budget,"* he called.

"How nice of you to take my budget into consideration, Mr. Riggs."

"Don't you have company at your own fucking table to worry about?" I growled at Leonard.

His mouth clamped shut and he raised his hands in a surrendering motion. "My bad. I was just trying to make conversation with the budget guru over there. Sheesh."

"Leonard, fu—"

"Forget him. He's just trying to get a rise."

My angry tirade was cut off not by Destiny's words but by the hand she'd placed on my thigh to garner my attention. My eyes dropped to the small, mahogany hand with pastel pink colored nails. A calm rushed over me, and before I realized it my right hand moved to cover hers, trapping it in place before she could think of pulling it back.

"You have my hand."

"That I do."

"Can I have it back please?"

My head was shaking no before she finished the question. "You gave up rights to this hand the moment you placed it on my body."

She frowned, forehead wrinkling as those umber eyes stared up at me in confusion. "I don't think that's how it works, Tyler."

"With me it is. But you're still learning."

Her mouth popped open. "Learning wh—"

"Destiny, did you get a chance to see the game?" Brenda interrupted, either not noticing our exchange or not caring. Either way, the disruption served to piss me off. I squeezed Destiny's hand in mine and she quickly spun her head back to me, mouth flopping open, trying to figure out who to place her attention on.

"Who didn't watch the game, Mrs. McClellan?" I called over Destiny's shoulder.

Brenda laughed. "Nice throwing, Ty."

I tipped my head at her. "Thank you, ma'am."

"What did I tell you about calling me ma'am?"

I shrugged. "My apologies, Ms. McClellan, just don't want to upset the big guy." I tipped my head in the direction of my coach and slightly leaned across Destiny to add, "You know he gets jealous of the affection you have for me." I pulled back, winking at Brenda, causing her to giggle.

The fingers of my left hand grazed across Destiny's soft shoulder, instinctively. I hadn't even noticed I'd thrown my free arm around the back of the booth we both sat at.

"That comes naturally for you, doesn't it?" she questioned, glancing up at me.

I lifted an eyebrow. "Touching you? Yes, it does." I nodded.

"No, charming the socks off women."

I frowned, not liking the tone she'd used, accusingly.

"Not just any woman. Only the ones who are worth it." I winked at her and went to say something else when the waiter, taking our orders, interrupted.

"I'll have the mixed green salad with the chilean sea bass," Destiny stated, handing the waiter her menu with her free hand. Her right, was still placed firmly in my hold. I noticed she hadn't tried to move it again, either.

I ordered the rack of lamb and the salad as well before turning my attention back on Destiny.

"No wine for you?" she questioned, looking at my empty wine glass.

"I don't drink during the season."

She lifted both brows in surprise. "Since when? The number of articles I've read on you—" Her statement faltered on her lips at the sight of my grin.

"You've been researching me."

She began shaking her head.

"Don't lie, Destiny." I leaned down, whispering in her ear, "Lying can get you into very deep trouble." I pulled back, satisfied, only when I saw her body shiver.

"I-I wasn't researching you, I mean, I was but not just you," she spat out quickly. "The whole team. I know Maynard comes from just outside of Chicago and grew up with his mom and stepdad, I know Riggs' mother left him and his father when he was just a baby. I know three members of your offensive line have gotten DUIs in their careers. I know—"

"You planning on running down the entire team's lives to me?"

Her mouth clamped shut at my jibe. She shook her head before saying, "I'm just proving to you that *you're* not the only person I took the time to read about. I like to study and get to know my clients is all

I'm saying." She lifted and lowered her shoulder on a shrug, and tried to pull her hand back once the food arrived at our table.

"I can't eat with your hand over mine."

I looked over at her left hand. "You have a hand free."

"I'm right-handed and you need to cut your lamb." Her head jutted in the direction of my plate.

I sighed. "So I do." Reluctantly, I pulled my hand from over hers. I instantly regretted my decision when the warmth her hand on my thigh provided, left with its removal.

"So, you're a football fan, Destiny? I never got a chance to ask you that with all of the dodging you were doing the last few weeks."

"I wasn't—" She stopped at the raise of my eyebrow. "Never mind," she huffed. "To answer your question, yes. I am a football fan. And yes, before you even ask, I am a diehard Cougars fan. My father would roll over in his gr—" She paused, as if stunned by something. Her eyelids lowered, her long lashes sweeping against the tops of her cheeks.

"When did he pass?"

She looked up at me, swallowing. "Over ten years now." She swallowed and took a sip of her wine before turning back to eat.

"You're not driving home, are you?" I phrased it as a question, but after seeing her take even a sip of wine, I knew I wasn't letting her get behind the wheel to drive anywhere.

"I took a Lyft here. I planned on catching one home."

I nodded.

"So you grew up watching football. Is that why you became a cheerleader?"

"Oh my God!" She rolled her eyes toward the ceiling. "I still can't believe Leslie showed you that picture."

"Why not? You should totally be proud of it. You were the best looking cheerleader at the top of the pyramid."

"I was the *only* cheerleader at the top of the pyramid."

"Really? I didn't notice. Didn't see anyone in the picture besides you. Could've been ten pyramids in the picture. You stood out."

Another sweep of those long lashes as she let out a small laugh before turning back to her plate.

I stared for as long as I could, watching the tines of her fork enter her succulent, soft lips before I needed to look elsewhere, otherwise I'd embarrass us both at this table. Well, I couldn't give a shit what anyone around us thought, even my coach, but I knew Destiny wouldn't take too kindly to my tossing her on the table and devouring every inch of her. At least, not until after our first date.

So instead of doing that, I continued to lightly graze my fingertips along her bare shoulder, while asking her probing questions about herself. I learned not only was she a cheerleader in college but had gotten to UCLA on a cheerleading scholarship, garnering her the opportunity to leave college without any debt, a fact she was personally proud of. She'd majored in finance and minored in English in college, and worked for one of the largest national investment firms for close to four years before striking out on her own. Career questions she was more open about answering but there were gaps that she wasn't filling.

"The team will be traveling for the next few weeks. Our regular season starts in two weeks and it's a home game. It's an afternoon game which gives me enough time to shower and change, do all of the post-game interviews, and still pick you up at seven for dinner," I told Destiny as we stood outside of the restaurant waiting for her Lyft to arrive.

She lifted an eyebrow. "Is that so?"

"That is correct."

"So you're asking me out on a date?"

I shook my head. "No, I'm letting you know, I'm taking you out so *you* know what time to be ready."

She laughed, lowering her head before looking back up at me. "That alpha male thing may work on the other women you—"

"You are highly concerned with the other women I'm supposedly seeing." I stepped closer, hovering over her. "I don't give a shit what you've read about me, Destiny. Only someone as special and unique as you gets this kind of attention. I'll see you in two weeks. Seven o'clock." I looked up just as a dark grey sedan was pulling up. "Your Lyft's here."

She blinked a few times and her partially opened mouth looked too inviting not to take a taste. Bending low, my hand moved to her waist. Feeling satisfied when I didn't sense any resistance on her part, I lowered until our lips met. I inhaled deeply at the first touch of my lips to hers, pulling her in more. When our tongues first touched, heat rushed through me. I pulled her in tighter when a small groan escaped her mouth. I became hungrier than I'd ever been, and considering I'd just finished eating, it wasn't for food. A honking of a horn forced us to pull apart. Destiny's breathing was heavy, mirroring my own breathing, as she stared up at me dazed and confused.

Another honking sound caught my attention, and I peered up at the Lyft driver who'd rolled down his window.

"Are you Destiny?"

Fucking douche, I thought to myself.

"Oh my God! You're Tyler Townsend!"

My frown deepened at this asshole's audacity. First he interrupts the best first kiss I've ever experienced, and next he's a blubbering fan.

I chose to ignore him for the time being, and instead, moved to the back door, pulling it open for Destiny to get in. When she moved passed me, I caught her by the waist.

"Two weeks. Seven p.m." I released her waist for her to get in before closing the door. Instead of stepping back to let the driver pull off, I moved around the front of the vehicle, crossing over to the driver's side door. I motioned with my hand for him to lower the window.

"What's your name?" I asked.

"Michael. I'm a huge fan. If you could ju—"

I held out my hand for Michael to shake. His smile dropped and his facial expression turned to a pained look when I tightened my hold on his hand. I lowered my head and pulled Michael toward me so his head was just outside the window and out of hearing distance of the woman in his backseat.

"Don't ever interrupt me when I'm with my woman again. Also, I need you to realize something very important Michael." I paused.

"W-what's that?"

I tilted my head in the direction of his backseat. "You've got precious cargo in your car. Make sure she gets home safely. So much as a hair on her head moves out of place and that's your ass. You understand what I'm telling you, Michael?" I squeezed his hand even tighter not caring that his face was beginning to turn red.

He sputtered a little before slowly nodding.

"Good." I loosened my grip. "Glad we had this talk." I released his hand and stood up to my full height, tapping on the roof of his car before waving and tossing a smile at Destiny, who I knew was staring at me. I watched as Michael drove off. He turned the car impossibly slow out of the restaurant's parking lot, no doubt, heeding my warning.

Knowing I was watching my future drive down the road, I watched carefully, ensuring that Michael indeed did pay attention to the speeding limits and stop signs. The next two weeks were going to feel like torture. And I'd never felt like that at the beginning of a football season. I was always anxious to get out on the field.

I turned when a low whistle sounded behind me.

"I told you women with them short, Nia Long, Halle Berry in the nineties haircuts would have your ass sprung." Kelvin laughed, shaking his head at me.

A smile eased across my face. "I'd be worried too if I didn't know she was just as sprung over me." It didn't matter that she tried to deny it, Destiny McDonald was going to be mine and she wanted it as much as I did. That, I was sure about.

CHAPTER 9

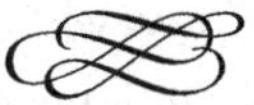

Destiny

"Maybe I'm just horny. You know it has been a few months since I had any action. Maybe—"

"Maybe that's why you're all goo-goo eyed over Tyler Townsend? Pssh! Don't fool yourself, girl. You. Are. Sprung."

I frowned as I stared into the screen of my phone, looking on at Resha. I'd stayed late at work, taking meetings with clients, one of which was the wife of a teammate of Tyler's. It seems my lectures hadn't fallen on deaf ears, as Janie, the wife of the one of the Cougar's offensive linemen, had come in with her budget in hand, asking how to best invest for their future.

"Nobody's sprung," I retorted, rolling my eyes and sitting back against my leather desk chair. I looked up and waved at one of owners of another small business in the office passed by. "Like I said, I'm probably just horny. It's been quite some time since I've had a satisfactory orgasm that wasn't by my own hand or a battery operated device," I mumbled.

"Well, nothing like a young stallion of a professional football player to get that engine revved up."

I pulled my head back, making a face into the screen. "Girl, what?" I shrieked.

Resha rolled her eyes. "Sorry. I met a damn race car driver," she mumbled.

"And now you're suggesting that I get my engine revved up? Hmph. I'm not the only one who needs to get their boots knocked."

"You know I'm ce—"

"Celibate? Yeah, I'm aware." I waved my free hand, dismissing her.

"I'm serious, D. This is what I need to do to spiritually cleanse myself of all of the toxic men I've dated in the past."

I rolled my eyes. "If you say so. Listen …" I paused, biting the inside of my cheek, debating whether or not I even wanted to bring this topic up. But Resha was my sounding board whenever I felt like I might be making a dumb move. It's why I'd confided in her about Tyler and why I'd need her input for the next conversation I was about to bring up. "Remember when I told you I got a funny feeling about the financial advisor Leonard Riggs was bragging about?"

Resha's honey-colored eyes moved skyward, trying to recall. "Riggs, that's the asshole kicker, right?"

I giggled. "Cornerback."

"Whatever." Resha wasn't a sports fan by any stretch.

"Doesn't matter. You remember, right?"

"Yeah. Why?"

"The other week when I went to dinner with the team, I stopped him outside of the restaurant to ask about this advisor. The one that's supposedly doubling his investment within a matter of weeks."

"Sounds like a scam to me."

"*Exactly.* You know that and I know that, but someone like Leonard who, though cocky as all hell and great with a football in his hands, wouldn't know that. And—"

"And there's a sucker born every minute," Resha interjected.

"Right, which means if Riggs is being ripped off, he's probably not alone. So, I asked him for his advisor's name. Unfortunately, since he has this stick up his ass where I'm concerned, he wouldn't give me a name. But he was more than happy … hell, giddy even, to tell me the name of his agent who'd referred him to the advisor. Guess who it is."

"I don't do guessing games, Destiny."

I huffed and threw my hand in the air. "Whatever. It's Darryl."

Resha stiffened, lips poking out in a confused manner as her head tilted to the side. "I'm sorry, I thought you just said Darryl, and the only Darryl I know is a two-timing son of a bi—"

"Yes, that's him. He went on to become a sports agent after he retired."

"A sports agent. Pssh!" she tutted. "His ass needs therapy, Jesus, and the Holy—"

"Resha," I warned.

She pushed out a breath on a sigh. "So why're you telling me all of this?"

I bit my bottom lip before continuing. "Because I'm thinking of going to see him just to ask about this financial advisor he's recommending." I rushed the last part out before flinching in anticipation of her reaction.

"Oh hell no, D! How could you even think to go see that son of a bitch again after what he did? How the hell would that thought even form in your mind? Have you lost it?"

"I know, I know," I repeated over and over to calm Resha's tirade. "Just hear me out. Leonard wouldn't give me the name or any other information on the financial advisor he's using. I even asked Mike McClellan if he knew the name but he didn't. And the more I think about it, the uneasier I get thinking this person is out there scamming these athletes. If Darryl is recommending this advisor to all of his clients, they could be losing millions of dollars. I can't just sit back and watch that happen if I can do something about it. This is why I got into personal finance in the first place. To help people manage their own finances better so that they wouldn't be at the losing end of some morally corrupt institutions or individuals who go out of their way to part people from their money. I—"

"All right, all right, Mother Teresa, I see what you're getting at," she stated flatly, holding her hand up.

I frowned. "I was just getting warmed up."

"Well cool it back down. You've convinced me. I don't like it but I see why you feel obligated to reach out to that slime ball rat of an ex-husband of yours. Hell, he could be in on it, too. And that means he might go to jail and *that* is something I can get behind," Resha finished with a lightness in her voice at the thought of Darryl facing prison time.

His involvement in this possible crime was something I'd briefly considered. I didn't believe he would be capable of setting his athletes up in such a manner, but hell, I'd been married to the man for eight years and thought he was faithful. I obviously didn't know him as well as I thought I had. In the intervening six years since our divorce, I'd had absolutely zero contact with him. A lot could change in six years. The reality was, I was contemplating walking into a situation I didn't know very much about.

"I know that look. Your mind's made up already," Resha stated, pulling my attention back to her.

I nodded.

"Just be careful, D. I don't fucking trust that ex of yours."

"That makes two of us." Were the last words before I hung up with Resha. As I turned off my computer, I set a reminder in my calendar for the next day to call Darryl Wright's office and make an appointment for as soon as possible. I'd found the number to his office online already. Resha was right, I had already made up my mind.

* * *

Tyler

"That's a wrap!" the director yelled from behind the three cameras that were all pointed in my direction.

I pushed out a breath and dropped the plastered grin I'd been wearing for this commercial shoot. I was doing a commercial for a deodorant brand that was one of my major sponsors. I was in Los Angeles and had an early morning flight out to head back to Williamsport and catch a flight with the team to head to our final scrimmage of the season which was on the East Coast. The season hadn't even officially started yet and my schedule was just revving up. Typically, I thrived on the early and pre-season energy, but as I discarded the fake football uniform I'd worn for the shoot and redressed in the jeans and button up T-shirt I'd worn to the set, I realized football was the last thing I wanted to think about.

"Hey there," a female voice purred behind me just as I placed the last of my belongings into my bag and started to head for the door.

I turned and internally frowned but outwardly I plastered on the same phony smile I'd adorned for the camera. "Hey yourself," I greeted Amy, one of the director's assistants. The gleam in her brown eyes told me what she wanted before her lips even parted. Too bad for her, this visit wouldn't go as the my previous one had.

"I was thinking we could go back to that sushi restaurant you loved the last time you were here, and then maybeee …" she purred again while letting her pointer finger trail up the middle of my chest.

My eyes lowered to her hand on my body before lifting to meet her eyes, shaking my head.

A pout formed in her pink-gloss coated lips.

"I've already got plans," I responded, shortly.

"With who?" she questioned, folding her arms across her chest.

I raised an eyebrow, frowning. "Not with you. Excuse me," was all I said before brushing past her and making a beeline for the door. It'd be a cold day in hell before I answered to any woman I didn't have a claim on. The car service the deodorant company hired for me was already waiting at the door as soon as I stepped outside. I quickly entered the backseat of the car and confirmed with the driver that I was headed back to my hotel, while pulling out my phone.

I pressed the button to FaceTime the only woman who held my attention these days. A frown marred my face when I got no response. Los Angeles was a few hours ahead of Williamsport and it was well after six p.m. here, so Destiny should've been home from work by then. I pressed the button once more, and again, received no answer.

I squeezed the phone as I lowered it to the seat, wondering if I should call her work number. But before I began dialing, my phone buzzed with a text message.

My Destiny: It's rude to FaceTime someone without at least sending a text beforehand.

I grinned before responding.

Me: Answer your damn phone, Destiny.

I laughed when she responded with multiple angry face emoji's. Thankfully, the car ride was rather short and I was dropped off in front of a private, back entrance at the hotel. I was able to avoid seeing anyone as I headed up to my hotel suite on the top floor. My sponsors always paid for most of my accommodations when I made trips like these, but due to my family's wealth and my own celebrity, I always got top floor suites as a matter of security. I often traveled with security. Though, they were obscured from the general public, they were with me ninety percent of the time.

Once I reached my suite, I FaceTimed Destiny again. I tossed my bag on the living room couch with my free arm as I headed to the bedroom.

"You're rude," she answered, eyes narrowed, lips jutting out slightly.

I had to tamp down on the biggest urge to run my tongue around those lips. The next time I saw her in person those fucking lips were mine to devour. Mark my words.

"I've been called worse." I shrugged, grinning at how cute she looked with what appeared to be a robe covering her body and a white towel twisted over her head, covering her hair.

"I was just getting out of the shower and washing my hair."

I frowned. "I am deeply sorry to have missed that. Want to get back in and let me watch?" I wiggled my eyebrows, smirking at her.

A soft giggled escaped her lips and her eyelashes lowered, bashfully.

Holy shit.

The confident, take on a room full of testosterone-laden football players, Destiny McDonald was hot as hell. This, just getting out of the shower, laughing and blushing over my corny jokes Destiny McDonald was hot *as fuck*.

"You're such a guy."

"Thank you," I dipped my head.

"That wasn't a com— Never mind."

I chuckled, plopping down on the large, king-sized bed.

"How's your trip going?"

"Slowly. Too slow."

She frowned. "Why? You don't like LA?"

"I don't like any city that you and I aren't both in."

She blinked. "We barely know each other."

"So?"

"So, how can you even say things like that? We haven't even been on a real date yet."

"Which, I've already told you I will be taking care of as soon as our first game of the season is over, next week. I hope you have an outfit picked out."

She shook her head, smiling. "This will never work."

I frowned, sitting up. "Why not?"

"Because, uh, because ... you're too young."

I cocked my head to the side. "Seriously? You're pulling the age card? You're an ageist? Is that what you're telling me, Destiny?"

Her forehead wrinkled. "Ageist?"

"Yeah, it's like racist but against people of a different age. Or maybe it is my race."

She sputtered. "I'm not ageist or racist. I've dated men of different races and ethni—" Her words were cut off when she looked up and caught the harsh expression on my face. Her eyes widened.

"I don't give a shit who you've dated before me. They. Don't. Matter," I growled.

"Tyler—"

"One day soon it'll be me with my hand wrapped around your throat, squeezing it just enough to constrict your airway only a little, with claw marks up and down my back because I'm a man who doesn't mind a little pain with my pleasure. It makes for a better experience. It will be my stiff cock pumping into your wetness with your walls clamping down around me, my body hovering over yours as you reach for your release, and my name on your lips when you come. And when you finally do, I guarantee our age difference will never be an issue again."

Her mouth fell open, and before I could say anything else, a knock on my door sounded.

"Shit. I gotta go." I had a dinner meeting with some executives of the deodorant company I'd just shot the commercial for. My agent was meeting me in the lobby of the hotel. "Next Sunday, Destiny. Seven p.m. I'm picking you up. And I won't be late." I gave her one last stare, more so to hold the memory of her dazed face with me until I could see her in person again, before hanging up.

"I'm coming," I yelled toward the door when another knock sounded. I was afraid I wasn't going to be great company with these executives tonight. While I could schmooze with the best of them, my head was still on the glossed over look in Destiny's eyes after my comments. Her eyes had widened, mouth opened, and the vein in her neck had increased its speed. She was turned on. I couldn't help the moan that escaped my throat at the thought of how wet she'd gotten from my words alone. A picture of her using her fingers to bring herself to a climax after hanging up the phone with me, began to torture me. I knew it was time to exit the hotel and get to dinner. It was either that or book the first thing smoking back to Williamsport.

I couldn't do that.

She wasn't ready for all of me just yet. Eventually, she'd be ready—I'd see to that—but right then she needed time to wrap her mind around what was happening between us.

CHAPTER 10

Destiny

How did seven days pass so quickly? One moment I was hanging up the phone with Tyler, barely able to comprehend my own name due to how turned on I was from his bold declarations. Soon after hanging up, I found myself with my hands inside of my panties, strumming my own clitoris, coming from the memory of the sound of his voice. What pissed me off is I was certain he knew exactly the power his words had on me. Now, here it was seven days later, the Cougars had just won their home opener against the Minnesota Bears, and I was anxiously looking through my closet to decide what to wear on my date with Tyler.

I'd had an outfit of skinny jeans, and my Lisa Perry dot print crepe wrap top, and a pair of strappy black heels to match. Though summer was winding down, and it was early September, the weather was still warm enough for the outfit which did have a deep neckline, and exposed a portion of my midriff. The outfit may have been a little risqué for a first date but my instincts told me to go with it. Thus, I stepped away from my closet, and discarded the fluffy robe I'd had for years, tossing it onto the arm of the rocking chair in the corner of my bedroom. I stepped into the dark blue lace panties I'd chosen to wear, not knowing why it mattered, it wasn't like Tyler was going to be seeing my underwear after only a first date.

Dismissing that thought, or more so, how my nipples hardened at the thought of Tyler actually seeing me in my panties and bra, I shrugged the shiver off that ran through me and continued to get dressed. Stepping to my full-length mirror, I adjusted the front tie of my blouse, so that the knot was secure and the two sides of the sash hung down, covering the center of my belly. I reached for my shimmer oil to rub into my chest and midriff areas, giving them a sun-kissed sheen to them. I placed a pair of diamond studs my father had bought me for my high school graduation in my ears, and adjusted a few strands of hair until my curls were perfectly coiled the way I liked them and my edges were sleeked down.

I twisted and rotated in the mirror, ensuring that I liked what I saw. Admittedly, I looked good. I felt good as well, save for the butterflies that ran through my belly. I placed my hand over my abdomen. It'd been a long time since I was nervous over a first date. Men hadn't intimidated me or made me go all goo-goo eyed in a very long time. I could hardly believe that Tyler Townsend had me feeling like a sixteen-year-old school girl all over again.

I looked up at the clock as soon as the buzzer for my front door rang. The clock had just struck seven p.m. A smile touched my lips. I strolled over to the intercom by my front door and pressed the button.

"Who is it?" I asked as if I didn't know.

"There better be only one man picking you up tonight," his smooth, silky reply came through the intercom.

More butterflies.

I swallowed and pressed the button that released the front entrance lock and waited. Not even three minutes later, a heavy knocking sounded on my front door. I inhaled deeply, taking one last opportunity to affix my clothing and hair, before pulling the door open.

My toes curled instantly at the smile that was plastered on his face. It was accompanied by a dimple on his left cheek. I was struck surprised when I noticed, for the first time, his left cheek dimpled on that smile. I'd never noticed he had a dimple, and trust me, I'd stared at that man more times than I cared to recall. None of his pictures circulating the media ever caught the dimple either.

"You are stunning." His voice sounded deeper than usual. Those hazel-green eyes sparkled with their usual mirth but they were slightly darkened.

"Th-thank you," I stated, clearing my throat. "Nice game," I complimented.

"You watched?"

"I told you I'm a Cougars fan."

"Just a fan of the Cougars?" he challenged.

I batted my lashes, lowering my head slightly. No, it wasn't just the team I was a fan of. Before I recognized what was happening, a strong finger slid under my chin, lifting my head to meet his piercing gaze. His lips were on mine less than a second later. The same thrill I'd felt during our first kiss was present for this one. My lips parted on a sigh, and Tyler's tongue swiped my lower lip before making entrance into my mouth. Another sigh broke free, and as if he was the only anchor I ever needed, my body rose to meet his. My arms reached up, wrapping around his broad shoulders, my feet going to their tiptoes even in the six inch heels I wore, my head tilting back far enough to grant him access to ravish my mouth just the way he was doing so.

His muscled arm snaked around my waist, pulling me to him as if even the slightest bit of separation between our two bodies was unbearable. If I didn't know any better I would've said that Tyler was staking his claim. That thought sobered me up. Reluctantly, I pulled back, breaking off the kiss.

"I thought … you we-were taking m-me out," I stuttered out breathlessly.

His eyes dropped to my kiss swollen lips, and he ran his tongue along his bottom lip, contemplatively. After a long pause he nodded. "That's what I said and I am a man of my word, Destiny."

My nipples, already hardened from the kiss we'd just shared, pebbled even more at the sound of my name on his lips.

"We should get going. Do you need to lock up?" he questioned.

I nodded. "Yeah, but first I should go retouch my lip—"

"Do that in the car." He stopped me, taking me by the hand, preventing me from excusing myself. The pleading I heard in his voice and saw in his eyes, pulled at something in me. He didn't seem to want me out of his presence. I nodded, agreeing—because I, too, didn't want to be out of his presence either.

I stepped over the threshold and out into the hallway expecting Tyler to take a few steps backward to give me some room. I should've known better. He gave me virtually no wiggle room and even pressed himself closer as I turned to lock my door with the key. Once I placed my keys in my black clutch, his strong hand covered mine as we strolled toward the elevator.

"A town car?" I questioned when we exited my building's front door and Tyler waved off the driver to hold the door of the car open for me.

"I would've driven myself but I didn't want anything to distract from giving you my complete attention," he answered smoothly.

I stepped closer. "You are good, Mr. Townsend." I giggled as I entered the car and heard his growl at my using his last name.

He slid into the backseat and moved close so that our thighs brushed one another's.

"You like testing me, Destiny. It's a trait I admire, but trust me when I tell you that tests will be met with consequences."

I frowned, dipping my brows. "What type of consequences?"

"Whichever type the situation demands."

"So what kind of consequences would me calling you by your last name demand?"

A twinge of nervousness moved up my spine at the grin that accosted his face. "The kind in which I might have to use my flogger and handcuffs to remind you exactly how I like hearing my name spill from your lips."

Oh. My. God.

My eyes floated closed at the damn flash flood that sprang in my panties.

Not again. Not again.

"What're you thinking?" he demanded with his hand on my knee.

"That I'm doing it again." My eyes popped open at the truth I'd just revealed.

"Doing what again?"

I swallowed and attempted to look out the car's window, in the opposite direction of Tyler, but my chin was caught by his hand.

"Doing *what* again?"

"Falling for another bad boy," I sighed and let out. They were always my kryptonite. In middle school and high school, I'd tried to put a lid on my attraction to them to appease my father who'd warned me off those types. The guys who skipped school, stole their parents' cars, always threw the best parties, and more. They were the boys I always seemed to gravitate toward and they to me. But my father was a strong influence, until I went away to college. Then, for the first time in my life, my parents weren't around to tell me who to stay away from. That's when I met Darryl, the ultimate bad boy. I knew it the first time I laid eyes on him. I promised myself I'd stay away but his pursuit was harder than my resistance. By the end of my first semester, freshman year, I was in deep. Two and half years later, we were married, the summer before my senior year, and the year he was drafted into the NBA. Eight years later it all fell apart because I'd gone ahead and listened to my heart and not my head.

"You think I'm a *bad boy*?" he asked as if it were the most ludicrous thought in the world.

Chuckling, I shook my head. "I don't think, Tyler, I know." I knew it like I knew my own damn name.

"Fine. So what's so wrong with that?"

My eyes ballooned, but just as I went to open my mouth he held up a finger, pausing me.

"Hold that thought." He glanced toward the door to his right, opening it. We had arrived. He got out of the car and then bent low, holding out his hand to assist me.

"Hope you like sushi," he stated just as I stood and looked up at the red and white marquee that read *Sogo Sushi.*

"This is one of my favorite restaurants in the city," I blurted out.

"I know."

I looked from the restaurant to Tyler, angling my head inquisitively.

"You mentioned it in one of the podcasts."

I smiled. "You're cheating, Tyler."

"I'd cheat, beg, borrow, or steal if it meant making you happy."

Another round of those goddamned butterflies. I pressed my hand holding my clutch to my abdomen, and once again, Tyler took my free hand, ushering us inside of the restaurant.

"Mr. Townsend. Your table is all ready," the hostess greeted right away.

Tyler led me by the hand, through the windy walkway of the Japanese restaurant. We were seated right next to one of the beautiful koi ponds that were housed in the restaurant. I was certain this seat wasn't an accident either. I'd likely mentioned my adoration for the koi ponds in this place on the podcast as well.

"Thank you," Tyler addressed the hostess, before navigating behind one of the chairs and staring at me, expectantly.

I moved to the seat, sitting down, and he pushed it in. I shivered as he brushed his fingers along the back of my neck before rounding the table to take his own seat.

The hostess placed the menus in front of us and told us our waiter would be with us shortly.

"Now," Tyler began, "back to what you were saying in the car."

I blinked, having forgotten the conversation just that quickly. "Oh, about the—"

"Bad boys. Is that a habit of yours?"

I blew out a breath and a humorless laugh. "Possibly."

He nodded. "I could see how."

I twisted my neck, looking at him questioningly.

He shrugged. "Men like challenges. You, Destiny, present us with a challenge."

"No I don't." I shook my head.

"You may not think so but you do."

"How so?"

He shook his head just as our waitress arrived at our table.

"My name is Asahi and I will be your waitress this evening. Can I get you something to drink to start off with?"

Tyler ordered a seltzer water with lime and I ordered a white wine. I remembered he'd told me that he didn't drink alcohol during the season. I briefly wondered if he was telling the truth.

"You don't have to do that," he leaned across the table and said once our waitress left.

"Do what?"

"Silently wonder or question. If you have something to ask, ask it. I'm an open book." He sat back, holding his arms out to the side.

Laughing, I shook my head. "If you say so."

"I do say so. But now back to the topic at hand. You wanted to know how you present us *bad boys,* as you referenced, with a challenge. It's the silent confidence you wear like a second skin. The aura of knowing exactly who you are and where you belong." He leaned back in again. "An aura that I, for one, find sexy as fuck, in case you hadn't picked up on it just yet."

I rolled my eyes and was grateful when Asahi brought our glasses to the table. I took a sip of my wine, simply because I lacked any sort of comeback. We gave our orders, and within a few minutes were alone again.

"Also, for the record, do yourself a favor and don't ever compare me to any other men in your life. I'm already running a mental tally of your transgressions worthy of the consequences we spoke about. Don't make me add comparisons to inferior beings to the list."

I couldn't help the smirk that my lips formed. "Inferior beings?"

He nodded while placing his glass back down on the table. "Any man who has had the pleasure of dating you and let you get away is clearly inferior to me. I learn from other people's mistakes instead of making my own."

Though the restaurant's dining room was dimly lit, the candle at the center of the table, clearly shone his face. The darkening of his eyes had my breath catching in my throat.

"You ... are intense," I pushed out in an almost whisper.

He shrugged. "It runs in the family, I guess."

"Your brothers are this ... excessive?"

He tipped his head. "Father as well. My mother never stood a chance." His mouth was shut but his eyes held a promise in them. *You don't either,* they said.

I peeled my gaze from his and took another sip of my wine. I was feeling hot, and I was certain it wasn't due to the effects of the alcohol.

"You're the youngest of four, right?" I questioned, trying to steer the conversation into safer territory.

"That's right. I knew you'd been researching me."

I waved him off, gazing out into the distance of the dining space. "Who hasn't heard of the Townsend dynasty? It's no secret you're one of four and your second oldest brother took over Townsend Industries once your father stepped down. That was an eventful day in the market."

He leaned in. "Was it?"

I nodded. "Oh definitely. I was new to my job as a financial advisor at *Portland Banking.*"

"One of the largest investment firms in the country."

"Yup, and I had about six clients then. They were calling nonstop that day wanting to know if their mutual funds had invested in Townsend Industries, and if so, they wanted to know if it was still safe." I shook my head. "Everyone knew the new CEO had worked at Townsend for years but he hadn't let on to his plans for the company. Was he going to expand nationally as your father had worked so hard to do, or was he going to contract? It was all a guessing game. Especially since he was so reluctant on taking interviews."

Tyler chuckled. "That's Aaron."

I nodded. "I should've known then."

"Known what?"

"That that world of personal finance wasn't for me. It was too salesy. Don't get me wrong, I *love* researching this stuff and figuring out P/E ratios and debt to equity and all that stuff, but the average investor doesn't need to do all that. Plus, the way they get raked over the coals in fees ..."

"Is that why you're such a Jack Bogle fan?"

I lifted an eyebrow. "Let me guess, the podcast?"

"Where else?"

I giggled. "Yes, that's why I'm a Bogle fan. The average investor doesn't have time, energy, or the know-how to sit and run the numbers, read all of the news on each company, and then make the right decision to time the market accordingly. No one can do that, save for the likes of Warren Buffett. Either way, I saw how streamlining your investments and finances in general was a much safer approach for the novice and average investor. Especially, for women. Don't even get me started on the ways in which women, even today, are still being left out of the market." I rolled my eyes.

"Finance is still an all boys' club?"

"Like you wouldn't believe."

Our food soon arrived and I realized how much I'd been talking. After taking a few bites of my salmon roll, I placed my chopsticks on my plate before asking, "I've given you my career history, how about yours? What made you go into football?"

"It was the one thing I was good at."

I don't know why that comment struck me but it did. I sat up. "I'm sure that's not true."

He gave a one shoulder shrug. "I sucked at school. My grades were terrible. I couldn't sit still worth a damn. Hell, I still can't for too long."

I frowned at the tone he'd stated those words.

"Attention Deficit Hyperactivity Disorder. Diagnosed in the second grade."

I lifted my eyebrows. "So sports was better suited for you?"

He nodded. "My father thought so. Around the third time he caught me jumping off the bannister of the staircase onto our living room's couch, he decided it was time to throw me in sports. Either that or my mother was going to strangle me."

I giggled. "She was fed up with you, huh?"

He chuckled. "Hell yeah. I was the last of four very headstrong boys. She was ready to kick me out by the time I was twelve."

"I can imagine."

"But she let me stay until I went away to college."

"I bet she misses you now."

"If her calling every other day is any indication, I'd say you're right about that."

"She's a mom." I lowered my eyes to the table, pressing my hand against my belly, wishing the sense of sorrow that passed through me to go away. When I lifted my gaze again, Tyler's eyes were firmly planted on me, inquiring. "Are you close with your brothers?" I asked, again, diverting the conversation.

He stared for another moment before he nodded. "Yeah, as close as we can be with me traveling as much."

"That's good"

"How about you? Any siblings?"

I shook my head. "No. I'm my parents' only child. Well, that's not entirely true. I'm the only child they had, but Resha, my cousin, as I'm sure you're aware, came to live with us when she was twelve. After that, we were raised as siblings."

"And you two are very close."

"We are."

We talked some more about our families in between finishing our meals. Once completed, Tyler waved the waitress over for the bill. He paid and then rose to pull my chair out before taking me by the hand again and escorting us out of the restaurant. We headed down toward the center of Williamsport where there was a walking strip that ran along a manmade river.

"Oh, I loved tossing pennies in that fountain as a kid." I smiled at the fond memories of my parents bringing me to this part of town on summer nights for ice cream and my father would always give me a penny to toss in the well to make a wish.

"Make a wish," Tyler said low in my ear at the same time I felt him press a penny into the palm of my hand.

I glanced down to see the shiny penny, heads up. I smiled up at him, and for a second got lost in those hypnotizing eyes. Another smile creased his face and that dimple I'd never seen before was back.

"Close your eyes."

My eyelids fell shut and I silently made a wish before opening my eyes and tossing the penny into the clear water.

"Your turn," I challenged, turning to him.

"I don't make wishes."

I tilted my head to the side.

"I make my own dreams come true."

I tossed my head back, laughing. "Uh, huh." I shook my head when he tried to pull me into him by the waist. "I made a wish, so you have to make one."

He frowned.

"Come on." I bumped him with my arm, causing him to chuckle.

"Fine." He pulled another penny from his pants pocket and went to toss it in.

"Close your eyes," I ordered, the same way he'd said it to me.

"Pushy, aren't you?"

"Tuh! You're one to talk."

"I am, aren't I?" He smirked.

"Make your wish."

He turned back to the fountain and briefly closed his eyes, mouthing something before opening them again and tossing the penny into the water.

"What'd you wish for?"

"That's not how it works, is it? I can't tell you unless I want it to come true?"

"Pssh. I thought you didn't believe in this wish stuff. You make your own dreams come true, right?"

"Right. So when it does come true, you'll be the first to know."

He'd barely finished his statement before he was pulling me into him, his lips covering mine. Apparently, I didn't mind it either, when my arms went up to encircle his neck, pulling him into me just as fervently. I moaned when I felt his thumb graze along my exposed abdomen. His hands were rough, callused from years of practice and playing football. And they felt divine against my sensitized skin.

"Let's get you home," he whispered against my lips.

"Yeah, home. Sure," I answered, breathlessly.

Again, I followed when Tyler's hand covered mine as we walked to the awaiting town car. The drive back to my place was about fifteen minutes. Tyler stood patiently behind me as I entered the code to the front door and then headed in the direction of the elevator. I only lived on the third floor and usually opted to take the stairs, but not in six inch stilettos and with Tyler breathing down my back. I was barely able to put one foot in front of the other.

"Want to come in?" I found myself asking, my voice husky as we stood in front of my door.

He looked as if he was debating something before finally nodding.

Turning, I unlocked my door, entered, and put my keys on the wall mount. I placed my clutch on the stand under the mount. As soon as the clutch was free from my hands, Tyler spun me around by my waist to face him, pinning my back against the door. He crowded my space as his lips descended over mine for the third time that night.

The kiss was frenzied when our tongues touched and tasted one another's. Tyler's hands ran up and down the length of my waist a few times until his fingers went under my blouse, cupping my breasts through the lacy bra I wore. He tweaked my nipples, causing me to gasp as pleasure shot through me. I pulled him into me by his forearms, loving the feel of his body against mine. His hands lowered and he bent low, scooping my thighs up to wrap around his waist.

His hand dropped to the waistband of my jeans. I tossed my head back against the door as his mouth lowered to my neck and the tops of my breast.

"Hsss," I hissed in air when his calloused fingers made contact with my swollen clit.

"This is what you wanted right?" he demanded, breathing harshly against my ear.

I blinked, trying to refocus my gaze and respond, but when he began making circles against my distended button, mewling sounds poured from my mouth. I'd never been this damn revved up, this quickly by any man.

"Is all that cream for me?" he taunted against my parted lips.

Of course, Tyler enjoyed dirty talk during intimacy. His words only served to make me wetter.

"I can't hear you, Destiny. Is all of this wetness for me?"

"Y-yes," I answered, panting and beginning to rock my hips against him. I needed a release more than a junkie needed their next fix.

"Yes, what?"

"Huh?" I breathed out, not comprehending.

"Yes, *what?"*

I racked my brain, trying to figure out what he wanted—nay, *needed* to hear to grant me my release.

"Yes, Tyler," I guessed.

I sighed in relief and tears blanketed my eyes when he dipped his hand lower, inserting a long finger inside of my aching canal while circling my clit with his thumb. My climax was quick. I tugged at his shoulders as I came, hips working against his hand. His lips crushed mine and I let out a moan into his mouth.

He kissed me through my orgasm before letting me up for air.

Slowly, I dropped my feet to the floor as I continued gasping for oxygen.

"You're not ready yet."

"I can assure you, I'm plenty ready." I appreciated him trying to ensure that I was wet enough for sex but had he not just noticed the major orgasm I'd had from his hand alone? I was more than ready.

A deep, humorless chuckle emerged from his vocal chords and he lowered his forehead to mine. "No, you're not but you will be. Soon." He lifted his head and stepped back.

I watched, confused, as his hands went to the waistband of my jeans, only this time to button them. He then moved back even more, straightening out his own clothes. I was dumbfounded when his hand reached for the door, pulling it open as I pushed away from it.

"Wh—" I began.

"You like hardwood floors?"

I looked around *really* confused now. "What?"

His eyes lowered to the dark hardwood of my living room. "Your floors are hardwood. Do you like hardwood? This color?"

I shook my head. He was entirely serious with this series of questions.

"Y-yeah."

"For the bedroom, too?"

"My bedroom is carpeted," I answered lamely.

He nodded as if storing that information.

The hell?

"Destiny?"

I glanced up. "Yes?"

"Decide where you want to go on our second date, next week once I get back into town." He leaned down, placing a kiss to the corner of my mouth. "And get some sleep," he stated low in my ear.

Sleep? Right. As if.

I watched as he turned and shut the door behind him. I was left standing there both dumbfounded, spellbound, and horny as all hell.

What the hell kind of game was Tyler playing?

* * *

Tyler

"What the hell kinda game were you playing out there, Riggs?" Kelvin shouted at Leonard as we all made our way into the locker room after the game. We'd just ended our second game of the season.

"Aye! What the fuck if your problem?" Leonard yelled back after Kelvin pushed him up against one of the lockers.

Dropping my shoulder pads and helmet, I quickly moved in between Kelvin and Leonard. Kelvin was usually the coolest guy in the room but Riggs had been pissing us all off lately. A few of his more recent sports interviews hadn't been too friendly toward our defensive line, and his showboating antics were getting on everyone's damn nerves. Including mine. However, I wasn't rattled by Riggs, but I wouldn't let him get under the skin of our best running back and my closest friend.

"Calm down, Kel," I stated, pushing him back with my forearm.

"Nah, Ty, you know as much as I do, this kid is asking for it," he growled, pointing the hand that held his gold and black Cougars helmet in Leonard's direction.

"Kid? I ain't no fucking kid!" Leonard snapped, pushing forward.

With the forearm I had planted against his chest, I pushed him back against the hardwood panel of our lockers.

"You need to chill the fuck out," I growled, looking toward Leonard. "What you did out there today was bullshit and you know it," I stated sternly. Riggs had caused the entire team a penalty when, after he caught a pass and made it into the endzone, he'd taken his sweet fucking time to showboat and do a long dance. That was just before he tossed the ball to the ground and ran to the bleachers, high-fiving fans in the stands.

"Ah, man, it was all in fun and shit. It's early on in the season, you two need to relax."

I glanced over my shoulder to see Kelvin sauntering off, shaking his head after giving Leonard one final glaring look.

I moved my arm, effectively releasing Leonard and trying to remind myself of coach's words about putting guys in their place the right way. This would be good training for my future coaching career.

"Early on in the season is the most pivotal time. It sets the tone for how the next five to six months are going to play out. It's more difficult to come back from a poor start in the beginning of the season than to keep the momentum up from a great early start," I replied firmly, crossing my arms over my bare chest. We were all in various states of undress, needing to shower and change after the game.

"Whatever, man. What're you trippin' for? We won, didn't we?"

I nodded. "But that penalty you cost us could've meant the difference between a win and a loss. I'm sure that fine you incurred with be a wake up call." I stepped closer, not quite crowding his space but close enough so he could see the serious look in my eyes. "And if it's not, the players on this team will be."

He frowned, wrinkling his forehead looking over my shoulder and side to side at the rest of the players around the room. I already knew some of them were staring at us. Riggs wasn't winning any friends on the team. At least when I fucked up, I hadn't pissed any of my teammates off. This guy still hadn't learned who his friends and enemies were.

"Whatever, man." He pivoted to walk away, but then stopped short, turning back to me. "You might not want to worry so much about me. Instead, worry about your girl."

He tried to walk off after that but was stopped by my open palm meeting the center of his chest. "You want to run that by me again?" I gritted out through clenched teeth.

He looked down at my hand firmly planted on his chest then back up at me. "Nothing." He shook his head. "Just thought I'd be a team player and warn you about the bi— female you're fucking with. My agent's her ex and she dogged him out. Probably'll do the same to you —" His words were cut off by my hand on his throat.

"I don't fucking like you. I can't stand your inability to take direction on the field. Your talent will only get you so far. I've kept all that to myself because I really don't give a shit about you either. I let a lot of shit slide. But let me be absolutely fucking clear, don't *ever* bring her up in any conversation with me or with anyone else again. She's off limits to you. Forget the name Destiny McDonald. I don't give a shit who you know from her past. Got it?"

"Everything all right?"

My coach's words behind me snapped me back to reality. I blinked but my gaze remained hard and focused on Leonard. Loosening my grip around his neck, I let my hand fall to my side as I took a step back.

"Everything's great. Just giving Riggs a little friendly advice. Isn't that right, Riggs?" I glared at him expectantly.

His eyes swung from me to our coach and back to me again. With anger in his own eyes, he nodded. "Yeah, Coach. Everything is copacetic."

"Everything's most definitely not copacetic," Coach began. "That fucking show out there was bullshit, Riggs."

I stepped back and let coach continue to chastise Riggs for the shit he pulled on the field. That was done, as far as I was concerned. It was his words about Destiny that had truly angered me. I moved away and headed to my own locker, planting my ass on my wooden stool in front of it before pulling it open.

I removed my phone from my locker and scrolled through the text messages to see if I'd received any new ones. Most were from my parents, brothers, sisters-in-law, and nephews. They always wished me luck before a game or sent congrats or *are you okay* texts after a win or loss. The message that had my smile widening even more was from the very woman I'd nearly taken Leonard's head off about. I'd sent her a message just before the game, asking if she'd be watching.

My Destiny: *I've been watching since before you were born.*

Me: *What'd you think?*

I typed out the question before putting my phone back inside of the locker as Coach McClellan began to talk to the entire team.

"Great effort by everyone …" he paused, looking Leonard's way, "almost everyone. Let's shower up. I'm opening up for post-game interviews in two minutes."

I opted to wait until after my post-game interview to shower and change into the suit I'd worn to the game. The interview lasted all of five minutes. I'd gotten used to five or six reporters at a time, shoving their recorders, cameras, and microphones in my face while they asked the same redundant ass questions. But I gave them my best wink and smile, all the while anxious to check my phone to see Destiny's response.

Once the reporters were gone, I grabbed my phone and clothes and headed to the shower. I grinned, staring down at the phone seeing I'd received a message.

My Destiny: *Riggs is an ass. That stunt could've cost us a loss.*

Me: *He's been told.*

My Destiny: *I'm sure he has … You were pretty okay out there.*

I lifted an eyebrow.

Me: *Pretty okay?*

My Destiny: *I can't compliment you too much. Your ego can barely fit through the door as is.*

"What're you reading?"

I glanced up, seeing Kelvin staring at me, smirking. He must've heard the laugh I just let out.

"Mind your damn business," I grunted, pushing past him to one of the private showers.

Me: *I'm sure you can manage my ego just fine, Destiny.*

I waited for her response, which had been rather immediate during this exchange. When two and then three minutes passed, I finally placed my phone along with the rest of my stuff on the bench and pulled the door open to shower.

After I got out and dried off, I checked my phone again, and still, there was no response. Frowning, I scrolled back through our conversation. I reasoned it'd been my last response that'd made her stiffen up, either that or she was preoccupied with something or someone. I inhaled deeply at the urge to kill at the thought of someone else taking her time while I was out of town doing my damn job. As much as I hated to admit it, Leonard Riggs' words began to creep back into my mind.

Destiny and I had talked about our pasts a little, but she'd conveniently skipped over the part where she was married. She had mentioned being married before on one of the podcasts but hadn't given much detail.

"Hey, you hanging out tonight?" Kelvin questioned as we made our way through the double doors of the stadium. We were in the Bay Area and knew of plenty of places that were more than happy to host us for a night on the town.

I shook my head. "Not tonight. Got plans already."

Kelvin and I slapped hands and fist bumped before parting ways. I took a car back to the hotel. I had plans that night indeed.

CHAPTER 11

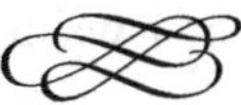

Destiny

"It'll be a walk in the park. Just go in, get the information you need, and get out. That's all," I murmured to myself as I stood in front of the high rise building in downtown Williamsport. This was the day Dawn was able to schedule my appointment with Darryl. I had her tell his office it was in reference to one of his athletes. According to her, the appointment was made without any problems.

"Okay," I sighed out and released one of my hands from the briefcase I held in front of me, in order to reach for the door handle. I crossed the threshold of the building's door, stepping onto the dark marble flooring inside. The security guard from behind the booth looked up when the noise of my heels on the marble sounded.

"Destiny McDonald, here for an appointment with Darryl Wright," I rushed out before I lost my nerve.

"Just one second." He looked down at something in front of him before nodding. "Here you are. I just need to see some I.D., please."

Removing my license from my wallet, I showed the guard. He nodded and handed me a visitor's pass with my name on it and directed me to the elevators that would take me to the tenth floor. I tapped my foot the entire elevator ride up, nervous energy coursing through my body. When the doors parted, I hesitated for one moment, wondering if I was seriously doing this. Was it even worth it? Maybe Riggs had made the whole thing up to get a rise out of me and here I was falling for it.

I stepped off the elevator, looking to my left and my right, seeing glass doorways on either side. The office of Darryl Wright Sports Inc., were to my left. I forced myself to push through my self-doubt. The worst that could happen is that I wasted a few hours of a work day, right?

"Hi, I'm Destiny McDonald in to see … Darr— er, Mr. Wright." I smiled at the cute blonde who sat behind the receptionist's desk.

"Um, let me see, oh yes. Mr. Wright will be out in just a moment. Can I get you any coffee, tea, or water?"

"A water would be great."

"I'll be right back," she answered, smiling and standing to head out of the receptionist area, rounding the corner that look like it led to a hallway. Less than a minute later, she appeared with a bottle of cold water.

"Thank you." I opened the bottle and took a long sip to satisfy my parched throat.

"It'll just be another minute. Mr. Wright is with a client."

I nodded and moved to the row of chairs directly facing her desk to sit down, but before I could even pull out my phone to check for any missed calls or messages, male laughter filled the hallway. My insides tightened at hearing the sound of Darryl's laughter for the first time in over six years. I uncrossed my legs and stood just as he reached the point of the hallway that opened up to the waiting area of his office.

He stopped immediately when he saw me.

I swallowed, taking in his tall stature, coffee-colored skin, and trimmed beard. As much as I was loathe to admit it, he'd aged well over the past few years.

"Destiny—"

"Mz. McDonald."

I blinked and pulled my gaze from Darryl to the man next to him, for the first time noticing that Leonard Riggs was even in the room.

"The hell are you doing here?"

I blinked at Leonard's tone and then snarled at him, remembering this wasn't his damn office, nor his business. Well, it sort of was, but not really.

Rolling my eyes, I dismissed Leonard and turned back to Darryl. "Mr. Wright, I made an appointment with your office. If this is a bad time, I ca—"

"What? No. Leonard was just leaving. I'll give you a call on the subject we discussed in my office." Darryl nodded and practically shove Leonard out the door as I looked on.

"Please, follow me. Jane, hold my calls," he tossed over his shoulder to the receptionist.

Out of my peripheral, I saw her nod her agreement before I turned to follow Darryl. I glanced around the office, taking in the door to my right that was shut, which I heard talking from behind it.

"That's Steve. Hired him as one of my junior agents," Darryl said, grabbing my attention.

I turned back to him, realizing we'd reached the end of the hallway. He was standing at the entranceway of his corner office, holding the wooden door open for me to pass through.

I took one glance at him and stood there. "After you." I tipped my head toward his office. I wasn't about to brush past him, making bodily contact for no reason at all.

I think I caught a frown before he turned and entered his office. Once inside, I didn't even bother to look around. I was sure Darryl had picked out the best office with the corner view that he could afford, along with the most high end, luxury furnishings he could find. He always wanted the best and most expensive. But that was no longer my business.

"So, how've you b—"

"Listen, I realize this is awkward ..."

"It doesn't have to be. We ca—"

"But I'm only here to get some information and then I'll be on my way, never to darken your doorstep again," I continued on as if he hadn't said anything.

"Damn, Destiny, it's like that? It's been seven years," he sighed out a frustrated breath, his shoulders slumping slightly as he sat on the corner edge of his desk.

"Has it? I hadn't noticed," I stated nonchalantly.

Though my eyes weren't on him, I could feel his gaze lingering on my body.

"Destiny, don't b—"

I held up my hand. "A few weeks ago, your client, Leonard Riggs, the one you were just chumming it up with, told me that you recommended a financial advisor."

"Oh, so this is what this is about." He nodded, a sly look overcoming his face. "You're salty, I didn't recommend your services to my athletes."

I frowned, wrinkling my forehead. "What? Why on earth would I expect … I told you years ago that I didn't expect a damn thing from you," I stated evenly.

He scowled. "You don't? Then why're you here?"

"This isn't about me, Darryl. Or you, to be honest. I just need the name of the financial advisor. Riggs wouldn't tell me, and I'd like to—"

"For what?"

I sighed. "That's a fair question. Riggs said they guy made some promises that to me, sound pretty absurd."

"To you it might be absurd but it might well be within that man's ability to perform."

I held back the temptation to roll my eyes. Darryl was trying to get a rise out of me. I could've saved him the trouble and told him that he no longer had the power to do that but that'd only make him act more like an ass.

"You're right," I said instead. "The advisor you recommended may just be better than I am. And if he is, I have zero problem admitting it." I shrugged. "Hell, I'd even recommend *my* clients to him if his investments perform as well as Leonard claims they do. I just need his name. Possibly a business card if you have one." I held my tone even and devoid of any emotion. I wasn't playing this back and forth game with Darryl. He had information I needed and that was it.

He sat there for a moment staring. I could see the wheels of his mind turning, trying to figure out how to play this to his advantage. Finally, he stood.

"You like my office?" He spread his arms wide.

For the first time, I glanced around, taking in the oak furniture, along with the dark shelves that were lined with articles and award that Darryl or some of his athletes had won.

"Yeah, sure," I agreed. "The name, Darryl?"

He let out a humorless chuckle. "Phillip Morris," he replied as he rounded his desk.

I lifted an eyebrow. "Like the tobacco company?"

He briefly looked up from his desk to me and nodded. "Yes, but he's got two Ls in his name instead of one," he answered while scribbling something down. He yanked the piece of notepad paper from its stand before coming around the desk again and handing the paper to me.

I looked down.

"I don't have his business card on me but that's the number to his office, address, and website of his company."

I nodded. "Thank you, Darryl."

"Oh, I'm Darryl now? Out in the lobby I was Mr. Wright."

I did roll my eyes that time.

"Like, I'm a damn stranger," he tutted and shook his head.

"We are strangers."

He stiffened at that. "We aren't—"

"We haven't seen or spoken to one another in almost seven years."

"At your insistence."

"And I appreciate your giving me this, Darryl," I lifted the paper, "but after today, we'll go on not seeing or speaking to one another. Thank you." I began backing up and turned toward the door.

"I hear you're dating again. Well, you've been dating for a while now, but I mean, athletes."

My hand paused on the door handle. I knew he was goading me but stupidly, I took the bait.

"What do you know about my dating life?"

"Just that Tyler Townsend better watch out. He doesn't know what he's in for if he makes a mistake."

"A mistake? Are you—" I shook my head. "How do you know about Tyler?"

He shrugged. "Word gets around, especially when the same woman dates more than one athlete."

My eyebrow spiked at his insinuation. I wasn't about to dignify his pettiness with a response. I pulled the door open.

"Maybe someone should tell Tyler not to let his heart get involved, seeing as how unforgiving you are."

I stopped, letting the door shut a few inches, but not all the way while my hand was still on the handle. "Are you serious right now? A mistake? Unforgiving? I wasn't the one who had a baby with another woman during our marriage."

"The baby wasn't even mine."

He was right. Months after our divorce was finalized, Darryl had a DNA test done on the baby of the woman who'd shown up on our doorstep. Turns out, the baby wasn't his. But that definitely didn't erase his many other transgressions.

"You got lucky with that one. But the baby that I was pregnant with was yours, and now it's dead because of syphilis that I contracted from you and your filthy di—" I stopped short, closing my eyes to prevent myself from lashing out. I wouldn't give him the rise he was looking for. I peeled my eyes open and they landed on the pictures he had sitting on the far corner of his desk. There were two children in them, one was about three and other about five.

They were his.

I inhaled.

I'd known Darryl had had children over the years. Try as I might, not hearing about him in any capacity was impossible. A friend or two would accidentally drop some information about him in a conversation.

"At least, you got to make up for what was lost." I looked back at his guilty gaze before turning and pulling the door open and shutting it behind me. I didn't even feel the need to slam it. Darryl couldn't piss me off anymore, and I'd shed all of the tears I'd needed to.

With the information that I was looking for in hand, I strolled down the hallway and out the door without another thought of Darryl Wright. He could rot in hell for all I cared.

I didn't stop moving until I exited the building. I inhaled deeply, filling my lungs to their capacity before releasing my breath. I decided to walk from Darryl's office to my own, though it was over ten city blocks. While walking, I pulled out my phone to see I had two missed calls from Resha.

My heart rate sped up as I pressed the button to call her back.

"I'm so sorry."

"What? What happened?"

"Shit! You haven't heard."

"Heard what? Is it Mama? Did the home call you? Why wouldn't they ca—"

"No, D, it's not about auntie. Where are you?"

I glanced around the street, looking at the passersby. "I'm leaving Darryl's office. We had that meeting today, remember?"

Another curse came from Resha's mouth.

"Resha, what aren't you telling me?!" I demanded.

"It's Tyler."

I scrunched up my face before my eyes ballooned. "Is he hurt? Was there an accident or something?" I picked up the pace to get back to my office. I figured the sports channel or website would have some information regarding a possible accident having to do with Tyler or his team.

"No, he's not hurt but his ass might be soon," Resha angrily responded.

"Tell me what's going on."

I stopped short in the middle of the sidewalk.

"Look, I'm going to tell you, but I want to do it while you're in your office. Away from people. Ju—"

I hung up the phone on Resha. She was pissing me off. I pulled open one of the social media apps I had on my phone and typed in Tyler's name, knowing any news headlines he was making would be posted on this app. My heart plummeted when the posts finally loaded. I saw why Resha wanted to wait until I was no longer in public to tell me this shit.

The first headline read *'Guess which famous quarterback was caught with his pants down!'* Against my better judgement, I clicked on the post, opening it up, and there it was, picture after picture of some woman half naked in Tyler's bed. His head was cut out of some of the pictures. But by the time I scrolled to the fourth picture, the hope that had blossomed in my chest was doused when Tyler's face was front and center as he laid there, with eyes closed next to the brunette bimbo, who was holding the camera.

I didn't need to see anymore. I closed out of the app, chest pounding as I began heading back to my office again. My heart thudded as anger filled every cell in my body. Then I began feeling stupid as all hell for even being angry. Tyler and I weren't a couple. He should be allowed to do whatever he wanted. *I just thought that—*

My thoughts were interrupted when my phone began ringing in my hand. I damn near threw the damn thing across the street when Tyler's name popped up on my screen. I wasn't going to answer it. Of course, I wasn't. So when my thumb pressed the button to answer the call, I had no idea why.

"What!" I fumed into the phone, loud and angry enough that a few passersby on the street looked on in concern. I gave them the stink eye and kept walking.

"I'm guessing you saw ..."

"Oh, I saw. I hope you had fu—"

"That wasn't me."

"Fuck off, Tyler. Your fucking face was on the photos," I snarled, surprising myself.

"I mean, yeah it was me, but I don't know that woman."

"Last time I check, you don't need to know someone to fuck them."

He growled at the other end. "All that cursing is going to get you a sore bottom."

I stopped short right outside the entrance of my office building's door. "What the hell did you just say to me?"

"You heard me. Look, we need to talk—"

"Talk? No, thank you. I told you once, but obviously, you're hard of hearing so I'll say it again. Fuck. Off!" I pulled the phone from my ear and hit the end call button before entering my building.

I made it up to my office's floor when my phone began ringing again.

"Tyler, I told you to f—"

"Damn, he called you already? The shit broke like an hour ago."

I pushed out a breath, my shoulders slumping at the sound of Resha's voice. I made my way through the outer office, head hanging low, as I passed through my own office door. Shutting it behind me, I pressed my back against it.

"So, how're we going to handle this? We could go old school and key his car, but he's rich so he probably has some high tech security. We don't want to end up in jail, though I would for you. You know that, right?"

I let out a laugh in spite of my mood. "And I would for you, too, Resh. But we're not doing any of that. Besides, you're still in Europe."

"I can bump my flight up a couple of weeks."

"No, you've got work to do and I'm fine."

"You're fine?"

"Yeah." I shrugged as if she could see me. "I mean, we went on one date a—"

"And talked every day, all day via text and phone calls since that date," Resha so rudely reminded me. "You talked to that boy more than you talked to me over the last two weeks."

I sighed. She was right but I wouldn't admit to anything. "It's no big deal. Listen, I've got some work to do," I stated at the same time my line beeped for another incoming call. "I'll give you a call later on."

I hung up with Resha to see Tyler's name on my screen. I immediately pressed the ignore button. Then I went to my recent calls and pressed Tyler's name and then blocked his number.

Shaking my head, I tossed my phone on my desk.

I was done with the bad boy types.

* * *

Two days earlier ...

Tyler

"Hey, hell of a game tonight." My coach patted me on the back as we exited the stadium.

It was another Sunday, early evening, and we'd just won our third game in a row. We were on a roll. I'd had over a hundred passing yards and one particularly beautiful spiral toss directly into Kelvin's hands who was planted right in the end zone. It was the highlight of the game for me. But as much as I loved this game, something was missing.

"You coming out tonight?" Kelvin patted me on the back as he came up from behind me.

I shook my head.

"Ah, man, come on. You never come out anymore. This ain't the Tyler I know."

I glanced up from my phone, looking over at Kelvin. "Maybe it's a different me."

Smirking, he shook his head. "Sprung. Just like I told you."

I laughed but didn't say anything else as we walked to the awaiting cars.

"All right, man, we'll be at Club Phoenix, if you change your mind."

I gave him a head nod and we clapped hands and fist bumped before going our separate ways. The driver was just barely pulling off when my thumb was pressing down to call Destiny's number.

"Nice game, Mr. Townsend," her breathy voice answered.

"What did I tell you about that Mr. Townsend bullshit?" I retorted.

"Aren't you touchy for a guy who just passed for a hundred and fifteen yards. Sheesh."

I smiled, something feeling right about the way she'd memorized my stats. She seemed to do that after every game.

"Trust me, Destiny, I'm not nearly as touchy as I'd like to be."

She giggled. "So you say."

"Are we back on this again?"

"*No.* We're not back on anything. That's the problem."

I smiled at the pout I heard in her voice. I wondered if her nose wrinkled up while she pouted like I'd seen it do before.

"There's no problem except what I've already told you."

I heard her push out a heavy breath and I just knew her dark brown eyes were rolling skyward.

"You seem to think I wasn't ready."

"You weren't."

"Tyler, I'm a grown ass woman. I know when I'm ready or not. Trust me, I was plenty ready."

"Not for what I had in store."

I heard her breath hitch.

I entered my hotel's room.

"I want to see your face. Hang up the phone," I instructed, shutting my door behind me.

"How do you know I want to FaceTime with you?"

"You do. Hang up the phone."

She hesitated, and a charge of electricity flowed through me. Her defiance turned me on more than she knew. It'd make it all so much better once she finally submitted.

She hung up the phone and I called her right back, this time via FaceTime.

"That's better," I stated as I stared into my phone's screen, taking in the rich hue of her skin and chocolate eyes. She wore an off-the-shoulder Cougars T-shirt I'd seen her wear once before during our FaceTime chats. I made a mental note to buy her a Cougars' jersey that had my name emblazoned across the back. Figured she might as well get used to wearing my last name as soon as possible.

"Aren't you tired? You just played a four hour game."

"Not anymore. We athletes have endless energy." I winked, causing her to roll her eyes. She was so damn cute when she did that.

"Don't I know it," she mumbled.

"What was that?"

"Nothing."

"Tell me about your day." I laid back against the bed, my head leaning against the headrest.

We talked for another forty-five minutes, Destiny telling me about her day and a couple of new clients she had met with. She brought up the fact that she and Resha had discussed doing a few live events of their podcast, once Resha was stateside again.

"You look like you're in a normal hotel room," she noticed after I got up and carried her with me to the bathroom to brush my teeth.

"I am tonight. The hotel didn't have any suites available." I shrugged.

"Your security's okay with that?" I'd told her about the private security my family hired to travel with me.

"I gave them the night off. I'm at the hotel for the rest of the night. I figured they'd want to go out and see the city." We were playing in New Jersey, but it was a short distance from New York.

"Are you sure that's safe? Kim Kardashian thought she was good in her hotel room as well." She frowned into the phone, a concerned expression marring her face.

"You worried about me, Destiny?"

"What do you think?"

"I *think* you'd be less worried if you'd taken me up on my offer. You'd be here with me tonight instead of worrying about me from home." I'd invited her to fly out for my game and to stay that night and catch the red eye with me in the morning but she'd declined.

"I couldn't," she reiterated the same excuse she'd come up with earlier. Which wasn't much of an excuse at all. Something had been occupying her time and she was being tight lipped on what it was.

"Next Sunday. It's a home game anyway. I'll get you into the box seats." I frowned at the way she was shaking her head.

"I ca—"

"It's not up for debate even if I have to carry you there myself."

"I'm sure you'd try."

"And succeed." I laid back against the bed.

"You need to get some rest."

I grunted. She was right. I had an earlier flight out than my team since I needed to head back to the West Coast for a half a day for some promotional stuff before making it back to Williamsport for practice the rest of the week.

"So do you," I retorted.

"I'm going to sleep in a little while. There's a personal finance book I picked up from the store today that I want to spend some time reading before going to bed."

I stared, admiring her beauty and her ambition. She was always working to improve her knowledge of her profession.

"Goodnight, Tyler."

"Night, Destiny."

I placed my phone on the nightstand by the bed and rose to change into a pair of plaid bottoms. I was feeling tired but I opted to take one of the melatonin pills I often carried with me, since I usually had trouble staying asleep throughout the night. I didn't use them every night, but considering how busy the next few days were going to be, and all of the time changes I'd been going through, I figured it was wise to try and get as much sleep as possible.

My head hit the pillow and I was out like a lamp. Needless to say, Destiny's face was the last thing I remembered thinking about before totally passing out.

* * *

"Destiny," I murmured against the soft skin I felt, stroking up and down my chest.

"Wake up, sleepyhead," a soft, female voice answered.

With my eyes still firmly shut, I smiled against that voice. Destiny's face came to mind as I recalled how fucking good it felt to have her legs wrapped around my waist. My dick instantly got hard as I remembered how wet she'd been when I slid my hand into the seam of those lace panties.

"Wake up," a voice whispered close to my ear, warm breath brushing over my neck.

This isn't right. Some internal signal went off in my gut, causing my eyes to spring open. I blinked a few times—trying to acclimate myself to my surroundings—and when I did, I was instantaneously pissed off.

"Who the fuck are you?" I roared, sitting up and moving to get out of the bed. I stood to my full height looking down at the woman dressed in a pink lace thong and bra set.

"I'm La—"

"How the fuck did you get in my goddamn room?" I demanded again, grabbing my phone off the nightstand. I pressed the button that dialed my security.

"A key, silly," she giggled, annoyingly.

She sat up on her knees, crawling toward me. I stepped back. "Get the fuck out." Seconds later, my large security guard came barreling through the doorway of the bedroom.

"Get her the fuck out of here. Now!" I looked toward them, dismissing this bitch that was in my bed.

"Hey! Get your hands off of me!" she shouted. "What the hell? What? He doesn't like women or something? Is that it? Are you ga—" I turned and stormed toward the bathroom, slamming the door behind me on her dumbass accusations.

I relieved myself in the toilet before flushing and then reemerging to find one of my security guards in the room, staring dumbly at me.

"How the fuck did she get in here?" I seethed.

"We were out. Checked on you when we got back in. You said you were good."

"That doesn't answer my question, Tone." I was just barely covering my anger. Tone was a contract employee of Townsend Security. He was new to my security detail, only being with me since the beginning of the summer.

I looked at the time on the clock on the nightstand.

"I have two hours before I need to be up for my flight. When I wake again, I better know who the fuck she is and how the hell she got into my room. Understood?"

Tone nodded. "Yeah, sure."

I turned my back on him as he exited the room. I switched the lamp off and laid back down to try to get some sleep. It was a fruitless endeavor. Not only had that random fucking woman in my bed pissed me off but it made me miss *not* waking up to the woman I really wanted even more.

* * *

"HOW DID SHE EVEN GET IN?" Aaron, my eldest brother, demanded as I stood in his office. It'd been three days since that bitch had shown up in my bed, and by now, the whole fucking world knew. At least that's what it felt like. Not like I gave a shit what the whole world thought, but the one person whose opinion I did care about knew, and the last words she'd said to me two days prior were *fuck off*.

Now, I was standing in Aaron's office, meeting with our head of security, along with Tone and Donovan, the two security staff that traveled with me.

"We went out and—"

"You went out?" Aaron fumed.

"I told them to," I interjected, knowing that expression on his face. Aaron was about to rage.

"You told them to? Why the hell would you do that?" he challenged, looking over in my direction from the head of his large conference table.

I stared at Aaron from the other end of the table. "Because I did. It was my decision."

Aaron's jaw ticked before he cut his eyes in the direction of my security. "That doesn't explain how she was able to get into the room."

"We checked. We checked the room before he entered. Nobody was in there."

"So she got in while he was asleep? That's fucking worse!"

Aaron was smaller than both of the men in stature but they both flinched at the tone of his voice.

"We think she was given a key by someone at the hotel. It's what these groupie types do. They finesse male managers for information on when ballers are coming into town."

"Is that supposed to make us feel any better?" Brutus, our head of security, finally asked. At six foot six, he was the biggest guy in the room and the direct supervisor of my two security guards.

"She wasn't able to steal anything. We checked and made sure. She didn't plant a bug or anything. We went over your phone and tablet with a fine tooth comb."

"But she was just able to take and upload a bunch of pictures of me asleep in my fucking hotel bed, making it appear as if I'd just fucked her." My voice was rigid with anger. I refrained from telling them how this bitch had just messed up the most important thing in my life.

"We need to discuss this," Brutus stated, standing from his chair.

"See that you handle these two," Aaron advised, standing as well. "I've got two newborns at home. I don't need to be here cleaning up after incompetence," he added. Patience had given birth to the two newest editions to our ever-growing family, a month and a half prior.

I eyed both Tone and Donovan as they followed behind Brutus on the way out.

I shook my head. "Fucking imbeciles." I turned to see Aaron staring at me, peculiarly. "What?"

He lifted an eyebrow. "I thought you'd be laughing this shit off."

My jaw tightened.

"That's what you usually do when shit like this happens."

"Yeah, well, maybe things have changed," I spat back, surprising Aaron. "I've got practice."

"Kyle's excited for Sunday's game," he said to my retreating back.

Wish I was as excited as he was. "I'll see you all there."

"I won't be there. Just the children with Mother and Father. I won't leave my wife home that long with two screaming newborns."

I nodded, but deep down I knew it's because Aaron couldn't bear to be separated from his newest editions or his wife for the entire length of a football game. He was enamored with his family. Something he only let those who were closest to him see. My heart squeezed in my chest. For the first time ever in my life, I was envious of my second eldest brother … hell, all three of my older brothers. They knew where they stood with the women they loved. Me, on the other hand …

"You need to make an appearance at the Tidas event."

I waited until the elevator doors that we'd just entered closed before turning to him. "What?"

"The Tidas Gala it's in a few weeks. I can't attend. Josh's wedding is the following day, so he can't. Carter will refuse, so that leaves you. Plus, you'll already be in town for the game with the Dolphins."

"You give me orders on my fucking schedule now?"

Aaron scowled, his usual face. "I'm asking, as a favor, if you could attend."

Didn't sound like much of a question.

"Yeah, whatever." I turned from him as the elevator doors opened to the garage of Townsend Industries.

We parted ways as Aaron sauntered off to the awaiting town car, and I made my way to the electric blue Porsche Cayenne that'd I'd parked earlier.

"And try to get the stick out of your ass before you get there," he said just before the driver shut the door behind him.

I snarled in his direction. "You're one to fucking talk," I mumbled. Truth was, I was acting more like Aaron these days, than he was. He was typically the scowling, demanding, move the fuck out of my way brother while I was known to be more laid back. But my jovial mood had disappeared the moment Destiny hung the phone up in my ear and had refused to answer any of my calls or text since then.

I ground my teeth as I slammed my door shut. For the first time in years, I didn't actually feel like going to practice. But duty called, and as soon as Brutus was done talking with my security detail, he'd be getting a call from me regarding a more important matter. I needed all of the details I could get my hands on Destiny McDonald. If she thought she'd gotten rid of me, she was sadly mistaken.

CHAPTER 12

Destiny

"You look divine, Destiny," Charlie's smooth as silk voice reverberated behind me.

I spun in the direction of my date, and just barely held my smile in place. "Thank you, Charlie. You look handsome as well."

Charlie was a former colleague of mine. He'd been invited to the Tidas Charity event as a representative of the company we both used to work for. When he'd heard through the grapevine that I'd be attending the event as well, he suggested that we attend together. Knowing what a big deal this annual event was, and not wanting to turn down the invite, I agreed. It made sense to go with Charlie since I'd flown all of the way to DC just to attend the event, at the insistence of two of my more prestigious clients. However, not knowing many people in attendance, knowing at least Charlie would help.

"Thank you." Grinning, he pushed his glasses up a little farther with his finger. Charlie was one of those guys who was handsome but had spent his most formative years with his head in the books and at math competitions. He'd been a late bloomer, according to him, and it wasn't until college that women had finally notice his intriguing dark brown eyes, curly brown locks, and Mediterranean good looks.

However, even years later, and a high six figure salary, Charlie was still that same nerd at heart. That's what also made him feel safe to be my date that evening. I didn't need any more men with huge egos and women fawning all over them in my presence.

"Everything all right?" Charlie asked, sounding nervous and looking down at his tuxedo, beginning to straighten out wrinkles that weren't there.

I then realized I'd just rolled my eyes as my brain started creeping back to thoughts of Tyler.

"Everything's fine," I lied. "Shall we go in?" I nodded in the direction of entranceway to the hotel where the event was being held.

"Of course." He nodded and placed his hand at the small of my back.

I gathered the silk material of the long, black gown I wore with my right hand, to prevent myself from tripping over it as I walked. We handed the door attendant our invitations and were soon let into the VIP event.

"So Brenda was telling me that your business is doing well. We haven't had the opportunity to talk much in the last couple of years."

I took one of the champagne flutes from the passing waiter as we entered the ballroom where the event was held. I pulled my eyes from all of the smiling people adorned in tuxedos and ball gowns to turn back toward Charlie.

"Brenda's right. Business is going well," I responded.

He shook his head. "I still can't believe you had the courage to strike out on your own. That takes a lot of guts. I admire that." His smile was friendly.

"Thank you." I would've told him leaving behind my old job to become one hundred percent self-employed hadn't taken much bravery at all. That once I'd left the eight-year marriage I'd been in, nothing after that seemed too scary. Except ...

"Hey, aren't you a huge football fan?" Charlie asked, interrupting my thoughts.

I gave him a perplexed look as he stared at something over my shoulder. "Yeah, why?"

"You're a fan of the Cougars, right?"

"Right again. Now, can I ask why you're talking about football out of the bl—"

"Because their star quarterback is here."

Immediately my back stiffened and I pivoted to stare across the room. My heart squeezed in my chest when Tyler's tall, built frame, draped in an expensive dark tuxedo came into view. I blinked, my breath catching at the first sight of him in well over a week. I'd even avoided watching that day's game just because I didn't want to be reminded of him. I wish I could say it'd worked but I'd be lying. And now, here I was, staring at the man I was working so hard to ignore.

"You think it'd be too much to try and get his autograph?"

I didn't even bother to respond to Charlie's inane suggestion. I wasn't about to go over there. In fact, it'd be best if I stopped staring and made my way across to the other side of this event. Besides, I was there to make potential new business connections, not ogle over lying football players … no matter how good he looked in that damn tux.

"N-no, I think we should—" I stopped talking the moment Tyler lifted those damn, hypnotizing eyes from the group of men he'd been talking with, and they landed directly on me. His eyes widened ever so slightly in surprise, before the irises that were usually hazel-green darkened to an almost olive color.

"He looks like he's coming this way," I heard in my peripheral.

I blinked, and sure enough, Tyler who'd been halfway across the room, was now only a few feet away. When his gaze shifted to my left, landing on Charlie, his jaw tightened noticeably, before shifting back to stare at me. It was then that I realized Charlie's hand was still at the small of my back, as if he was preparing to introduce me as his date.

Something about the expression on Tyler's face told me that would not be a good idea.

* * *

Tyler

"That was a tough loss out there today," Jamie Norman stated, staring at me, as the three men who accompanied him nodded in agreement.

So this is how it's going to be tonight? I thought as I looked over the four men. Jamie was right, the Cougars had lost to the DC Titans earlier in the day. It was a tough loss only made worse by my already sour mood. And while I usually didn't mind helping my family out by attending a charity or even business event that requested the Townsend name, I wasn't in the mood that night.

"We'll get 'em next time," I replied to Jamie.

"We know you will," another man standing to Jamie's right added. I couldn't quite remember his name, nor did I really care to either. I just needed to show my face for a little while and get the hell out of there. I was considering moving my flight up, to leave that evening instead of the following morning like I'd originally planned. Joshua's wedding was the next day and I needed to be back home by mid-morning to make it on time.

"Tyler, we understand that neither Aaron nor your father could make this charity event tonight due to Joshua's wedding. We appreciate you coming in their stead, since you were already in DC an all."

"It's my pleasure, gentlemen," I lied and nodded.

"Tidas Industries is especially dedicated to renewing our commitment to green energy and we understand that Aaron is making a push to go green with your company's products as well ..."

Here we go, I thought, as Jamie began to make his push for Townsend Industries to buy-in whatever the hell it was their company sold. Aaron had sent me the company's prospectus days before but I never bothered to read it. I couldn't care less which way my brother decided to go on this project or whatever it was they were proposing.

"Jamie, before you get any further into your sell, I want to assure you that my brother does not take a possible joint venture with Tidas as a laughing matter. I'm sure Aaron is diligently weighing all his options, and—" I stopped the bullshit response I'd made up in my head the moment my eyes lifted and caught with Destiny's.

For the first time in days I was able to inhale deeply, as we stared across the room at one another. I was struck, not for the first time, by her rich, dark skin, and high cheekbones that looked as if they were glowing. She wore her hair in its short style, curled coming down covering her forehead. The right side of her hair was held back by some sort of shiny butterfly clip. My eyes scanned lower—her petite frame was covered in a sleeveless black, three tiered ruffle gown, that displayed an acceptable amount of cleavage. I mean, not nearly as much as I'd like to see but acceptable enough for her to be adorned with this dress out in public.

"We appreciate that, Tyler, and any concern Townsend Industries might have …"

"Jamie, I will pass the message on. If you'll excuse me." I stepped around the group of men and was damn near halfway across the room in no time at all. It was then that I realized there was a male figure standing next to Destiny. I peeled my gaze from her to the imbecile who had the audacity to have his arm terribly close to my woman, and to top it off, it looked as if he was smiling at me.

I looked back to Destiny, who for the first time, since I'd known her, had a deer-in-headlights expression on her face. That look didn't last too long, however, before she lifted her chin, staring at me defiantly.

My girl couldn't help but poke the beast, could she? I grinned inwardly.

"Mr. Townsend, it's such a pleasure to meet you," the douche next to Destiny began just as I approached them. "I'm Charlie and this is—"

"Destiny," I cut him off and stated, glancing from him to Destiny.

"You two know each other?"

I turned back to the douche. "You didn't think you needed to introduce me to my woman, did you?" I glared at the man who was about three inches shorter than I was.

"Y-your …"

I looked back to Destiny when I heard her gasp.

"I-I wasn't aware you two kn—"

"Now you are."

"Destiny?" he questioned, peering down at her.

I squeezed my hands into fists, hating him for even thinking he could dare to speak to her.

"Mr. Townsend and I aren'—-"

"Careful, Destiny. *Consequences,*" I blatantly reminded her of the conversation we'd had on our first date.

Her mouth snapped shut, her eyes narrowing on me.

Such fire. She had no idea how much she was turning me on.

"Charlie, can you excuse us? It'll just take a moment," she added.

I cut my eyes toward *Charlie.* "No it won't," I stated, firmly, before taking Destiny by the elbow and pulling her away from the douchebag toward a nearby hallway that looked empty.

"Take your hand off of me," she growled as she snatched away, spinning to face me.

"Calm down."

Her eyes ballooned. "Are you telling me to calm down? After what you just did?"

"What did I just do besides tell the truth?"

"Truth? Telling Charlie, my date—"

"Your what?" I questioned, dangerously low.

"My—"

"Think long and hard before you say whatever you're planning to say next."

"Where the hell do you get off acting all jealous and possessive when *you're* the one who was screwing some random Instagram groupie less than a week ago?" Her nostrils flared as she whisper-yelled her question at me.

She was fucking cute.

"I wasn't screwing anybody."

"Pictures say otherwise."

"What pictures? Of me screwing that tramp? No. Because they don't exist. I was on the phone with you that night. We hung up and I took a fucking melatonin pill to help me sleep, and that was that until I woke up with some tramp in my bed. My security had to haul her ass out of there. She must've taken the photos before I woke up."

"Pssh, yeah right, Tyler. Am I supposed to believe that?"

"Yes, you are because that's the fucking truth. I don't know that bi—" I inhaled and pinched the bridge of my nose. "It's the truth," I started again. "And I think you know it is." I advanced on her, crowding her personal space.

"You know what, whatever." She waved both hands in the air. "It doesn't even matter because this thing between us wouldn't work anyway. No way I'm going to deal with constant groupies sneaking in and out of your hotel room. Not a—" She cut herself off, shaking her head and looking away from me, out into the distance.

Not again.

That's what she'd been about to say.

"Your mouth is moving but your body's contradicting your words," I began, lowering my eyes to see the outline her hardened nipples were making through the material of her dress. "You've missed me as much as I've missed you the last few days."

I caught it when her breathing began to increase as I let my pointer finger run along the outside of her ear and down the column of her neck.

"Don't t-touch me," she tried to say forcibly, but it came out on a stutter. She made no move to create more space between our two bodies.

I moved closer. "Is that what you want? Because this little vein in your neck is telling me that you want me to keep touching you. And not just with my hands either. I think you want my hands, mouth, and cock to touch you a lot more."

A deep intake of air sounded when Destiny looked up at me, her eyes pleading for me to do exactly when I'd just mentioned. She bit her bottom lip, refusing to let the actual words come out.

A moan sounded from my own throat at the sight of her plump lip being fondled by her teeth. It was my turn to fondle that lip.

Without more preamble, I lowered my head until our two mouths met. Her words had said one thing, but when Destiny's mouth opened up for me, allowing my tongue to collide with hers, her words held no weight at all.

I took her by the waist with both of my hands, pulling her into my body, kissing the life out of her. I pressed my hips into her, letting her feel the effect just being in her presence had on me. She did the same, when she openly moaned into my mouth, breaking free of the kiss to whisper my name.

"Let's take this upstairs," I stated against her lips.

CHAPTER 13

Tyler

I waited for Destiny's response. When she lowered her eyelids I thought she'd try to come up with another lie about not wanting me to touch her. But worry turned to the most fulfilling sense of relief I'd ever experienced, when her eyes rose to mine again, and she nodded.

Everything behind us was forgotten about. The Tidas Event. The men begging for Townsend Industries' approval, and that lame ass date she'd told she would be back to in just a minute. It all faded into nonexistence as I took Destiny by the hand toward the back bank of elevators at the hotel, to deliver us up to my suite. Thankfully, I had a private elevator that led directly to my room, as per my request.

"You're staying at the hotel?" Destiny asked after I stepped on the elevator after her.

I moved closer, cupping her face between my hands. "No," I shook my head, "*we're* staying here," I answered just before locking lips with her again.

This kiss was more feverish than the last one. Both of us panted against each other's lips as we kissed. Destiny's small hands pulled me by the shoulders as if I were an anchor. A sense of pride and need swelled in my chest as the elevator door beeped and pulled open. I didn't take the time to give Destiny the tour of my suite, as I scooped her up in my arms and carried her to the bedroom.

I kicked open the door to the bedroom and carried her to the bed, setting her down as if she were the most precious jewel. Because she was.

"Told you, you wouldn't be back in a minute," I taunted, pulling the bow tie of my tuxedo from around my neck.

My woman didn't disappoint when she sat up on the bed, on her knees, and reached out, pulling me by the lapels of my jacket to her. "Shut up," she growled before planting her lips to mine.

Goddamn this woman was going to drive me insane.

I reached around over her shoulders, rubbing my hands down the silky skin of her bared back, pulling at the tie in the back that held the dress together. The sides of her dress fell to my hands, and I began tugging it the rest of the way down. I broke away from the kiss, needing to see her body being revealed to me for the first time.

I thanked myself for having left the light in my bedroom on earlier. I had a full view of her perky tits as they stood out, dark chocolate nipples pebbled as if beckoning me. My mouth watered and I lowered, taking one into my mouth. Destiny moaned, tossing her head back, her hand reaching around to cup the back of my head.

I delighted at discovering how sensitive her breasts were. I moved to the other breast, clamping my lips around it and sucking. Again she moaned. I reached my hand up to massage the tit that wasn't in my mouth, my mouth watering at the idea of how wet she was growing from my foreplay.

I moved up her chest, kissing as I went, reaching her neck and then ear. "You like having your titties sucked?" I asked directly in her ear.

She nodded.

"No, no, Destiny. You answer with your mouth when I ask a question," I growled, lifting my hand to cup the back of her head, pulling it back by her hair. I used just enough force to lift her face to meet mine but not enough to be painful.

"I said, do you like having your titties sucked?"

Her lips formed a scowl and eyes narrowed, and my dick grew incredibly hard. I ran my hand down the middle of her chest, moving lower, to pull her dress farther from her body. I tightened the hold I had on her hair.

"Yes," she finally responded, tightly.

I grinned. "See? That wasn't so bad, was it?" This time I didn't wait for an answer when I used my hands to pull the dress all of the way down to her knees along with the thin underwear she'd worn underneath.

My own jaw tightened at the sight. "You wore thongs for him?" I growled. The thought alone had me ready to not only fuck Destiny into next week just so she knew exactly who she belonged to, but after doing so, going back down to the charity event and beating the shit out of the douche she'd shown up with, just because of the possibility that he might've seen her in these panties.

"No," she answered, shaking her head. "The dress didn't look right with any other pair of panties. I-I hadn't planned on sleeping with Charlie."

Right answer.

It was the right answer that tamed the beast in me just enough to push anymore thoughts of *Charlie* out of my mind.

Wordlessly, I pushed her back by the shoulders so that she was laying against the bed, while I continued to remove her clothing. Briefly, I considered allowing her to keep her shoes on but nixed that idea. There'd be time for that later on. Once she was completely naked, I stepped back to get the full picture of her naked body laid across my bed—my bed for the night, at least. The woman, however, was all mine, even if she didn't quite know it.

"Open your legs. I want to see that pretty pussy," I ordered while undressing myself.

Slowly she spread her knees apart, revealing her second pair of lips.

"Use your fingers to spread her open. Let me see how wet she is for the last cock she'll ever know." I caught Destiny's shocked expression at my words. I lifted an eyebrow. "Open," I ordered more forcefully.

Swallowing, she moved her right hand down her body, using her pointer and middle fingers to open her second pair of lips for me. I licked my own lips when I saw the moisture that'd already began seeping out.

"See? She knows who see belongs to," I said just before covering Destiny's body with my own.

Despite our differences in size and weight, she took all of my bodyweight willingly, opening both her arms and legs to receive me. Needing to taste those soft, succulent lips again, I kissed her some more.

I moaned into her mouth when at the same time our tongues touched, the tip of my cock made contact with her pussy. But I couldn't move that quickly. I'd cut off my own dick before I took my pleasure before she received hers.

Destiny gasped when I rolled us over, so now my back was against the bed and she laid on top of me.

"Come here," I ordered, Grabbing her waist, I pulled her little ass up until her pussy hovered just above my face.

"Tyler," she panted over and over.

"Hold onto the headboard," I growled just before pulling her body down on my face so that her pussy was now my meal. A guttural sound escaped my throat at the taste of her pussy on my taste buds. She was sweet like cotton candy, and I ate like the starved man I was. I'd been starved of her snappy comebacks and attention for days. And now, here she was riding my fucking face like a joyride. I was in heaven.

Destiny bounced her ass up and down, making the most adorable moaning sounds, which turned me on like no other woman ever had.

I felt the reverberations of the headboard when she smacked or punched it. Her body was rigid with its need to release, and being the generous man I am, I locked my lips around her clit and sucked, giving her just what she needed to come.

Those tiny hips of her bounced up and down and around; her thighs clenched tightly around the sides of my head as she came.

"Th-that was … thank you," Destiny panted as she slid down off my chest, onto her back.

"You didn't think I spent years lifting weights just to toss some pigskin across a field, did you?" I retorted.

My chest tightened when she let out a giggle before wrapping her hand around the back of my neck, pulling me to her mouth. She surprised me when her tongue outlined my lips as she moaned. She was enjoying her own taste on my mouth.

I pulled back. "My girl is nasty."

She gave me a mischievous grin that was soon replaced by my lips covering hers. I moved over her again, positioning myself between her legs, our lips still locked together. Her legs went up, crossing behind my back as I rocked myself against her over and over. Both of us were panting and ready for me to make entrance when Destiny's hand went to my chest.

"Wait, wait …" she begged through heavy breaths. "C-condoms. We need protection."

I squeezed my eyes shut and lowered my head to the crook of her neck. I could be a reckless son of a bitch at times but never like this. Ever since I was eleven years old and had even hinted at noticing girls from the first time, my father had drilled into me the necessity for protection. Being a player in the NFL had solidified my father's warnings. I'd seen and had plenty of interactions with groupies more than willing to pop out a kid by an athlete just to collect a check.

"Tyler."

"I know," I responded. I moved back, reaching for my wallet which was in the pocket of my tuxedo pants that laid on the floor. Swiftly, I pulled out the condom, undid the wrapper, and sat up on my knees to put it on. I watched Destiny as she observed me sheathing myself in the magnum condom. She worried her bottom lip and swallowed, pensively. I grinned inwardly. The magnum wasn't just for show or an ego boost. It was the only brand I purchased because it was the only brand and size that fit my length and girth.

"You want me to go slow or fast?" I leaned down and asked after giving her another peck on the lips. I wrapped my arms under her shoulders, forcing our bodies together from the chest to where my cock was about to enter her.

"You're letting me decide something for once?"

I smiled and nipped at that plump bottom lip. "This time," I answered and placed myself right at the entrance of her canal.

"Fast," she responded.

I nodded. "Slow it is," I retorted cockily as I began to penetrate her with achingly slow movements of my hips.

"Tyyy," Destiny growled, raising her hands up to the backs of my shoulders, her nails going into my skin.

I ducked my head into the column of her neck. "This too fast for you?" I taunted, still only about halfway inside of her.

"F-faster."

"What did I tell you before? About playing games?" I questioned and lifted my head to stare down into her glassy-eyed gaze.

"What?" She moaned when I moved deeper another inch.

"The game only ends when *I* say it ends. You don't get to ignore me for three days and then get to call all of the shots in the bedroom, Destiny." I moved another half an inch deeper.

"Tyy—"

"Goddamn, I thought I loved the way you said my name before. But with my cock inside of you, my name is even sweeter on your lips."

"Please," she begged, head thrashing against the pillow, back arching.

I took one look at her pleading expression and the games were over. As much shit as I liked to talk, I knew when to say when. I pushed all of the way in, causing Destiny's breath to hitch, before pulling out again all of the way to the tip, and diving back in. Her legs wrapped tighter around my lower back, fingernails dug into my skin even deeper, and the scent of her arousal all served to heighten my own pleasure.

With her little body wrapped around mine, I pumped into Destiny with the force of a drowning man, straining for his last breath. The difference was I didn't want to come out from underneath this type of drowning. I lowered my mouth until our lips locked again, and kissed her with the same intensity that my cock was making its acquaintance with her inner walls. It was as if her pussy was made for me and only me. I don't know how long it took, but soon enough the tingles down my spine that were a signal of my impending orgasm were occurring. I wouldn't let that happen until Destiny came again for the second time. Two to one, those were the odds I could live with.

"Come for daddy," I crooned into her neck.

"T-Ty—"

Reaching down, I lifted her left leg higher as I reached underneath it, giving myself the ability to enter her another inch deeper.

"Come for me, Destiny," I implored when I felt her walls tightening around me. I moved my free hand to pinch her right nipple, playing with it between my thumb and forefinger.

"Oooh," she sang as her orgasm made its appearance.

"Hss shit!" I cursed at the feeling of her pussy milking me as she came. My damn vision blurred and my own orgasm barreled through me, causing my rhythm to slip. I gripped the top of the headboard, not wanting the entirety of my weight to crush Destiny. I came harder than I ever could remember.

The last coherent thought I can remember having was if our coupling was this good with a barrier still between us, we were in trouble when I finally entered her with no protection whatsoever.

And for the first time in my life, I was highly looking forward to the days when I could slip between a woman's legs, unprotected, to give her my future babies.

CHAPTER 14

Destiny

I'm such a skeezer, I thought to myself as I carefully peeled myself from under Tyler's heavy ass arm. I climbed off the bed and stood unmoving, trying to make sure he was still fast asleep. The man slept like a damn rock. No wonder that tramp had been able to get into his room and bed without him realizing it.

I shook my head.

I was not supposed to be thinking about Instagram hoes or anything else. I needed to get my shit together and haul ass out of there. I began to groan at the soreness between my legs, but then covered my mouth to keep myself quiet. Tyler was much larger than I'd expected. No wonder he walked the earth so cockily. Not only had he come from wealth and privilege, but he was one of the best players in the NFL *and* he had a big dick to match. Deadly combination. He'd be my undoing most assuredly. I had no choice but to hightail my ass out of there.

I stepped into the thong I'd worn the night before and put on my dress, tying the bow at the back to keep it in place. I carried my shoes and the clutch I'd brought with me toward the bedroom door. I glanced over my shoulder one last time, and sure enough, Tyler's eyes were still firmly closed, mouth parted as a tiny snore escaped his lips. My gaze lingered on that mouth, remembering how it'd brought me pleasure the night before.

"No," I admonished myself, shaking my head. No time to think about any of that. I turned and headed to the main exit. I cursed when I remembered that the exit was an elevator. A very loud elevator from what I'd remembered from the night before. But I'd have to take the chance.

However, just as my finger went to press the door open button, a much larger hand made impact with the door close button, halting my anticipated escape.

"Remember what I told you about consequences, Destiny?"

* * *

Tyler

My chest heaved up and down as I stood over Destiny, my hand firmly pressed against the door close button of the elevator. She stood completely still, back facing me, obviously stunned by my sudden appearance.

In general, I'm not a hard sleeper, save for when I take a sleeping pill, or apparently after spending a night in between the legs of the most intriguing women I'd ever been in the presence of.

"Move. Your. Hand," she ordered, still not turning to face me. Her back to me pissed me off more than her daring to give me such an order. Second only to the fact that she'd honestly tried to slip out of my bed and this suite without my knowing.

"Turn your ass around," I growled, still hovering over her.

"Ty—" she began as she turned but stopped short. Her eyes widened, mouth popped open before she quickly clamped it shut. "You don't have any pajama bottoms? Sheesh!" she stated, annoyed, presumably at her own body's reaction to my nudity.

"You didn't seem to mind my lack of pajama bottoms last night."

I already anticipated the eye roll my comment was going to elicit. She didn't disappoint, this time adding a stomping of her bare right foot. That was when I noticed the high heel shoes she'd worn the night before were clutched to her chest. Again, another sign she'd gone out of her way not to make noise in order to sneak out of here.

"Where the hell did you think you were going?"

"I didn't *think* anything," she retorted, tossing a hand on her hip. "I *am* going back to my hotel to gather my belongings and to catch my flight back home."

"I can guarantee you your day isn't going to go as planned."

She pushed out a puff of air, looking annoyed. "Tyler, look ... last night was great and all—"

"Great *and all*?" She was lying her ass off.

"But it was just one night. This thing, whatever it is between us, isn't going to work. Let's not try to fool ourselves into thinking it will. You're always on the road, random women sneaking into your room and whatnot. I just—"

"I'm not your ex-husband." My tone was sharp.

Her eyes enlarged again. "Y-you know about him?"

I nodded. "But obviously not from your own mouth. Is that what happened, Destiny? The NBA player ex couldn't keep it in his pants and you finally had enough?"

"Shut up," she demanded.

"It is, isn't it?"

"That's none of your damn business."

"See, that's where you're quite wrong. Anything involving you, past, present, or future is my damn business."

"Tyler, just stop! This is nonsense. Besides, don't you have a wedding to go to?"

I frowned, wrinkling my forehead. It was the day of Joshua's wedding. I looked around to find a clock to see what time it was. I was supposed to leave first thing in the morning to make it to Joshua's wedding on time. But the night before the only thing that'd been on my mind was Destiny. Just as I located the clock on the far wall of the hotel suite and read the time as being seven-thirty in the morning, the elevator's door beeped just before opening. During the back and forth with Destiny I'd let my hand drop, releasing the button.

"Oh shit!" my security yelled as he stepped off the elevator, seeing me standing there, completely nude.

"Destiny!" I called, pushing past the security as she took the distraction as an opportunity to hop on the elevator and press the down button. "Goddamn it!" I grunted, slapping the elevator doors as they closed.

"Mr. Townsend, we're sorry," Donovan began, turning his head away to avoid looking at me.

"What the hell are you doing up here?" I demanded. "Get the fuck out!"

"It's just you're late for your flight and your father's been calling—"

"Get out!" I yelled again, storming to the bedroom and slamming the door shut. The wheels in my mind spun as I decided what to do. It would take too much time to attempt to find out what Destiny's hotel was. I could have my security chase her down, but after being reamed out by Brutus and Aaron, I was certain they wouldn't leave my side. Plus, there was the matter of Joshua's wedding. I was supposed to be on a plane an hour ago.

"Dammit!" I clapped my hands, cursing, hating the feeling of powerlessness this damn woman was beginning to have over me. She had me chasing my coattails and I didn't fucking like it at all.

CHAPTER 15

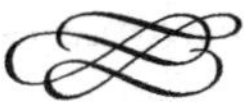

Tyler

"I'm here," I grunted into the phone, completely annoyed and frustrated. I was on the phone with my father, who'd called me at least three times while I was in the air. After landing, I had to stop by my place to change into the navy blue tuxedo that Joshua had chosen for all of his groomsmen, before actually heading over to the church.

Joshua and his soon-to-be wife, Kayla, were getting married in one of the oldest churches in the city of Williamsport. I pulled up in the town car as guests were arriving and being seated. I swore under my breath knowing Joshua would probably be pissed at me for being so late. Add to that my already dour mood due to the woman I couldn't stop thinking about and I wasn't the best person to be around at that moment. So when I felt a hand on my left forearm, I turned, ready to ream out whoever it was before my security could.

"Remove your hand, ma'am," Donovan called out, immediately getting between the woman and I.

I glanced up and the woman's blue eyes reminded me of someone but I couldn't place my finger on who.

"I'm so sorry. It's just that, you're Tyler, right? Joshua's brother?"

the older woman—who appeared to be closer to my parents age than Joshua's—asked.

"Why?" I nearly growled. I instantly felt a sense of guilt in my gut when she flinched.

"I-I'm, uh, an old friend of Joshua's. Can you please pass this along to him?" She held out a pink envelope.

"What's in the letter?" Donovan demanded.

However, something in the woman's eyes led me to conclude that whatever she held was harmless.

"It's okay, Don. I got it." I took the letter from the woman and gave her a nod, before turning to head down the long hall and up to the changing rooms on the second story of the church.

I waved my security off when they told me they'd be in with the rest of the guests. Joshua had enough security for his wedding that mine didn't need to be on call at the moment.

"About fucking time," Joshua exclaimed as I entered the room where all three of my brothers, father, and my four nephews were.

"Whatever," I grunted in response to Joshua. I brushed passed him, seeing the bottle of scotch on one of the tables. Without a second thought I charged over to the table, grabbed the first glass within reach, and poured myself a shot. Usually, I abstained from alcohol during the season, but with my mood, I needed something to take the edge off.

I didn't even stop to notice how all four men in the room had paused to carefully watch me. Not until my father spoke up.

"There's only one thing that makes a Townsend man drink like that."

And just like the assholes they were, all three of my brother's responded, "A woman."

"My, my, how the tables have turned," Joshua added, grinning like a fucking Cheshire cat.

"Whatever," I grunted again. "Oh, here." I practically tossed the envelope the woman from earlier had given me.

"What's this?"

"Hell if I know. Some woman asked me to give it to you in the hallway. One of your guests. Didn't know her, but she reminded me of …" I snapped my fingers, trying to remember.

"Chelsea," Joshua stated as he stared at the writing of his name on the envelope.

"Yeah!" I agreed. Chelsea had been a long-time friend turned girlfriend of Joshua's. His first love, according to my mother. But she'd died of cancer in their early twenties. Kayla, the woman Joshua was marrying in less than thirty minutes, was actually best friends with the both of them growing up. Apparently, they'd become more than that. I saw that one coming a mile away but whatever. I rolled my eyes and poured another shot, downing it.

"Don't fuck up your brother's wedding," my father growled at me.

"Wouldn't dream of it, Father."

"I need to see Kayla!" Josh demanded, catching all of our attentions. Before anyone could react my older brother was charging out of the room, intent on seeing his bride-to-be.

"What's going on?" Diego questioned, looking up at Carter.

"Let's find out," his father answered.

I trailed behind everyone, including my father and Aaron who were each carrying one of Aaron and Patience's newborn sons. The boys named, Thiers and Andreas, were close to two months old, and thankfully sound asleep for all of this commotion.

"You can't see her," I heard my mother telling Joshua as I rounded the corner. "You will be seeing her in the next thirty—"

"It's important," he insisted. Apparently, whatever was in that letter riled him up.

Less than a minute later, Kayla's voice called out from somewhere behind the door and Joshua was led inside, with his eyes closed. I shrugged and followed behind Carter and Aaron as they started back for the changing room.

"These damn boys are just as bad as you," I heard my mother mumble.

I happened to look up to catch the smile and wink my father tossed her before planting a kiss to her lips. "No smear lipstick. You're learning," he said low, but I was still able to hear it.

"Pretend all you want, but I know you well enough to know how much you like the sight of my lipstick smeared."

I shook my head and picked up my pace just as my father growled something to my mother, causing her to giggle. The sight of their affection no longer grossed me out but it did, for the first time ever, cause me to feel a twinge of jealousy. No, not a twinge, a fucking mountain full of jealousy. Here I was at my third oldest brother's wedding while my father and other two brothers were all present with their wives and children, and I was alone. Now, I'm not an insecure man at all. And I certainly could've had my pick of women to accompany me to this wedding. But the one I wanted to bring had fled from my hotel suite before I even got the chance to ask her.

"It's going to be a long fucking day," I mumbled to myself just as Joshua entered the room again, grinning from ear to ear.

* * *

"YOU WANT to tell me what's been up your butt today?"

I adjusted the frown on my face, turning it into the best smile I could manage before facing my mother.

"You look ravishing, Mother." I grinned in her direction.

In spite of herself, she smiled. "You always were my favorite."

I nodded. "That's what I've always told them all." I nodded in the direction of my brothers, all three of which were on the dance floor, in the middle of my parent's massive back lawn at Townsend Manor. Joshua and Kayla had opted to have their reception here, which came as no surprise since it's where both Carter and Aaron had their own weddings. Townsend Manor spanned nearly six acres, hosted a lake out back, and had plenty of greenery and space for a dance floor and children to run about.

"Don't get too full of yourself. I tell that to all four of my boys when they look as down as you're looking."

For the first time since that morning, a sincere grinned touched my lips. Leaning down, I placed a kiss to my mother's rosy cheek.

"I'm fine," I assured her. To my dismay her frown deepened.

"My Tyler would never say something as dull as *I'm fine* if he were actually doing fine." She pointed her head in the direction of the dance floor where the children were running around the couples who were dancing. "You've barely played with the children. Diego keeps asking me what's wrong with Uncle Ty."

Damn, even the children noticed my sour mood.

"Our boy is fine, Deb." My father's voice interrupted my mother and I.

She turned to him, frowning. "He's not f—"

"No, but we've raised a good boy with a good head on his shoulders."

"Thank you, Father."

"Even if he is a smartass at times."

"Apple doesn't fall far from the tree," I retorted.

My father grinned. "See?" He lifted an eyebrow in my mother's direction, bending low to kiss her lips. "I think Kennedy wanted to tell you about the latest book she picked up from the library," my father told her.

Mother looked over at Kennedy who, much to her delight, had her head stuck in a book, at one of the tables. My mother laughed before giving my father and I one last look and moving toward her only granddaughter.

I took a sip of the champagne I'd swiped from one of the passing waiters. It wasn't scotch but it'd do for now.

"Want to tell me her name?" My father's deep voice broke the silence of the moment.

Instantly a picture of Destiny filled my mind. I no longer saw Joshua dancing with his new wife, or the large pond beyond the greenery, or the blue sky that was broken up by the reds, oranges, and yellows of the changing fall leaves. Just Destiny's smiling face.

"Keeping it to yourself, I guess," my father murmured. "I'd always knew you'd be the youngest when you married."

That comment was what made me turn back to him. I lifted an eyebrow.

"You need the stability of your own family more than the other three," he continued.

"How so?"

"You're my wild child but a family man at heart. Only a strong woman with a big heart could settle you down. However, I knew you'd find her early on. Probably your crazy antics that kept you from finding her sooner, but alas, it looks like she's giving you a run for your money." He had the damn nerve to chuckle.

The frown was back on my face instantaneously.

"One more question, is she falling for you the way you've fallen for her?"

I stared into my father's brown eyes and swallowed, contemplating that question. "Yes, she is," I answered with certainty.

"Then you better make fucking sure you catch her," Carter's voice suddenly filled my presence.

I glanced from my father to my eldest brother who was standing next to him, arms folded, same intense expression on his face as his eyes burrowed into mine.

"With both fucking hands," Aaron chimed in. His hazel eyes were just intense as the other two.

"And hold on tighter than the grip you use on that goddamn pigskin every Sunday," my father finally stated.

I looked all three squarely in the eyes and nodded before turning back to the dancefloor seeing Joshua and Kayla wrapped arm in arm, swaying to the music. They stared into one another's gazes as if no one else in the world existed. One by one, my father and brothers left my side and swept their own wives up in their arms. Even Aaron, who everyone knew was a terrible dancer, somehow convinced his wife to accompany him on the dancefloor. I loved my family dearly and their words solidified in my mind what I needed to do.

I pulled my cell phone from my pocket and dialed Destiny's number. Unsurprisingly, she didn't answer. When her voicemail picked up I decided to leave it all on the line.

"I told you games end when I say they do. Consider this your official warning. Game's over, Destiny. There is no denying the inevitable anymore. I might've let you walk away for good before you let me in between those sweet, silky thighs of yours. But you did, so there's no more running after last night."

I hung up the phone and immediately went to seek out Brutus. The information he'd given me on Destiny was limited. It told me that she was previously married, to whom and for how long, but I needed more. Starting with her address.

CHAPTER 16

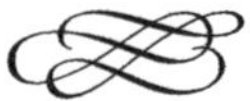

Destiny

"Game's over ..." I listened to Tyler's message for the third time, as I emerged from the Lyft I'd been riding in from the airport. Yes, I'd unblocked his number from my phone and was now able to hear his voicemail message. A shiver ran through my body at the deep edge his voice held. I could just imagine those usually light eyes of his darkening as he left this message. My entire body felt as if it'd been engulfed in flames. I worried my bottom lip, strolling toward the elevator of my building, trailing my suitcase behind me.

"S'cuse me," I pardoned myself after nearly bumping into the woman who was coming off the elevator. Moving to the side to give her space to depart, I quickly entered the elevator, pressing the number three for my floor. It was after ten o'clock at night. I'd remained in DC until early that evening, meeting with a few clients for lunch and an early dinner, before leaving for my flight. Though I'd managed to make it through my meetings with relative ease, the whole day my primary focus had been on Tyler. I was a coward for running out on him like that. I don't even know why I'd done it. Sure, maybe the issue with the groupie scared me a little, but the scariest part was I believed his story. I believed him when he'd said he hadn't slept with that woman.

While waiting at the airport, I took the time to find the tramp's Instagram page. She had all types of photos with male celebrities, mainly professional athletes. She obviously wasn't new to this world at all. Though, it didn't necessarily prove that she'd lied, it did give credence to Tyler's story, that this chick was fame hungry and would do anything to be seen with an athlete, thereby making her more suspect in my eyes.

"Holy shit!" I cursed when I stepped out of the elevator to head toward my condo—which was right across the hall—and nearly collided with Tyler. "What are you doing here?" I rushed out, feeling hot and anxious at the same time.

A slow, lazy smile spread across his handsome face, and my insides tightened. Especially when that dimple emerged.

"You got my message." It wasn't a question, he could tell I'd gotten it. I suspected he even knew I'd listened more than once.

"Waiting outside of someone's home like you're damn John Cusack in 'Say Anything,'" I stated, trying to sound annoyed.

His face scrunched up. "Who?"

Sighing, I pushed out a puff of air. "See? That's why you and I would never work. You don't even know classic eighties movies. You weren't even born when that movie came out."

Tyler was the one to roll his eyes next. "We're back to the age bullshit again?"

"I'm just saying—"

"Did it feel like I was too young when I was in between your legs last night, Destiny?" he asked, stepping closer.

I took a step back until my butt brushed against my doorknob.

"I can't hear you. Did it feel like I was too young last night?"

I parted my lips to reply but nothing came out. He seemed to have that effect on me.

"Didn't think so," he answered his own question before connecting his lips with mine.

My hand loosened around the suitcase I'd been dragging. Not even the loud popping sound it made as it hit the hardwood floor of the hallway broke the kiss. Tyler's arm swung around my waist, sealing our bodies together. His lips were insistent as his tongue outlined lips before making contact with my tongue. He tasted like some sort of champagne. If my brain hadn't been short-circuiting I would've noticed the navy blue tuxedo he was wearing.

He was the first one to break away from the kiss. Thank goodness, as I needed oxygen, but didn't have the good sense to seek it out. All good sense left me when he kissed me like that.

"You don't have to tell me what happened between you and your ex. Not tonight. One day you will, and it's my sincere hope that on that day I'll have enough restraint not to kill him for whatever it is that he did to you."

My eyes widened in shock. I stared up into his eyes. Not mirth or humor was present. He was as serious as a heart attack.

"H-how do you know he did something to me?" According to all of the gossip blogs and magazines that were popular when Darryl and I had broken up, I was the gold digging baller's wife who left her husband when he was down and out. Darryl's career ending knee injury had been pinned as the reason I left him.

"Because any man who was lucky enough to have you and then lose you, had to have done it to himself. And because whatever he did is making it that much more difficult for you to trust me." Anger flashed in his eyes.

"Ty—" I was cut off with another peck to my lips.

"Destiny, I just spent the last few hours watching my third youngest brother confess his love to the woman he plans on spending the rest of his life with. I also watched my oldest two brothers and father barely leave their wives' sides throughout the entire day, and all it did was make me miss you even more."

I frowned. "So you want something with me because you're envious of what your brothers have?" I pushed against this chest but his hold on my waist was firm.

"You're so fucking cute when you're angry. But no," he paused to kiss my lips again, "I don't envy my brothers. Not in the way that I'd want to steal their happiness, anyway. I'm happy for them. And never, before you, have I ever coveted what they had with their spouses. Hell, I was the brother who teased the shit out of them relentlessly and reminded them of the days they'd said they'd never marry. But my father told me something today that reminded me of the fact that while I'd said a lot of shit in my day, the one thing I never said was that I wouldn't marry. I've always been honest about wanting my own family. And I knew when I met the right person I'd just know." He stopped, staring down on me.

I was sure my heartbeat was pounding so fast and so hard that he could hear it.

"I knew the day you walked into that lecture hall."

What was I supposed to say to that? How was I to respond? No coherent thought could even manage to make its way to the forefront of my mind.

"Now," Tyler began, just before dipping his head and pressing another kiss to my opened mouth, "open the door, Destiny."

An order.

That's what his words were. An order. And I was the last woman to take orders from a damn man. So when I turned, key in hand, and began unlocking my front door, I knew I'd officially lost my damn mind.

Tyler Townsend had driven me insane.

That was the only explanation that fit. But even that awareness didn't get much more than a passing thought when Tyler bent low behind me, his hot mouth connecting with the side of my neck. I closed my eyes and pressed backwards against the hardness of his body, as we fumbled into my condo, neither of us alert to the fact that my lights were already on.

I swung my arm out wildly, searching for the wall switch, only then realizing then that it was in the upright position. Again, that was quickly dismissed as I assumed I'd likely left my light on when I left the previous day. Tyler's moans in my ear and his lips and tongue on my body had left me with no awareness of my surroundings save for him.

I spun to face him, briefly opening my eyes just before his mouth covered mine again.

"Please, don't let me interrupt anything."

Resha's voice caused me to jump out of my skin. I was pulled firmly against Tyler's body, as he stood erect, looking over my head. His arm was so tight around my body that I could barely breathe.

"Resha?" I asked out loud, my back still facing her thanks to the tight hold Tyler still had on me.

"Who else would be in your place this late?" she retorted.

I sighed. "It's okay," I whispered to Tyler, consolingly. Only then did his grip loosen just enough for me to turn around. I had to struggle a little just to be set free from his hold.

"What're you doing here?" I questioned, rushing over to give her a hug. It'd been nearly a month since we'd seen each other in person. Thanks to her work, Resha was often traveling.

"And you must be Tyler," Resha stated after we hugged, entirely ignoring my question.

I turned to watch my cousin and best friend move into the living room space of my open-floor plan condo, to stare Tyler down. I watched as the two sized one another up. Resha liked to pretend she was intimidating, when in actuality she was barely an inch taller than I was, and though curvier in a size twelve body, she was much more dainty.

Tyler's face finally expanded to his charming smile—funny how I was now able to discern which smile he was adorning at any given moment.

"Glad to see you made it back safely from Europe," Tyler finally stated as he moved closer, taking her hand in his and pressing a kiss to it.

Resha actually dipped her head, giggling.

I rolled my eyes.

Seriously?

Resha was supposed to be my eyes and ears when my own discernment had gone out of whack. Tyler caused my entire thirty-six years worth of common sense to short-circuit. I needed Resha to be the one to knock some sense into me where he was concerned, yet here she was being charmed by him as well.

"Like I said, what are you doing here?" I placed my hand on my hip, breaking up the little love fest. I'll admit there may've been some jealousy on my part as well.

"Sheesh. It's been four weeks since you've seen me. You'd think she'd be happy," Resha tutted. "I was stopping by to make sure you got in safely but I see you got in just fine." Her voice rose a little as she looked toward Tyler. "Also, I wanted to talk about the live show of our podcast. We need to discuss the details on that. Plus, I need to tell you how my trip went. And I stopped by—"

"Resha," Tyler's deep voice sliced through the air, cutting Resha off.

Her mouth clamped shut. Now *that* was something I hadn't seen before.

"As you know, Destiny just departed off her own flight. I'm sure you need to catch up on your own rest, seeing as how you're likely dealing with jet lag and all. How about you two reconvene in the morning? I'll have breakfast delivered so you two can meet."

I just knew that was going to get a rise out of Resha, but again, Tyler had the magic touch when he moved over to Resha, placing a hand on her shoulder, and gently guiding her toward the door. They even struck up a conversation about her return flight on her way to the door. Before I knew it, he was ushering her out while confirming that breakfast would be here at nine the next morning for our meeting.

"Good thing she lives in the building," he stated, turning from the door back to me.

I tilted my head to the side. "I mentioned that in a podcast?"

His eyes moved to the corner of the room before turning back to me. "You must've."

I shrugged. I didn't recall saying that, but how else would he know Resha and I lived in the same building, albeit she lived one floor up?

"Now," he started, his voice deepening as he strolled toward me, "where were we?"

Again, my heart rate spiked when the usual darkening of his eyes occurred. The same look that always happened right before his lips covered mine.

"Tyler," I whispered his name, breathlessly, in between kisses.

"Where's your bedroom?" he demanded, his lips pressed to mine.

I had one arm wrapped around his neck and with my free arm I managed to point down the hallway, in the direction of my bedroom. Before I took my next breath, I was hoisted up his body, my legs wrapping around his waist. As if he were carrying nothing more than a bag of feathers, he swiftly carried me down the hall, kicking the door of my bedroom open.

Once we reached the doorway, I leaned over his shoulder, flipping on the switch to lighten the bedroom. Tyler lifted his head from me, glancing around, his pupils narrowing in on the white, tufted sleigh bed that lay in the center. His footfalls were absorbed by the plush carpeting that lined the floor of my bedroom, before he gently laid me down on the bed.

I went to reach for the button of his tuxedo jacket but soon found both of my wrists encircled in one of his large hands. My breath hitched when he raised my arms over my head as he slowly came down, covering my body.

"I want to touch you," I whined, at the same time lifting my head to make way for his lips as he kissed down the column of my neck.

"Do you?" he challenged.

"Yesss," I hissed when he used his free hand to pinch my right nipple through the sweater I wore.

"Your nipples are so sensitive," he groaned in my ear. His hand slipped underneath my sweater, eliciting goosebumps up and down my abdomen. Before I knew it, my sweater was up and over my head, Tyler's quick hands already trapping my wrists against the mattress before I could move.

"You're too fucking fast," I grunted, pushing with my hips against his body.

His deep chuckle reverberated against me, causing my core to clench. "That mouth is going to get you into trouble, precious."

His mouth covered mine again, and just to prove that he didn't have me right where he thought he did, I bit his tongue. Not hard enough to draw blood, but harsh enough to sting.

"Woa-ow!" I yelped when Tyler flipped me over so fast, my head spun, and then the stinging in my ass as he spanked me through the jeans I still had on moved up my body.

He leaned down, covering my back with his upper body. "You like trouble."

"Just as much as you do," I retorted.

Another laugh and then I was being stripped of my clothing. In record time, he had me bare ass naked, on my back in the center of my bed. I didn't mind at all, save for the fact that he was still fully clothed, the exception being his tuxedo jacket.

"Remember those consequences we discussed, precious?"

I wrinkled my forehead, wondering what he was getting at. His right hand slowly made its way into his pocket, pulling out a black, velvet box. Curiosity got the best of me as I watched him carefully open the box.

My mouth fell open when my eyes landed on a pair of rose pink, diamond encrusted nipple clamps.

"You can't be serious."

"Oh but I am. Running out this morning like you did is going to cost you. And since these chocolate kisses of yours are so sensitive, what better way to experience your first punishment?"

I inhaled sharply as he reached down, pinching my already protruding nipple between his thumb and forefinger.

He moved farther between my thighs, causing them to separate even more to accommodate his big body. With his eyes still trained on me, he removed the nipple clamps from the box, tossing it over the side of the bed. He hesitated, holding up the clamps, his eyes requesting my consent.

"Do you want me to use these on you, precious?" he questioned.

I squeezed my eyes shut, as his thumb grazed one of my nipples. I was a huge fan of nipple play. I loved it, but no man had ever had me in this position so early on in a relationship. Hell, I hadn't even allowed any man aside from my ex-husband to get this close to me with a pair of clamps. But with Tyler …

"Yes," I answered just above a whisper, opening my eyes.

A deep moan came from Tyler's throat as he reached down, applying first one then the second clamp, that were attached by a chain. My entire body began vibrating with need and sensation as the pinch of the clamps turned into pain and slowly edged its way into pleasure.

I bit my bottom lip, lifting my chin, beckoning Tyler's kiss. He didn't disappoint, leaning over and connecting our lips. This time the kiss was slow, torturous almost, as his tongue whirled around my mouth, savoring and tasting every portion. I could feel the wetness seeping from my core. I was sure I was leaving a huge wet spot against the pants of his tuxedo. Tyler obviously couldn't care less, as he began pumping his hips against my pussy.

"Ahh!" I tossed my head back, groaning when he tugged on the chain that connected the nipple clamps, causing them to briefly squeeze even tighter.

"No more running, Destiny. I won't allow it," he said with a certainty and a steeliness that most men twice his age could barely muster.

But me being me, I had to have the last word. "I didn't run," I challenged, only to find myself hissing and writhing against the bed again when he pulled at the chain once more. I growled low in my throat.

"So fucking cute," he retorted, grinning and displaying that damn dimple again.

I didn't have time to respond when he moved from the bed and hurriedly removed the rest of his clothing. My mouth watered as I took in the perfection of his body. The previous night I'd been in too much of a rush to have him inside of me to really look over his body. He was the perfect specimen of a man. Beautifully sculpted muscles made possible by his years of amateur and professional athletic training. Unlike most redheads, he tanned quite well. Smooth tanned skin covered the hard mass of six pack muscles, pecks, biceps, and triceps. But even the excellence of his upper body paled in comparison to the gorgeous monstrosity of his cock. He was huge, and the red tip was already dripping angrily with precum. His large hand covered the base of his shaft.

"Since you like back talking so much, I've got something to fill that mouth of yours."

I grinned at his words. "I'm not sure you could fit," I taunted saucily, sitting up for him to lay down on the bed.

"Make it work," he answered.

I moved, as he took his place at the center of my bed, and I leaned down between his legs, sitting on my knees. With one last look up at Tyler between my lashes, I bent lower and licked the tip of his cock, tasting the tangy precum that'd seeped from his body. I swallowed, delighting in his flavor. I covered the tip of his shaft with my mouth, using my tongue to make it nice and wet so I could easily maneuver up and down his length. I hadn't totally been lying when I said I wasn't sure if he would fit. But I wanted it as badly as I wanted my next breath. I lifted my head until his cock spilled out of my mouth. Spitting onto his shaft, I glanced up at Tyler to see his eyes at half mast, lips twisted up almost as if he was in agony. I used my tongue to swirl my spit around his tip before covering the entirety of it with my mouth again. I was able to go another inch lower, and then lower still, until he hit the back of my throat.

I didn't have much of a gag reflex. I was thankful for that when Tyler's hips began pistoning up and down off the bed, sending him deeper and deeper down my throat. I took all of him. I, like he, derived pleasure from seeing my partner fulfilled. The loud moans and frantic movement of his hips told me that he was enjoying this, which caused me to grow ever wetter.

"That's feels good, precious," he grunted. "Shit!" he cursed when I reached up to play with his balls while his cock was still in my mouth.

When they firmed up and his cock swelled, I knew he was ready.

"I'm going to come," he ground out as if warning me.

I increased the speed of my bobbing head. Soon enough, my mouth was being filled with the sweet taste of his semen. I closed my eyes and let his juices squirt onto my tongue. I swallowed, anxiously anticipating the next spurt.

I didn't get the chance to take the rest of him when I was unceremoniously flipped onto my back as Tyler made quick work of sheathing himself with the condom he'd still held in his hand. Again, his hand took both of my wrists and lifted them over my head as he entered my body.

"Fuck! You're so wet," he grunted against my lips.

I lifted my head, licking and then biting his lower lip, pulling it into my mouth.

"Mmm," I moaned against his mouth when he pushed all the way inside of me until our hips met. I released his lip, inhaling deeply at the feeling of being so full.

"Not talking so much anymore," he taunted.

I gasped again when he thrust into me with extreme force, daring me to try to respond to his taunting. I growled and wrapped my legs tightly around his lower back. Just when I had begun to think I was gaining the upper hand, he tugged at that damn chain again, causing my pussy walls to clench as the sensations coursed through me.

"Tyyyy," I moaned, throwing my head against the pillows. I twisted my wrist, trying to break free. I wanted to touch him or punch him. He was driving me so damn crazy I didn't know what I wanted to do.

"Mine," he growled against my mouth. "Say it!" he demanded.

"Fuck you," I retorted. "Ahh!" I yelped at the smack on the ass and another pull of the chain that'd retort had earned me.

"Smart ass," he chuckled at the same time he pulled completely out of me, flipping me over. "Arch your back," he ordered.

He couldn't even finish the order before my back was bowing, anticipating his breaching me from behind.

Smack!

"Shit!" I cursed at the stinging from his hand.

Smack!

My breath caught in my throat and I let out a silent scream when another smack caused my breasts to jiggle, pulling the nipple clamps tighter. Tyler reached in between my legs from behind, using his pointer and middle fingers to rub circles against my clit. I moaned and thrashed my head against the pillow, and he hadn't even entered me yet. A fact I was oh so painfully aware of when my clenching pussy muscles tightened around nothing.

"Tyler!" I gasped. The man was torturing me

"Something you need, precious?" His warm breath brushed against my ear as he leaned over my body to question me.

"You … I need you," I answered honestly.

A deep sound emerged from his throat and I felt the tip of him begin to breach my core. "How much of me, precious?"

My hands tightened into fists around the white sheets covering my mattress. I swear if I could kick his ass, I would. But I needed him to fill me more than I needed to win this battle. So I finally said, "All of you, Tyler. I need all of you."

I gasped and my mouth fell open as he responded by completely filling me to the hilt, his hands moving to cover my breasts as he began pounding me from the back. I squealed and moaned as my ass bounced off of his body. His large hands massaged my breasts, every so often tugging at the chain of the nipple clamps. My entire body began shaking with the need to release.

"Ty-Ty," I panted, unable to get his full name, let alone a full sentence out. Thankfully, I didn't need to.

"Come for me, precious."

That was all she wrote. My body erupted as my eyes crossed with the intensity of the orgasm that rushed through every cell of my being. From the soles of my feet to the top of my head I felt like my body was being stretched and pulled beyond capacity as the orgasm rolled over me.

If this was how I'd leave this earth then so be it.

CHAPTER 17

Destiny

"Who the hell is this?"

My eyes sprang open at the angry tone in Tyler's voice. I glanced up at the clock on my night stand. It read 6:03 a.m. I blinked a couple of times, trying to recall what day it was. I thought it was Monday.

"What the fuck are you calling my woman so early for?"

"Shit!" I cursed. No. It was Tuesday.

I hopped out of bed and ran into the living room where I spotted a pacing Tyler, completely naked in my living room. I had to ignore the way my body heated at seeing him like this in my home.

"It's JT."

"JT."

Tyler and I both said at the same time. He turned to me, my phone still pressed to his ear. Annoyance filled both of our gazes.

"Don't ever call here so damn early again." He lowered the phone, pressing the end call button.

"The hell did you just do?" I stomped my foot, hands on my hips. It wasn't until Tyler's heated gazed scanned my body that for the first time I realized I was nude as well.

"Who the hell is JT?" he demanded just as sharply, ignoring my question.

"My personal trainer."

"And what the hell is he calling so early for?"

I rolled my eyes. "He calls every Tuesday and Thursday because I have a tendency to oversleep."

"And does he always call you baby when you answer the damn phone?"

"You wouldn't have heard that if you hadn't been answering *my* damn phone in the first place!" I stomped my foot again.

"You were sleeping. I didn't want it to wake you if it wasn't an emergency."

"Right," I countered. "Can I have my phone please?" I held out my hand, demanding he place my phone in it.

He worked his jaw, staring down at me. Reluctantly, he placed my phone in the palm of my hand. "Luckily, I already told him what'll happen if he calls my woman so goddamn early again."

"You're insane."

He didn't even try to counter my claim. Simply grinned at me and nodded, moving closer as if he was going to kiss me. I turned my head and his lips landed on my cheek. It shouldn't have turned me on the way it did. but hell ... obviously I'd lost any good sense.

"I'm going to meet my trainer," I told him, proud of myself from keeping the tremble out of my voice.

"Great. We can work out together," he answered, following on my heels as I made my way into my bedroom.

Two hours later, I pushed back into my condo again, after having a great workout with JT, though it was a bit awkward with Tyler being there the first twenty minutes of my session. To make matters worse, he'd only had the tuxedo he'd worn to my place the night before to wear. If it hadn't been for the fact that he had his own training he needed to get to, I was certain he would've remained there throughout my entire workout.

I had to apologize to JT once Tyler left and that seemed to get our training session back on track. However, JT was a lot less flirtatious and less hands-on throughout the workout. I didn't mind it but I also knew it was because of whatever Tyler had threatened him with. I wasn't quite sure how to feel about that.

"Is breakfast here yet?" Resha questioned, bursting through my door.

I would've been startled if I hadn't expected it. She rarely knocked, instead using her key to enter my place. I had a key for her place as well, though I rarely used it, save for when she was out of town and I needed to drop off her mail and water her plants.

"Good morning to you, too. Breakfast will be here soon. I'm going to shower."

"Good, 'cause you stink." Grinning, she waved her hand in front of her nose, screwing up her face.

"Heffa!" I told her, tossing my gym towel at her.

"Ew!" she screeched. Resha acted as if she was allergic to all things involving sweat and physical exertion.

I waved her off and went to quickly shower, moisturize, and style my hair before I heard the buzzer of my front door sound.

"Food's here!" Resha called.

"Let him in," I yelled back.

Tyler had kept his word and ordered Resha and I breakfast for our morning planning session, even though I'd tried to tell him that wasn't necessary.

I always keep my word.

That's what he'd said to me. The look in his eye when he'd said it chipped away just a little bit more at the wall I'd been trying to erect between he and I.

I stepped into the black knee-length skirt, ankle booties, and the white silk blouse that was patterned with multi-colored lips all over. I loved this shirt.

"Oh, I love that top on you," Resha remarked, obviously agreeing with my taste as I emerged from the bedroom.

"Thank you."

"You've got meetings today?" she questioned.

"Yeah, I'm finally meeting with that financial advisor I was telling you about," I answered, scanning my glass dining table at the array of food.

"Yeah, he went all out," Resha said what I was thinking.

There were Belgian waffles topped with strawberries, and another topped with peaches, fruit salad, turkey bacon and sausage because Resha nor I ate pork, toast, eggs, coffee, and grapefruit and orange juice. I shook my head.

"I don't know what that look is for but I'm gonna eat. And if you were occupied all night with what I *suspected* you two were going to do when he kicked me outta here, you need to eat, too." She handed me one of my white ceramic plates before she began filling her own.

I took some eggs, fruit, and half of a waffle before sitting down.

"So, business or personal first?"

I looked at Resha.

"Business."

She swallowed and nodded. "I think our first live show needs to be around December or January some time."

I frowned. "You don't think that's too close to the holidays? People will be traveling, spending money on gifts and such. You think they'll want to fork out more money to see us live?"

Resha hesitated, her honey eyes moving toward the double glass doors that lead to my balcony. "Good point. But, I still think it's a good time. We could do it in between Christmas and New Years'. Most people take off during that week. We could start selling tickets in early November and people could buy tickets as holidays gifts."

I chewed on the forkful of eggs I just taken, thinking over her suggestion. I nodded. "That could work," I answered after swallowing. "Let me figure out the logistics. We'd need to pick a venue soon."

Resha clapped, excitedly. "I've already looked at a couple. I really liked the New Town Theater. In total it seats about five hundred people—"

"You think we'll get that many?" I asked.

"Girl, you've got to stop thinking so small," she admonished.

"Okay, we need to talk prices and timelines."

"I got the prices and everything here. I spoke with the event scheduler at the theater and looked in the venue yesterday afternoon after I landed. For my money, it looks good, but I want us both to be on the same page, so I made an appointment for later this week for us to take a look."

I nodded, perusing the flyer. "Just let me know the date and time and I'll work it out. In the future, we'll need to hire a manager or event planner or someone to coordinate this stuff if we keep doing these live shows. Especially with you traveling so much."

"Agreed, but let's cross one hurdle at a time."

"Okay."

"Now this financial advisor you're meeting with today. This is the person that scallywag ex-husband of yours told you about?"

I giggled. "Yeah."

"I'm sure you didn't call his office and say 'Hi, I'm Destiny McDonald and I think you're full of shit. Can I have a meeting with you?'"

"No," I shook my head, laughing, "I certainly did not say that. I called and gave a fake name. Said I was the widow of a wealthy man and looking for ways to invest the money I'd just inherited."

Resha nodded. "You don't think he'll recognize you?"

I shrugged. "From where?"

"You were married to a famous basketball player."

I rolled my eyes. "Don't remind me. I mean, I thought of that, but Darryl and I were over years ago. Plus, we were mainly private about our relationship. It wasn't until after our split that more photos of me leaked but even then, it was only a handful. I've cut my hair since then so I'm hoping time works in my favor. I think he and Darryl have only been working together for the last two years, way after we broke up."

Resha paused with a glass of orange juice at her lips, mulling over my explanation. "That might work. Social media wasn't as ubiquitous back then."

I nodded.

"Now that business is out of the way, tell me how you go from I'm not speaking to Tyler Townsend anymore to kicking me out of your home so you could screw him all night long, in less than seventy-two hours."

I pushed out a breathe and sighed, closing my eyes.

I knew that was coming.

* * *

Tyler: *Do you like Ethiopian food?*

I grinned down at the text message that stared back at me. Shaking my head I responded.

Me: *Yes.*

Not even a full ten seconds later my phone buzzed again.

Tyler: *Good. I'll see you tonight at six.*

He was coming over and apparently bringing Ethiopian food with him. My stomach rumbled at the thought. It was well past three o'clock and, yet again, I'd forgotten to have lunch. It was a byproduct of back-to-back meetings, before rushing out of the office to make it to my appointment with Phillip Morris on time.

"Welcome to Phillip Morris' office, how can I help you?" The cheerful receptionist greeted me as I breezed through the glass doors of the office.

"Hi," I stopped to look down at the name on the placard that sat on her desk, "Stephanie. I'm Jesse Pritchard. I have a three-fifteen with Mr. Morris today."

Stephanie nodded. "Yes, Ms. Pritchard, have a seat."

"Mrs. Pritchard," I corrected.

Stephanie blinked. "I'm sorry, of course, Mrs. Pritchard. Please have a seat."

I smiled and nodded, noting the expensive decor that decorated the lobby of the office. There were two flat screen televisions that sat high in the corners of either end of the lobby, beautifully hand-carved statues that sat on the wooden bookshelves, along with magazines and newspapers of all of the major financial and business news outlets from around the world. Along the far wall, was a huge waterfall that spilled over into a pool of water below. I walked over to the waterfall and was surprised to see there were actually fish swimming around in the pool below. Nothing about this office said cheap or inexpensive. I wondered how Mr. Morris could afford these amenities. Of course, it could be just that he was that good and business was doing well. On the other hand, it could be something much more sinister.

"Mrs. Pritchard."

I turned to find a man who appeared to be in his mid-forties to early fifties but looked good for his age. At six feet even, Phillip Morris towered over me, even in heels. His tanned skin, beach blond hair, and pale blue eyes gave him an almost surfer, California native look.

"Mr. Morris, I presume," I greeted, extending my hand to his.

"Please, call me Phillip." He shook my hand firmly then moved to my side to face his receptionist. He instructed her to hold his calls before directing me down the hall to his office. "So, Ms. Pritchard, what can I do for you?"

"Mrs. Pritchard," I corrected before sitting in the leather chair across from his very large cherry wood desk.

He cleared his throat. "Excuse me."

I shook my head. "No, I'm the one who's sorry. I'm just not used to the new title. I loved being a Mrs. You know? And now that my Michael is gone …" I trailed off, sniffling. I looked up and gave a half smile through watery eyes, taking a couple of the tissues from the box that Phillip offered. "Thank you."

"Please, Mrs. Pritchard. No need to apologize in a situation such as this. You said your husband died of a heart attack?"

"Yes, that's right. I was out shopping one afternoon just a month ago. We were coming up on our three year anniversary. I wanted to get Michael something special. He was always spoiling me. I wanted to do the same for him. Anyway, I got a call from a friend he'd gone out golfing with, saying he had a heart attack and was being rushed to the hospital."

Phillip nodded and jotted something down on the notepad in front of him.

"He died two days later." I sniffled again and dabbed my eyes with the tissues, hoping I was coming across as believable.

"I'm so sorry for your loss, Mrs. Pritchard. These things can never be predicted and can be so sudden. What type of work was it you said your husband did?"

I swallowed, clearing my throat. "He owned his own landscaping company in San Diego but he sold it two years ago soon after we married. He'd made a great amount of money over the years and the sale of the company had been a very lucrative one for him. He planned on us having children and being able to be home to spend time with them. Unlike with the children from his first two marriages." I hiccupped and dabbed at my eyes some more.

"Do you two have any children?"

I shook my head and hesitated.

"I'm so sorry."

"It's fine. Well, not fine but that's life, isn't it?"

Phillip nodded. "And now you have this inheritance from your late husband and are looking for ways to invest it for your own future, is that correct?"

"That is correct, Phillip. I haven't brought my documents with me. They're all tied up with lawyers and whatnot, but I should be getting a lump sum payout soon and I am just so confused on what to do. I read books and articles, and one says to invest in real estate, the other says put everything in stocks and let it ride out, another says bonds, a fourth says precious metals. I'm just so overwhelmed. I never had much money before Michael, and we were together for five years before we married. Throughout our whole relationship he handled the money stuff and told me I never had to worry about it." I pushed out a breath to display how over my head I felt.

Phillip, placed his pen down and clasped his hands in front of him. "Mrs. Pritchard, it's great you're doing research and trying to get a handle on the best ways to invest. The trouble with all of these financial books and articles is they don't personalize their information. Each person needs a plan to meet their own financial goals. You may want to have children in the future or to remarry and protect your investments from a future divorce, or a kid's college fund or your own retirement. These are all things that need to be considered and that can change over time. What I do with my clients is I consider their individual cases and make the right investments for them, based on their goals. That is not something any personal finance book, made to be read by millions of people can do. Now, exactly how much do you think you will be getting?"

"Uh, I'm not certain but I recall Michael said he had about ten million in total assets."

Phillip nodded.

"And did you two have a prenup?"

I shook my head.

"And how many children did Michael have?"

"Two. One each from his previous marriages."

"Okay, with that said, and assuming he has no other children coming out of the woodwork, you may be looking at, at least three to three point five million coming your way. Now, with the way I have my clients invest, you could double that amount inside of a year's time."

My eyes bulged. "Double?"

Phillip gave me a serious look, nodding his head. "Absolutely. And the way the market is going, you might be able to do better than that."

"Really? Is it risky?"

"Well," he began, holding out his arms, "there is certainly risk in every investment, but I am very cautious to protect my clients. And I am always working to look out for your best interests. You will receive financial status reports every month on how your investments are doing. Let me show you how they look. I have a sample from last month's investment portfolios."

Over the next thirty minutes, Phillip Morris showed me financial portfolio after portfolio of the different funds he managed. He claimed, due to my age, he would place me in an aggressive stock fund but again, I needn't worry about risk since he often hedged his bets. When I questioned how, he gave some convoluted answer as to how he researched stocks price to earnings ratio and through his connections was able to get information on how a company performed. Phillip was a fast talker, and to someone who was as clueless as I'd tried to make myself appear to be as Mrs. Pritchard, he sounded like the real deal. However, as Destiny McDonald, I knew he was full of shit. And that pissed me off.

"Thank you for your time, Phillip."

"You're absolutely welcome, Mrs. Pritchard," he returned, shaking my hand and walking me to the front lobby.

"Please, I think we're past that. You're going to be investing my money. You can call me Jesse."

"Well, Jesse, it's been a pleasure and I look forward to doing business with you. As soon as you hear from your attorney in California don't forget to give my office a call and we will get started right away on investing your money."

I nodded. "Thank you."

I pushed past the double doors of his office and out into the elevator bank of the building, frowning. Phillip Morris was full of shit. I knew it but I also knew I'd have a hell of a time proving it.

CHAPTER 18

Tyler

"Do you always get enough food to feed an entire football team?" I questioned, staring down at the mountain of food Tyler had purchased that was spread all over my dining room table. This was our third date in a row, spent at my home, and he'd always ordered a ton of food.

He gave a one shoulder shrug before tossing the bags the food had come in on my granite countertop. "Figured I'd order more than necessary just in case you skipped lunch again today."

I groaned and lifted my head to the sky. "One day I skip lunch and every day since you order an entire restaurant. You're so over the top." I lifted my head to see him standing directly over me. My body warmed instantly. I was starting to get used to my body's physical reactions to just being in his presence.

"It was only one time you told me about, but I'm sure you've skipped lunch more than once. You won't be doing that as long as I'm around."

I rolled my eyes, remembering that he'd actually had lunch delivered to my office that day. "I don't make it a habit," I retorted.

"Nor will you be from here on out." He bent low, beckoning a kiss.

I turned my head, as if denying him a kiss, until he began tickling my ribcage.

"Stop it!" I yelped, giggling. "Stop!"

"Lips, precious," he ordered.

"No!" I challenged, trying to break free of his hold but doing a piss poor job of it due to my incessant giggling.

"Lips," he growled.

"O-okay," I answered, shivering. I turned my face to meet his insistent lips. The moan that fell from my mouth was unstoppable. Too soon, he pulled back, ending the kiss.

"You need to eat."

"Let's eat in the living room," I told him, grabbing the meal of split lentils with some type of garlic and onion sauce and a side of collard greens. Tyler had ordered Ethiopian for the second time that week. I'm certain that had to do with the fact that I'd practically been drooling over our previous meal from the same restaurant.

"You don't mind eating in the living room?" he questioned, standing over the couch with his food in his hand.

"No." I shrugged. "Don't tell me you've never eaten on the couch before." I patted the dark grey cushion of the couch for him to sit.

"Not growing up," he began, sitting next to me, his thigh brushing up against mine. "At least, not while my mother was around. She hated for us to eat in the living room, or anywhere near her furniture."

"So naturally, when she wasn't looking, you did," I stated as I took a forkful of collard greens.

"Naturally," he responded, winking at me.

My belly flip flopped.

"She's not a snob. My mother. She just knew we were careless and taught us to eat in the dining area. She once found two-week-old tuna in my brother Carter's room so she banned us from eating in our bedrooms."

"Another rule I'm sure you broke."

Tyler chuckled. "Try this." He held out a piece of the injera with cheese on it.

Instinctively, I opened my mouth to allow him to serve me the food. I closed my eyes and ran my tongue along the tip of his pointer finger as he slowly pulled it free from my mouth. A growling sound made deep in his throat is what caused me to open my eyes to see him staring at me hard.

I chewed slowly and licked my lips lustfully.

"After dinner," he warned.

"You're such a tease," I sighed. I slipped off the couch and crawled along the vibrant pink and purple area rug to move in between Tyler's legs. He dipped his head, planting a kiss in the spot where my shoulder and neck meet, eliciting another shiver.

We ate and talked about his day of practice. My stomach twisted when he reminded me the following day he would be on the road again for another away game. But I wouldn't whine about his job no matter how much I wanted him to stay here with me until we both grew sick of one another. If that were to ever happen. The way I was starting to feel, it never would.

"What're you thinking about?" His deep voice broke through my thoughts. He trailed a long finger back and forth over the line of my shoulder and collarbone.

I pushed out a breath and tilted my head back so it rested against his strong thigh. "How come you don't have any tattoos?"

He angled his head, surprised but not thrown by my question.

"It just seems odd. Most athletes I know have lots of tattoos. It's practically a rite of passage. But you have none. And trust me, I have looked over every inch of your body, more than once, and you don't have any. Why?"

"Every inch?"

"Ty," I laughed, nudging his knee with my head.

He laughed before taking the half empty plate of food from my hand and placing it carefully on my glass coffee table next to his.

"Because, precious. When you look this good no need to mess it up with shoddy artwork." His voice held a hint of laughter but he was also dead serious.

So fucking cocky.

"Are you serious?" I questioned, laughing.

"Would I lie about something as important as my looks?" he questioned, wiggling his eyebrows when I looked up at him.

I stood, turning to him and straddling his legs with my own. His hands went to my waist, holding me in place.

"No, I don't think you would."

"So, I never felt the need to." He shrugged. "My good looks needn't be marred by ink."

"You never felt the pressure to? Like, to be part of the team? I know my ex—" I clamped my mouth shut. *Stupid.*

"Your ex was an athlete ..." Tyler prodded.

I looked up at him, staring him in the eye, and the intent stare he was giving me reminded me of his words about what he might do to my ex once he found out what happened between us. I briefly wondered if he was capable of it. The gleam in his eye at that moment was telling me I didn't have to wonder.

"Yes," I finally answered. "Darryl Wright, a former NBA player. Anyway, he had gotten his first tattoo with his teammate on a dare his sophomore year."

"Weak minded," Tyler exhaled, sounding disgusted.

"But isn't that what teammates do to, like, bond, or whatever?"

"Some. I'm not one of the some. I do what I want because I want to not because someone will or won't think less of me."

I nodded, knowing he was telling the truth.

"Have you always been that way?"

"No choice but to be. It's how we were raised."

"We?"

"Townsends. My parents raised us all to be our own men. After Carter decided to basically give the middle finger to the family business, and join the army and later the Williamsport Fire Department, my father realized he'd done too good a job raising us to be individuals." He chuckled.

I smiled down at him while intertwining my fingers with his. "You definitely are your own man." I pressed a kiss to his lips just because. "Thanks for dinner."

"Don't thank me for feeding my woman. Now you want to tell me what had you so busy this week at work that had you forgetting to eat?"

I rolled my eyes, lifting my head to the ceiling again. "Are we back on that again?"

"Hell yes. New clients? Overbooked yourself? You need your own assistant?"

I giggled. "Yes, to all three." That was the truth. "But I kind of took on something that's a little out of the ordinary."

Tyler scrunched his face up, obviously not liking my tone.

"Don't get worried," I rushed to say. "It's just a new financial advisor I'm looking into."

"What, he's competition or something?"

I shook my head. "Nothing like that. He's just … off. I don't think he's to be trusted, and he works with people with a lot of money. He could be harmful to their financial well-being." I wouldn't give Tyler the full details since it was a teammate of his who'd first led me to Phillip Morris. But Tyler was sharp. He wasn't falling for my half-hearted answer.

"Harmful to their financial well-being. Meaning what exactly? You think he's stealing from them."

"I can't exactly say that, but—"

"You believe he's stealing from his clients," he said again.

"Yes."

"And you're involving yourself in this why?" His tone was hard, serious.

"Because it's my responsibility as a professional in this field. There are too many financial planners and advisors who are taking their clients for a walk. It's why I left the company I used to work for."

"I get all of that, and trust me when I say I find your passion for it sexy as fuck. But why the hell are *you* investigating this guy? Aren't there agencies or prosecutors who should be doing this?"

I sighed. "I'm not *investigating* really, just doing a little background research. Brenda has a friend at the SEC. I'm planning on calling Bren in the morning to talk with her about it. After that, it'll be out of my hands."

I tightened my fingers around Tyler's as they were still intertwined.

"You haven't gone to see him, have you? This financial advisor?"

"What?"

"You said you weren't investigating him. That means you've just been doing a little internet research, right? You haven't made any appointments with him?"

I swallowed and shook my head. "No," I lied.

His jaw ticked.

I leaned down, making a trail of kisses down his strong jawline.

"I haven't spent anything I've earned in the NFL."

I pulled back to stare down at him. "Really?"

He nodded. "Not a dime."

"Why?" It was a silly question. Tyler was born into a family that guaranteed a lifetime of never having to worry about money but I still found it interesting that he hadn't spent his NFL earnings.

"I invest it. To have something that I earned to pass down to my children and my wife, should I die first. They'll have the inheritance that comes with my last name, of course. But I wanted to give them something earned from my own blood, sweat, and hard work."

"Even what you earn from endorsements?" Tyler's NFL salary was already in the seven figures per year but that was a pittance of what he made from his various endorsements.

"Most of that is invested too."

"You've thought about having kids?"

He nodded. "Since earning my first paycheck. And a wife."

I was speechless. Didn't know what to say. Tyler was so different from my first impression of him. Beneath the seemingly reckless, don't give a shit exterior was a grown ass man who knew how to handle his business.

"You want to have children?"

My heart leapt into my throat. I went to answer but no words came out. I slowly nodded, unable speak to just how much I wanted to be a mother. I didn't have to when Tyler moved quickly, flipping us, so that I was on my back and he covered my body.

He moved his hand to something in the back pocket of his jeans. Out of my peripheral I saw something that looked like two tickets.

"What's that?"

"Tickets to the box seats of next week's home game. I got two in case you wanted to bring Resha or your mother. I can get another one if they both want to come."

My heart melted.

"Resha hates football and I doubt my mother would want to attend." While she still tried her best to remain active my mother shied away from going out amongst people she didn't know or larger crowds.

"Run it by them and see what they say."

Smiling, I pulled Tyler's head down until our lips connected. "Thank you."

"Show rather than tell," he retorted before sucking my lower lip into his mouth.

I did show my gratitude for his generosity for the remainder of the night.

* * *

"THANK YOU," I told the huge, bald man who towered in front of the door that led to the elevators up to the skybox section of Williamsport Arena, where the Cougars were playing. It was the following Sunday, and as planned, I was attending Tyler's home game for the first time. Unfortunately, I was alone since Resha had to make a last minute trip to Boston for work. And as I guessed, my mother wasn't up for an outing at a football game. I figured I would be fine, however. I loved football, and even without anyone to watch the game with I'd enjoy seeing it live from the view in the sky. I'd seen Tyler every night that week. In fact, he'd slept over every night the previous week. So much so, that his belongings had taken over one of the top drawers of my dresser. When I asked how come we never stayed at his place he shrugged and said he liked my place more.

I rotated my neck after stepping off the elevator, searching for the door that would lead to the box seats.

"I.D.," a deep voice sounded.

I looked up and up some more until my eyes collided with the dark gaze of another bald and extremely large man. His stern face, stature, and standing with his hands positioned in front of him shouted that he was more security.

"Sure," I answered, a little caught off guard. I realized security was tight in this section of the stadium but I'd already shown my I.D. and badge to the first security guard.

"Thank you, Ms. McDonald. You may pass." He stepped aside and I entered through the entrance into the luxury seating area, expecting to see a number of faces I didn't recognize, likely wheeling and dealing. That's what usually happened in these particular seating areas. Most times, half of the seat holders had no interest in the game down on the field, but in who they could rub shoulders with in the luxury seats. It was a world I happened to be very familiar with.

So when I entered the room and my eyes first collided with the scowling face of Aaron Townsend, I shouldn't have been too surprised. However, I'd specifically asked Tyler if his family members were going to be in attendance and he'd said they weren't.

Mother and Father are away. Aaron and Patience are too busy with the babies to attend a football game. Joshua is still celebrating his honeymoon, and Carter is likely working and Michelle isn't too interested in football.

He was wrong. Oh, so wrong.

My gaze shifted from Aaron's scowl to a surprised looking Joshua who stood next to him, arm in arm with a woman with big, curly, auburn hair.

"Hi!" a soft voice interrupted the silence.

I glanced down to see a boy with the same hazel eyes as Aaron, caramel skin, and curly dark hair staring up at me. My heart instantly melted.

"You're a friend of Uncle Ty's," he stated with assuredness.

"I-I am."

His smile was wide and my heart caught in my chest. I had to look away from him. Reluctantly, I looked back up at the man I presumed to be his father, *the* Aaron Townsend.

"Kyle, take your drink to the table," he ordered in a stern yet gentle voice. For some reason that voice surprised me. From what I'd read, heard, and seen of Aaron Townsend the man didn't have a gentle bone in his body. Of course, that was how outsiders described him. Whenever Tyler did, it was with an affection one held for their older brother.

"Well, come in."

I glanced over and sighed at the sight of a smiling older woman with bright blue eyes. Deborah Townsend. Tyler's mother.

"I'm sorry. I'm Destiny McDonald," I introduced at the same time she took me by the arm, walking us toward one of the circular wooden tables at the center of the room.

"I'm Deborah, and that's my husband, Robert." She tilted her head to a tall man with greying hair who was speaking to another man. As soon as she touched his arm, he turned dark eyes on her. I shouldn't have been shocked at how handsome Robert Townsend was in person. I'd certainly seen his pictures in business articles before. However, in person the magnetism that was even apparent in photos, was tenfold in person. And every one of his sons had inherited it. All of them.

Each one of the Townsend men was there with their significant others. I was able to put faces to the names Tyler had been telling me about for weeks. Joshua and his new wife, Kayla, Aaron and his wife, Patience, as well as their four children were all in attendance, along with their eldest brother, Carter, his wife, Michelle, and their sons, Diego and Samuel.

"How did you and Tyler meet?" Patience asked me as she bounced one of her fussy twins over her shoulder. We were standing at the bar in the box seating area. I swallowed the sip of my diet cola. I smiled at Patience who was approximately the same height as I was, at least she would've been but I had decided to where my favorite stiletto booties to go with the skinny black jeans and the Cougars jersey with the number seven, which was Tyler's number.

"I was hired by the team during this past summer's training camp to teach about financial planning. I'm a financial advisor."

Patience nodded as she rubbed the baby's back, her loose hanging sisterlocks swinging as she moved her head.

"That's interesting. Was it difficult working with the team?"

Raising my brows, I pondered the question. "Well, some of them did bristle at my presence initially, but most came around. A few of them have since taken me on to work with them directly."

"I'll bet Tyler was a handful from the beginning."

I turned to the female voice that'd interrupted and was greeted by Kayla.

My smile widened a little. "He wouldn't be Tyler if he wasn't," I answered, feeling comfortable with these women for some reason.

Both giggled in response.

"Game's starting!" one of the men called out.

The three of us headed toward one of the tables that gave us a window seat and a perfect view down onto the field. The Cougars with their home advantage took possession of the ball on offense first. My eyes zoomed in on Tyler's every move. I might try to kick his ass for not warning me his family was actually going to be there, but I couldn't not stare at him on the field. The way those tight uniform pants hugged his ass was to be admired.

"First down," I mumbled as the game started. I watched in earnest as Tyler scrambled, looking as if he were stumped on whether to pass or toss the ball. Soon, he did a fake pass to Leonard, causing a few tackles to chase him. Then Tyler stepped back and tossed an eleven yard pass to Kelvin who easily caught it before being tackled.

"Nice!" I called out, my adrenaline pumping. I watched intently as the Cougars worked steadily to gain yardage. "Third down," I mumbled, my heart pounding. On that run, Tyler did pass it to Leonard who ran the ball in for the first touchdown of the game. "Yes!" I cheered, standing up on my feet. I stopped, looking around and noticing the grins from the members of Tyler's family staring at me. I lowered my arms but turned back to the game, shrugging.

I was passionate about football and my man. The rest of the first half went well and The Cougars were up nine to six as both teams headed back to the lockers. For the first time, I realized I hadn't sat down since I first stood up.

"Anyone want something to eat?" Kayla called out as she stood.

"I'll go with you," I answered, moving closer to her to head over to the bar to order some food.

"You're a football fan?" she asked as we walked.

I nodded. "Since I was a little girl. Watched every Sunday with my father." I smiled at the memories.

"He was a Cougars fan?"

"Through and through. I'm pretty sure he bled black and blue," I giggled along with Kayla.

"I'll have the turkey salad sandwich with extra pickles, please," Kayla ordered. "Oh, and a roast beef sandwich minus the pickles. You know what, just add those pickles to my sandwich."

"You would've stolen them from my plate anyway."

I turned to see a grinning Joshua Townsend, green eyes sparkling as he eyed his wife.

Kayla shrugged. "You would've let me have them. I'm just saving you the trouble of giving them to me."

"You'll probably have half my sandwich, too."

"I *am* eating for two," she added nonchalantly, rubbing her belly.

My eyes bulged as I glanced down at her rounded stomach.

"We told everyone last week. Except for Ty, he was out of town," Kayla looked at me and stated.

"He'll be pissed to be the last one to know," Josh chuckled.

"I won't tell," I added quickly, thinking they slipped up by saying something about the baby in my presence.

"It's fine. We were planning on telling him after the game anyway," Kayla responded.

I smiled. "Congratulations," I stated, again glancing toward her stomach.

"Wings?"

The bartender caught my attention as he handed me the plate of wings and onion rings I'd ordered.

"Those smell delicious." Kayla practically drooled.

I held them toward her. "Please, have some."

"She would've swiped them from you anyway. Trust me, she's good for that." Joshua chuckled before placing a kiss to Kayla's forehead and sauntering off.

We both headed back to the table with our food.

"Andreas, shhh," Patience tried to console one of the twins.

I glanced around to see Aaron had stepped outside of the doorway to take a call.

"Do you need some help?" I asked Patience as I watched her struggle with both twins.

"Yes, please. They don't usually go to new people, but—" She didn't finish her sentence before she placed one of the twins in my arms.

I smiled down at the honey-toned baby whose eyes were at half-mast. "Poor guy. You're fighting sleep, huh?" I cooed. "Aww." I bounced him up and down and began humming a little. Soon he was nodding off.

"They usually don't like new people," Patience said low next to me. "I need to add you to the babysitting list," she joked.

Smiling, I gazed down upon the sleeping baby in my arms. Just then, Carter and Michelle's oldest son, Diego, passed in front of us as he played some game with Kyle.

"How old is he?"

"Nine," came Michelle's answer as she sat down in the seat to my right. "Going on twenty-five."

We all laughed. But soon enough I found myself staring at the children in awe, a heaviness settling over my heart. It took me back to the conversation I'd had with Tyler the previous week in which he'd told me about him saving his income to pass to his own family.

"I need to get something to drink."

"I got him." Aaron's voice sounded above me as he reached down, plucking his son from my arms.

I didn't have time to even ask where he'd come from. I was on my feet and heading to the bar before I gave it much thought. I didn't order anything—instead, just standing off to the side, trying to get my bearings underneath me. I wasn't usually this emotional but being surrounded by all these children and babies …

"I know that expression."

I looked up to find Tyler's mother standing only a few inches from me. Her eyes dipped to my hand that rested on my abdomen.

"I've worn that expression. The look of mourning only a mother could wear."

All of the air escaped my lungs. I clenched my teeth and shook my head. "I-I wasn't a mom. H-he wasn't even born yet," I stated, honestly not understanding what'd made me share this with this woman who was a practical stranger. Save for the fact, that she'd raised the man who I was sure I was falling in love with.

Deborah Townsend moved in front of me, taking my hands into hers. "You were." She nodded before pulling me into a warm hug. It was the type of hug I'd wanted to get from my own mother but I was more her comforter than the other way around for the last six years.

"I needed that," I stated, when she pulled back.

She took my chin in between her thumb and forefinger. "I know." She smiled. "Game's about to restart."

I inhaled and watched Deborah Townsend head back to where she had been sitting next to her husband during the first half of the game. I ordered a water with lemon from the bar and then resumed my previous seat to watch the Cougars beat the Broncos twenty-one to ten.

Tyler

"I really should kick your ass," Destiny growled at me as I strolled down the hall toward the elevator bank that led up to my penthouse condo.

"How're you going to do that when you're not even standing?" I questioned, nuzzling my face in the side of her neck, while I firmly held her in my arms.

"Put me down so I can. Why are you even carrying me? You just played a four hour game. And you got tackled pretty hard in that third quarter. That damn Nichols is a goddamn brute," she chided, angrily.

"Now you want to kick his ass?"

"Hell yeah, tackling my man like he didn't have any sense." She twisted her lips and rolled her eyes as I stepped onto the elevator.

"He was doing his job. Punch in five, four, three, eight," I told her. The code for the private elevator.

"Are you sore?" she questioned, looking me directly in my eyes, concerned.

A smile touched my lips. "Thirty seconds ago you wanted to kick my ass and now you're asking if I'm sore?"

"I still want to kick your ass for not telling me your family would be there but not if you're injured." She gave me a sly look.

I chuckled as the elevator doors spread open. At the same time, Destiny tightened her arms around my neck and leaned in, catching my earlobe between her teeth. A tingle moved down my spine.

"Little minx," I growled, squeezing her ass.

"Great game, baby," she whispered in my ear. "And congratulations. You're going to be an uncle again," she added.

I smiled. After the game, Joshua and Kayla had told me of their good news. I'd suspected as much for weeks but waited for them to tell me. Apparently, I was the last to know, even after Destiny.

"I love being an uncle," I responded as I moved through the huge living room space of my condo and into the bedroom. There I placed Destiny on the massive California king bed I had especially made for me.

"I don't even get a tour of your place my first time here?"

I shrugged. "Later." I went to cover her body with mine but she moved out of the way.

"No!" She stood up, looking down on me. "You need a warm bath so you won't be sore in the morning. Preferably in epsom salt. And are you hungry? When's the last time you ate?"

"I was planning on eating something," I growled while reaching for the button of her jeans.

"Stop that," she said, smacking my hands away. "Where's your epsom salt? No pro athlete lives in a home that doesn't carry epsom salt."

I grunted. "Under the bathroom sink."

"Great. I'll run a bath with the salt. Get undressed."

I wrinkled my forehead. "Since when do you give the orders?"

"Since always." She shrugged and moved into the bathroom. Seconds later I heard the water running.

I tilted my head to the side and sighed. "True." She was right. She'd run away with my heart from the first moment I laid eyes on her. I stood, removing the tie, button-up top, dress pants, and shoes I'd worn for the game. I left my suit jacket in my car. Completely unashamed, I strolled into the bathroom, coming up behind Destiny, placing my hands at her waist. She gasped when my cock bumped up against her ass.

I began kissing down one side of her neck before moving to the other side.

"You have no fucking clue how hot it is seeing you wear my name," I commented on the jersey she was still sporting.

"Nooo," she whined, pulling away, giggling. "You need to get in. The salt has melted."

I angled my head, staring down at her.

"Seriously, Tyler. You're pumped up on adrenaline and ..." her eyes dipped to my semi-erect cock, "sex hormones, but if you don't soak for a little while you will be feeling it in the morning."

I worked my jaw, knowing she was right and hating it.

"I'll give you a massage once you get in."

"Fine, but only if you're naked when you do it."

"Ty—"

"No ifs, ands, or buts ... well, only the butt that's covered by those jeans." Grinning, I winked at her.

"You're so corny," she laughed. "In."

I stepped in the freestanding, stone resin tub and let my body become completely submerged up to the midway point of my chest.

"Now, get naked," I growled.

"Wait." she stood back, holding a finger up.

I frowned.

"You need to eat. What do you have in your—" She didn't even finish her sentence before she was out the door, heading in the direction of the kitchen, I presumed.

I had half a mind to climb my ass out of the tub and drag her back in there with me, pulling the clothes from her body. But she was right, even after some icing and a quick shower after the game, I was already starting to feel the soreness in my muscles. I had opted not to get a massage by one of the trainers when I looked at my phone and realized my entire family had, in fact, shown up to the game. I knew Destiny was thinking I'd set her up but I hadn't.

Much to my relief, I exited the team's locker room and staging area where the reporters were to find my woman and my family getting on great. Their approval, though not necessary, still meant a great deal to me.

"I found one of those prepared meals. I have that same delivery service. Salmon and quinoa salad. I warmed it up in the microwave. Here." She shoved a forkful of salmon in my face.

I opened my mouth and grabbed her wrist at the same time. "Delicious. Now take your clothes off," I ordered after swallowing.

"You need to eat some more." She pulled her wrist free and pushed another forkful of food my way. I accepted it, because, once again, she was right. I was hungry after the game. She sat on the edge of the bath, feeding me until the meal was complete.

"Now ..." I started, tugging at the jersey she still wore. "This is sexy but it'll look better on my bathroom floor. Take. It. Off."

She giggled, standing. "So impatient. I should make you w— Okay!" she screeched when I moved to stand.

I settled back into the warm water of the bathtub only when she was fully nude. She moved behind me, climbing in.

"I want to see you."

"I promised you a massage." She let a few droplets of water fall from her fingers onto my shoulders and the back of my neck.

I moaned, dropping my head when her little hands began working the muscles of my arms and upper back.

"See? Told you, you were sore," she taunted when I flinched.

Reaching back, I squeezed her thigh. She kissed the back of my shoulder where it was a little tender from the tackle she'd mentioned earlier.

"What are you doing tomorrow after work?"

"Hmm, nothing."

"I'll pick you up at five, then I want to show you something."

"A surprise. I don't like surprises," she added.

"Too damn bad," I growled, turning my body so that I could grab her, and pulled her around to the front of my body. I had her straddle my hips, just right so that her pussy aligned with the tip of my cock. "Now, say yes," I urged, biting her earlobe.

"Mmm." She shivered in my arms, pressing her breasts to my chest.

Despite the cooling water, I was getting hot all over.

"Say it," I growled, squeezing the globes of her ass.

"Yesss," she hissed just before I slide her down the length of my cock.

"I-I wasn't f-finished with your m-massage," she insisted, her hips flexing.

"You're going to finish massaging my cock with this beautiful pussy of yours." I lifted my hips, pushing into her. Both of us let out a groan. Water sloshed over the sides of the bathtub as I pulled her hips down to meet mine again, over and over. I leaned down and took a chocolate-tipped nipple into my mouth, twirling my tongue around it.

Destiny's entire body began shaking and convulsing as she tossed her head back. Her hands went to grip the sides of the bathtub for leverage as I drilled into her from the bottom.

"Oh my god!" she screamed as her eyes popped open and she stared at the ceiling.

"Shit!" I cursed, having forgotten that the overhead mirror was even there. I'd had it installed when I first moved in but hadn't even used it with any other woman. "Goddamn," I cursed. Seeing our coupling from that angle was hot as fuck. "Keep looking, precious," I demanded, one hand going to pinch and tweak her nipples. Her hips began jumping wildly once I did that. My girl loved having her nipples played with during sex.

"That's it," I growled when she squeezed her inner muscles around my cock. "You like watching daddy fuck you?" I growled, staring down at her as she kept her eyes trained on the mirror above.

"Y-yess!" she hissed in between pants.

I lifted my hips, rotating them to hit the insides of her walls. Destiny rolled her hips against mine, panting heavily. When she began twitching I knew she was close. I lowered my thumb to draw circles around her clit at the same time I pulled one of her nipples into my mouth. Within seconds she was yelling my name as she came. That was the sweetest sound on earth

My release came so fast I didn't even have time to prepare. I felt the orgasm as tingles shot down my spine and legs, my cock twitching with its own release. I held Destiny to me until the last droplet of semen poured from me.

"I've been preparing all my life for you," I stated firmly once I caught my breath, staring into the eyes of the woman I was certain had been made for only me.

I took her lips in a kiss just so she could feel how serious I was.

CHAPTER 19

Tyler

"And you're still not telling me where we're going?" Destiny asked for the second time since I'd picked her up from work.

I glanced over at her. "You look beautiful, precious. Give me a kiss." I leaned across the tanned leather of the center console, beckoning a kiss.

"No," she pouted, turning her head. "But if you tell me where we're going I—"

"Kiss," I growled. A horn sounded behind me and I glanced in the rearview mirror before looking ahead to see the light had turned green.

"Tyler, go!"

"Not until you put your damn lips on mine. Fuck everybody behind us."

She inhaled sharply. "That's so selfish."

"I'm not the one that's holding everybody up, precious. Kiss," I beckoned again.

"You're a spoiled brat."

I grinned. "I know, right?" Another horn sounded behind us. I merely looked toward Destiny expectantly.

She sighed before throwing her hands in the air and turning to me so I could kiss her. Only once I pulled back from the kiss did I move my foot from the brake to the gas pedal.

"I should make you take me home." She tried to sound pissed.

"We are going home," I answered while signaling to make a right turn. I glanced over at her, noting the confused expression on her face before turning back to the road.

"How? This isn't the way to my place or yours."

"Not where we live now," I stated casually. "Just sit back and enjoy the ride. We'll be there in about ten minutes. Are you hungry?"

"I swear you're trying to make me gain weight. I couldn't possibly be hungry with the huge lunch you sent over today."

"Just making sure you ate."

To my surprise, she leaned against the console and placed a kiss to my cheek. "Thanks for caring."

I lifted an eyebrow, noticing the sincerity in her voice. My grip tightened on the steering wheel. How could a woman as stunning, caring, and wonderful as this have never had a man properly cater to her before? At that point, I was certain her ex-husband deserved the ass beating I'd wanted to give him ever since I learned he even existed.

"Cedarwoods," she stated as we passed through the gates of the community where most of my family lived. "Isn't this where—"

"My brothers live? Yup," I answered.

Destiny gasped.

"Ouch!" I yelped after she punched me in the arm. It didn't hurt but I had to pretend like it did.

"Oh stop! That didn't hurt." She rolled her eyes in that cute ass way she often does when she's trying not to smile. "You're taking me to meet your family *again* without telling me."

I shook my head. "Not my entire family. Just Joshua. And this meeting isn't about them."

"It isn't?" She scrunched up her face.

"Nope," I answered before putting my car into park right outside one of what appeared to be a huge hole in a large piece of property.

"It's about us," I finished before getting out of the car and walking over to her side to hold the door open for her.

"Thank you," Destiny stated, slipping my hand in hers as I helped her out.

I admired the V-neck, light grey sweater she wore along with the black pencil skirt that hugged her body masterfully. Even in her four inch heels, the top of her head came to just the midway point of my chest.

"Now? How is this about us?" she questioned, appearing confused at the mount of dirt.

"This will be our home."

Her head jutted backwards before swinging upright to stare at me in surprise to my casual statement. "What?"

"Pretty sure I was speaking English. Do you like the community?" I questioned, looking around at the homes that lined the street. "Aaron and Patience live in that one over there." I pointed at the top of a home that was the next block over. "Carter and Michelle live right next door to them, although you can't see their house from this angle. Josh and Kayla's home is a few doors down to the left of Aaron's. I wanted to be close but at least a block away from my brothers."

"Tyler, what are you talking about? Why did you bring me here?"

"Damn, Ty, didn't even bother to tell your woman why you brought her all the way out here before we met?" Joshua chuckled behind me.

I turned to my brother, frowning. "You're late."

His eyebrow peaked. "Since when are *you* a stickler for time?"

"Since you kept my lady waiting." I reached out, instinctively, placing my arm around Destiny's waist.

Joshua nodded at Destiny. "Pleasure to see you again. And you have my brother running on time for once."

I felt Destiny stare up at me, though my eyes were narrowed in Josh's direction.

"Pleasure, as well, Joshua. And we're on time but apparently I'm the only one who has no idea what this meeting is about."

Josh simply laughed. "I'll let you tell it, Romeo."

"Fuck you," I growled before turning to Destiny, ignoring more laughter from my idiot brother. "Do you like this community?" I asked again.

"Ty—"

"Do you?"

She sighed, narrowing her gaze at me, and bit her bottom lip. I barely held back the groan that nearly spilled out, remembering when she did that exact lip bite the night before as her hips sank down onto my hard cock as she rode me.

"I mean, it's beautiful." She shrugged, glancing around. "And obviously safe. But," she waved her hands shaking her head, "why. Are. We. Here?" she insisted.

"I bought this property more than two years ago." I jutted my head in the direction of the two acre plot of land. "Like I said, I wanted to live close to my brothers and parents. They don't live in this community but are only ten minutes away. But it never felt quite right to build ... until now. With you."

Her mouth fell open.

I tightened my hand around hers, unaware that I had even been holding it but not shocked. It was rare that whenever we were in the same space some part of me wasn't touching her.

"You keep saying how you're rarely at a loss for words, but this isn't the first or second or third time you've come up with nothing to say," I stated, tugging her hand so she would face me again.

She blinked. "B-because you keep leaving me speechless. I-I ..."

"Sheesh, you just sprung this on her?"

I blinked, narrowing my gaze at my dipshit brother who I'd forgotten was still there.

"Any fucking way," I dismissed him and turned back to Destiny. "Let me show you the design I was looking at before you answer. Plans," I said to Joshua who wore a lopsided ass grin that I wanted to wipe off more than anything.

Still speechless, Destiny followed me toward Joshua as he laid the iPad he'd been carrying on the hood of my car to pull up the designs of a colonial, Spanish-style home that featured five bedrooms, a finished basement, sun room, upstairs playroom, four full bathrooms, and two half-baths, as well as a three car garage.

"It's huge," she finally breathed out after looking through the main designs of the house for a second time.

"Just over five thousand square feet. Not too big. Little brother didn't want to go too big," Josh added.

Destiny looked up at me. "That's one of the smaller designs?"

I nodded. "There're larger ones if you like. But I figured you'd like the Spanish colonial look the best. Do you?"

"Do I what?" she asked, still looking a little dumbfounded.

"Like it?"

She nodded. "I do. I love it."

"Come here." I took her by the hand toward the property. "Watch out for the dirt," I warned, not wanting her to get stuck in the dirt with her heels. "This is where the driveway would be that leads to the three car garage. The mudroom will be right there as you enter from the garage ..." I continued to point out where each of the rooms would be to help her visualize our future home.

"You're really good at painting a clear vision."

"He's always been that way. Also helped him on tests," Josh came up behind us, stating.

Destiny turned to him with a raised eyebrow.

"He didn't tell you? Our kid brother got a perfect score on his SATs. Damn near failed all his classes but managed to scrape by with perfect scores on all his tests. A real idiot savant this one is." Josh tapped me on the shoulder.

I moved to grab Josh by his collar just as he jumped backwards, laughing. At the same time Destiny's hand firmed around my forearm.

"He did tell me," she giggled, answering Josh. "He also told me how his older brothers couldn't wait to give him shit once he finally fell in love. Payback is a bitch in heels," she laughed.

I turned to her, my heart racing. She'd mentioned the L word.

"He—" She was cut off by my lips on hers. I needed to kiss her more than I needed my next breath. I took my time, savoring the kiss, but too soon she pulled back.

"A-are you asking me to move in with you? Is that what this is?"

I shook my head. "I'm *telling* you this is where we will make our home once it's completed."

"About a ten month build time," Josh yelled behind me.

Destiny stared at him over my shoulder then turned those brown, doe eyes back to me. "You're telling me?"

I nodded. "I am, precious. We'll have a lot of work to do between now and the time we can move in."

"You think?"

I chuckled.

"We haven't even talked about living together," she whispered, not wanting Joshua to overhear, I supposed.

"What's to talk about?"

Her eyes bulged. "Are you seri—" She stopped when Joshua's laughter behind me increased.

"He's a chip off the old block. You'll get used to it."

"Josh, if you don't take your stupid ass back home to your wife, I'm going to embarrass the shit out of you in front of my woman."

"Stop being so mean," Destiny chided, tugging my hand.

"No worries, Destiny. He's behaving nothing short of a Townsend. Ty, let me know of any changes you two come up with and we'll set up meetings to begin breaking ground."

I barely glanced Josh's way as he got in his car and headed back to his house, I presumed.

"You could have given me some type of warning or heads up or—"

"Are you hungry?"

She blinked and her shoulders slumped as she pushed out a breath. "Don't try to change the—"

"I'm not changing subjects. I just assume this is going to be a longer conversation and the least I can do is feed you while I convince you of the many reasons you're going to love living here." I slipped my hand around her waist and guided her back to my car as she ranted on why this wasn't a good idea, or that we should at least wait. I merely nodded every now and again, letting her have her say. In the end, I knew the end result. I was playing for keeps.

* * *

Destiny

"You don't even know my favorite color," I insisted, as I sat across from the lunch table, staring at Tyler. We were at the Williamsport Stadium. Tyler had practice and had asked me to join him for lunch since I was working from home that day. It'd been two weeks since he'd taken me to view his property and we were still going back and forth over whether or not we were ready to move in together.

"It's pink," Ty quickly responded around chewing and swallowing the turkey sandwich on rye bread he was eating. "You don't like people to know that because you don't want them to think you're too girly so you hide it in buying small things like headphones, your phone case, jewelry, or my favorite pink negligee you wore for me the other night."

"Ty!" I whisper-yelled, glancing around, hoping his teammates that were mingling about hadn't heard.

"What?" He looked up at me, genuinely confused.

For the life of me, I couldn't help the internal sigh that went off at the sight of those hazel-green eyes.

"Nothing," I murmured. "Besides, you bought that negligee for me," I reminded him, remembering myself when he'd had it delivered three weeks ago while he was on the road. I'd worn it for him while we FaceTimed that same night.

"I knew pink was your favorite color then and I figured the color would look hot as hell against your skin. I was fucking right," he added, sounding like he'd won the jackpot.

I lowered my head, smirking.

"I'm right, aren't I? Pink is your favorite color and you have no more reasons as to why we shouldn't live together once the house is built. Hell, we practically live together now."

I bit the inside of my lip. He was right. He was either always at my place or I at his, though we stayed at my place more frequently.

"You're not even halfway through your season. You should be focused on that right now."

"Trust me, precious, I can concentrate on more than one thing at a time. Especially, if one of those things is *you.*"

"That was some smooth shit."

I turned my head in the direction the voice had come from to see Leonard Riggs standing not too far from our table.

Tyler was on his feet and in Leonard's face before I could even register what was going on.

"Can I fucking help you?" he growled.

"Tyler," I said, standing up and looking around, hoping we weren't making a scene.

"Nah, I was just paying the star quarterback a compliment," Riggs stated, backing up while wearing a stupid grin. "My *agent* probably used to say the same—"

"Oh God!" I yelped when Tyler's hands clasped around the collar of Leonard's T-shirt. "Tyler, enough. It's not that serious. He's your teammate." I was talking fast, trying to drill some sense into Tyler before this thing escalated unnecessarily.

"Leonard, why don't you come have lunch with me," Kelvin Maynard insisted, showing up out of nowhere.

I watched as Kelvin eyed Tyler, both men silently communicating something between one another before Tyler released Leonard.

"You gonna get enough of putting—"

"Let's go." Kelvin hooked his arm around Leonard, practically dragging him off while Tyler stared as the two men left. Just as Tyler turned back to face me, I saw Riggs narrow his eyes on me, his face scowling as if I'd personally done something to displease him.

I shrugged him off. "Hey," I said to Ty, my hand making contact with his arm. "You okay?" I asked tentatively. It always stunned me how Tyler could go from affable to insanely intense to downright badass in the blink of an eye.

"Are you okay?"

I shrugged. "Of course. He doesn't bother me. I'm more worried about you. He's your teammate. I get you don't like him and you don't have ,to but you should do your best to get along with him."

"As long as he doesn't cause trouble for you, he and I can get along just fine." He bent low, summoning my lips for a kiss.

I stepped closer, wrapping my arm around his broad back, and tilted my head upwards. "He can't cause any problems for me."

Ty bent the rest of the way and our lips connected. He deepened the kiss as his tongue invaded mine. A light moan emanated from my throat.

"I have to go."

My eyes squeezed shut and I sealed my mouth shut against the groaning whine that wanted to break free. I was an adult. I could go a few damn hours being separated from my man.

"Enjoy the rest of practice. I'll make sure there's a hot bath waiting for you when you get home." The words slipped from my lips as if I'd said them hundreds of time before. When Tyler's eyes lit up like a Christmas tree I knew I'd just hammered yet another nail in the coffin of my 'it's too soon for us to live together' argument.

"You said it, not me."

I rolled my eyes. I had said it. "Bye," I responded, before grabbing my bag, jacket, and phone from the table and sauntering off.

Just as I rounded the corner to head to the parking lot my phone rang. "Hey, Bren."

"Destiny, sorry it's taken so long to get back to you. Will, my guy at the SEC, wants to meet with you for lunch this week to discuss this Phillip Morris character."

"Nice. You name the time and place and I'll be there."

I'd told Brenda all about my suspicions about Phillip Morris and his dubious investments. She, in turn, talked to her connect at the Securities and Exchange Commission, the agency that was responsible for investigating suspected crimes of this nature.

"So, he thinks this guy is full of shit, too?" I asked Brenda after she gave me the restaurant where she, Will, and I were going to meet.

"Not only does he think so, as it turns out, Phillip Morris has popped up on the SEC's radar before but they never were able to follow through with anything. I'll let Will tell you what he can, but I think you're onto something with this guy."

"I knew it. Thanks, Bren, for setting this up. I'll see you on Thursday for lunch."

"See you then."

I hung up the phone with Brenda, frowning. I really hated lowlifes like Phillip Morris who fed off the ignorance of people who were just searching for ways to best invest their hard-earned money.

"Still here? Looking for someone else to push up on once Townsend gets tired of you?"

I groaned inwardly before turning to see a scowling Leonard Riggs. I was so not in the mood for this fool.

"Look, Leonard, I don't know what your problem with me is—"

"My *problem* with—"

"Oh no," I held up my hand, cutting him off. "That certainly wasn't an invitation for you to tell me what your problem is. I really couldn't care less. Your problem with me is just that. *Your* problem, not mine. And I suggest you handle it as far from me as possible. Now ex—"

I was stopped from turning away from Leonard when he grabbed the top of my arm, squeezing it tightly. "Take your goddamn hand off me!" I growled, pushing at his chest with my free hand. He barely budged, and in fact, squeezed my arm tighter.

"It's bitches like you that run around from athlete to athlete looking for a good time and a come up that make me sick."

"Get off me!" I insisted again, that time punching his chest. He loosened his grip just enough that I was able to snatch my arm free. "I don't know what you think you know about me or what your *agent* has told you about me, but who I am and what I am is none of your damned business. Don't ever put your fucking hands on me again or you will get a taste of my pepper spray." I held up the canister of my pepper spray that was attached to my keychain.

For the first time since the beginning of this little exchange, Leonard acted like he had a brain in his head and took a step back.

He tutted. "You ain't worth it."

I rolled my eyes, knowing he wanted to elicit some sort of response from me. I wouldn't give him one. My self-worth didn't rest in the eyes of any man, let alone Leonard fucking Riggs. He could think what he wanted.

I moved back, turning to head in the direction of my car. I had more important things to worry about.

CHAPTER 20

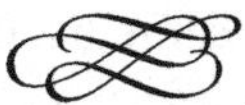

Tyler

"What's on the 'my man orders too much food for just two people' menu tonight?" Destiny joked, grinning as she opened the door of her condo for me.

My gaze traveled down the beige off-the-shoulder sweater she wore with a pair of black leggings. I even noticed the shiny plum color nail polish that adorned her feet and matched the color of her fingernails. I never liked dark polish on a woman before—hell, I barely even noticed that type of shit before—but with her all of my senses were heightened.

"Greek," I answered, holding up the bag containing the cartons of greek salad, chicken and pork gyros, and baklava for dessert.

Destiny groaned, tilting her head to the ceiling. My body went rigid. I loved when she did that.

"So many carbs," she whined, stepping aside and allowing me to pass.

I headed directly to the couch instead of the dining area. We usually ate in the less formal living room area, with Destiny sandwiched between my legs.

"What do you care about carbs?" I questioned, pulling cartons out of the bag and placing them on the coffee table.

"Easy for you to say, Mr. I play sports for a living so it's nothing for me to burn off excess calories."

I chuckled as I slipped my jacket off, handing it to Destiny for her to put on the coat rack next to the door. I took one of the plates she'd set out and placed some of the salad and her chicken gyro on the plate, handing it to her as she came back over. She took it and waited for me to fix my own plate and sit on the floor in front of the couch before she stepped between my legs and lowered herself to sit. It'd become such a natural practice for us that neither one of us thought twice about it.

"Tell me about the rest of your day," I inquired as we ate.

She began telling me about speaking with Brenda and how they were meeting with this guy from the SEC to share their impressions of this financial advisor, Destiny thought wasn't on the up and up.

"And you're just meeting with him, right? Passing along some information. That's it?" I asked, still not liking her involvement in this shit. I understood her desire to report on the activity of a professional who wasn't living up to ethical or even legal standards of their profession. What I *didn't* care for was the fact that to do so, it felt like my woman was possibly putting herself in harm's way. Call me paranoid, but taking a lesson from my brothers' experiences, the women in my family tended to run into people who weren't always the most savory of the bunch. And well, the men in my family, myself included, were well versed in breaking heads if it fucking came to it.

"Yes. That's it. I'm just going to give him the information I know and be done with it. Phillip Morris won't even know it was me who blew the whistle."

I raised an eyebrow to Destiny as she turned in my lap, sitting back on her knees. She may not have known it but she was sitting in the perfectly submissive position. When her eyelids closed, covering her irises from my line of sight, and she slightly lowered her head, demurely, I started to believe she knew exactly what she was doing.

My eyes dipped to her bared, mahogany shoulder, more skin being revealed as she reached up, taking my plate from my hands, causing the sweater to shift.

"I promised you a hot bath. Are you sore from practice?"

She was so good at changing the subject. But I was better.

"Oh!" She yelped when I swiftly reached down, cupping the globes of her ass and pressing her body toward me.

"We'll change the subject for now. But no way in hell will I forget where we left off, little minx," I stated with a warning in my tone just before sucking her left earlobe in my mouth.

"Hmmm," she hummed, her lips against mine.

I squeezed her ass again before moving my hands up her back and then to the tops of her arms, tightening my hold just enough to pull her closer to me.

Destiny pulled back slightly, flinching.

I stiffened, noticing the pained expression on her face that she quickly tried to mask.

"What was that?" I knew I hadn't held her tight enough to cause any real pain.

"Nothing." She shook her head, and I knew she was lying.

I cupped her chin in my hand. "What the hell was that?" I asked again, my voice low and deep.

"It's nothing. Just a minor bruise on my arm."

I pulled down the side of her sweater over her shoulder and noticed a dark purple looking bruise running around the width of her arm.

Everything inside of my body stilled. "Is that a handprint?" Even I hadn't ever heard the tone my voice had taken on.

"It's fine." She pulled back, covering her arm with her sweater again.

"Who did it?"

"Tyler, it's nothing. Don't—"

"Who. Did. It?" I knew it wasn't me. The bruise hadn't been there that morning.

Sighing, Destiny tried to stand. She was halted by my hands at her hips. "Do you really want to make me have to find out myself?"

"It's nothing. Leonard and I had a lit—"

"Riggs? Leonard fucking Riggs?" Before his full name was out of my mouth, I was on my feet, keys in hand.

"Tyler, where're you going?" Destiny demanded behind me.

When I didn't answer she ran ahead, pressing her hand against the door, trying to prevent me from opening it. The only thing I saw was red.

"I'll be back," was all I said, placing a kiss to the top of her head and lifting her off her feet and out of the way of the door.

I slammed her door shut behind me and moved in the direction of the stairs, lacking patience to wait for the elevator. I didn't even think as I pushed through the door of the parking garage that was attached to Destiny's building. I piled into my Cayenne, and for the first time in a long time was grateful to have all of the horsepower of a Porsche under the fucking hood.

I knew exactly where Riggs lived and that was the first place I pointed my car in the direction. Over and over as I drove the knowledge that Riggs had dared to put his fucking hands on Destiny served to press my foot harder against the gas pedal. Ironically, Riggs' stupid ass lived in the same Cedarwoods community that my brothers—and soon I would—live, though he lived four blocks over. The previous season he'd thrown a number of parties at his place. I'd attended one of them out of the spirit of team unity and all that bullshit. But tonight, was a different story entirely.

I threw my car in park and didn't even bother to take the keys out of the ignition as I jumped out of the car. Seeing the lights on and figures moving behind the glossy window panes of the large, wooden door, I began pounding on it with my open fist. I don't know how long it took but eventually Marco, one of our second string guys, opened the door.

"Ty, hey. You—"

"Where the fuck is Riggs?" I demanded, pushing Marco aside with my arm. My eyes darted around the entryway of the house before I looked up the top of the double staircase and saw Riggs standing there grinning with his eyes planted on one of the two women he had his arms wrapped around. Just then his dumbass looked down and saw me.

"Silver spoon! You decided to join us!" he cheered as if this were a friendly gathering of the minds.

It took me less than a half a dozen steps before I was up the stairs, reaching over one of the women, I hadn't bothered to look at, and grabbing Riggs by the T-shirt he wore.

"I fucking told you about leaving alone what's mine, right?"

The first blow to Riggs' jaw caught him by surprise. It was my right hook that did the initial real damage.

"The fuck?!" Riggs cursed while ducking my next left jab.

I didn't let that deter me as I sent a blow to his ribcage. I ignored the screams and the shouts of the women and the people, likely many of which were our teammates, around us.

"I knew you were fucking stupid as hell but I didn't realize you had a death wish!" I yelled at the same time another one of my fists hurled Riggs' way. He dodged that one and I stumbled just enough for him to land a fist in my ribcage. I felt the hit but no pain. In fact, it served to make me angrier. I blocked his next blow and another one of my fists made direct contact with his abdomen.

I made an effort to advance forward, only to feel two pairs of arms holding me back.

"Get the fuck off of me!" I yelled to whoever thought it was their fucking civic duty to break this shit up. They could get some of what I planned on giving Riggs, as well.

"Tyler, calm down. He's on our team, man."

"Fuck off me, Marco!"

"All this over some used up pussy?" Riggs had the audacity to yell even with the bloody lip he was holding.

His comment enraged me more.

"The only used up pussy you better be referring to is the one you came out of, you piece of shit."

Riggs's eyes doubled in size with anger. I knew that comment would get to him and he began charging me. I broke free of Marco and whoever else was holding me, and ducked the wild fist Leonard sent my way. I countered with another hook to his ribs, sending him stumbling to the ground.

"Get off of him!" came shouts behind me, both male and female.

Before I could really end Riggs the way I wanted to, I was being pulled off, this time by more than two pairs of hands.

"Tyler, calm down!" one of our defensive linemen shouted.

Four bodies now stood in between Riggs and I.

"Fuck you and that bitch!" he shouted from behind them.

"Tyler, no!" everyone shouted as I charged him again. Words were inefficient for expressing how much I wanted to rip his fucking head off.

"Let's go," someone said as they pulled Riggs farther down the long hallway.

I squinted, looking toward one of the women that was next to him, helping him as he limped along.

"Hey! Hey!" shouted our teammates as I bulldozed past them, grabbing the woman by the arm and spinning her around to face me.

"Let go of me!" she bellowed.

My hand immediately dropped from her body as I recognized the same woman that'd woken me up in the middle of the night nearly two months earlier in my hotel room. I looked to Riggs and went to charge him again.

"You set me up! What is she, a fucking hooker?" I charged, realizing that this same woman being in Riggs' house was no coincidence.

"I ain't no hooker!" she screamed, but I ignored her.

"Yeah, Charlene did me a little favor! You should be thanking me. I know she gives good head!" he yelled while being carried down the hall.

Again our teammates moved in between us, stopping me from being able to get to him. I snatched my arm free and spun around, ready to head down the stairs, only to be facing a familiar face. We'd never met in person but most people knew who Darryl Wright was. Unfortunately, I knew him as more than just an athlete, and although he stood there, saying nothing—and technically, I had no reason to be pissed at him—I had half a mind to deck him as well, just because.

I gave him the same scowling looking he was giving me. "Something you need to fucking get off your chest?" I questioned, fists tightening at my sides.

His jaw worked but he remained silent.

"Didn't think so."

I headed back down the same steps I ran up, taking two at a time. Thankfully for them, no one tried to stop me or got in between me and the door. When I reached my car, I pulled out my phone and dialed my coach's number.

"Tyler?" he answered, sounding confused.

"Just so you know, I'll gladly take this suspension and the fine. I'll even throw in another hundred thousand to donate to charity."

"Wha—" he asked, but I'd already hung up on him.

I was too charged up to explain, but I'd seen the cell phone cameras out by a number of people who were present. Hell, at this point, I wouldn't put it past Riggs to post this online himself. Within a few hours everyone would know how I tried to take his damn head off. My only regret was that I hadn't been successful, if I were being honest.

The only person whose opinion I cared for had called three times since I'd left her place. I knew she wouldn't be happy about how all of this went down, but those bruises on her arm ...

I shook my head.

No way in hell was I going to let that fly.

* * *

Destiny

"I cannot believe this," I growled, staring down into my phone, reading the latest gossip blog that was reporting on Tyler's suspension. More importantly, they were reporting on the reason behind his suspension. A video, in which you can clearly make out Tyler lunging and yelling at Leonard Riggs, proceeded the all-out brawl in Riggs' home.

"Watching it again, huh?"

I jumped, startled, and turned to look over my shoulder as Brenda stared down at the screen of the phone in my hand.

"I can't believe him." I shook my head and sighed.

"Believe it. Proof's right there." She tilted her head in the direction of the phone. "Rumor has it, that display was over you." She raised a brunette eyebrow at me.

I closed my eyes before peeling them back open. While the video footage was out, there were many rumors swirling as to why Tyler and Leonard got into a fight. Some blogs were reporting that Tyler was pissed that Riggs wasn't showing up to practice on time and possibly dragging the team down. Others stated it was over an incident that happened at practice. One blog even mentioned that the woman who had snuck into bed with Tyler months prior was now with Leonard and that's what caused the fight. I'd grown irrationally pissed when I saw that particular blog.

"You don't listen to rumors, Brenda."

She grinned. "So, I lied." She tossed up her hands, shrugging with a grin on her face. "My gut tells me it was over you. You want to tell me I'm wrong?"

"You're wrong."

"And you're a liar."

I laughed out loud at her accuracy.

"Whatever his reasoning, I'm sure Tyler had a legitimate excuse. Anyway, let's get down to why we're here, shall we?"

"Please," I answered. We were at the Portuguese restaurant where I'd met Brenda and the rest of the team at the end of their training camp. It was also the night of the first time Tyler and I kissed, so this place held a special place in my heart. Even though I was still pissed at him, I couldn't help but smile at the memory.

"Will called me and said he's running a little late but he's on his way."

"Good," I replied as we settled into our table that sat right next to the window looking out into the parking lot. We would know exactly when Will arrived.

We ordered our drinks—a seltzer water with lemon for me, and a diet cola for Brenda—before we began talking about the issue at hand. I went over again with Brenda why I didn't trust this Phillip Morris, finally confessing to her that I'd gone to meet with him in person under a fake name. Brenda was just about to let me have it when she noticed Will pull up.

"After this meeting, I'm going to kick your butt," she stated low enough for me to hear as Will approached our table.

We stood as Brenda made the introductions. Will towered over both Brenda and I by at least a foot. As it turns out, they'd known each other since college, when Will and Mike played football together.

"So, Ms. McDonald, tell me what you've got."

"Destiny, please."

He nodded.

I pulled the information I'd gathered about Phillip Morris from my briefcase and explained it all as I handed each piece of paper to Will. I hesitated, but eventually told him about my meeting Phillip in person and how that had confirmed my suspicions.

"He's stealing from these clients. I know it," I added, summarizing my argument.

Will's serious looking face was still turned downward, perusing the forms I'd presented him with. His salt and pepper eyebrows were bunched together as he read the papers Phillip had given me when I went into his office impersonating the part of the wealthy widow.

"Have you had any contact with Mr. Morris since that meeting?"

I nodded. "He's called me once to follow up but I haven't met with him since."

"Would you be open to meeting with him again?"

My eyes widened in surprise. I hadn't been expecting that one at all. "Uh, well ..." I looked to Brenda.

"Will, she can't do that. Don't you have your own investigators or whatever?"

Will nodded. "We do. But, Destiny, you've already made contact with him. If you were to follow up with a few meetings we could gather information much more quickly, and if he's doing what these files suggest he's doing, we can form an actual investigation much more quickly with your help."

Sitting back in my chair, I stared down at my half-eaten lunch of broiled salmon with steamed vegetables. I used the fork to move the food around the plate as I thought about it.

"What would it entail?"

"A few meetings spread out over a few weeks. Just to get enough information that we could decipher the ins and outs of his business. We won't need much of your time."

I turned to Brenda.

"Will, there isn't another way?"

"There is but it would take longer. And in the meantime, Mr. Morris is meeting with clients everyday who are basically just throwing their money at him."

I sighed. "Okay. You tell me what we need to do. I'm in."

"Destiny, are you sure? You don't have to do this. You've done enough."

"I know, Bren. But you know me. Once I start something I have to see it through. If Will and the SEC need more information, then that's what I'll get for them."

"Stubborn," Brenda tutted, causing me to smile.

I was glad when she didn't try to talk me out of it. Now all I had to do was not tell Tyler about my decision. Out of everyone, he would be the least pleased with it.

CHAPTER 21

Destiny

"I seriously need my own assistant," I groaned as I slumped against the leather chair in my office. After my lunch with Brenda and Will, I'd had three back-to-back meetings with clients, and a potential client who'd dropped in, fifteen minutes before five o'clock. I'd just finished up with that meeting and noticed it was getting close to six p.m. I didn't even dare to look at my phone, knowing I'd see messages and likely a missed call or two from Tyler asking where the hell I was.

"Long day?"

I startled and sat up in my chair, turning toward the deep voice that'd asked the question. My stomach dropped when I saw my ex-husband's tall form taking up space in my doorway.

"What're you doing here?" I demanded.

"You're not that hard to find, Destiny," he answered, moving into my office as if he were invited. "Especially, when you have men fighting over you."

I shook my head. "Nope. This conversation is over before it even started. Please, leave."

Darryl's head jutted back as if he were appalled. "You can stop by my office but I can't return the favor?"

"I made an appointment with your office. You knew I was coming and had ample opportunity and time to refuse said meeting. This little drop-in of yours is not the same thing, because trust me, if you had called and requested a meeting, it would have been denied. Leave."

"Jesus, Destiny. Are you still this upset? It's been seven years. We were married for eight years, together for ten. We can't even have a civilized conversation?"

"Darryl, you and I have nothing to talk about."

"Oh no? How about what's going on between you and Tyler Townsend?"

"I *know* that's none of your fucking business."

My heart began pounding at the sound of Tyler's tight voice from my doorway. I inhaled sharply when I turned to see him standing there, fists clenched tightly at his sides, handsome face scowling as he eyed Darryl.

Oh shit.

We seriously did not need a repeat of what'd happened earlier in the week.

"It's time for you to go," I sternly told Darryl.

"It's been fucking time … like after the first time she asked you to leave."

Damn. How long had he been standing there?

When Tyler moved in Darryl's direction, I nearly leapt from behind my desk to move in front of him, pressing my hand against Tyler's abdomen as if that would've stopped him if he really wanted to beat Darryl's ass.

"Leave. Now." I managed to keep my voice controlled, not wanting to raise it and have others who might still be in the office overhear.

Darryl eyed Tyler for a few heartbeats before glancing my way and shaking his head as he moved toward the door. I tugged Tyler by the arm, pulling him toward me to grant Darryl enough space to move past and exit. When he did, I shut my door behind him, closing Tyler and I inside.

"You are just determined to get into more trouble, aren't you?" I folded my arms across my chest.

Tyler shrugged. "I'm not afraid of a little trouble."

"I've noticed. Don't touch me." I swatted his reaching hand away from me. "I'm still pissed at you for getting your ass suspended for two games. And what are you doing here?"

"I called to see where you were. I wanted to know how your lunch meeting went today."

"It went fine," I stated looking over the papers on my desk.

"Fine as in the SEC is taking over this shit and you're done with it?" he asked, lifting my head by my chin to face him.

"Yes. The SEC is taking over looking into Phillip Morris."

He nodded.

"I had a few meetings that ran over and a drop-in. That's why I'm still here and didn't get a chance to call you. Then Darryl showed up."

"He was there."

I wrinkled my forehead. "Where?"

"The other night at Leonard's."

I nodded. "He's Leonard's agent."

Tyler scoffed. "Figures. He regularly shows up like that?"

"No, not at all. I've barely seen him in the last seven years."

"Barely?"

I flinched, wishing that hadn't slipped out. "Look," I started, knowing he was wasn't going to like what I was about to say, "the financial advisor I told you about? Well, it turns out he was working with Darryl, or at least, Darryl was pointing his athletes in his direction. So, to get Phillip Morris' information I made an appointment with Darryl. That was weeks ago and I haven't heard from nor seen him since. Until tonight."

"Until tonight," Tyler stated cautiously.

I shrugged. "Probably all of the stuff with you and Leonard …" I waved my hands in front of my face, dismissing the entire issue. "He's not important. What *is* important is that I'm starving and want to go home."

"Yeah, about that …"

I gave Tyler a funny look.

"How would you feel about not going home?"

"Hmm?"

"Instead, I want you to come away with me for a few days."

"Away? Where?"

He shrugged. "Anywhere you want."

"Tyler, that doesn't make any se—"

"I'm suspended for two games. No practice until next week. We can make it a long weekend. You can move any appointments around, right?"

"Yeah, but … You don't even have a destination in mind. We don't have anything packed. I'm sure you'll get in trouble for just up and leaving even with your suspension. Plus, how? We'd need to book tickets somewhere and—"

"Belize and Roatan Island. Those are our destinations. We'll get there by boat."

"Boat?"

Tyler shrugged. "Yacht, actually. My family owns a yacht. We, mostly my parents, use it for personal time. Vacations. You can teach me to scuba dive."

"I'm not certified to teach. Just to dive."

Another shrug as he stepped closer, his arm going around my waist. "Then we'll get an instructor for me and we'll dive together. Roatan has the best diving around, right?"

I nodded. "Yes, but …" I hesitated. It all sounded crazy, but the gleam in Tyler's eyes as he stared down into mine, kept me from saying no.

A slow smile crept across his face as if he just knew he'd won. "Your bags are already packed. We leave in an hour."

I sputtered. "Y-you packed my bags? How? Why? You didn't know I'd agree to this impromptu vacation."

"I knew," was all he said before pressing a kiss to my lips.

"Don't touch me." I pulled back from the kiss. "I'm still pissed at you for getting your ass suspended in the first place. You shouldn't be allowed to go on vacation. Like in school, if you get suspended for fighting, you don't get to go to Disneyland. You are made to stay home and write book reports and do chores all day. You're put on punishment." I knew I'd used the wrong word when that damn smile grew and that goddamn dimple came out to play, as if it was winking at me.

"You want to punish me?" He wiggled his eyebrows and I couldn't help the giggle that spilled from my lips.

"What clothes of mine did you pack?" I couldn't believe he'd gone in my closet to pack. Though, on second thought, I totally could believe it. Tyler practically lived at my place. Much of his belongings were at my condo and I'd given him a key weeks ago.

"Nothing. We don't need clothes."

"Tyler."

He chuckled. "A few bathing suits, dresses for going out at night, and shoes."

I sighed. "How do I know you packed all of the right stuff and that they match?"

"Whatever I forgot, we can pick up. Let's go. We need to meet the plane. The yacht's docked in Miami so we leave from there."

I couldn't believe I was doing this. "Wait, my laptop—"

"Is in the bag although you won't be getting much work done," he answered, tugging on my arm.

I had no choice but to follow his lead. It'd been a long time since I'd acted so spontaneously, least of all, with a man. For six years I'd guarded my heart just enough that I could date and enjoy a man's company but never fall for them. Not like I'd fallen in the past. Yet, in the blink of an eye, not only had Tyler Townsend caused me to trip and fall, but to completely wipe out. I closed my eyes, as he pulled me by the arm toward my office door. I made a silent wish that he was there to catch me when I landed, because I was certain I couldn't stop myself from tumbling even if I'd wanted to.

CHAPTER 22

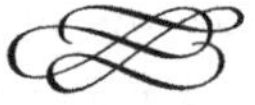

Tyler

"Is there anything else I can get you, Mr. and Mrs. Townsend?" the flight attendant on our chartered plane questioned, leaning over as she smile brightly at Destiny and I.

"Oh, we're not—"

"We're fine. Thank you." I nodded, dismissing the flight attendant.

Destiny turned to stare at me, eyebrows wrinkled. I knew what she was about to ask so I cut her off at the pass.

"You're going to be too hot in the sweater you are wearing where we're going. You should take it off." I nodded at the black turtleneck sweat she adorned.

"Get naked right here?" she questioned, eyebrow quirked.

Grinning, I held out my hands. "If that's what you'd like, I sure as hell won't stop you."

She rolled her eyes.

"Or you could just use one of the private bathrooms. But again, I'm not opposed to you changing right here out in the open."

"I'm fine in my clothes."

"That, we can agree on. But you'd be more fine if you were over here." I patted my lap.

Destiny glanced around, I assumed looking for Rachel, the flight attendant who was catering to our needs while we were on board. She'd just taken the cups and plates from the dinner that'd we'd been served not long after takeoff. I had made sure to have dinner on the flight since I knew Destiny hadn't eaten before we left.

No longer accepting the distance between us, although she sat less than three feet away from me, I undid my seatbelt, folded up the table that sat between us, and moved to undo Destiny's seatbelt. She gave little resistance when I picked her up, so that her legs wrapped around my waist, and then sat down so that she was now sitting atop my lap, facing me.

"That's better," I growled, my face nuzzling her neck. I inhaled some type of floral scent mixed with her own natural essence, and I couldn't get enough of it as her arms closed in around my shoulders.

"Are you sure you know what you're doing?"

I pulled back and stared up at her as she bit her bottom lip.

"I always know what I'm doing. Even when I don't."

"You better," she responded, just above a whisper.

I pressed my back against the leather seat of the plane, bringing her upper body closer to me. Her head lowered until our foreheads touched.

"Talk to me," I encouraged.

"I haven't seen him in months … years before that," she began.

My jaw tightened ever so slightly, knowing she was talking about her ex-husband. A man I hated for the simple fact that at one point in time in her life, he'd had her heart.

"We met my freshman year at UCLA. He was a sophomore. It was … typical. I was a cheerleader, he was the star of the basketball team. We didn't have practices together or anything, so the first time we actually met was at a home game. He crashed into me, literally. We were sitting on the sidelines, waiting for our turn to perform at half-time, and he got fouled really hard. He tripped and came barreling down on top of me …" She paused, shaking her head. "After that, he pursued me, relentlessly. But I tried to keep my distance. I just knew he'd break my heart."

She sighed before continuing.

"Eventually, he wore me down and before spring of my freshman year we were known around campus as the 'it' couple. At the end of my junior year, he made the decision to sign up for the draft. And the night before, he proposed. I said yes. And by the time he played his first NBA game, we were married.

"I still had to finish my senior year of college but I tried hard to be the best wife. I chose to give up my career ambitions initially because he said he needed me to be at home, there for him when he wasn't working. I did. I joined all of the basketball wife organizations, joined all types of philanthropic engagements, but mostly I was there for him. I learned the best massages to give when he was sore, to cook the foods he liked, listen when he had problems. I did it all, or so I thought."

Stopping, she looked down into my eyes.

"Seven years into our marriage I decided it was time to start a family. I was mostly tired of being alone in the big ass house he bought, when he was on the road. The social clubs and foundations and whatnot were no longer fulfilling. I wanted to be a mom. So we tried. Not long after I got pregnant. I was so happy. I planned everything out. His room, where he'd go to school, everything I could think of. It was a boy. But when I was six months pregnant, something went wrong. I began bleeding. Darryl wasn't home so I called Resha. She came over and saw how much I was bleeding and called 911. I was rushed to the hospital but it was too late. By the time the baby was born h-he ... didn't make it."

Destiny inhaled deeply, her eyes watered, and her hands clasped tightly around my shoulders. Holding onto me for strength.

"That wasn't even the worst part. The worst of it was when the doctor told me the reason I'd gone into early labor was because I'd contracted a sexually transmitted infection. Syphilis. In some cases it can cause premature birth of a baby which can lead to death. My husband had been the only person I'd been with sexually for over ten years at that point. But obviously, I hadn't been his only person."

She shook her head before lowering it to my shoulder, hugging me tightly.

I rubbed my hands up and down her back, carefully. I fought the rage that threatened to bubble up inside of me. I loathed men who betrayed their family. My father taught me there is no deeper betrayal than hurting your family. To top it off, this was the woman I loved, and despite the fact I hadn't known her all those years ago, it obviously still affected her now. That alone was reason to call for Darryl Wright's head on a platter.

"You want me to kill him?" My voice was tight but controlled.

Destiny pulled back, her eyes searching mine. I found myself surprised when a small smile found its way to her lips. She shook her head.

"That won't be necessary. As hard as it was, I forgave Darryl."

I wrinkled my forehead, confused. "Forgave?"

She nodded. "Yes. I hated him for a long time after that. I divorced him and refused to take anything from him just because I knew it'd hurt him more. I only ended up shooting myself in the foot. My divorce lawyer went on and on about how much of his wealth I was entitled to. But it felt like blood money. The thought of having anything of his made me sick. But a year and a half after our divorce I picked up a newspaper and saw an image of him smiling as he held the hand of his new fiancée. She was five months pregnant with their son. That was the moment I knew I needed to let my hatred go. It was killing me, not him. So, I started seeing a grief counselor. With the money I'd saved from working, I booked my first solo vacation to Italy where I got my scuba certification. A year later I started my own side business that would eventually become my full-time job. Resha and I started our podcast and I began dating again. But most importantly, I prayed for him to find happiness. That was what one of my counselors suggested I do. Pray for all of the good things I wanted for myself for Darryl. It was hard but I did it. Slowly, my hatred melted into anger, which eventually dissolved into annoyance and then … nothing."

I sat back, staring, ponderingly. "Nothing?"

She shrugged. "Not nothing, totally, but mild annoyance at best. I don't hate him anymore."

I grinded my teeth together, hating the question I couldn't stop myself from asking. "Do you still have feelings for him?"

Destiny pulled back sharply, staring at me as if I were insane. I just might've been but I needed to know.

"Hell no. I just don't hate him anymore. I forgave for *me*, Tyler. Because my anger and bitterness was holding me back. I spent two years trying to think of ways I could get Darryl back for the pain he caused me, and what I found out was the best way to get him back, was to let him and the pain go. So I could live my best life. And if I hadn't I wouldn't have been free to ..."

"Free to what?"

"To fall in love with you."

I won't bother trying to describe whatever it was that flowed through me at hearing those words, because it was a feeling beyond any description I could muster. All I knew, was that the imaginary weight that'd fallen on my chest ever since I laid eyes on Destiny McDonald months earlier had lifted. I knew I was a goner that first moment—the weight was composed of the stress of waiting for her to come around to the same conclusion. And she had.

"I love you more than I ever knew was possible," I responded, my voice raspy, strangled by all the emotion bubbling through me. My hand was at the back of her head, pressing our lips together. I would've thought hearing her say those three words would've satisfied my hunger, but as we continued to kiss and take our fill of one another, I grew hungrier for more. More of her. More of this. More of us. Just more of everything.

* * *

Destiny

"Oh my God! What is this music?" Tyler questioned out loud, looking around the expansive interior space of the yacht. Seriously, calling this thing anything other than a mansion on water was an understatement.

The yacht, or the Supernova, as his parents named it, was over three hundred and fifty feet in length. Contained a large dining and living room space that housed all leather furniture. I loved how the interior had been decorated in woods and earth tones. The outer portions of the yacht boasted a whirlpool and jacuzzi, a helipad because you never know when someone needs to drop in from their helicopter, and three spacious bedrooms and bathrooms, throughout the first and second decks of the yacht.

"What do you have against Coldplay?" I demanded.

He grunted. "No wonder Resha calls this your *white boy music*."

I giggled. We had been on the yacht for less than a half an hour and I'd set up my Spotify playlist to play throughout the yacht's speaker system. Apparently, Tyler wasn't a huge fan of the Coldplay, Five for Fighting, or the Train songs that had played thus far. I suddenly regretted telling him how Resha constantly got on me about my supposed love affair of pop and soft-rock from the early two thousands.

"Fine, I'll play something just for you." I bounced over to the granite bar where my phone rested, picking it up and changing the song to bring up something a little more recent that Tyler just might appreciate.

"A little Kanye West?" he had the nerve to ask.

I squinted at him as I peered over my shoulder. "We do *not* acknowledge that man as long as he insists on supporting the current executive administration." I sucked my teeth and rolled my eyes.

Tyler chuckled. "I can agree there. Hell, Jay-Z then."

"Nope." I placed my phone down as Maroon Five's "Girl Like You" began playing. "Sound familiar?"

Tyler's face scrunched up as he stood from the low sitting armchair but, as if a lightbulb went off in his head, his eyes narrowed at me. He remembered.

I began swaying my hips, throwing my arms in the air, moving to the rhythm of the music.

"This is the first song you danced to for me."

I laughed, "Excuse you? I wasn't dancing for *you* at that lounge."

"Oh, precious. You may not have known it but you were dancing for me."

Dammit.

He always got me. I stumbled, my heartbeat erratic at hearing the deepening of his voice. But, his arms were right there, catching me.

"I told you, you'd be uncomfortable in this shirt." He tugged at the bottom of my sweater before he pulled it up and over my head, leaving me in the lace bra I wore underneath and the pencil skirt, nude tights, and brown booties I'd worn to work.

"I was perfectly comfortable in my shirt."

"Yeah? Let's see how comfortable you can get butt ass naked on this boat," he growled before dipping his head and sucking my earlobe into his mouth.

I giggled but looked around over his shoulder. "What about the staff? Should we take this to the bedroom?" There was a staff of about fifteen on the yacht just for us, and that didn't include the captain and co-captain.

"They know not to come in here unless called."

"Mmm," I moaned when his tongue trailed along the pulsing vein in my neck. "Are you sure?"

"Tell me you love me again," he demanded.

I gasped when he picked me up, my legs instantly wrapping around his body. "I love you."

"How much?" His hand went to the zipper at the back of my skirt and began sliding it down.

I swallowed. "A lot."

"Enough to make it permanent?"

My eyes widened. Tyler stared, searching my gaze for something.

"What do you m—" My question was cut off when he fused our lips together as he carried me somewhere in the room. I couldn't see where we were headed as my eyes had sealed shut against the pleasure that rolled through my body from his touch and kiss.

I did, however, feel the hard wood of the dining table when Tyler placed me down on it once he'd pulled my skirt down around my thighs. His previous question escaped my memory between his kisses and the hand he moved down my abdomen to reach the top of my dark lace panties.

"Tyler!" I yelled when I heard the ripping of my undergarment.

"Told you, you wouldn't need clothes. You chose to wear them anyway," he retorted before pushing against my belly, laying my back against the table.

I couldn't pretend I was upset about the underwear. They weren't even my favorite pair. Hell, if they had been, when Tyler discarded the rest of my clothing, and hoisted my thighs up over his shoulders and leaned down to run his tongue along my outer lips, I wouldn't have given a damn then either.

"Mmm," I breathed out, rolling my head from one side to another on the table. My hips lifted slightly when Tyler's hot tongue found my throbbing clit. "Tyler," I sighed his name on a plea, begging for more.

The man was nothing if not a deliverer of dreams. He used his two fingers to separate my labia and to give his tongue space to do what it wanted to my pulsing button. I wiggled my hips, lifting them, searching for more. Tyler's free hand wrapped around my right thigh, essentially holding me in place as he had his way with me.

"Fuck!" I yelled out, pounding my fist against the table. The man was a crook. That's exactly what he was. It such a short amount of time he'd stolen my heart, my sanity, and my body, making it his. My body was his to pleasure. He didn't say it with words but his mouth was spelling it out all over my thirsting vagina.

"Tyler!" I yelled out his name as I came, my vaginal walls squeezing, searching for something to milk.

Tyler aimed to please because before I could even catch my breath, he was sliding his thick rod into me. And just as quickly, another orgasm began to build deep inside of my body. I lifted my hands, reaching for his broad shoulders to hold onto. My hand went to the back of his head, pulling him to me. Our lips met in a frenzy, our tongues tasting, licking, and slurping at one another as if we hadn't tasted anything this wonderful in years. Never had I ever hungered for someone as much as Tyler, and that was saying a lot. So much, that I had to squeeze my eyes shut against the gravity of my realization.

"I knew," he began saying, and grunting while he continued to pound into my body. "Since that first day in training camp …" he drilled into me relentlessly, "I knew you were mine." His teeth sunk into the flesh of my neck.

"Oooh," I whined, overcome by the mix of pain and pleasure.

Tyler interlocked his hands with mine, raising them over my head against the table. He went completely still, his eyes intent with that fire that was always present behind the mirth. "You can still be pissed at me over Riggs if you need to, but know this … another man will never hurt or put his hands on my woman without feeling any repercussions. That goes for Riggs, your ex, and any other fucker who wants to act as if he has a death wish. Riggs is lucky he only walked away with a busted lip and bloody nose."

"Ty-Ty—" I panted, unable to form anything near a coherent thought. I was on the verge of coming and he was talking about killing his damn teammate.

"Just making that clear for you," he stated before taking both of my wrists in one of his massive hands and moving the other one to my clit. "Now, you can come for me," he ordered while pressing circles into my clit with his thumb and stroking my inside walls with his hard cock.

My mouth parted, back arched, and eyes rolled back into my head as the orgasm flooded every fiber of my being. My toes curled and my heels dug into Tyler's back as he continued to pump into my body, reaching for his own release. I felt it the moment he released into me. I should've been terrified given my history. I should've demanded he pull out. But when he leaned down over my body, staring into my eyes just before he took my lips in another heated kiss, there was no fear. Just acceptance of the reality that I, indeed, belonged to Tyler Townsend.

CHAPTER 23

Tyler

Tonight's the night. That was the first thought I had as soon as my eyes opened that morning. It'd been a day and a half since we'd left Williamsport for the yacht. Our first stop was Belize, as I'd wanted to spend as much private time with my girl on the yacht as possible. Once we made it to Belize, we ate, had our bags placed in the luxury room I'd rented for the night that sat right on the beach, and headed to do some scuba diving.

Much to my surprise, or I shouldn't have been surprised, but weeks earlier Destiny had shown me pictures of her trip to Italy in which she'd become a certified scuba diver. She discussed going on trips over the past three years, but never having made it to Roatan Island which supposedly had the best diving in the western hemisphere. Needless to say, that planted the seed for this trip. While I'd originally planned to wait until after the season, my suspension, and in all honesty, my lack of patience, had propelled me to book the trip months earlier.

"I can't wait to see Roatan. It looks so beautiful from these pictures," Destiny beamed, staring at her phone. "Look." She stood from the large, king-sized bed in the bedroom of the yacht and walked over to me, plopping down in my lap. I sat out on a chair on our bedroom's second story deck.

Leaning back, I kicked my feet up on the railing, and adjusted her body so she was tightly snuggled against mine.

"It's beautiful," I stated before kissing her shoulder.

"You didn't even look." She frowned. "You okay? You've been quiet this morning."

I lifted an eyebrow.

"I didn't get much sleep last night or the night before that."

She giggled and swatted at my shoulder. "That's your own damn fault for being so fine."

I winked at her and sat back deeper into my chair. Sighing, she turned her back to lay against my chest. I wrapped my arms tighter around her waist, holding her firmly to me. I ran my hands up and down the sides of her exposed abdomen, thanks to the two-piece, bright pink bikini she wore. I'd made sure to pack that one when I first saw it in her dresser.

"What're you thinking about?"

"Life."

She pivoted her head to stare up at me.

"I was a twin." I moved my gaze from her to the mass of blue water that met up with the mass of blue sky at the horizon. "Identical twin. He died at birth."

Destiny gasped, sitting up. "Tyler, I'm so sorry."

"It's weird. It's like I can feel him sometimes. Or at least, I used to. When I was a kid. Always felt like there was a piece of me that was missing. I'm pretty sure that's what also caused me to act out. I felt like I needed to live life to the fullest for the both of us, since he didn't get to join the party, ya know?"

Destiny tilted her head to the side. "It kind of makes sense."

"I think he led me to you."

"How so?"

I shrugged. "If I hadn't been such a pain in the ass as a kid, maybe my father wouldn't have put me into sports. I know after the first time I was tackled on the field, my mother insisted that I be taken out. My father was only able to convince her to keep me in by pointing out how much more disciplined I was while playing. And if I hadn't continued playing, I never would've been recruited by the Cougars and maybe I wouldn't have come across you. My destiny." I reached up and kissed her lips before turning her to face the ocean again as I wrapped my arms around her waist.

Yup, tonight would be the night.

* * *

Destiny

"That was awesome," I gushed. As we sat down on the outside portion of the deck, one of the waitstaff on the yacht began serving us our lunch of seafood, salad, and rice pilaf. I smiled over at Tyler, my body warming up at the water that still trickled from his body.

We had just come back from snorkeling on the second largest reef in the world. The array of brightly colored fish and life that was so close I could touch it was awe inspiring.

"Being underwater always reminds me of how insignificant I am," I sighed.

Tyler paused from drying his hair with the beach towel to give me a funny look.

"I'm serious. I mean, how insignificant we all are. The ocean is *huge* ... so huge that even after thousands of years on this planet, humans still have no idea what's under most of it. There are still forms of sea creatures we haven't even discovered yet. Can you imagine? So cool."

Tyler leaned down, kissing my lips. "I can't imagine," he stated before pulling back.

"Water has healing properties, too. I think it's why I took up scuba diving after I started getting counseling. Something drew me to the water. Sounds silly, right?" I shrugged.

Tyler chuckled. "Well, you didn't laugh at me when I told you I could still feel my dead twin even though he and I never formally met. So, I don't get to tease you about this, I guess."

I scooted closer to him on the leather loveseat, pressing my lips to his cheeks. "Thanks."

He grunted and held a scallop up to my lips. "Eat. You've been swimming all morning."

I rolled my eyes but opened my mouth, letting him slide the tines of the fork inside. I moaned at the taste of the succulent scallop that'd been cooked in a garlic butter. It was delicious. So much so, my stomach actually began growling for more.

Tyler, ever one to deliver, especially where food was concerned, was more than happy to feed me throughout the rest of our lunch.

Once our meals were finished, Tyler motioned with his hand and one of the servers quickly came to remove our plates. Tyler leaned over to tell the server something in his ear. I didn't pay much attention, just assuming he was telling him of our dinner plans or something.

I yawned. Snorkeling and the delicious food had begun to tire me out.

"Tired?"

"A little."

A smile touched my lips when I heard music playing. "We should go dancing tonight." I looked over at Tyler.

His eyebrows raised pensively. "If we have time."

"Time? What else are we doing?"

He paused, looking over at me. His expression was serious. Just then, the server from a moment ago returned and placed something in Tyler's hand before leaving us alone once more. I glanced down but couldn't see what Tyler held. I looked back up into Tyler's eyes.

"Getting married."

I barely had time to comprehend those two words. Tyler opened his hand and lifted it up for me to see.

Slowly, I let my gaze drop and my mouth fell open when I saw a beautiful square cut diamond encased in a rose gold infinity setting.

"Wh-what are you doing?"

"Asking you to be my wife."

"You want to get engaged?" I asked, my eyes still planted on the ring.

"Hell no."

My gaze shot to his, confused.

"I want to get married. Here. Today. I don't need a fiancée. I need a wife. More specifically, I need *you* to be my wife because you're the only person that fits me. You're the only person made for me to spend the rest of my life with."

I inhaled sharply, still unable to wrap my mind around what was happening. I glanced around the scenery, the yacht, at anything but Tyler. Because I knew if I looked into his eyes that clear thought wouldn't even be possible. Hell, it was barely possible without staring directly into his heated gaze. And that's when I heard it.

The smooth vocals of Pat Monahan as he sang Train's "Marry Me". My vision went blurry as the tears filled my eyes.

"Destiny," Tyler's voice beckoned me.

I turned to look at him and was nearly bowled over by the sharpness of his gaze.

"I only know how to live one of two ways. All in or not at all. There's no point of half-assing anything, not especially when I know something is mine for the taking."

"Tyler, we've barely been dating two months."

"And?"

"I ..." I searched for something that made sense. "You haven't even met my mother yet."

"I'll meet her when we get home."

"Y-your family's not here. *My* family's not here. Resha will kill me for marrying without her here."

"She'll have to get through me first."

My shoulders sagged. I opened my mouth but he beat me to the punch.

"I only know how to play the game one way."

"What game?"

"Life. I only play it one way, and that means when I find something that's mine, I don't hem and haw and I don't waste time wondering what anyone else is going to think. I'm not built that way. We've been dating for two months but I've known way before that, that you and I were in this thing for the long haul. It was you who needed time to get used to it. I play for keeps, Destiny. So I was patient. Now my patience has all but run out. Tell me you don't want to marry me and we'll call the whole thing off. I'll never bother you again."

My heart truly began racing at those words. The thought of Tyler walking away completely nearly caused my knees to buckle. Thank God I was sitting down.

My eyes closed, and I felt Tyler lift my left hand and slide the ring onto my finger. My eyes popped open when he grabbed me around the waist, moving me to straddle his long legs, facing him.

"Okay," I said just above a whisper.

"Okay, what?"

"I'll marry you … today."

The majestic water behind us with the sun high in the blue sky couldn't compare to the beaming smile that crossed Tyler's face. My heart actually stopped at that moment. I was such a goner.

Burying his face into the crook of my neck, he nuzzled it. "Thank you." He pulled back to look up at me. "Oh, even if you had said no, I wouldn't have walked away. I was lying when I said that shit."

I tossed my head back and laughed. "I know," I responded.

"Ha!" he cheered, standing up and twirling around with me still locked around his waist.

"Mr. Townsend, are we ready?"

Tyler stopped and I had to press against his shoulder for him to put me back on my feet. Once he did, I spun around to see a tall, regal man, dressed in all white. I squinted. He was our ship's captain.

"We are." Tyler nodded.

"Tyler?"

"This is Larry."

I nodded, already knowing his name since he was introduced when we first boarded the yacht two days earlier.

"He's also an ordained minister and licensed to marry us."

"What? Now?" I questioned, looking at Tyler before glancing down at the two piece, high waisted, African, dashiki printed bathing suit I wore.

"Right now, precious."

He really only had two speeds. Fast and furious or zero. Inhaling deeply, I placed my hand in his outstretched one, and let him guide me over to where Larry was standing. Minutes later I was reciting wedding vows as a handful of the yacht's staff stood in the background, serving as our witnesses.

"You wanted to know what my wish was at the well the night of our first date. I told you I'd tell you when it came true. This was it. For you to be my wife," he stated just before lowering his head and giving me our first kiss as husband and wife.

And that is the story of how I became Mrs. Tyler Townsend.

CHAPTER 24

Destiny

"I cannot believe we did this," I breathed out, holding my left hand up in front of me as I passed through the door of my condo. I angled my head, marveling at the new infinity tattoo that adorned my left ring finger. Our actual rings were being custom made. How had he talked me into this?

"Believe it, precious," Tyler growled low in my ear, his arms wrapping around my waist, pulling be backwards to his body.

I looked down, taking his left hand in mine, holding it up for my inspection. Like mine, his ring finger bore the identical infinity symbol tatted on the outside of his finger. His first tattoo ever. However, unlike mine, his had a little "D" hanging from the center of the symbol. D for Destiny, of course. My heart swelled in my chest. So much so that it threatened to burst.

"I love you," I told him just because.

"I love you," he returned. "But don't get too mushy just yet. There's something I need you to do."

My eyes widened. "You haven't asked enough of me already?"

Laughing, he began walking us toward my bedroom. "Not even close, precious."

He pushed the door open and flicked the switch for the light. I blinked when I noticed that on my nicely made white sheets and comforter, was a cheerleading costume.

"There were some left over from Halloween. I had my assistant pick one up."

"You're planning on dressing up as a cheerleader?"

"Haha!" He growled, slapping me on the ass.

"Ouch!" I yelped and turned to rub my ass.

"Since I never got to see you in your *actual* cheerleading outfit back in the day, I figured the least you could do for your new husband was dress up while you showed me one of your old cheers."

"Tyler, are you insane?" I regretted the question as soon as it came from my mouth. Of course he was. "Don't answer that." I held up my hands, waving off my silly question. "I am not—"

"Of course you are, precious," he stated as if it were a foregone conclusion.

"And what makes you so damn sure?"

He peeled off the light bomber jacket he'd adorned, once we'd deplaned in Williamsport. Then he reached for the asymmetrical jacket, I wore, unbuttoning it and tossing it to the armchair where he'd tossed his.

"Because ..." he began as he walked over to one of my wooden dressers at the foot of the bed, where he'd been keeping his belongings. He pulled out a wooden box and opened it. "If you're good to me, tonight, I'll return the favor, tenfold."

I slowly crept over to him, peering inside the box. A tiny gasp escaped my lips as I took in the different instruments he kept inside.

"I've wanted to use the Wartenberg pinwheel on you for months." His voice was so calm, steady, and full of need. It called to every cell in my body. The hairs on my arms and neck stood on end as he held up the metal pinwheel. It looked intimidating, but not as intimidating as the man wielding it. My nipples ached to be teased by him just from the image alone. I could only imagine the type of pleasure it could bring. The idea didn't scare me.

It aroused me.

So when I found myself changing into the red, black, and white cheerleading costume that Tyler had laid out on my bed, a minute later, I wasn't surprised.

"I need music," I told him.

He rose from the bed. "I'll choose."

I grinned, knowing he was thinking I'd likely pick what he now termed *white boy music,* too.

I angled my head when a familiar song began playing.

"How am I supposed to cheer to this?" It was Beyoncé's "Dance For You". I loved the song but it wasn't cheerleading music. It was …

"Lap dance music," he mused, finishing my thoughts. "I got a lap and you got the dance." He sat at the edge of the bed, legs parted.

I shook my head and smirked but began swaying my hips just the same as I sauntered over to him. If I was going to give my husband a lap dance, I was going to make it look good. I spun so my back was to him and dipped low, coming up slow with my ass pressed against his groin. I could already feel him growing hard beneath his jeans.

As Beyoncé began singing the first line of the chorus I turned around, bracing my hands on Tyler's thighs, and dipped my head low, moving up slowly as I swiveled my ass high in the air. I moved to straddled his lap, circling my hips over the bulge in his pants. His large hand moved over my thigh and began sliding the skirt up. I smacked his hand away before hopping off his lap. Spinning again, I moved farther away, putting my hands in my hair and body rolling, exposing just a little bit of my abdomen, before reaching down and pulling the top of the cheer uniform off entirely.

"We didn't strip while I was cheering, but I'll make an exception for you," I teased and winked at him.

"Good choice," he growled.

When Queen Bey began singing about popping it, I turned around and popped my ass back before reaching behind me and undoing the zipper of the skirt. As another round of the chorus played, I allowed the skirt to slip from my body, leaving me in only my silk undergarments. Slowly, I hooked my hands into either side of the panties and rolled them down my legs. Standing, I tossed them at Tyler. He snatched them out of the air and brought them to his nose, inhaling deeply.

I leaned back, laughing.

"I need the real thing," was the last thing I heard before he stood and reached me in less than two steps, lifting me off my feet.

All I remember was my back hitting the bed and Tyler quickly moving over top of me, covering my body. That wasn't the first time we'd made love since saying I do. Our marriage had been thoroughly consummated already, but that night as Tyler used that pinwheel on my body, having me call out his name over and over, any doubts I had about what we'd done while away were put to rest.

Now, it was time for the remainder of the world to find out.

* * *

Tyler

"I can't fucking believe you had the nerve to go on a fucking vacation while you were suspended," Coach Mike growled in my face.

I sighed and had to keep myself from shrugging off his anger. I respected my coach, but if he expected me to apologize for anything I'd done over the previous two weeks, he'd be waiting a hell of a long time.

"The owners were pissed," he stated, pacing back and forth.

We were just outside one of the business offices at Williamsport Stadium. Myself, Mike, Riggs, and the owners were scheduled to meet there at nine that morning. Supposedly, the meeting was to be a time for peer mediation or some bullshit. They were trying to resolve the conflict between Riggs and I, to ensure we could still play on the same team. Apparently, while I'd been away he'd threatened to sue me or press charges or whatever the fuck his lawyer had said. I hadn't paid much attention to the threats. Riggs liked talking big shit. Shit talking, I could handle with no problem. Putting his hands on Destiny again would ensure the end of his life. As long as he was aware of that particular fact, I didn't have much else to say to the fucker.

"Are you even listening to me? You still haven't given me a clear explanation as to what that whole fight between you and Riggs was about."

"I heard you, Coach."

"That's it? You heard me."

"Yeah, so did I."

I turned to see Riggs standing there, eyeing me as if I gave a shit.

"Great. Now that you both are here, we can get an explanation as to what happened that night." Coach questioned.

"You saw the video," I responded, still staring at Riggs.

"That's not an answer."

"Riggs just needed to learn to keep his hands to himself." That was all the explanation I was ready to give to coach. I'd decided I'd handle Riggs in my own way.

"What the hell kind of cryptic—," Coach began, but was interrupted by one of the owners, James McCroy.

"Let's take this inside, gentlemen."

I shrugged and followed James inside while Mike placed himself between Riggs and I. I moved to the opposite side of the large conference table just so I could look Riggs in the eye when necessary. Within minutes a few more of the owners began piling in, along with a few of the team's legal staff. I rolled my eyes knowing most of this was for show. The owners had made clear their displeasure with what'd happened between Riggs and I. They'd gone so far as threatening to end our contracts and require back pay for what we'd been paid thus far. I was three years into a five year contract. Unbeknownst to the owners, not a dime of what I'd been paid had been spent. They could take it all, with interest, and I wouldn't be hurting at all.

I wasn't so sure Riggs could say the same. That's why a sense of satisfaction rolled over me when I looked across the table and saw him squirm in his seat as he glanced at the owners as they conferred with their legal team.

"Let's get started."

"Let's," I agreed as I stared at James at the head of the table, with my hands clasped in front of me on the table.

"As both of you know, we are here because of the incident that occurred between Mr. Riggs and Mr. Townsend."

My eyes shot across the table when Riggs grunted as he stared at me. Lifting an eyebrow, I angled my head. "Something you need to say?"

"Fuc—"

"Now, gentlemen, please!" James began, voice raised as I started rising up out of my chair.

"Tyler, sit down," Mike ordered. "You too, Riggs. James, let me take this on," he requested.

Only when I saw Riggs sit his ass down did I plant my ass back in my chair.

"Look, you two don't like each other. We get it. But you are on the same team. We have a real opportunity to win the entire thing. The fucking Super Bowl. I'll be damned if I let you two fuck it up over some bullshit spat—"

"It wasn't bullshit," I stated calmly but firmly, looking my coach directly in the eye. "Mike, I respect you more than anyone in this room, and you were the first phone call I made after whooping his ass." I glanced across the table at Riggs.

"Fuck you!" He spat. "You didn't do shit."

My lips split as I chuckled, staring at Riggs. "I'll let you show off for the room, but the evidence is filmed." My smile diminished. "Of course, we could do a reenactment right the fuck here and now," I growled, remembering the original reason I'd gone to Riggs' home in the first place. The memory of bruises on Destiny's arm from this piece of shit …

"Cut it out!" Mike growled as the rest of the owners began fidgeting in their chairs. "You're on the same goddamned team and I don't give a shit if that doesn't mean something to the two of you. It means something to me. Fuck whatever this is all about. Tyler, you're the quarterback. The leader on the field. And we both know your career ambitions once your time in the league has ended. Riggs, you and I both know this is the best thing you've got going and you need not fuck it up. So with that said, I expect the both of you to have your asses on the field for practice within the next thirty minutes." And with that, Mike nodded at the rest of the owners and left the room.

I turned to face Riggs. "As long as you keep your hands where the fuck they belong from now on, I've got no problem," I lied. His ass was still mine. No way a motherfucker was going to get away with putting their hands on my wife and just receive a minor ass whooping. But the plans I had for Riggs could be put on hold. For now.

I stood and nodded at the owners who were still talking, but as far as I was concerned, the need for talk was over. I was headed to practice, and then I had an even more important date with my wife.

* * *

Destiny

"Yes, Brenda, I know. I know," I groaned into the phone. "Look, it was no big deal. I just talked with Morris for about thirty minutes. I passed along the same information that Paul told me to. As far as Morris is concerned, I am just a heartbroken widow who is looking to invest with him," I explained my phone meeting with Phillip Morris earlier that day to Brenda. At the prompting of Paul, I engaged with Phillip once again, telling him that I had gotten some money from my supposed deceased husband's estate and I was ready to invest. He was more than a little excited to take me up on my offer. He went around and around in circles explaining the supposedly complex investment strategies he utilized that he'd said would no doubt provide me with a pretty hefty return on my investment, in a matter of months. As the fake widow I feigned excitement over the prospects. As a seasoned professional in personal finance, I knew he was completely full of shit.

"This guy is a scumbag. I can't wait until he is busted for this. There are real people behind the piles of money he is stealing. I did a little bit more research on him. Did you know he owns two homes? One, a two-thousand square foot condo in the exclusive Williamsport Towers, and another on the edge of town. The cost of both is close to one million dollars. You *know* he didn't buy those properties with his own investment gains."

My voice was full of anger from just thinking about Morris' extravagant lifestyle. I would never begrudge someone of partaking in all that life has to offer with the money they earned, or even with money they inherited. However, what I absolutely would not condone is a man who was literally stealing from unsuspecting clients to fund his extravagance.

"He'll be caught," Brenda assured me.

"He better be and soon. I'm not sure how long I can keep this going."

"Keep what going?"

My head swung in the direction of my office door. Leaned against the doorframe was the man I'd missed since I'd gotten out of bed that morning. He was dressed in a light green button-up top that actually brought out the green color in his eyes. He'd paired the shirt with dark blue jeans. His hands were tucked into his pockets as if he was unassuming but the small smirk that played at his lips, coupled with the sparkling mirth I'd come to always look for in his eyes was there.

"I gotta go," I told Brenda. I hung up the phone and stood. Before I was even completely upright, Tyler was reaching for me, outstretching his long arms, wrapping them around my waist. The feeling of coming home again, that I'd become used to in such a short amount of time, appeared as I melted into his body. I reached up on my tiptoes to meet Tyler's approaching lips.

"How was practice?"

He shrugged. "Practice was practice."

I frowned. "You know what I mean." I tugged a little at either sides of his collar. "You and Riggs ..."

"He's still breathing." His lips formed a frown as if he'd hated to say that statement out loud.

"Despite your annoyance with his breathing, that's actually a good thing."

His forehead wrinkled. "How so?"

I wanted to giggle at the absurdity of his questioning but, in all seriousness, he seemed to be serious about ending Riggs' life. "Because it means my husband isn't sitting in a jail cell for murder."

His lips turned upward. "Say it again."

I gave him a perplexed look. "What? I'm happy you're not sitting in a jail cell?"

He shook his head. "No, the part about me being your husband."

Grinning, I wrapped my hands around his triceps, pulling his body closer to me. "I'm glad *my husband* isn't in a six by eight foot cell instead of here with m—" The last syllable was cut off when his lips captured mine. I'd been expecting the kiss ever since that smile that showed his one dimple made its appearance. I was learning that particular smile was just for me.

"You ready?" he questioned, pulling back and placing his forehead against mine.

I bit my lower lip.

He tipped my chin. "What's that about?"

"I'm nervous."

"Destiny Townsend? Nervous?"

A chill ran through my body at hearing my married name. He'd made it a point to say it whenever he got a chance.

"McDonald-Townsend," I reminded him. I insisted on hyphenating my last name.

Tyler frowned. "We'll see about that."

I sighed.

"Anyway, let's go. We don't want to keep your mother waiting."

I nodded, still feeling nervous. Tonight was the first night that my mother and Tyler were going to meet. Oh, and that we were going to reveal that we were married. Talk about laying it on.

"Mothers love me," Tyler reassured me as we made our way to the building's elevator. "I mean, what's not to love? I'm charming, wealthy, great-looking, nice ass to boot …" He pivoted, turning his ass toward me so I could see.

I tossed my head back, laughing.

"And I'm funny as hell." He wiggled his eyebrows.

Butterflies in my stomach began flapping their wings in agreement with my cocky husband.

"Whatever," I stated, rolling my eyes and stepping off the elevator, not willing to agree. Lord knew he already had an ego the size of the building we were exiting. No need to inflate it even more.

He opened the electric blue door of his Cayenne for me to get in. Moments later, he was climbing into the driver's seat and we were on our way. Pushing out a breath, I hoped for the best.

* * *

"HEY, MA," I greeted my mother as she opened the door partially upon hearing my knocking. I'd called her and let her know I was coming, and even though I had a key, I still wanted to respect her privacy by knocking. Especially, since the huge man standing behind me was present.

"Hey b-baby." My mother smiled at me as she widened the door. Her eyes sparkled as she took me in, but then widened when she glanced up overhead, behind me. A wrinkle in her forehead indicated she was trying to place exactly who Tyler was.

"Ma, this is Tyler. Tyler Townsend," I introduced, stepping to the side so she could see him.

She took a step back and widened the door. I was surprised to see her dressed in a three-quarter length sleeve dress that was cinched at her waist and reached past her knees. The dress was patterned with purple, green, and electric blue. Her hair, was styled in her usual twist out that nicely framed her face, just barely grazing her shoulders.

"It's a pleasure to meet you, Mrs. McDonald," Tyler stated, taking her shaky hand in his and kissing it.

I blinked away moisture from my eyes at hearing the tenderness in his voice.

"P-pleasure," she got out. "Come in." She stepped back, allowing us to enter her apartment.

Tyler stood aside, allowing me to enter first and then shutting the door behind us.

"I hope you don't mind, Mrs. McDonald, but Destiny told me you have an affinity for Chinese food. And well, I do, too. So …" He held up the two bags of food he'd insisted on purchasing for this dinner.

My mother smiled brightly and nodded. "Table's here." She gestured to the table in her tiny dining room space.

Suddenly, a wave of guilt fell over me. I had just spent the previous week on a yacht more than twice the size of my mother's apartment. Tyler was constructing a house that could fit my mother's apartment in just one of the bedrooms, for us to live on, and my mother …

"Destiny."

My head snapped in my mother's direction. "Yes."

"G-get your head out of the clouds, girl," she stated, causing me to smile.

"Sorry, Ma."

"We need to eat."

I nodded at my mother and went to help her with her chair but Tyler beat me to it. He pulled out one of the ebony, wicker, slide chairs that matched the rectangular dining table, and assisted my mother in sitting down as he slid it closer to the table.

My heart squeezed in my chest. 'Thank you,' I mouthed to Tyler as he moved to the side of the table to pull out my chair.

He didn't respond verbally, instead he pressed a kiss just behind my ear. Once seated, I looked over to see my mother smiling at the both of us.

"Your hair looks nice, Ma."

She grinned a little, slowly reaching up to pat some of the curls. "Resha was over earlier before her flight. I told her you were bringing someone. S-she dressed me and did my hair."

Smiling, I nodded. Resha had told me she was visiting Mom before her flight back to New York. She knew I was introducing Tyler to Mom tonight also. She just didn't know I'd have additional news to share.

"You are a sight for sore eyes, Mrs. McDonald," Tyler interjected.

My mother dipped her head, grinning. It was the first time I'd seen her act bashful in years. Not since her diagnosis had she been very receiving on compliments.

Tyler made my mother and I remain seated while he found his way around her kitchen, placing plates, forks, and glasses in front of us.

When he was done with that, he served us our food before fixing his own plate. Again, my heart melted. I already knew I loved this man beyond reason. Heck, I'd married him in the middle of the ocean after only a few months of dating. But to see him so gentle, loving, and kind with the woman that'd given me life, made my heart skip a beat, quite literally.

"Ma, I have something to tell you," I began after we finished our main course. I looked over at Tyler.

He took my hand in his, holding it on the table. I noticed my mother's eyes drop to our clasped hands.

"Mrs. McDonald," Tyler began, cutting me off before I got a chance to speak.

I turned to him and he simply squeezed my hand, glancing at me, silently informing me that he would be taking the lead on this one.

"I love your daughter with my entire being." His eyes slid from me to my mother. "She is my world and I will spend the rest of my life making sure she knows it. That is why I asked her to marry me." He looked back to me, I knew because I hadn't taken my eyes off of him since he'd started talking. "And she said yes."

Finally, I looked to my mother whose lips quivered a bit as a smile broke out on her face. "Y-you're engaged?"

I shook my head slightly.

"We were married last week while on vacation," Tyler continued. "We wanted our privacy to share in the moment, just for us, but I am sure there will be another, larger ceremony for both our families once the house is completed."

"House?"

"Yes, ma'am." Tyler nodded. He went on to tell her about the house in Cedarwoods, going so far as to promise her one of the bedrooms that would be open for her to live in.

As I suspected, my mother shook her head at the idea of moving in with us. My heart sank. I wanted her close to me, especially now. I didn't feel right about living in such a large home surrounded by Tyler's side of the family nearby while my own mother lived alone.

"I think you'll feel differently once you become a grandmother,"

Tyler stated confidently.

My head whipped around to glare at him. He simply smiled and pulled my hand to his, kissing my knuckles.

"Y-you're pregnant?"

I gasped and shook my head vigorously. "No."

"I-is that why you married so fast?"

"Ma, no!" I insisted. "I'm *not* pregnant."

"Yet."

I cut my eyes in Tyler's direction who gave me a nonchalant look and a shrug.

"Only a matter of time, precious."

I ignored the tingling in my body at the pet name he used, as well as bit the inside of my cheek to keep the smile off my face.

"Anyway, Ma, I'm sorry you couldn't be there when we married, but you're the first to know from either of our families and we … I never wanted you to feel left out."

My mother sat back in her chair. She reached a wobbly hand out for me to grasp. I took her hand in mine. She turned to Tyler. "My daughter doesn't m-make impetuous decisions. And she isn't one to make the same mistake twice. If she said yes, then she must really be in love. You h-have my blessing."

I squeezed her hand, eyes blinking rapidly to clear away the tears that threatened to spill over.

"And you have my word, you'll never regret your decision. Either of you."

I hadn't even realized the first tear slipped until I felt Tyler reach up and wipe it away with his thumb. Jesus, I usually wasn't this damn emotional. I swallowed and leaned in for the kiss my husband offered, feeling safer and more secure than I could ever remember feeling.

We spent another hour over my mother's. Once I told Tyler how much my mother loved sweets, he'd insisted on bringing an entire chocolate truffle cake with us for dessert. They both indulged, and for once, I didn't admonish my mother for taking a second piece of cake. I was too busy trying to rein in my own emotions after watching Tyler feed my mother her cake once he noticed the trembling in her hands preventing her from enjoying her dessert. Her trembling often got worse at night and when she was tired.

I helped my mother change and get to bed before Tyler and I left for the night. I checked at the front desk to make sure the staff new to check on my mother throughout the night and have someone help her early the next morning. I called her facility daily to check in on her, but still wanted to make sure they knew my mother had someone in her corner at all times.

"You can also add me as the contact person for Mrs. McDonald."

I was shocked when I glanced up to see Tyler speaking to the head night nurse, who sat at the front desk.

"Oh, and your name is—"

"Tyler Townsend."

"Your relation to Mrs. McDonald?"

"Son-in-law."

I quietly watched as Tyler informed the woman of his contact information to be contacted in case of an emergency.

"That's one down and one more family to go. Minus Resha." He smiled at me as we exited the complex.

"I'll let you tell her on your own," I joked.

Tyler shook his head. "Oh hell no, that's one conversation I'll leave to you."

"Hey? What happened to all the *you can count on me, Mrs. McDonald* stuff?"

He shrugged. "I lied." He ducked, laughing loudly when I punched his arm.

"Jerk." I tried to snatch away when he caught me in a hold around my waist, pulling me against his chest. He dipped his head, nuzzling his face into the crook of my neck.

"You want me to tell Resha or anyone else you're my wife, I'll do it with bells on."

I shivered. "You're still a jerk."

"I know. But you married me." He laughed and reached down, squeezing my ass through the dress pants I wore.

It was a good night.

CHAPTER 25

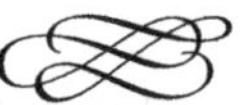

Tyler

"Why are you biting your lip like you're nervous?"

"What? I don't bite my—"

"Yeah, you do. Sometimes when you're horny as hell you bite the bottom corner. When I have you bent over with your back arched, long stroking you, you suck your entire bottom lip between your teeth. But when you're nervous, you bite just the inside center of your lip. Like right now." I tilted my head toward her bottom lip.

"Tyler!" she whisper-yelled.

I wrinkled my brows. "What?"

"We are standing at your parents' front do— What are you doing?" she questioned as I punched in the code to my parents' front door and pushed it open once the lock disengaged.

"Walking in," I answered, pulling her by the hand with me. "Anyone home?" I called out. Within seconds I could hear the quick footfalls of who I suspected were my two oldest nephews.

"Uncle Ty!"

I grinned at the sound of Diego's voice, soon followed by Kyle's.

"Hey, guys," I greeted, scooping down to pick up both Kyle and Diego, giving them a kiss before placing them back down.

"Hi!" Kyle waved behind me.

I turned to wrap my arms around Destiny who was smiling down at the boys.

She waved. "Hi, Kyle and Diego."

A heartbeat later more footfalls gave way as the other members of my family came piling out of the kitchen and downstairs family room. It was Christmas Eve and we were finally able to celebrate with my entire family all together.

"Uncle Tyler, Daddy said that Ms. Destiny is your girlfriend," Diego giggled as the entire family stood around greeting us.

A tiny laugh escaped Destiny's mouth and I turned to look down at her. She peered up at me and the smile that was only reserved for her touched my lips and I winked at her. I bent low, crouching down to get eye level with Diego.

"Tyler," Destiny began, a note of warning in her tone. That only made my smile grow.

"No, buddy, not for the first time in his life, your daddy is wrong …" I glanced up at Carter who was frowning at me, confused.

"Tyler, maybe we should—"

"She's my wife," I stated, huge grin on my face as I stared up at Carter and the rest of my family, before turning back to Diego. He looked just as surprised as the rest of my family. I heard my mother gasp, along with the rest of my sisters-in-law.

I stood up and wrapped my right arm around Destiny's waist. I gave her a smug look in response to the scorching look she was giving me. We had planned on waiting until sometime after dinner to tell my family that we had married. Destiny had wanted it that way.

"You didn't want me to lie to my nephew, did you?" I whispered and then kissed her lips.

"I fucking knew it." Joshua was the first to speak up. "Remember how pissed he was at my wedding? You must've been giving him a run for his money," Josh stated, grinning at Destiny.

"No more than he was giving me," she quickly responded.

"That's bullshit if ever I've heard it. You gave me all types of shit."

"Tyler, your mouth," my mother insisted.

"Sorry, Mother."

"Destiny, please come with us. We were just leaving the men to do whatever it is they do," my mother said, taking Destiny by the arm.

Reluctantly, I let my mother take her. I watched as Destiny, my mother, Patience, Michelle, and Kayla headed toward the back of the house.

"I can't believe it," Carter exclaimed.

I peered over at my eldest brother who was shaking his head.

"I figured you would be the one to pull one over on us," Joshua added.

"Makes sense."

I looked to Aaron who'd just spoken.

"I told you to get the stick out of your ass. Looks like you did."

I chuckled at my second oldest brother's attempt at a joke. He had indeed told me to get the stick out of my ass. I suspected he knew Destiny had something to do with why it was there in the first place.

"Is this woman the reason you've had so much trouble this season?"

I turned to my father, frowning. "So much trouble?" I repeated.

"The woman breaking into your hotel, you getting into a fight with your teammate, being suspended for two games." He lifted a dark eyebrow.

"She's not the reason any of that happened." My voice had turned hard.

My father's jaw worked as he stared at me. I could feel my three brothers glancing between the two of us. I respected my father more than any other man in this world, but even he didn't get to talk negatively about the woman I'd married. That was how he had raised me.

Finally, he nodded. "Then what happened?"

I looked between my brothers and my father before telling them the issues between myself and Leonard Riggs. I explained for some reason, out of some dumb loyalty to his agent, who was Destiny's ex, he had it out for her. Therefore, somehow getting that woman he'd obviously screwed to sneak into my hotel room and take pictures to post on social media. Then about how he'd man handled Destiny while she was leaving after having lunch with me at the stadium.

"Why didn't you tell us before? I would've cracked his head open myself," Carter growled, while cracking his knuckles. Aaron, Joshua, and my father all had the same angered expressions on their face as Carter. I was certain their looks mirrored my own.

"I didn't need to tell you. I handled it on my own. Took my suspension and got married. Riggs still has what's coming to him."

My father raised another eyebrow at me.

"But for now, we have a season to finish. Now, let's eat. I'm fucking starving," I stated, rubbing my belly. "And where's my wife?" I called out, clapping and rubbing my hands together.

"Jesus fuck. I can't believe this nitwit got married."

Carter chuckled in response to Joshua's comment. "Soon enough he'll be a fucking father."

"God help us all."

That was Aaron.

I glanced back at my brothers, grinning. "Jealous because I beat you all to the punch?"

"Hey, hey!" my mother called out when I ducked a swing from Joshua. "You all stop that. I swear you would've thought I raised a bunch of farm animals." She sucked her teeth.

Since the women had been cooking much of the day, my brothers and I served the table. It was sort of a tradition in our house, when the food wasn't catered. I held out one of the wooden chairs for Destiny to sit, pushing it toward the long, glass table. I sat next to her as my mother insisted we say grace, and then began eating.

"Destiny, you were saying you're a financial advisor?" my mother began.

"Yes, Mrs. Townsend."

"Please, call me Deb or Deborah, or Mom, if you'd like."

My chest swelled as my mother's blue eyes wrinkled as she smiled at my wife.

"Thank you, Deb."

"I've listened to your podcast. Been listening for a while, actually," Michelle spoke up.

"Really?"

"Yeah, I just didn't want to say anything the first time we met."

Destiny and Michelle laughed.

"What's a podcast?" my mother questioned.

"Um, it's like an online radio show. I host it with my sister. Well, technically Resha is my cousin, but we were raised together. So for all intents and purposes, she's—"

"Your sister," Patience finished Destiny's statement.

Everyone at the table understood that. Given that fact that technically speaking, Aaron, was my cousin by DNA but after his biological parents were killed in a car accident caused by his father, my parents adopted him. He was raised right alongside us as brothers, no difference.

"So are you one of those financial advisors that advises all your clients to invest the funds that will bring you the highest returns but cost them the most in fees."

"Aaron, what the fuck?" I growled across the table at the shitty questioned he'd so arrogantly lobbied across the table at my wife.

"It's okay," Destiny responded, tightening her hand around my arm, pulling me back from the table.

"It's not okay. It was fucking rude and di—"

"No really. It's okay," Destiny began, placing her hand on my thigh. "I get it. Unfortunately, financial advisors don't have the best reputation and with good reason. There are a shit load of mutual and investment funds with outrageous fees. Excuse my language, Deb." Destiny gave my mother a remorseful look.

My mother nodded and smiled at her.

"Everyone should question their financial advisor's loyalty. I don't charge my clients by which investments they make. I charge them based on the time I spend with them. Thus, if they only see me for an hour a month, that's all they're charged for. I don't continually switch my clients' portfolios around, trying to chase the next big stock rise. I make it clear my strategy is to invest with two strategies in mind. For diversity and for the long haul. I left my full-time job at one of the biggest investment banks in the city because they encouraged stock picking and chasing fees over what was best for the client. I choose not to do that in my business. I've been successful thus far," she finished, tilting her head in Aaron's direction before smiling up at me.

Goddamn, I love this woman. Leaning down, I pressed a kiss to her lips before turning a sharp gaze on Aaron.

"Any further questions, I expect will be directed my way and not toward my wife," I growled.

Aaron didn't have anymore questions and the rest of dinner went off without a hitch. After dinner we opened presents and not for the first time I couldn't wait until Destiny and I had our own children to unwrap presents by the tree with.

* * *

Destiny

"I can't believe you convinced me to come with you," I grunted as I laid back against the hotel's huge bed. It was a few days after New Year's and Tyler had his first playoff game of the season. The Cougars had been on a total winning streak since he and Riggs had returned from their suspensions. Despite the fact that both men hated one another off the field, they were beasts once they stepped onto the greenery.

"Believe it and weep, precious," Tyler retorted, smacking my jeans' covered ass as I turned over.

"It's *read it and weep.*"

He shrugged his huge shoulders. "Whatever. Besides, I needed my good luck charm with me this week. We win the next three games and we're going to the big one."

I smiled at the excitement in his voice. He wanted to win the Super Bowl so badly *I* could taste it. I sat up on my knees.

"And you'll finally get the ring you always wanted," I stated, wrapping my arms around his neck.

Tyler shook his head. "Not even close. I got the ring I always wanted." He held up his left hand that wore the white gold wedding band that'd finally arrived two days earlier. Mine matched his. "Winning the Superbowl will just be icing on the cake." He kissed my lips.

I pulled back. "When you say shit like that it gives me no choice but to do this." I released his neck and stepped off the bed, turning his body and sinking down to the floor. I released his belt buckle and the button of his jeans, tugging his pants and boxer briefs down until his semi-hard erection sprung out.

I looked up into his eyes which had darkened and the smile that was accompanied by the dimple was there to match. Without another word, I opened my mouth, letting my lips encircle the rim of his cock. I used my tongue to moisten the tip of his cock. I tasted the tangy taste of his precum and swallowed. Still keeping my eyes on the now nearly forest green eyes of my husband's, I began to slide my lips and mouth over his rod. The moan that emanated from the back of his throat increased my own need, and I began bobbing my head in rapid succession on his thick member.

I felt Tyler's large hand slide over my shoulder to my neck and then the back of my head, trapping it in place. When he tightened his grip in my hair, my own body heat increased. Tyler began working his hips, sliding his cock farther down my throat. I raised my hands to his hips to hold on as he used my mouth to find his own release. His breathing increased, as did his grunts as he reached toward his climax. Moments later a deep, guttural moan came from the back of his throat, and I felt the first splash of his semen onto my tongue. I continued sucking, trying to obtain every bit of his come.

"Hey!" I yelped when he moved suddenly, pulling himself free and picking me up and tossing me on the bed.

"You're mine," he growled as he climbed over top of me.

"Don't you have a game to p-prepare f-for?" I teased, stuttering at the end as he began running his teeth up and down the vein in my neck.

"This is the only game I care about right now."

With that, he began tugging at my jeans. Needless to say, the few hours before he had to head to the game were well spent.

CHAPTER 26

Destiny

"Destiny McDonald-T ... How may I help you?" I hadn't exactly been using my full married name at work just yet.

"Destiny, it's Paul. Listen, so the FBI is taking over the investigation into Phillip Morris. We'll be working with them to complete this investigation. What you've given us so far is great and will likely go a long way to end his career and hopefully put him away. That being said, your role in this investigation is completed."

I pushed out a breath as my shoulders sank. "Wow, that's good news, I guess."

"You guess?"

"Yeah, I mean, I kind of wanted to see the whole thing through 'til the end."

"I know, but the SEC has limited power in this and from the information we've gathered so far, it looks like Morris could face time in jail for what he's doing with clients' money. That is out of our hands and into the hands of the FBI. They have their own procedures to handle all of this."

"I get it. But can you tell me how long this investigation will go on?

Are his clients still going to be kept out of the loop on all of this while they continue to invest with him?"

"As of right now, I'm on strict orders not to give you anymore information about this investigation."

"Seriously, Paul? I'm the one who's met with him on more than one occasion and given you guys the information," I fumed.

"I know, Destiny, but it's out of my hands. Really. Once the FBI gets involved they take over. The SEC will do what we can to end his career and make him pay. But it's the FBI that has the power to put him away."

I sighed heavily.

"The truth is, it's better this way for everyone involved. We want this thing put to bed as quickly as possible and we want to keep you out of harm's way."

"Harm?"

Paul pushed out a breathe. "It's just safer this way. I'm not saying Phillip Morris is any sort of threat to you, but you never know how someone will react when they learn they're being investigated. Morris doesn't know you were the one to blow the whistle, nor does he know your first name just yet, but chances are, with you making the news in the future—"

"The news?" I blinked, wondering what Paul was referring to.

"Sports news. Brenda informed me that you're now married to Williamsport Cougar quarterback, Tyler Townsend."

I pursed my lips. I'd told Brenda … well, technically, Mike had told Brenda after Tyler told him and she came to me for confirmation. So far, we hadn't made the news public yet, wanting all of our family and friends to know before we did. And since Resha was constantly on the go, I hadn't been able to tell her yet. Apparently, the secret was starting to get out anyway.

"It's only a matter of time before you're photographed with him at some event. Morris would definitely find out. Now is the perfect time to pull you from this investigation. While he is still in the dark on the information being gathered on him."

I sighed again. "You're right. I still hate the thought of him continuing to deceive people. Even the likes of Leonard Riggs." I sneered as I said his name but it was true. Even Riggs didn't deserve to have his hard-earned wealth stolen by a snake like Morris. Scumbag though he might be, in his own right, Riggs still busted his ass on the field every week to help the Cougars win.

"Hey, speaking of the Cougars, you think I could get an autograph from your husband?"

Paul's question pulled me back to the fact that I was still on the phone with him. I frowned. "Yeah, sure," I answered half-heartedly.

"Thanks. Listen, I've gotta go. I can't say I'll keep you informed because I won't be able to, but once anything becomes public I'll give you a call to let you know first."

I rolled my eyes, knowing that was the best Paul could offer. SEC and FBI investigations were private until charges were filed publicly. It was necessary to preserve the integrity of the investigation. I understood it, even though I didn't like it.

"Thanks," I murmured.

I hung up the phone with Paul, ready to get back to what I'd been working on before the call, when there was a sudden knock on my door.

I glanced up and smiled. "Hey you."

"Hey, you like my ensemble?"

My eyes scanned down the length of Resha's black, knee-length wrap dress and I frowned, lifting an eyebrow. "It's a little plain for you."

She nodded and stepped into my office. "I thought you'd say that, but I figured it'd be the most appropriate thing to wear to your funeral."

My eyes widened. "Ouch! What the hell was that for?" I growled, frowning at her and rubbing the arm she'd just pinched.

"That ..." she pointed at me as she rounded my desk to sit opposite me, "is for lying to me for weeks now, heffa!"

"Lie about what?"

"Oh, I don't know, the fact that you're *married.*"

I gasped. "Who told you?"

"See? You don't even deny it. Just wanna know who spilled the beans."

"Mama," I groaned, raising my head to the ceiling.

"Don't blame Auntie. She was only looking out for her favorite niece since her daughter is a lying, backstabbing, cheating—"

"All of that, Resha?"

"Yes," she answered, smacking her gloss colored lips together, pouting as she folded her arms across her chest.

Rising, I moved around my desk to stand in front of her. Her light brown eyes pinned my every move. I could see the hurt in them.

"You know you were the *first* person I wanted to tell. Even before we told Ma. But you were out of town so much and it's something I wanted to tell you in person."

"We talk damn near every day, D. Why couldn't you just say it over the phone?"

I took Resha's hands in mine. "Because I knew you'd have questions and I wanted you to be able to look me in the eye, and before you say it, no, doing it via video chat or FaceTime wouldn't have worked either. You were my biggest support after the divorce ..."

"You didn't think I'd support your marriage to Tyler?"

"She knew you would."

I glanced up at the deep voice that'd just entered into the conversation. I couldn't help the smile that arose at the sight of Tyler's large frame standing in my office doorway. His eyes slid from Resha to me, that smile he reserved just for me opening up. He winked at me before looking back to Resha.

"Destiny wanted your approval more than anything. She knew you would think our marriage was fast," he began as he entered the room.

"It *is* fast," she retorted.

"Maybe, but when you know, you know." Tyler looked to me. "I'll tell you the same thing I told Mrs. McDonald. I will spend the rest of my life proving to Destiny that she made the best decision by becoming Mrs. Townsend. I don't make promises I don't keep. I do play for keeps, however."

I swallowed the lump in my throat as I stared up into the eyes of my husband. He had such a way of making me trust that everything was going to be okay. And if it wasn't okay, he would make it so.

"Oookay," Resha dragged out, causing Tyler and I to suddenly remember she was still in the room.

I'd forgotten just that quickly.

"I mean with the way you've been playing lately, I keep hearing you're unstoppable. I'm betting my sister has something to do with that."

"She has everything to do with it. She's my good luck charm." He leaned down and I rose to my tiptoes to meet his beckoning lips.

Tyler and the Cougars had been on a roll over the last few weeks. They were one game away from winning a chance at the Super Bowl. I had no doubt in my mind that they'd make it, and my husband would be the one carrying them to the finish line. I couldn't wait to cheer them on. Suddenly, I was more than a little relieved that Paul's call had come earlier. Not having to worry about Phillip Morris any longer freed up some mental space for me to be one hundred percent there for Tyler as a support system.

"Hello? I'm still here," Resha uttered.

I grinned her way.

"Anyway, I'll head on out—"

"We were just going to get dinner and head home. How about you join us? I know you two have some work for the podcast to discuss," Tyler chimed in.

My heart swelled as I squeezed his hand, not even realizing that I'd been holding it but I should've.

"We do need to talk about our first live show. It'll be the week after the Super Bowl."

I nodded and looked up at Tyler. He leaned down and kissed the corner of my mouth, silently conveying it was okay to spend a few hours with Resha.

On the way home, I promised my husband a bath and rub down of his sore muscles once Resha left. He was more than happy to accommodate us, allowing time for Resha and I to not only talk about work but to catch up on one another's private lives.

* * *

Tyler

"You ready for this?"

I glanced up at Kelvin who was standing over me as I sat in front of my assigned locker in the stadium. We were minutes away from entering the field to kickoff at the biggest game of our careers. Though he tried to hide it, I could see the nervous energy coursing through Kelvin from the look in his eyes.

I stood up, placing my arm on his shoulder. "I've already made the biggest commitment I'll ever make in my life. I thought playing the Super Bowl would be my big day but nope." I shook my head and then chuckled at Kelvin's confused expression.

"Man, what the fuck are you talking about? You cracking up on me or something?"

I shook my head. "No. I'm telling you, I wasn't nervous two months ago when I married Destiny, and I ain't nervous now, either. My good luck charm will be watching with the rest of my family up in the box seats." I winked at Kelvin.

"Married? Good luck charm? From the man who said superstition was for fools?"

I gave a one shoulder shrug. I had said that in the past. It's no secret that many athletes were superstitious in one way or another. Some wear the same pair of underwear on game day, brush with the same toothbrush before a big game, wear a certain pair of sneakers, drive one specific car to and from games. All of it I found to be utterly ridiculous. But my wife? She was my good luck charm. The last few months had proved it. I'd been on fire, playing the best football of my career and that was saying a lot. It was no accident we'd advanced to the big game the same season I met and married the woman of my dreams.

"Maybe I lied," I simply stated to Kelvin.

"What? Look, we ain't got time now, but once this game is over and we win this shit, you and I are going to have a talk about this wife of yours. More so, this wedding I wasn't invited to." He frowned.

"Wife? Wedding?"

My face instantly contorted into a scowl at the sound of Leonard's voice. "Your mother never taught you not to butt into private conversations before she left?" I stated, pointedly to Leonard. I grinned when he tried to step closer as if he wanted to take a swing at me. It was no secret that Leonard's mother had abandoned him and his father before he was five years old. I suspected it was one of the main contributing factors to his obviously sour attitude toward the opposite sex. And while my comment was particularly assholish, I didn't have any qualms hitting Riggs where it hurt. After he'd put his hands on my wife, all bets were off. As far as I was concerned the fact that he still had functioning legs and his trachea was still in place was a testament to my growing patience.

"Don't ever mention my—"

"Fuck you and your mother, Riggs. As for you, don't ever mention my *wife* again or question me about her. That goes for you and your piece of shit agent who failed to hold on to her. I won't make his mistakes. Trust. And after this game is over, you and I have zero to discuss. Ever," I growled.

Riggs would become a free agent after this season, and his likelihood of staying with the Cougars was slim to none, if I had anything to say about it. And I did.

"All right, let's bring it in!" Mike shouted from the entranceway of the locker room, garnering all of our attentions.

Just as everyone was stuffing their unnecessary belongings into their lockers to make their way over to the coach, my phone buzzed. I figured it was Destiny and my family wishing me luck before the game. While I knew the team needed to huddle up and head out, something nagged at me to check the message.

I opened up my text message from my father.

Destiny still hasn't arrived from the hotel. Will text when she gets here.

My entire body stilled. A million different thoughts infiltrated my mind as I wondered what could possibly be holding her up.

"Townsend, let's go!" Mike yelled.

"Fuck!" I cursed as I tossed my phone into my locker and slammed it shut. This was not how I wanted to go into this game.

* * *

Destiny

I swear if I made it up off the floor, I was never going to have sex with my husband again. My phone rang from the bed of the hotel's bedroom that we were staying in.

"Shit!" I cursed. It was probably the car service that was to take me to the stadium where the Cougars were playing the Hornets at the New Orleans field. The game was on neutral territory for both teams. I'd flown down with Tyler's family the day before.

"Girl, what are you doing?" Resha bellowed into the phone. She had also come with us to cheer Tyler and his team on. My only other family member, my mother, had opted to remain at home, although I'd tried to convince her to come. She still got anxious being around people she didn't know that well given her illness. But I knew she and a few of her neighbors were watching the game at her place. It comforted me knowing she wasn't alone.

"Hurling up this morning's breakfast," I murmured to Resha.

"What?"

"Nothing."

"I'm on my way down there. Tyler's whole family has left already. We need to go."

I groaned. "I'll be ready in five minutes." I stood up from the bed and held my arms out, steadying myself. I'd been queasy for the past three days. That morning after Tyler had left for the game I'd thrown up once and began dry heaving throughout the rest of the afternoon. I'd snuck off to a local pharmacy to pick up a test. It'd confirmed what I'd already knew. I hadn't told anyone just yet, wanting to give Tyler the news first. But that was if I could make it out of this damn room.

I took a couple sips of water to satisfy my parched throat, and after praying that it stayed down, I opened the door when Resha began knocking.

"Let's go," I rushed out, grabbing my coat and checking to make sure I had my wallet and bag.

"You don't look so good." Resha frowned at me.

"Gee, thanks."

"I'm serious."

"I'm fine. Just a little bug or something. We gotta go." I hurried, shutting the door behind me and leaving Resha to catch up with me toward the elevator.

Thankfully, my driver was still there and the drive from our hotel to the stadium was a short one. By the time we made it to the stadium, passed security, and up to the sky box seats where Tyler's family was already waiting, nearly an hour had past.

"Hey, you made it. We were starting to have our doubts," Kayla greeted, grinning at us.

"This one likes to take her sweet time," Resha pointed at me. She'd already been introduced to Ty's whole family the day before. Much like me, she got on well with the rest of the women.

I rolled my eyes at Resha. I was already feeling guilty for missing the start of the game. Even if it was due to a good reason.

"Well, at least you got in before the end of the first quarter," Patience stated as she joined us while bouncing her son, Thiers, on her hip.

I nearly melted as his large, honey-colored eyes looked up into mine. A small smile creased his lips. My hand went to my belly, but this time a feeling of joy and anticipation filled me instead of the sadness that had claimed me before.

"We ordered plenty of food. It should be served in a few minutes," Michelle told us, and jerked her head to guide all of us over to the seats closest to the window.

The nauseous feeling that still accompanied me fell to the background as I took my seat amongst my husband's family—or my family as well now, too—and watched the players returning to the field after the start of the second quarter. I grinned as I watched Tyler stroll out onto the field with the rest of his offensive line. For the first time I glanced up at the scoreboard and frowned. The Cougars were down fourteen zero.

"He nearly had two interceptions so far." I glanced up, looking over at Carter, Tyler's oldest brother. His attention was on me.

I wrinkled my forehead, frowning. Tyler didn't throw interceptions. He was the most precise player on the field.

"Come on, baby," I murmured to myself, turning back to the game.

"Why isn't he throwing?" Joshua demanded as we all watched Tyler pass the ball to Kelvin for the third time in a row. Kelvin was quickly tackled, gaining less than three yards.

"They need to get on the scoreboard before halftime," I stated out loud to no one in particular. Just as those words slipped from my lips, the Cougars' head coach made the decision to go for a field goal. I held my breath as the kicker ran to the field to set up for the attempt. Thankfully, the Cougars' kicker easily made the nearly forty yard goal, gaining the first three points the team earned of the game.

Everyone in the skybox exhaled a sigh of relief but it was only minor. The Cougars weren't performing and that's because their leader wasn't.

"Chicken?" Patience asked as she passed a plate of chicken wings in front of me.

My stomach instantly recoiled and I slapped my hand over my mouth before hurriedly standing and rushing to the private restroom in the seating area. I slammed the door shut, and as soon as I turned to the toilet, the little bit of contents my stomach had managed to hold onto that day were emptied out into the bowl. My back arched and stretched as I continued to dry heave for god knew how long. After a few minutes without anymore dry heaving, I moved to the sink and splashed my face with some water.

"We've got to pull it together, kid," I urged, rubbing my belly. "Your daddy's not doing so well on the field," I continued to talk as if the fetus in my womb could understand what I was trying to get at.

I grabbed a few paper towels and patted my face dry before tossing them and moving to the door. As soon as I opened it, I was greeted by

Resha, Patience, Michelle, and Kayla, all four giving me a sympathetic look.

"These helped me tremendously in my first tri," Michelle stated just above a whisper, handing me something.

I looked down, forehead wrinkled as I noticed what looked to be a piece of wrapped candy.

"They're ginger candies. Great for nausea."

I sighed, relieved, and snatched the candy, unwrapping it and popping it into my mouth. "Thank you."

"Are you feeling all right? I guess we now know why you were late," Patience asked.

I nodded. "I'm okay. Just uh ..."

"Overwhelmed?" Kayla spoke up.

I nodded.

"Here." Resha pushed through the other three ladies and handed me my bag. "You look like you've been through the wringer. Go make yourself up."

"So encouraging, you are," I teased.

She shrugged. "Maybe send your man a picture or something. It may help him do better."

"The game. How's it going out there?" I asked, looking between all of the ladies.

"They just went into half-time and they're still down by eleven."

I sighed. "Michelle, do you have anymore of those candies?"

"Here, take the whole bag. I never took them out after Sam was born. They might be a little old though."

"That's fine. I just need something for this damn nausea and these are helping. I'm going to take Resha's advice and freshen up a little bit."

They all nodded and stepped away from the bathroom door, as I shut it. I pulled my lip gloss, concealer, and powder from my bag to help me touch up the bags that'd formed under my eyes from all of the throwing up. Once I coated my lips with my favorite gloss I pulled out my cell phone.

911 Answer your phone.

I sent the text message to Tyler, and before I could even hit send to dial his phone, my own phone was ringing.

"Destiny, baby, what's wrong? Where are you?" he demanded, his voice strangled with worry.

"What's wrong is that this kid of yours is giving me hell already. I spent half the damn day in the bathroom hurling up everything I've eaten in the last forty-eight hours and then some. And once I finally arrive to the game, once your kid has given me a break, I end up watching my husband perform like it's his first game."

There was a long silence on the other end of the phone.

"Wh-what did you say?"

"I said you're playing like shit."

"About the kid."

"Oh yeah, it turns out you're going to be a father and this kid is going to be just as much of a hellraiser as you are."

Tyler's breathing increased. I could picture in my mind his nostrils flaring as he took in what I'd just told him, but I wasn't finished just yet.

"And while you're digesting that little bit of news can you do me a favor?"

"Anything."

"Tell me how I'm going to explain to our son or daughter why their father choked in the big game. Why he played like it was his first damn game in the little leagues? Can you do that?"

"Father said you hadn't arrived. That they were waiting on you."

His voice was still strained with worry.

"I'm fine, babe." My voice softened to a reassuring tone. "I promise. These ginger candies Michelle gave me are helping with the nausea. I might even be able to eat something. But not if you keep playing the way you are. Think you can do something about that?"

"A boy."

"What?"

"It's a boy. We're having a son. I can feel it." His voice had taken on a new energy.

"Yeah, well I'd hate for him to tease you for the next twenty years about sucking in the first Super Bowl you played in. And trust me, I will give him all of the ammunition he needs for his jokes. I'll be the first one to show him footage of this game. Every Christmas, Thanksgiving, hell, even Halloween we'll play footage to scare the trick or treaters."

"He'll see this game and the ring I won when it was all over." His voice was full of the determination and confidence I was so used to.

"We'll see you on the other side. Love you."

"I love you more than you know. And our little man, too."

I grinned as I hung up the phone, not bothering to tell him that *I* had a strong inclination that I was having a girl. Let him think what he needed to for the moment. I had a game to go watch.

I stuffed my phone back into my bag and exited the bathroom, pulling the door shut behind me.

"You missed all of the halftime show. I know you love Maroon 5," Resha stated as I sat down.

I shrugged. "I had more important things to do. The next half is not going to go like the first half. I guarantee you that."

Simply hearing the joy in Tyler's voice at finding out that he was going to be a father was more than enough for me not to even care about missing one of my favorite bands perform. There was a much better performance on the way.

CHAPTER 27

Tyler

"Tyler, Tyler, over here!"

"Over here!"

I blinked as the incessant lights from flashing cameras and yells from the reporters who'd swarmed our locker room went off. The scene was chaos as just about everyone of my teammates shook and sprayed a bottle of champagne while shouting in celebration.

The second half of the game had not gone like the first half at all. The news Destiny had shared with me lit a flame under my ass that nothing else could. Knowing the woman I adored and loved more than life itself was carrying my son was all I needed to hear to pull my shit together. That, and the fact that I believed her when she said she'd use my poor performance as ammunition to tease me for the next twenty years. I couldn't allow my future son to think his old man had choked in the big game.

"Congratulations, Mr. MVP!" Kelvin yelled over the raucous of the crowd, clapping me on the back.

I slapped my hand against his open palm and pulled him in for a hug.

"Something lit your ass in the second half."

"My wife telling me I'm going to be a father!" I gushed, unable to contain myself or the good news.

"Ah, man! We need fucking cigars and champagne!"

"Keep Destiny's pregnancy to yourself, though," I told Kelvin.

I didn't give a shit about anyone finding out about our marriage. I'd sing that from the rooftops myself, but I knew I was the first person Destiny had told about her pregnancy. Seeing as how we were surrounded by reporters, I didn't need that news getting out before we could tell our respective families.

"Tyler, did you think after that dismal first half you would now be in this position?" a reporter from the *Sun Times* asked, thrusting his microphone in my face.

"What the hell else was I supposed to think? That was over after the first half? You think I've been playing sports for a damn week? I knew we still had a hell of a chance," I growled at the reporter, annoyed by his asinine question.

"Tyler, tell us what you were thinking as you tossed that seventy-five yard pass to Gellman as the final play in the third quarter for the touchdown that took you over the Falcons?"

"I was thinking *he better fucking catch it*," I stated honestly, causing the reporters standing around to laugh. But I wasn't kidding. That was the longest pass of my career, a perfect spiral right into the hands of one of our receivers who'd been wide open in the end zone.

"Anything you want to say to your fans and people watching?" another reporter asked.

I turned and looked into the camera next to him. "I want to thank the Cougars' fans for always supporting us, my family of course, and most importantly, my wife, my good luck charm for giving me the best gift I could ever imagine. I love you, precious." With that, I stood and pushed passed the reporters to celebrate with the rest of my teammates.

The rest of the time in the locker room was a blur. There was a ton of celebration, champagne splashing, yelling, dancing, and more. And while I took it all in with my teammates, the real celebration for me began once I laid eyes on my five-foot-three dynamo of a wife. A wife, who I knew was pregnant with my son.

"I'm so proud of you," Destiny gushed as I pulled her into my arms. "And you smell."

I tossed my head back, laughing while also picking her up. "You still planning on bad mouthing me to my kid?"

She giggled. "Only a little but you'll probably deserve it for one reason or another."

I shrugged. "True."

I lowered my mouth to hers, taking my fill of her plump lips and kissing her with all of the energy I had left in my body. "I love you," I murmured against her lips.

"And I you."

My face turned serious as I placed her back on her feet. "How're you feeling?" I questioned, my hand going to her belly.

She looked around at the few passersby who were exiting the tunnel from the locker room to the exit. Most of my team had left to continue their celebration elsewhere. I'd needed to wait to see my wife before showering and heading back to the hotel.

"Better. I even got to eat a little bit."

"What'd you have?" I questioned, frowning.

"Chicken noodle soup. It was really good, and I kept it down which is a plus. We need to see if a convenience store is still open to pick up some of those ginger candies Michelle gave me."

"I'll call my assistant to have them at the hotel by the time we get back."

"You don't have t—"

Her refute stopped mid-sentence at the scolding look I gave.

"I'm just saying your assistant probably wants to enjoy tonight as well, not work."

"He can enjoy it once he picks up what you need."

Destiny's grin was a mile wide, surprising even me when she nuzzled my chest with her head and wrapped her arms around my waist.

"I love you," she sighed.

"I thought you said I smelled," I teased.

"You do, but I love you too much to care right now. That all right with you, Mr. MVP?" she asked saucily as she stared up at me.

"Fine with me but we need to shower."

"Hey!" she yelped when I scooped her up and began carrying her little ass toward the locker room. "Where're we going?"

"To shower. I need some help getting those hard to reach areas, you know? Also, I could use one of those massages of yours."

"Don't you have personal trainers for that?"

"Yeah, but I don't plan on throwing their thighs over my arms and ramming my cock into them while they call my name over and over as they come. You, on the other hand ..." I wiggled my eyebrows and continued walking, pushing the door of the locker room open.

Destiny's laughter remained and echo in the tunnel as we made our way toward the shower.

CHAPTER 28

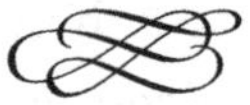

Destiny

"What the hell are you doing?" Tyler growled as he peered at me through the screen of my phone.

"I'm sitting down!" I huffed out, barely able to breathe. "That's all I do these days," I groaned.

"'Cause you're as big as a house."

"Screw you, Townsend! It's your damn fault I'm like this." Pouting, I rubbed my protruding belly. I thought about trying to kick my feet up on the coffee table that rested a few inches from the couch but then thought better of it. The chances of me getting up were slim to none since I was alone.

I glanced around the living room of our home. "At least we got the living room finished."

"It could've waited until after camp was finished." Tyler frowned, that worry vein in his forehead protruding again. I'd become accustomed to that look over the last few months. Ever since the doctor told us that both Tyler and I were correct in our gender guesses. We were having a girl, and not one but two boys.

Yup. I was pregnant with goddamned triplets. Hence, my inability to breathe and sit without needing a damn crane to lift me up.

"By then, I'll be even bigger than I am now and unable help with *anything.*"

"You better not be helping with anything now. Where the hell is Resha? And Joshua and Carter? They were supposed to be helping with things today."

I rolled my eyes. "Babe, it's barely seven thirty in the morning. Your brothers will be over in a few hours and Resha ran out to pick us up some breakfast."

At the mention of food my stomach growled. Despite the prevailing notion that pregnant women get to eat whatever and however they wanted, that hadn't been the case for me. Three babies took up a whole lot of space in my small body which meant that even a normal portioned meal got me full pretty quickly. I had to change up to eating a number of small meals throughout the day as to not get too full too fast which was super uncomfortable.

"I don't like that you're alone there."

I grinned at the look of consternation that crossed my husband's handsome face. It'd been just under three weeks since we closed on our home in Cedarwoods. Joshua, as CEO of Townsend Real Estate, had pulled some strings to get our home built in a timely manner once he found out we were pregnant with triplets. We officially moved in right before Tyler had to leave for training camp. Since he'd been gone his entire family stepped in to help me complete decorating and getting the nurseries together. Resha had been staying over and took time off to travel less for work just so I wouldn't be alone. My mother even stayed over a couple of nights, using the room that we'd designed especially for her on the first floor. I tried to tell Resha, my mother and Tyler they didn't need to worry so much but they refused to listen to me, of course.

"I'm not alone. Resha will be back soon. And today we're going shopping for some last minute items to add to the nurseries."

"You can wait until I get home," he reiterated.

"But I don't want to. I can't just sit around this big ass house and do nothing. I'm nesting. How's practice going?" I asked to change the topic.

"It's going. New guy is fitting in well."

I nodded. Leonard Riggs had been traded in spite of his performance. The Cougars had opted for a new wide receiver.

"That's a good thing, right?"

"Yeah, it's good."

"You don't sound so thrilled about it."

"I am. I'd just rather be there with you. You sure you're all right?"

"I'm fine. And don't ask me again. Are you okay? You're starting to worry me a little." Tyler wasn't a typical worry wort.

"Yeah, just a feeling. I'm sure it's due to not being as close to you as I should be while you're pregnant."

The Cougars had moved their training camp to a university campus that was two hours away.

"We're good here. You'll be done and back home before you know it."

"And then I'll be on the road for the season and for sponsorships." The worry vein in his forehead appeared again as he frowned.

"Hey, what're you thinking?"

"I'm thinking this … was the life I wanted, but maybe not so much anymore. Hell, even coaching would require long hours away from you and the kids."

"But not as much."

He shook his head. "Definitely not as much."

"Nothing needs to be decided today. We'll talk when you get home."

"All right. Love you."

"Love you."

"Show me the belly," he ordered, grinning.

I laughed and pointed the phone down toward my belly so he could see it. He told each one of the babies that he loved them, by name. We'd picked out their names months ago.

As soon as I'd disconnected the call the doorbell rang.

I sucked my teeth. "Dammit, Resha," I grunted. She was always leaving her key behind. "I'm coming. I'm coming," I called to the door, after back-to-back ringing sounded. "I told you to take your da—"

My words died on my lips when I opened the door and saw that it wasn't Resha at my door but Phillip Morris. What alarmed me even more than the fact that he was on my doorstep was the disheveled and crazed look in his blue eyes.

"Phillip Morris."

An eerie smile crept across his face. "That's my name. And yours is Jesse Pritchard, or no, is it Destiny? Destiny McDonald-Townsend. Congratulations, by the way ... on the wedding and the ..." His eyes dropped to my stomach.

My hand instantly went to my belly, protectively.

"Pregnancy." He stepped forward.

I went to slam the door shut, knowing this was not a social call. The FBI and SEC had done their jobs and continued their investigation into Morris. I hadn't heard anything from Paul for months until about a month earlier he called and told me that charges had been filed by both the SEC and FBI for money laundering and a number of other crimes. While the SEC's charges would, at most, lead to Morris being publicly banned from practicing as a financial advisor again and having to make financial retribution, it was the charges by the FBI that could put him in jail for up to seven years.

The last I'd heard, Morris had done his best to prove his innocence but the truth was, he was guilty. Eventually, he'd pleaded as such and was now awaiting his sentencing trial, which was to be in a few weeks. Apparently, he was out on bail while he waited.

"See, I'd been trying to figure out over and over in my head who ratted me out. Why would the SEC randomly decide to come after me?"

"You need to get the hell off my doorstep!" I demanded while attempting to close the door in his face. I was stopped by his hand on the door. I tried to push it shut with all of my strength but I was already winded from that tiny bit of exertion.

"What's the matter? Don't want to hear what I have to say?" he demanded, pushing the door all of the way open one final time. He pushed it so hard, I stumbled backwards a few feet, knocking me down onto the second step of our stairway.

My heartbeat thundered in my ears as I watched Morris slam the door behind him and lock it. I immediately went for my phone, thinking it was in the pocket of the relaxed fit pants I wore. My heart sank when I discovered I'd left it on the couch all of the way on the other side of the room.

"Get the hell out of my house!" I demanded, trying to sound intimidating, despite the tremor in my voice.

"Why? You came to my fucking house and wrecked it all up! Things were going fine! Fine! But then you waltzed into my office pretending to be a poor, broken down widow who needed some help with her money. Then boom! My life is fucking flipped upside down."

He moved closer, threateningly. I glanced over his shoulder and saw my phone resting on the huge couch I'd just gotten off of.

"I didn't do shit you didn't deserve. You stole money from people!"

"They didn't deserve it!" he yelled loudly, face contorting into one of rage.

That was when I braced my arms on the stair behind me and kicked at his knee as hard as I could. I missed his knee but managed to land the kick to his thigh.

"Ow, bitch!" He growled loudly, crouching low.

It gave me just enough time to jump off the stair and make a dash past him toward the living room where I'd left my phone. Unfortunately, I was much slower these days, barely able to jog, let alone sprint for the phone. Morris quickly rebounded and was on my heels just as I reached my phone.

"Ow! Get the hell off of me!" I yelled and swung my arms as he grabbed me from behind by my hair and the shirt I wore.

"You ruined my life!" he snarled while wrapping his hand around my nose and mouth.

I began panicking with the loss of oxygen. At the same time the babies in my womb began moving, reminding me that I wasn't in this fight for myself. I had to protect them. With all of the strength I could muster, I swung my right elbow back as hard as I could, making contact with the soft flesh of Phillip Morris' abdomen.

He crumbled low, grunting in pain. His grip loosened and I gasped for much needed air. I quickly tapped the power button on my phone and glanced over my shoulder to see Morris straightening up. I turned back to my phone and slid the Emergency SOS button left to right, hoping that it did the job and automatically dialed the emergency contacts in my phone. Tyler had insisted months ago that I set it up, once he learned that I hadn't even known about the feature.

"I'm going to kill you!" Morris taunted, lunging at me.

I yelped and just barely escaped his grasp as I turned and ran toward the staircase. Our bedroom was on the second floor and had a lock on it as well as security features. I figured if I could get there ahead of Morris, I'd be okay.

"Come here, bitch!" he growled as he chased me through the living room and up the stairs.

I began breathing intensely as a sharp pain ran down my spine, slowing my progress. At the same time, Morris was on me, once again pulling me by the hair and the T-shirt I wore. I lost my footing and my hand slipped from the wooden railing, and I crashed down against Morris' body, causing him to tumble as well. The next thing I remember was my back slamming hard against the hardwood of the stair below me, before everything faded to black.

* * *

Tyler

"Where the hell is my wife?" I demanded of the nurse behind the desk.

"I-Um, who—"

"Where the fuck is she?" I growled at the nurse, pounding on the desk.

"Ty!"

I turned and looked toward Carter who was waving me over from the entrance of the E.R. into the main area of Williamsport General Hospital.

"Where is she?" I demanded, following Carter as we crossed the hallways toward the elevator.

"She's … okay."

"What the hell aren't you telling me?" I watched as he pounded the button for the fifth floor.

"The doctors say she's stable but that could change."

As soon as the words were out of this mouth the elevator dinged and the doors opened. My attention went to the worried expressions on the faces of my mother, mother-in-law, and sisters-in-law. My father stepped out from behind my mother, followed by Aaron. Knowing my entire family was here when I couldn't be filled me immense gratitude and love. The entire two hour drive from training camp back to Williamsport had been filled with anxiety and rage.

I'd had a nagging feeling for weeks, which was why I wasn't too thrilled about leaving for camp in the first place. It was also why I'd convinced Resha to stay with Destiny while I was gone. Two months earlier Destiny had finally told me her involvement in the Phillip Morris investigation. Once it looked like he was going to jail for a while, she felt comfortable enough to tell me she'd been working with the SEC to provide some inside information that was then passed to the FBI. I was pissed, finding out the truth and the fact that she'd been put in danger. But she'd assured me that Phillip Morris had no idea who she was and that he was indeed going to jail. That helped ease my fear slightly. Now, I felt like a fucking idiot for not checking on it myself.

At the end of our first practice for the day, I immediately checked my phone and saw the emergency call from Destiny. I called just about everyone in my family and ran off the field, not even giving my coach an explanation. It was only when a nurse glanced at me, in my practice uniform, that I even realized I still had it on.

"Where is she?" I demanded of my father as I walked closer.

"Room 510, but she …" His words fell to the background as I brushed passed him in search of my wife.

I didn't bother knocking on the door, instead, barging in. And the first thing I heard were loud screams.

"No, no, no!" Destiny demanded.

"Destiny, baby!" I yelled, running to her side and taking her outstretched hand. She was laying in the bed, her legs squirming and her free hand gripping her stomach. Her face was contorted in pain.

"Tyler! It's too soon!" she gasped.

"Destiny, we have to get these babies out now."

That was the first time I even noticed Destiny's OB was in the room. A middle-aged Indian woman named Dr. Mehra.

"Tyler, we have to deliver your children now," she stated, looking to me and then nodding at the nurse.

"No! It's too soon. They're too young," Destiny wailed, squeezing my hand. "Tyler, tell her. They're too little. They won't make it. Please!" she begged with tears in those brown orbs that I loved so damned much.

"Dr. Mehra, do they have to be delivered today?" I questioned.

"I'm sorry, Tyler, but yes. It's more dangerous for mom and the babies if we don't deliver. But at thirty weeks there is still a great chance they will all survive."

"No!" Destiny cried.

"Precious, listen to me." I crouched down low, running my hand along the side of her face. "You can do this. Okay? Dr. Mehra's going to deliver all of our babies and they're going to be fine. They need you to be strong right now. We've got this. It's game time."

"Tyler, I can't lose another baby."

My heart squeezed in my chest. I pressed a kiss to her forehead. "With everything in me, I swear on this earth, you won't."

"Ty—"

"We've got to go. It's going to be a C-section." Dr. Mehra began barking out orders to the hospital staff.

Before I knew it, I was holding Destiny's hand as her hospital bed was being wheeled out of the room and down the hall, toward what I assumed was the operating room.

"I'm sorry, Tyler, you can't be in here for this," Dr. Mehra threw over her shoulder before pushing past the double doors.

"Get the hell off me! I'm going wherever the fuck my wife goes!" I growled at whoever was pulling me away from Destiny.

"Tyler!" she called out as our hands disconnected.

"I'm right here," I yelled as she moved farther away from me. There was a heavy weight holding me back that I fought hard to get rid of. It took me a minute to realize that it wasn't one but two people—men keeping me from reaching my wife as her bed was wheeled past another set of double doors.

"Mr. Townsend, calm down. Please!" grunted an unfamiliar male voice.

"Get the fuck off of me!" I growled in an attempt to swing at the owner of said voice, but my right arm was being held by whoever was assisting him.

"Tyler, calm down!" It was a feminine voice, one I'd known since the womb. My mother. However, even her initial pleas didn't halt my fight to get free and get to my wife and children.

"She needs me!" I demanded.

"She needs you to be calm and to keep it together for her and those babies."

I felt my mother pull my face between her hands. It was another minute before my eyes focused enough to stare into her burning blue eyes.

"She needs you right now. But when all of this is over, and your children and wife are home healthy and safe, you will do what you need to." My mother's voice was low and calm but filled with the steeliness that always belied her and my father's love for all of us.

"Son," my father called me, placing a strong hand on my shoulder, "your children and wife need you now."

I turned back to my mother who still cupped my face. My jaw firmed as I ground my teeth together.

"Morris?"

"He's in police custody," my father answered.

On the way to the hospital my family had sent me text messages explaining how Morris had attacked Destiny in our home.

"Everyone involved in this will lose their damn head," I grunted.

"Eventually." My mother nodded, finally releasing my face.

I looked above her head to the double doors where my wife had been taken. I hated this feeling of helplessness. Dr. Mehra was a world class physician. But even knowing that didn't lighten the burden of not being able to be in the room where my wife and children needed me. I worked hard to tamp down on the rage I felt and focused on pulling my shit together for when they were out of surgery.

I'd have plenty of time to get out my anger. And let it out I would.

CHAPTER 29

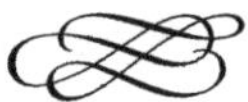

Destiny

I felt his presence even before I opened my eyes. I turned my head toward the warmth and safety that seemed to emanate from him and slowly opened my eyes. My vision was blurred at first, but after blinking a few times, I looked directly into those hazel-green eyes that always seemed to welcome me home.

"Hey, sleeping beauty," his deep, low voice called.

I cracked a smile. "Hey," I whispered, my throat feeling super dry. "Wh-where am I?" I looked around the room and wrinkled my forehead as I took in the white walls, flat screen mounted in the corner of the room, and the ugly wooden, hard chairs meant for family visitors. I blinked again. I was in a hospital.

I squeezed my eyes shut. "Why am I in the hospital?"

Suddenly it all came back to me.

Phillip Morris.

The attack.

The fall down the stairs.

"The babies!" I yelled out, reaching my arm to feel my belly. But it wasn't right. It was soft. "What happened?"

"Hey, it's all right."

"No! They were hurt. They were so little. They didn't make it!" I began shaking.

"Destiny, look!" Tyler had to grab my arms as he jutted his head to the other side of the room.

I followed the motion of his head, turning to my left, and stilled at the sight of three incubators.

"The doctors tried to say all three had to remain in the neonatal unit, but after I raised a little hell and reminded everyone including the CEO that I wasn't the one to fuck with, they did some rearranging to bring all three in here."

I glanced at Tyler, and then back to the incubators. "Th-they're here?"

"They're here. They need to stay in those incubators to help develop their lungs and some other shit the doctor said they need, but. they're perfect. All three of them."

I swallowed and turned back to Tyler. "Are you sure?"

He nodded.

That was when I lost it. All of the tears spilled out as I began sobbing so hard my entire body shook. I sniffled and tried to pull it together but that only made the sobbing worse. I barely felt the bed move as my six-foot-two husband climbed into the bed, wrapping his arms around me, and held me as I cried on his shoulder.

It must've taken at least ten minutes for all of the tears to empty out before I could pull it together enough to get my first real glimpse of my children outside of my stomach.

With the aid of a few hospital staff, Tyler assisted me off the bed and into a wheelchair so I could move closer to the babies.

"Tristen is our first born," Tyler began telling me the order of our children's births since I had been put under anesthesia for the C-section. "Followed by Annalise," he continued, moving down the row of incubators. "And finally, Travis."

I insisted on Annalise as our daughter's name while Tyler wanted the boys' names to begin with Ts since he couldn't exactly name both boys after himself.

"They're perfect," I stated, my voice filled with awe as I stared at the tiny creations we'd made.

"Their mom is perfect." Tyler leaned down on one knee next to my wheelchair, pressing a kiss to my hand.

"Their dad's no slouch either." Turning, I looked at him, and let out a giggle when I realized he was still wearing his practice uniform.

"My father and mother went to our place to pick up some clothes for us. I wasn't leaving your side."

I cupped his face and pressed a quick kiss to his lips. "Thank you," I whispered.

"Nope. Thank you."

He stood and we continued to ogle our children.

* * *

Robert Townsend

I always knew my youngest would be my most rebellious one yet.

"You thought you could come into my fucking house and attack my goddamned wife?" Tyler yelled.

Even I flinched as another punch to Phillip Morris' ribs ended with the cracking of bones.

"You almost killed my children."

Another punch to the soft flesh of Morris' abdomen.

"Help!" Morris shouted. At least that's what it sounded like. The layers of duct tape that covered his mouth made it difficult to discern. Even still, had he been able to clearly speak, I would've remained in the exact spot I was in. About twenty feet away from the huge tree that he was tied to by the rope that circled his body and the tree. I shook my head.

Tyler's idea.

"This guy's not gonna last much longer," Joshua grunted beside me.

I peered over my right shoulder at my third youngest son. "You want him to?"

Joshua turned those emerald green eyes my way. "We've been out here almost two hours."

"He deserves worse," Aaron grunted from my left.

"Much worse." That was Carter, the eldest of the group.

"Fucking scumbag!" Tyler yelled, landing a vicious elbow to Morris' face. I'm sure that one cracked his cheekbone.

"I'm just saying, we've all got better things to do than to watch this piece of trash take his last breath. Can we end it and go home to our wives and kids?" Joshua insisted. "He could be here all damn day." Josh turned to me.

I slowly nodded my head. He was right. It was high time to put an end to this. I casually looked around the forested area. I knew no one was there besides us. We were on privately owned land that had been in the Townsend family for generations. I took one step, then another. The crunch of the leaves beneath my running shoes didn't deter Tyler from continuing his torment on Morris.

"Ty," I called.

No response as he murmured something in Morris' ear. Whatever he said caused Morris' one non-swollen eye to bulge open, and he began squirming again, trying to break free.

"Tyler!" I called again.

And again, he didn't even acknowledge my presence.

Little fucker.

He was always the most hard-headed of the group, which was why I insisted that he be put in sports in the first place. Even when Deborah disagreed with me. He needed more discipline and structure outside of the home as well as inside just to keep his ass in line. Football gave him that.

"I'm going to kill everyone you love and ever thought about loving. Even your pet goldfish won't survive once I'm fucking done with you!" Tyler growled, low next to Morris' ear.

"Tyler Joseph Townsend! That's enough!" I stated firmly.

Though I could only make out his profile, I saw when he blinked. Slowly he turned his head toward me. His eyes were so foggy, filled with rage and hatred for the man who'd dared to do harm to his family. I knew that look. I was the first to wear it in the family. But that was a story for another day.

"Finish him so we can all get back to our families," I ordered.

Tyler narrowed his gaze on me, and I just knew he was itching to defy me. His eyes went over my shoulder to his brothers before returning to me. He was warring over what to do as he turned back to face Morris. His hands tightened into fists.

"Destiny, Travis, Annalise, and Tristan," I reminded him.

That seemed to do the trick. His chest deflated a little as he pushed out a heavy breath. His hands loosened, no longer balled into fists.

"I have a guy that'll drop him back off at the prison. Make it look like a casualty of jailhouse fight. It's time to wrap this up."

Tyler nodded.

I turned my back and began walking back in the direction of my other sons. I heard the final blows of Tyler's that ended Phillip Morris' life. Once I turned around, I watched Tyler cut the rope from the tree with the scissors he'd used on Phillip Morris earlier. The limp body fell to the ground. Tyler stepped over it and began removing his bloody T-shirt.

"Come on, bro. You need a fucking shower," Joshua commented. "I got somewhere to put your clothes," he stated, holding his hand out for the clothing.

Tyler nodded.

Within thirty minutes, Tyler had cleaned himself up and changed into an entirely new outfit, the clean up crew had retrieved Morris' body and sent him on his way back to the jail, to be found the next morning, and my boys and I were on our way back to Williamsport, to our wives.

I know, I know. Pretty unconventional way for a father to spend quality time with his sons. But to know me is to understand there isn't very much that's conventional about me.

"Time to head home—"

"No, I've got another stop to make. Josh," Tyler called. "You've got what I asked for?"

"Right here." Joshua tossed a now cleaned off Tyler a vial of something.

"I'll be home in an hour," Ty stated before heading out in his own car.

* * *

Tyler

I flexed my fingers as I waited patiently in the dark living room of Darryl Wright's penthouse condo. I frowned, looking around at the fancy shit he kept in his place. I hated this fucker even more than I hated Phillip Morris.

I flexed my fingers again, feeling the swelling in my knuckles from the beating I'd put on Morris' body.

"Yeah, Leonard. I hear you. We're gonna figure this out. You just focus on getting better and out of the hospital," Darryl said into the phone as he entered his front door. He didn't even see me as he wandered directly over to the glass table where he kept his nightly drink.

I smiled inwardly hearing him trying to console Leonard. Unfortunately, Leonard had had an *accident* while driving his motorcycle weeks earlier. A motorcycle he was forbidden to drive due to his contractual obligations to the league. Nevertheless, he'd insisted on purchasing the damn thing, and even worse for him, I not only knew about it but also knew where he lived, and therefore where he kept it, to inform my guy who knew how to tinker with anything on wheels to make them unsafe to drive. Although, they looked fine from the outside. As I'd said, I hadn't been finished with Leonard once he'd set me up and putting his fucking hands on my woman.

"I got you, Leonard. We're going to get every cent you are owed from the Cougars. Then we'll get you rehabbed and you will be back on the field in no time."

I rolled my eyes at Darryl's lies. Leonard's back had been broken in the accident. Though he'd walk again, he'd *never* play at the level he once had. He was lucky I'd waited until after we'd won the Super Bowl to get revenge. At least he had a ring to show for his short NFL career.

"I gotta go. Got my damn kid tonight," he grunted as he frowned and loosened his tie with his free hand.

I glared at this asshole even harder. He really was a piece of work.

"You really shouldn't be making promises you can't fucking keep," I stated after he hung up and tossed the phone in his leather couch.

"What the fuck?" he yelped as he spun around, seeing me emerge from the shadows behind his front door.

"Surprised?" I asked darkly.

"The hell are you doing in my house?"

"Decided we needed to have a little talk."

"A talk? Fuck you! Get out of my damn house before I beat your—"

"My ass?" I questioned, eyes narrowing and stepping closer. "Let me tell you all of the ways in which that'll never fucking happen," I growled, moving even closer. Darryl Wright was taller than me by a few inches but I'd have no problem putting his ass to the ground. However, I was trying my best to restrain myself. "Like I said, we need to talk."

"We have nothing to talk about."

I watched as he twisted his neck, running his finger around the collar of his white button-up shirt, just before taking another sip of his drink.

"It was you, wasn't it?"

He frowned, a deep V settling between his eyebrows. "Me what?"

"Who told Phillip Morris where we lived."

His eyes widened in surprise, telling of his guilt.

I shook my head. "You gave him my home address once he figured out Destiny was behind the initial investigation into his company. It was you who told him I was out of town at training camp and she'd be home alone. Your punk ass sent a man to my house to attack my pregnant wife!" I seethed as I lunged forward, grabbing him by the collar of his shirt.

He struggled to push me off but his body was already weakening.

"I-I-she's my wife!" he blurted out. "She was mine first! She fucking left me after one fuck up!"

"You killed her fucking kid you selfish son of a bitch!" I pushed him backwards, causing him to stumble.

"Sh-shut up," he struggled to get out in between coughing. He unbuttoned the top buttons of his shirt as if searching for relief from being overheated.

I peered down at his crouched over body, watching him inhale deeper and deeper to get fresh oxygen into his body.

"She was never your wife. She was *always* meant for me. You just got in the fucking way. You were never man enough for her."

"Sh-shut u-up," he stuttered.

"She intimidated you. That's why you had her put her career ambitions aside, had her catering to you, why you bought her to flashiest and best of everything, and why you fucked anything in a skirt when you had her at home waiting for you."

"Y-you don't know sh—" His words broke off as he gasped for air. He looked up at me, eyes filled with terror. "H-help me."

I took a step back. "It'll be over soon enough. The pain you're feeling is from the arteries of your heart constricting." I looked him up and down. "The calcium gluconate I had injected into your IV via the specialty nurse concierge services of yours is finally kicking in." Thanks to a little background research I had done on Darryl, I discovered that he got weekly nurse concierge visits to his office after yet another recent surgery on his knee. After that, it was pretty easy to figure out how to get the heart-attack inducing calcium gluconate into his next IV. The alcohol he'd drank once he arrived home likely didn't help his heart as it began to slow down due to the lack of electrolytes in the body caused by the drug.

"You're dying, Darryl," I gritted out low in his ear. "As you do, I just want you to know that *my* wife will never spend one second mourning you. She's too busy taking care of our children and me, her husband, while running her own company. You will be nothing more than a memory." With that, I took a step back, watching as Darryl gasped for air as he fell to the ground.

I waited for another thirty minutes, making sure that he had truly stopped breathing, before reaching for the doorknob of his condo with my gloved hand. Quietly, I made my way down the right hall—toward the staircase I knew had no cameras—and out of his building.

Weeks later it was reported that Darryl Wright died of a massive heart attack. His body hadn't been found for three full days. He was supposed to have picked up his oldest son that same night, but when he didn't show up the child's mother, Darryl's ex-fiancée, just figured he'd flaked … again. After her phone calls went unanswered she didn't try to reach him any longer. It wasn't until the following Tuesday when Darryl's assistant showed up at his condo and found his body that the truth was revealed. By then any trace elements of the drug I'd had him injected with were long gone. His official cause of death was ruled a myocardial infarction. His body was cremated after the funeral.

EPILOGUE

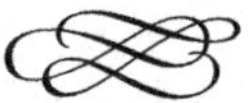

Seven months later
Destiny

I held my hand up to the fingerprint scanner that unlocked the front door of our home. Since the attack, Tyler insisted on completely upgrading all of our security measures in and around the home. We now had a gate that only he, myself and his immediate family knew the access codes to. Not even our security team knew the code.

"I'm home!" I called out as I kicked my sneakers off and pushed them to the side of the door where we kept the shoes upon entering. That also was at the insistence of my husband. A couple of weeks after the babies were born he'd read an article about tracking dirt through the house and how bacteria or whatever can be harmful to children. Now, we're not allowed to walk around with shoes on in the house.

I'll have to break us free of that rule soon. But for now, I let my husband think he was in charge.

"Hey, precious."

My heart rate sped up a little bit when that dimple appeared with that smile.

"I would get up but I'm being held hostage at the moment," he teased.

I laughed at the sight of Annalise crawling over Tyler's waist, apparently trying to grab the rattle that Travis was shaking with his right hand while he worked hard to lift himself by pressing his left hand against Tyler's shoulder. Tristan was perched on the navy blue velvet couch that Tyler rested his back against, trying to climb over Tyler's head.

"You do look a little occupied." I giggled, watching the man I loved with all of my heart lovingly playing with the children who were my world.

"How was your workout and lunch?"

I strolled over to my family and lifted Travis so that I could take his spot on the floor right next to his father. I pressed a kiss to my baby boy's cheek and then answered, "It was great. Zumba is always a fun time. Lunch was great but Resha is going through some type of identity crisis."

Tyler gave me a look. "Sounds serious."

I shrugged. "Serious but maybe a good thing." I paused and smiled as Tyler pulled Tristan from the couch and nuzzled him and Annalise, causing both of them to giggle. My heart swelled.

"This whole Mr. Mom thing looks good on you," I teased for the umpteenth time. After the attack and birth of the children, Tyler took a leave of absence from the NFL. I'd insisted that wasn't necessary and that his team and fans were counting on him, but he'd been even more adamant that his one and only priority was the well-being of the four of us.

I leaned my head on his shoulder and smiled when his lips made contact with my temple. "I love you."

"Oh yeah? How much?"

"So much that you don't have to cook dinner for a whole week."

He grunted. "We don't cook. We have a chef."

I frowned and then giggled. He was right. He nor I wanted to cook but we also wanted to feed our family well so we sprang for an all-natural, organic chef who even made pureed baby food. It was well worth the hefty price tag.

"What else you got, precious?"

"I love you enough to give you three healthy babies."

"That I put in that womb of yours."

When I sat up he nipped my earlobe, causing me to squeal and Annalise to giggle.

"You think your daddy's funny, huh?" I asked, pulling her onto my lap. "Just wait until you find a guy who'll make you reconsider everything in your life. Just you wait, little girl," I taunted her while nuzzling her belly. Her giggles filled me with such joy.

However, when I peered up at Tyler the frown that marred his face was unexpected.

"What's that look?"

"You're talking about my daughter finding a man one day. I'm the only man she'll need in this world."

I rolled my eyes. "That's what my father said, too," I told Annalise, ignoring her father while nuzzling her cute button nose. She giggled in the way that made my heart beat faster.

"Don't go putting ideas into my baby girl's head. In fact, give her to me." He reached over and grabbed Annalise, placing her onto his lap. I stared at Tyler with her. Out of our three children, Annalise was the only one that'd inherited Tyler's auburn locks.

At that moment, Tristan crawled over onto my lap, grinning up at me. That same mirth that his father's eyes held, were behind his toffee brown irises as well. Tristan would be the troublemaker. He'd already proven as much by keeping us up most nights while his brother and sister slept peacefully.

"Your poor sister," I told my boys. "She's not going to be able to date until she leaves for college."

"Not even then," came Tyler's quick reply.

"What're you going to do? Keep her under lock and key?"

"If necessary."

I shook my head and yawned. "I need to shower."

"I'll join you. It's their nap time soon."

"Oh no! You're liable to have me making another one of these kids."

"What's wrong with that?" He tilted his head to the side, as if perplexed.

"Tyler," I growled.

He shrugged. "Fine. We can take it into the bedroom. We haven't used the ceiling mirror since last week anyway."

"The same mirror you forgot to retract last week. Making it possible for our eight-year-old nephew to walk into our bedroom and ask why we had a mirror on our ceiling in front of the entire family?"

I was mortified when at our family dinner that we'd hosted the previous week, Diego came to the dining room table asking why Uncle Tyler and Aunt Destiny had a mirror on the ceiling over our bed. Yes, it was Tyler's idea to have the damn thing. Usually, he was good about retracting it or at least, keeping our bedroom door closed, but Diego saw it while he was using the upstairs bathroom.

Tyler smirked, cockily. "Kid's gotta learn sometime."

"You're impossible."

"And yours. For keeps," he retorted, wiggling his eyebrows, leaning over and beckoning a kiss. And as always, I leaned up to give him what he silently requested.

* * *

WANT to read more about the Townsends? Find out how it all started with their parents love story. Click here to read Until My Last Breath.

WANT to read about Destiny's cousin, Resha? Click here to read No Coincidence.

KEEP IN CONTACT WITH TIFFANY

Looking for updates on future releases? I can be found around the web at the following locations:

FaceBook private group: Tiffany's Passions Between the Pages
Website: TiffanyPattersonWrites.com
FaceBook Page: Author Tiffany Patterson
Email: TiffanyPattersonWrites@gmail.com

More books by Tiffany Patterson

THE BLACK BURLES SERIES

BLACK PEARL

Black Dahlia
Black Butterfly

Forever Series

7 Degrees of Alpha (Collection)
Forever

Safe Space Series

Safe Space (Book 1)
Safe Space (Book 2)